Isabelle in the Afternoon

Douglas Kennedy's previous thirteen novels include the critically acclaimed bestsellers *The Big Picture, The Pursuit of Happiness, A Special Relationship* and *The Moment*. He is also the author of three highly praised travel books. *The Big Picture* was filmed with Romain Duris and Catherine Deneuve; *The Woman in the Fifth* with Ethan Hawke and Kristin Scott Thomas.

His work has been translated into twenty-two languages. In 2007 he was awarded the French decoration of *Chevalier de l'Ordre des Arts et des Lettres*, and in 2009 the inaugural *Grand Prix de Figaro*. Born in Manhattan in 1955, he has two children and currently divides his time between London, Paris, Berlin, Maine and New York.

ve you'

D0418534

Also available by Douglas Kennedy

Fiction

The Dead Heart
The Big Picture
The Job
The Pursuit of Happiness
A Special Relationship
State of the Union
Temptation
The Woman in the Fifth
Leaving the World
The Moment
Five Days
The Heat of Betrayal
The Great Wide Open

Non-fiction

Beyond the Pyramids
In God's Country
Chasing Mammon

Douglas Kennedy

Isabelle in the Afternoon

arrow books

1 3 5 7 9 10 8 6 4 2

Arrow Books
20 Vauxhall Bridge Road
London SW1V 2SA

Arrow Books is part of the Penguin Random House group of companies
whose addresses can be found at global.penguinrandomhouse.com.

Penguin
Random House
UK

First published in Great Britain by Hutchinson in 2020
First published in paperback by Arrow Books in 2020

www.penguin.co.uk

A CIP catalogue record for this book is available from the British Library.

ISBN 9780099585237
ISBN 9780099585244 (export)

Typeset in 11.35/16 pt Adobe Garamond
by Integra Software Services Pvt. Ltd, Pondicherry

Printed and bound in Great Britain by Clays Ltd, Elcograf S.p.A.

MIX
Paper from
responsible sources
FSC
www.fsc.org
FSC® C018179

Penguin Random House is committed to a sustainable future for
our business, our readers and our planet. This book is made from
Forest Stewardship Council® certified paper.

'Same bed, different dreams.'

– Chinese proverb

One

BEFORE ISABELLE I knew nothing of sex.

Before Isabelle I knew nothing of freedom.

Before Isabelle I knew nothing of Paris – where sex and freedom are two of its eternal themes.

Before Isabelle I knew nothing of life.

Before Isabelle . . .

Seen through that rear-view mirror called remembrance . . .

Before Isabelle I was nothing more than a boy.

And after Isabelle?

After 'the before' and before 'the after' . . . that is the stuff of all stories. Especially those shaded by matters intimate.

And with Isabelle it was always intimate.

Even when there wasn't an afternoon entwined together.

Afternoons and Isabelle.

The constant trajectory of that little story, which also happens to be, for me, a big story. Because it is the story of my life.

All lives are transient tales. Which is what makes my narrative, your narrative, *our narrative*, so essential. Every life has its own import, no matter how fleeting or peripheral it may seem. Every life is a novel. And every life, if allowed, has its afternoons with Isabelle. When all is possible and infinite – and as fugitive as a sandstorm in the Sahara.

Afternoons and Isabelle.

That one address where, at a certain juncture, I intersected with that most elusive of constructs:

Happiness.

Paris.

My first sighting of it came in my twenty-first year. Nineteen seventy-seven, 8.18 in the morning, according to the watch on my wrist. Three minutes later I passed beneath an art deco clock overhanging the chilly expanses of the Gare du Nord.

January in Paris. All *noir et blanc* and endless encroaching darkness. I'd fallen off the night train from Amsterdam. An eight-hour trek, punctuated by moments of fleeting sleep sitting upright in a cramped carriage. All the way south the space between my ears was still clouded by pre-departure weed inhaled in a coffeeshop on the Prinsengracht. At the entrance to the Métro there was a small boulangerie where I quelled the effects of a night without food with a croissant and a short black shot of java. Adjacent to that was a *tabac*. Three francs bought me a packet of Camels and a day of smoking. Moments later, just like everyone else awaiting the southbound *ligne 5* train, I was deep in thrall to an early-morning cigarette.

The Métro. At this post-dawn hour there was still elbow room in one of its second-class carriages. Everyone was exhaling clouds of smoke and frosted air. The Métro back then: a pervasive aroma of burnt wood and undeodorized armpits. Dim fluorescent lights casting a subterranean, aquamarine glow in its wooden carriages. And notifications asking that you give up your seat for those mutilated in the war.

I had an address of a hotel at Jussieu. The 5th arrondissement. Not far from the Jardin des Plantes. A half-star hotel with a half-star price: forty francs a night. Six American dollars. Leaving me another forty francs per day with which to feed and water myself and go to movies and smoke cigarettes and sit in cafés and . . .

I had no idea how to finish that sentence. I was operating without an agenda or any preconceived stratagem. I had just graduated early from one of the state universities in the Midwest. I had already accepted a scholarship at a law school that guaranteed its graduates a clean trajectory into the higher echelons of national life.

The fact that the money Dad had spent on educating me could now be justified meant I was finally deserving of his highest praise: 'You've done good, son,' he told me. What was not good, according to his world view, had been my announcement over Thanksgiving that, as soon as the Christmas holidays were behind us, I would be flying the Atlantic.

My father. A distant, taciturn fellow. Not a monster. Not a terrifying disciplinarian. But absent. Even though he never traveled and was home most nights by 6 p.m. An insurance man with his own small company. Himself and a staff of three. His own father had been a career soldier, always referred to as 'the Colonel'. Dad told me once in a flicker of rare candor – after my mother died of a virulent, fast-killing cancer – that he spent most of his own childhood in fear of that martinet of a man. Dad was never stern with me – especially as I was always the careful kid, the good student. I kept my head down and turned myself into a grind, hoping to please a father unable to show me much in the way of affection.

My mother was a stoic. A quiet woman who taught school and seemed resigned to her chilly fate with the man she had agreed to marry. She never had an argument with my father, always played the dutiful housewife, and raised me to be 'a good boy destined for bigger things'. Mom interested me in books. She bought me an atlas and got me curious about the world beyond our hayseed frontiers. Unlike Dad, she was carefully affectionate with me. I did feel her love, albeit in her own measured way.

When she got sick I was just twelve. My terror of losing her was vast. From diagnosis to death was a six-week nightmare. I was only told that she was in the endgame of her cancer ten days before she left this life. I knew she was sick. But she listened to my father and kept denying the finality enveloping her. The day she admitted to me that her time amongst us was coming to an end was the night before she was rushed to a hospital an hour away from us in Indianapolis. I walked around in a state of silent trauma for days afterwards. That Friday, Dad arrived unannounced at school, conferring in whispers with my home-room teacher, then motioning for me to leave with him. Once we were outside he told me, 'Your mom only has hours left. We have to hurry.' We said little more to each other on the drive to the hospital. But my mom had slipped into a coma by the time we arrived. My dad let the oncologist on duty do the official thing and confirm that there was no hope she would survive the evening. Mom never came out of the coma. I never got to talk with her again, to say goodbye.

A year after her death my dad announced to me that he was marrying a woman named Dorothy. He'd met her at his church.

She was a bookkeeper. She came from the same reticent side of the street as Dad and treated me with aloof courtesy. When I went off to the state university for my first year of college, Dorothy convinced Dad to sell the family house and buy a place with her. I was actually relieved when this came to pass. Just as I was pleased that Dad had acquired this chilly woman. It took the pressure off me to be there for my father, even though he himself never expressed a nanosecond of neediness. Because that would have meant showing vulnerability to his son. And Dad could never do that. Dorothy told me that I should consider the guest room my home. I thanked her, and used it on the big holidays like Thanksgiving and Christmas, but otherwise stayed away. Dad and Dorothy made all the right noises when I got into that pinnacle of law schools. But as a man who distrusted the big bad world beyond his own narrow experience of life (he'd never once left the country, except for a stint in the navy during the war), he was not pleased when I told him I was heading to Paris.

'This should have been discussed, son.'

'I'm discussing it now.'

And I quietly explained how all those summers clerking for a local law firm, and the ten hours a week stacking books at the university library, and the strict application of his oft-preached virtue of frugality, had given me enough capital to fund a few months beyond American frontiers. An extra course load undertaken over the past two semesters meant I would be free of college – and its attendant costs – in just a few weeks.

'I don't approve, son.'

But he didn't raise the issue again – especially once Dorothy pointed out that I had just saved him a few thousand dollars by getting my degree a semester ahead of schedule. Dad drove me to the airport on the night I left and even handed me an envelope with two hundred dollars in cash as a 'going-away gift'. Then he gave me one of his cursory hugs and told me to drop him a line from time to time. His way of telling me: you're on your own now. Though truth be told, I was always just that.

On the Métro, a woman only a few years older than me eyed my blue down jacket, my backpack, my hiking boots. I could see her making an instant assessment: *American college kid abroad and lost.* I felt a sudden need to break out of this identikit image; to smash all the limitations and cautious conformities of my life until now. And I wanted to ask for her phone number and tell her, 'Wait until you see me in cooler clothes.' But I had no French.

At Jussieu there was an army surplus store that sold black pea jackets – *Importé des États-Unis.* I tried one on. It made me look like a Kerouac drifter. It cost four hundred francs: a steep price for me. But it was a coat I would wear every day of this winter. And it was a coat that would allow me to blend into the cityscape; would not call attention to my anxious American-abroad status.

And I was anxious.

Because I was alone. And deficient in the language. And friendless. And lacking the rigid direction that had defined my life until now.

Anxiety is the dizziness of freedom.

I now had freedom.

And Paris.

And a black pea coat.

And the sense, for the first time ever, that my life was a tabula rasa.

A blank slate can often induce dread. Especially when you have been brought up to believe in the necessity of narrow certitude.

At the hotel I handed over a week's rent, took the key, went upstairs and slammed the door for a few unconscious hours, awaking with this thought:

I am bound to nothing and no one.

A vertiginous realization.

*

My hotel room. An elderly brass bed with a wafer-thin mattress. A sink of stained porcelain and semi-rusted taps. A pockmarked mahogany wardrobe, an old café table and one chair. Floral wallpaper yellowed by age and cigarette smoke. A small radiator that banged percussively. A view of an alleyway. Walls that leaked sound. A clacking typewriter. A man with an endless hacking cough. I still slept. And woke in the late afternoon. The bathroom was down the hall. A stand-up, squat-to-shit toilet. Grim. A small shower stall next door, framed by an old green vinyl curtain. There was a hose with a hand-held shower head. The water was hot. I soaped up my body and hair, washing away the all-day siesta. I used the harsh bath towel left on my bed to dry off and hide my nakedness during the dash back to my room. I dressed and went out into the world.

7

Snow was falling. Paris had been bleached. Hunger was speaking to me. I hadn't had a proper hot meal in over a day. I found a small place tucked away behind the boulevard Saint-Michel. *Steak frites*, a half-liter of red wine, a *crème caramel*: twenty-five francs. I thought: I am too conscious of money, of the price and conflicting values of everything. Frugality and self-denial were two central household credos indoctrinated in me at a premature age. I now wanted to jettison them all. But I also wanted somehow to get through the next five months without needing to run home and find work. There was a summer clerkship with a federal judge awaiting me in Minneapolis on June 1. There was law school and all its future implications come September. Before all that I had this juncture, this space, without obligations – outside of staying within my budget.

I wandered for much of the evening, oblivious to the cold, the still-falling snow. If you have not grown up around epic urban grandeur – or anything that even begins to hint at historic monumentalism – Paris is humbling. But though its great architectural set pieces dazzled me, my peripheral vision was leading me elsewhere: to its backstreets, its spindly labyrinth of alleyways. And there was the sense that sex was everywhere – from the women of the night trawling for custom on the edges of sidewalks to the couples locked in tangled embraces against walls, lamp posts, even the stone balustrade of the Pont Neuf. I followed the path of the Seine: dark frigid water in a relentless drift. I envied the lovers. I envied anyone who had connected with someone else; who didn't feel alone in the dark.

*

I learned to drift.

My first week in Paris was just that: an extended, aimless ramble. Daybreak now for me was around ten in the morning. There was a café next door to the hotel. I ate the same breakfast every morning: *citron pressé, croissant, grand crème*. It was a place frequented by local workers – the trashmen, guys doing roadwork – which kept it cheap. The owner – bad teeth, tired eyes, ever professional – was always behind the counter. After I was there for the fourth day running he greeted me with a nod: '*La même chose?*' he asked. I replied with a *bonjour* and a nod back. We never exchanged names.

A daily *International Herald Tribune* was beyond my budget. But the café owner always had yesterday's edition behind the bar. He told me: 'A compatriot of yours from the hotel always buys it before breakfast, then leaves it on the table when he departs.'

Or at least that is what I thought he told me. I understood barely more than I could speak.

'*Il arrive quand?*' I had bought a notebook, a cheap fountain pen, a dictionary and a book of basic verbs. I had set myself the daily task of learning ten new words and two new verbs conjugated in the *présent, passé composé et futur proche* every day.

'Every morning at seven. I think he doesn't sleep much. A man with eyes that are far too bruised by life.'

I loved that description so much – *Un homme aux yeux trop mâchés par la vie* – that I wrote it down in my notebook.

The café was called Le Select, its name a contradiction. There was nothing select about it. It was small, basic, with a handful of tables and no real amenities. I had no experience of cafés. Only American coffee shops, American diners, American drip coffee. Juke boxes and grubby linoleum and waitresses who chewed gum and wore battered smiles. Here at Le Select booze was an accepted part of the morning ritual. Most of the trash-tossers – *les éboueurs* – would down a Calva with their coffee, just as a pair of gendarmes often stopped in for *vin rouge*, poured from label-less liter bottles. They never paid for their drinks. Le Select taught me the art of loitering with intent. I would sit there until noon with my breakfast, my day-old newspaper, my cigarettes, my notebook and fountain pen. I was never told to move along, never disturbed. As a result I came to understand a key construct of cafés: their sense of improvised community and heated refuge amidst the cold dispassion of city streets.

Around midday I moved myself along to loiter elsewhere, often to the cinemas on the rue Champollion. Old Westerns. Old film noirs. Obscure musicals. Directors' festivals: Hitchcock. Hawks. Wells. Huston. All in the original English with French subtitles dancing at the bottom edge of the screen. A place to hide for ten francs per *séance*.

Séance: a screening. But also a gathering. A ritual form of meeting.

Another word for my notebook.

I took a decision to explore, on foot, all twenty arrondissements. I haunted museums and galleries. I was a regular at English-language bookshops. I went to the jazz joints on the rue des Lombards. I ate a tagine for the first time. I found myself desperate to keep busy; an antidote to the solitude of my days and nights. I told myself: floating will tamp down the loneliness. Instead, floating augmented the emptiness within. I was not unhappy in Paris. I was unhappy in myself. I could not pinpoint the reason why. I wasn't missing home. I wasn't longing for things stateside. I was reveling in the newness of all before me. But the sadness – like a stubborn stain – refused to wash away.

The couple in the room next to mine were always fighting. The night man on the front desk – Omar, a Berber from the south of Morocco – told me they were Serbians. Refugees. And always furious at each other.

'Their world would come unstuck if they showed kindness to each other. So they keep up the anger.'

The typewriter clacking was also a constant night-time feature of hotel life. I didn't mind it. It had a metronomic effect on me, the *tap, tap, tap* lulling me into the underworld of sleep. One night in my second week, falling in late from a *séance* at a jazz club I saw the door of my neighbor's room ajar. The light within was clouded by smoke.

'You may enter,' came a voice from deep within the fumes. An American voice.

I pushed open the door. I found myself in an identical version of my own room, albeit one where the tenant had taken up full-time residence. Seated in the bentwood chair was a guy in his mid-twenties. Shoulder-length blond hair, round steel glasses, a cigarette between his teeth, a fogged-in smile.

'You my neighbor?' he asked. 'Should I be doing this in bad French?'

'English works.'

'Is the typing keeping you awake?'

'I don't sleep in my coat.'

'So you saw my door open . . . and just decided to say hello?'

'I can leave.'

'You can also sit down.'

This is how I met Paul Most.

'Yeah I write. No, I have not published a word. No, I am not going to tell you what this novel is all about – which shows great restraint on my part. Yes, I am a New Yorker. Yes, I have just enough of a trust fund to ruin me.'

He was a refugee from an authoritarian father. An investment banker. White shoe. Connected. Park Avenue. High Church Episcopalian.

'The whole prep school/Ivy League trajectory. I got into Harvard. I got thrown out of Harvard. Lack of interest in work. Two years in the Merchant Marine. Hey, it worked for Eugene O'Neill. I got back into Harvard. Daddy connections. I scraped through. I spent a Peace Corps year teaching the hopeless cases of Upper Volta. I worked my way through gonorrhea, syphilis, trichomoniasis. I exchanged Ouagadougou for Paris fifteen months ago. I found this hotel. I negotiated a deal. Here I sit, typing into the night.'

'Your father hasn't tried to force you back home and onto Wall Street?'

'Daddy has written me off. While in Upper Volta, and having a deranged moment brought on by dengue fever, I wrote the *Harvard Magazine* in response to a request for Class Notes. And what words did I send them? "*Paul Most, Class of '74, lives in West Africa with a permanent case of the clap.*" Well, I thought it witty.'

12

'Did it make it into print?'

'Hardly. But Ivy walls have ears. Papa wrote to me care of American Express in Paris telling me I was now on my own, without his largesse in the big bad world. Of course, he knew he could not stop me benefiting from a trust set up by his father for his five grandchildren. My share of the interest of the principal became payable to me as of my twenty-fifth birthday . . . which happened to be seven months ago. Right about the time that Papa defenestrated me. I now have a nice and tidy monthly allowance of eight hundred dollars. Considering that I have negotiated the management of this scruffy establishment down to twenty-five francs a night, I have my little sliver of bed space in Paris for just over one hundred dollars a month. And they even change the sheets twice a week.'

He then asked me where I'd grown up. I told him. His reply:

'What a dull little place to call home.'

I pointed to the eau de vie. A Vieille Prune. He poured me a glass. I took one of his Camels. He asked where I went to college. I gave him the information demanded.

'My word, aren't you Mr State U.? And now? Are you having the budget grand European tour before heading back to join Daddy's agrarian insurance practice?'

'I enter Harvard Law in September.'

That got his attention.

'Seriously?'

'Seriously.'

'*Chapeaux*. A fellow Harvard man.'

And one who didn't get there courtesy of Daddy.

13

But that subtext remained unarticulated.

He changed the subject, never once asking a further question about my life.

But two cigarettes and three eaux de vie later, he offered this observation:

'I know why you stood outside my door tonight. The agony of Paris. The city is cruel to anyone on their own. You see everyone intertwined and it points up your little-boy-lost status. And the fact that you are returning home to an empty bed in a cheap hotel.'

'That makes two of us.'

'Oh, I've got someone. Just not here tonight. But you're flying solo. And unable to connect.'

I wanted to contradict this. Wanted to protest. Wanted to slap down his cruelty. But I knew that would send me down a defensive street. Which was where he wanted me to end up. I could see the snare he was setting. So I said:

'Guilty as charged.'

'My, my – an honest man.'

'Any thoughts how I can become less lonely here?' I asked.

'I presume you speak little or no French.'

'It's very basic. Far from conversational.'

'I could invite you to a party tomorrow night. A book-launch thing. A friend of Sabine's.'

'Who's Sabine?'

'The woman who should be here tonight. Don't ask me to explain.'

'Why would I ask that?'

'A farm boy with teeth.'

'I wasn't raised on a farm.'

His reply was a smirk.

'If I invite you, I must warn you: I will not act as your chaperone. Nor will I introduce you to anyone.'

'Then why invite me?'

'Because you said you were lonely. Call it an act of mercy.'

He reached for a notepad and scribbled out an address.

'Tomorrow night at seven.'

He eyed up my flared gray denims, my brown crew-neck sweater, my blue button-down shirt.

'It's Paris. You might want to wear black.'

*

I returned to the army surplus store. The same boxer-faced man served me. I told him what I needed. I indicated my budget was limited. He looked me over, taking in my size. 'Skinny boy.' Then he went scavenging through the shelves. He pulled out a black wool turtleneck for thirty-five francs and a pair of black wool trousers for forty-five francs. He had to shake the dust off before I tried them on. They both fit me just fine.

'I have black winter boots from la Légion étrangère. Soft leather. Already broken in. Warm but not heavy – and with a good sole. Perfect for Paris. Sixty francs.'

I tried them on. They worked.

'Give me one hundred and ten francs for everything,' he said. 'And now you are *une symphonie en noir*.'

*

15

'You look like you just walked off the USS *East Village*.'

Paul Most's greeting to me before I made my way into the bookshop.

'You told me to change my style.'

'And indeed you did, Sailor.'

The bookshop was called La Hune. Most was standing outside it, a Camel on the go. A woman was with him. Rail thin, frizzy hair, a biker jacker, a black silk scarf.

'Meet Sabine,' he said.

I extended my hand. Sabine regarded this action with amusement. She leaned over and gave me a kiss on each cheek.

'My greenhorn friend here has no idea of local protocol,' Most said.

Sabine's response came out as a verbal slap.

'*Tu sais que je refuse de parler en anglais.*'

Most responded with a flood of fast French, an aggressive tone creeping in. Sabine pouted, barking back at him:

'*T'es un con.*'

She'd just called him an asshole. Appropriate.

'See what you caused?' Most said to me, all smiles.

He motioned to the door.

'Catch you at the bar.'

The bookshop was not a big space. There were brimming shelves everywhere. Books piled high. A dense crowd. I sought out the bar and reached for red wine. I backed into a bookshelf, above which was a sign: PHILO. I glanced down and found myself staring into a cliff face of volumes: de Beauvoir, Deleuze, de Maistre, Democritus, De Morgan, Derrida, Descartes, Diderot, Dworkin . . .

'*Êtes-vous obsédé par les philosophes dont le nom commence par "D"?*'

The voice: quiet, resonant, teasing. I spun round. I found myself facing a woman. An abundance of wavy red hair. Deep green eyes: pellucid, ever observant, witty. Her face soft, freckled, open. Her dress black and tight. Black stockings. Black boots. A cigarette between long fingers, the cuticles somewhat chewed, a band of gold on her left ring finger. My first thought: vulnerable. My second thought: beautiful. My third thought: I am smitten. My fourth thought: that damn wedding ring.

'American?' she said.

'I'm afraid so.'

'No need to be embarrassed about that.'

Her English was flawless.

'I am embarrassed about my lack of French. Why is your English so good?'

'Practice. I lived in New York for two years. I should have stayed. I didn't.'

'And now?'

'Now I live here.'

'Doing what?'

Another amused smile.

'You like to interrogate. Are you a criminal lawyer?'

'I'm heading that way. But let me guess. You're a professor?'

'Why are you so determined to find out what I do?'

'My natural need to pose questions.'

'Curiosity is commendable. I am a translator.'

'English to French?'

'German to French as well. Both ways round.'

'You're fluent in three languages?'

'Four. My Italian is reasonable.'

'Now I do feel like a rube.'

'There's a word I don't know – "rube".'

'Someone from the sticks. A hayseed. A yokel.'

'And let me guess – the inventor of this "argot" was from New York?'

'No doubt.'

She reached into the small black leather bag suspended from her shoulder and brought out a small black notebook and silver pen.

'How do you spell "yokel"?'

I told her.

'I love argot. It is the true local color of all languages.'

'Give me an example of Parisian argot.'

'*Grave de chez grave.*'

'*Grave* is "serious", right?'

'I am impressed – for someone who says he has no French.'

I explained my daily vocabulary discipline.

'Such diligence. Then you are definitely not *grave de chez grave*, which means "stupid".'

'Sometimes I feel that way – stupid.'

'In general, or just here in Paris?'

'Here. Now. In this bookshop. With all these smart, worldly people.'

'And you telling yourself *I'm just a "rube"* – have I pronounced that right? – *from the sticks?*'

'You pick up argot quickly.'

'When you are a translator words are everything.'

'So you are curious too.'

'Ever curious.'

She lightly touched my arm, letting her fingers linger there for a moment. I smiled at her. She smiled back.

'I'm Isabelle.'

'I'm Sam. Funny you asking me that question about philosophers. I looked at all those names on the spines of the books – all the *D*'s – and thought: I know so little.'

'But acknowledging that you have gaps in your knowledge – that you want to venture into intellectual places you've avoided until now – is wonderful. For me curiosity is all. So stop telling yourself you are a "rube". You found your way here tonight. You walked into an event so absurdly Parisian. Do you know the book being launched? The author?'

'I'm a gatecrasher.'

'I admire you even more for that. Look over there at the rather petite woman with the wild curls. That's Jeanne Rocheferand. *Philosophe. Normalienne.* She will be an *académicienne* before the end of the decade.'

She was tiny. In her sixties. Beyond thin. Leopard-skin print pants. Leopard-skin top. Big black hair. Hovering next to her a guy around twenty-eight. French biker type. Green aviator shades. Bored with the talk. His hand on her ass.

'I understand none of those terms,' I said.

'And why would you? They mean a great deal in our own world here. Stay here long enough, learn the language, it will all make sense.'

'I only have a few months over here. And I might move on.'

'Then you won't learn much – which perhaps is not the idea here.'

'I have no idea what the goal is.'

'"Goal". Such an American word and notion.'

'Is that a problem?'

Another light brush of her fingers across my arm.

'It's sweet. Here no one will ever speak of objectives, goals. We are all being far too theoretical. Dazzling ourselves with our cerebral verbiage. But everything in life is about permitting ourselves that which we want. Or creating limitations, frontiers for ourselves.'

'Are you a free person?'

'Yes and no. And yes, I permit myself certain things, and stop myself from crossing over into places where more freedom might just be found. The usual risks and compromises inherent in a certain kind of metropolitan life.'

'I am not metropolitan.'

'You are here. It is a start.'

A glance at her watch.

'The time, the time. I have a dinner . . .'

Without thought or premeditation I took her hand in mine. Her eyes closed. Then opened. Her fingers loosened. She stepped back.

'A pleasure, Sam.'

'A pleasure, Isabelle.'

Silence.

She broke it. 'So ask me for my number.'

'May I please have your phone number?'

She met my gaze.

'You may.'

A quick dive into her bag, the emergence of a single small card.

'Here it is. I am at this number most mornings and after-noons.'

She leaned over and kissed me on each cheek. I felt a charge of longing for someone I had only just met. She sensed it. She smiled.

'*À bientôt.*'

And she was gone.

I stood there, holding the card. I stared down at its simple black typeface:

ISABELLE de MONSAMBERT
Traductrice
9 rue Bernard Palissy
75006 Paris
01 489 62 33

I pulled out my wallet. I put the card in a small slot. I wanted to believe I would make that call in the next day or so.

'So you got Isabelle's phone number.'

Paul Most talking. Paul Most now by my side, a bottle of wine in his hand.

'How do you know her name?'

'Met her at another book thing last week. We got talking. I asked for her number. She didn't give it to me. Looks like you're the chosen one, fella. If you choose to be chosen. You've been given the card. The question now is: can you play it?'

*

Most disappeared with Sabine the Petulant. I nodded at the writer – a hail and farewell. She smiled. The biker boyfriend scowled. I looked around. The party was breaking up. I headed out into the black Paris night. I glanced at the menu of the Café de Flore. Beyond my means. I wandered back into the 5th and found a cheap brasserie where I ate a croque monsieur and drank two glasses of *vin ordinaire* while replaying the conversation with Isabelle. I opened my wallet. I looked again at her card. I kept thinking about the wedding band on her left ring finger. Her invitation. '*À bientôt.*' If I chose to make the call.

I pulled out an aerogramme – scored at a local post office – and my fountain pen. I wrote my father a simple note telling him I was alive and flourishing, that Paris was 'interesting' (he preferred understatement), that I was looking forward to my summer with the judge and Harvard thereafter. I threw in that last bit to reassure him that I was definitely going to do the right thing and come home. Because I still needed to answer to that voice of authority he represented. Had Dad been a completely removed man it might have been easier to compartmentalize his detachment from me. But the fact that he was never arctic with me, but also never there . . . it just augmented the guilt; the sense that something within me was responsible for his endless reticence.

I signed off the letter *Love, Sam.* I finished my last glass of wine, smoking down a Gauloise before heading back to the hotel. Isabelle's card got transferred from my wallet to a corner of the table I had turned into a desk. I placed it under a notebook. It sat there untouched for two days. I did my daily breakfast thing, my daily cinema thing, my daily drifting-around-town thing. I knocked once on Paul Most's door, in search of company. No answer. I filled more pages in my notebook. I saw two Westerns in a cinema on the rue Champollion where I was the only patron in the theater. I found Chinatown in the 13th arrondissement and ate Szechuan pig's feet for no better reason than to eat Szechuan pig's feet. I slept in fitful bursts. I kept telling myself: pick up the card, make the phone call. I imagined her amused voice letting me know: 'I am hardly interested in a yokel like you.'

Late that night, around three, I heard the couple next door fighting again. The man hectoring her. The woman crying. Trying to supplicate him. Suing for peace. It didn't matter that Serbo-Croat was a Martian language to me. The vernacular of rage expressed by a couple needs no translation. Whether uttered in a flood of reproachful words or evinced through lengthy silences at a dinner table (my parents' preferred form of message transmission), that sense of contempt is unmistakable. *Contempt*: was that the underlying sentiment which marked the endgame for most intimate relationships? I got out of bed and poured myself a glass of wine from the liter bottle of fifteen-franc rouge I'd bought yesterday. It was drinkable, cheap. I lit a cigarette. I listened as the fight hit a crescendo – the woman now lashing out, berating her man, submerging him in her disdain. Now it was his turn to sob and plead. I reached over and turned on the little transistor radio that had crossed the Atlantic with me. I found a jazz station on the FM dial and heard a woman sing in a melancholic mezzo of her search for 'someone to watch over me'. That universal yearning . . . even though, at this early juncture in my life, I was beginning to fathom: everyone is, at heart, out on their own in the mess of life.

I drank more of the wine. The singer continued to catch, with syncopated longing, the search for that elusive soulmate. Next door some object was hurled. It smashed. Screams ensued. Doors opened. Voices were raised in complaint. I turned up the jazz, finished my cigarette. I fingered the card half lodged under my notebook and resolved to call Isabelle when day overtook this dark night.

*

There was a pay phone at Le Select. It had a *jeton* – the token you bought to operate it – jammed into its slot. I asked the guy behind the counter if I could use the red Bakelite phone he kept next to the bottles of Pernod and Ricard. He placed it in front of me on the zinc counter. The rotary dial clicked like a spinning roulette wheel as I dialed the number.

'*Oui, allô?*'

She'd answered on the third ring.

'*Bonjour*, Isabelle?'

'*Oui?*'

She sounded tentative. As in: *Who is this?*

'*C'est moi* . . . Sam.'

'Sam?'

'*L'américain*. Three days ago . . . the bookshop.'

'Oh . . . *Samuel*. A lovely surprise.'

Sem-you-el. She gave my name a quirky musicality.

'I was just wondering . . .'

I couldn't complete the sentence. *Merde.*

'Would you like to meet for a drink?'

24

She'd just completed the sentence for me. Double *merde*.

'Yes, I would like that.'

'Good.'

I could hear amusement in her voice. I could sense her thinking, *A boy. A scared little American boy.*

'If you have my phone number, then you also have my address.'

I glanced down at the card. This was all vertiginous new territory for me.

'Yes, I've got it.'

'Do you have something to write with?'

I scrambled in my jacket pocket for my notebook and pen.

'Ready.'

She gave me the door code. She told me the street was off the rue de Rennes and that I should take the Métro to Saint-Germain-des-Prés.

'At five?' she asked.

'When?'

'Today. Unless you are busy.'

Busy with what?

'I'll be there.'

'*À très bientôt.*'

The last time – the only time – we'd spoken she had ended the conversation with '*À bientôt.*' Now that 'See you soon' had been upgraded with a *très*. My French was still basic. But I had started to discern the subtle intricacies, the signs and meanings contained in the addition of a more alluring *très*.

A crystalline January day. Cold. A hard blue sky. I walked and found myself deep in the 10th. A canal. Grubby streets. Tumbledown buildings. More walking to quell the anxiety within.

25

The canal ran right down to the Bastille. Why this intrinsic fear? That afternoon on the canal, when I tried to walk off the worry – was that the moment when a perception began to take hold? My childhood had been infused with sad culpability. A belief – reinforced by my father – that I merited being kept at arm's length. Not really worthy of love. A parental viewpoint that now had me wondering: how could a woman as rarefied and cerebral as Isabelle find this naive child of the Midwest worthy of her interest?

The canal ran out. I ducked into the Métro. Some minutes later I was above ground in Saint-Germain-des-Prés. Night. The electric dance of street lights and car beams and neon. I crossed the rue de Rennes. Bernard Palissy was a short, narrow street, number 9 a broad, low building. A publisher occupied the ground floor and had a severe display of its latest titles in a small picture window. I punched in the code on the pad. The door opened with a decisive click. I walked on into the courtyard. Cobblestones, narrow windows. Isabelle had told me to head to the far end and find her name on a list of bells. I rang once. Another decisive click. I opened the door to face narrow stairs. A voice – her voice – from above:

'It is an alpine climb.'

The banister was an oiled rope. The staircase was an upward spiral. It was a serious ascent. On each tiny floor were two doors painted maroon. I reached the fifth landing. The summit. Isabelle was standing in an open doorway, wearing a black turtleneck and a long, narrow, black wool skirt that held tight to her long, narrow frame. She had a cigarette between two fingers. I could see her sizing me up. She smiled, then leaned forward to kiss me on each cheek.

'You deserve a drink after that effort.'

I followed her inside. I was in a tiny apartment. A narrow rectangle of a place. The ceiling was low. It almost grazed my head.

'I was worried you might be a tight fit here.'

'The disadvantages of being tall.'

'I like your height. The majority of French men are small – on every level.'

She took my coat, her fingers touching the sleeve of my sweater. I wanted to envelop her. Instead, I lit up a cigarette. Isabelle reached over to a shelf in the kitchen alcove and took down two large bulbous glasses. Putting them on the table, she reached for a bottle of wine and a corkscrew. She extracted the cork with instinctive ease. She poured out about three fingers of wine into each glass. A swirl of deep tannic red. I wanted to reach for mine and down it in one go. Dutch courage and all that.

'We need to give it five minutes. A wine must breathe.'

I took a deep steadying drag on my cigarette. Isabelle reached for me, threading her fingers through my free hand. I sat on the sofa, telling myself: don't pull her toward you.

She came down beside me. Her grasp of my fingers tightened.

'Kiss me.'

One beat later we were entwined. My mouth deep against hers. Her hands around my head. Her tongue within me. Her legs open, then thrown around me. Rocking me back and forth, back and forth. Augmenting passion: immediate, crazed. Pulling off each other's clothes. Her underwear: black, simple. She grabbed for my belt. Pulling down my jeans. Her hand taking me. Her

27

skin freckled like her face, translucent. Her triangle of hair. My finger stroking her. She let out a hushed howl. She grabbed me, guiding me in. I pushed down. As deep as I could go. Now her howls were not hushed. Now she was digging her nails into my back. We were possessed. Amok. No past knowledge of such craziness, such freedom. I tried to hold back as long as possible. I came in a wild burst, the effect electric. I muffled my gasps. I slumped against her. She was still shaking. I was aware of the rapid metronome of her heart. The dampness of our skins. The way we were conjoined. Her hand taking mine. Clutching it. The solidarity of shared passion. She moved a hand to either side of my head. Grasping me. Looking long and hard into my eyes. I saw questions. She kissed me. She ran an index finger down from my forehead to my lips.

'You can come back,' she said.

I smiled, trying to cloak my anxiety. The anxiety of being so smitten. She lit us cigarettes. She reached for the wine glasses, handing me one, then she clinked her glass against mine.

'*À nous*,' she said.

To us.

*

That night I knocked on Paul Most's door.

'I'm writing,' he shouted over the lethargic clack-clack of his typewriter.

'I'm buying the drinks if you want an excuse to stop writing.'

'Excuse accepted,' he said.

Five minutes later we were huddled over Calvados and cigarettes in a corner of Le Select.

28

'So when did you fall in love?' he asked me.

This question threw me. Because it also had me wondering: am I that transparent?

'I don't know what you are talking about,' I said.

'Bullshit. You've just become a resident of that country called Smitten. Let me guess, the beautiful, elusive Isabelle . . .?'

I said nothing, staring down into the dark copper veneer of my apple brandy. Most reached for my pack of cigarettes.

'Your silence says it all: guilty as charged.'

Now it was my turn to light up a fresh smoke.

'Have you ever fallen hard?' I finally asked.

'Sure. Around thirty-three times. And always with a high sense of irony accompanying the downward plunge. But that's not you, sonny boy. "*How ya gonna keep 'em down on the farm after they've seen Paree?*"'

My lips tightened. I drew down hard on my cigarette and threw back the remains of my Calvados.

'Go on, call me an asshole,' Most said.

I remained silent.

'That's you – the ever-polite farm boy.'

'I wasn't raised on a fucking farm,' I hissed.

Most smiled. And said, 'Checkmate. Let me guess: you've never felt this way before, never known passion like—'

I held up my hand, like a cop halting traffic.

Most smiled again.

'Here's the thing,' he said. 'I've had one or two of these arrangements during my time here. They work just fine as long as you understand the married Frenchwoman is playing by one set of rules . . . and you won't get hurt as long as you accept her rules and don't think you can impose yours on it. Trust me: your heart isn't going to get what it so badly wants.'

To which I could only think what I could not express:

How could Isabelle and I have made love like that and not both be in love?

*

I phoned at ten the next morning. A mistake. Too early. Too eager. As the roulette-wheel dial phone at Le Select spun round, I told myself: *Not yet. Not now. Wait.* Even though she had said to 'Call me tomorrow' as I left her that first afternoon. Since then I'd played back every moment of what had just transpired. Blindsided by it all. Now fearful of its possible loss.

Is that what's called a duality? Does your introduction to proper passion set up a terrible dance of headiness underscored by the prospect of it all slipping out of your grasp? Which makes you even more anxious to try to shore it up. Even though you have no idea at such an early juncture what, if anything, this might be.

'*Bonjour*, Samuel. You are calling rather early.' Her tone formal, amused, corrective. 'How've you been since yesterday?'

'Missing you.'

Fuck. Too heart-on-sleeve.

'Lovely to hear that. It was a wonderful few hours.'

'When can we have the next wonderful few hours?'

'*Mon jeune homme . . .*'

'I could come over later.'

'I would truly like that. But I must head off for the weekend in a few hours. Monday, 1700 hours?'

'Uh . . . sure.'

'You sound hesitant.'

'Not hesitant. Just stupid.'

'You are hardly stupid, Samuel. I look forward to our next rendezvous with great pleasure.'

I felt despair. Why was I getting the impression: this is a one-sided crush? But as soon as these questions formed between my ears, I silenced them. Instead, I said:

'Monday it is then.'

'*Merveilleux. Bon weekend, Samuel.*'

End of conversation.

I must head off for the weekend in a few hours.

Monday now seemed a faraway date, protracted, distant. My reckless-desire scenario: to call her back, insist on a passionate hour today. Or to show up at the rue Bernard Palissy and . . .

Destroy everything with the immaturity of the impulsive.

I pushed away the phone. I ordered another coffee. I went back to my newspaper and notebook. I opened *Pariscope* and programmed the films and jazz gigs and free organ recitals in churches that would fill up the time until Monday. I gave myself the illusion of staying busy.

The weekend bled away. I tried not to live in the realm of raised expectations. I tried to tamp down my fear of her last-minute cancelation (even though she'd given no indication so far that this could be on the cards).

Monday morning landed with the slam of an outside door. Heading down the hall to the bathroom, I saw Paul Most in the hallway, two suitcases by his feet.

'Well, hello, stranger,' he said.

'I knocked twice. No answer.'

'Otherwise engaged. Now, otherwise leaving.'

'Any reason why?'

'My father left this life two nights ago.'

'I am so sorry.'

'The platitude is appreciated.'

'It was meant.'

'I know that. I am in a sour place. Papa was not a nice man. But I must do the correct thing. The burial is Wednesday. My mother tells me I was not cut out of the will. Which was also her way of informing me: show no disrespect, be there for me, and I won't go legal and legislate against you.'

'So this is it. The final exit. No return?'

'I've done my time here. I'm now at that juncture where I would have to stop living as a transient and get a place, get a *carte de séjour* and find work and declare Paris home. To get the papers I would need to marry. There are candidates. But beware these bohemian Frenchwomen who espouse free love and no strings. They all have this bourgeoise underside. They will start talking commitment, property, babies. It's all programmed into them at an impressionable age. The veneer of sexual freedom often disguises future domestic entrapment.'

'Will you dodge all that back home?'

'Of course not. Within five years I'll be married and doing something academic and limiting. Unless I decide before then to make the big Faustian pact and follow Dad into advertising. He was the ultimate J. Walter Thompson exec. Slick, smart, all success, no presence. Never rated me.'

I reached out and put a hand on his shoulder. He shrugged me off.

'Is this your idea of consolation?' he asked.

'Solidarity.'

'What will that bring me?'

'The momentary belief that someone else gets it.'

He hung his head, then hoisted his bags.

'America beckons.'

'I look forward to reading your book.'

'It will never see print.'

'How can you say that?'

'Because I know trash when I read it.'

Declining my offer of assistance, he trudged down the stairs. I peered in his room. All his books had been left behind. Stacks of unused notepads. Bottles of wine and booze. I called down to him.

'What about all your stuff?'

'Past tense. Help yourself.'

'That's kind of you.'

'I'm anything but kind. And I know that in time this Paris idyll will also seem to you like the last illusion of freedom before you did what most of us Yanks end up doing: the usual conformist dance.'

Our last words. A front-door slam. He was gone.

I went into his room. More than a hundred books. A stack of yellow writing pads. A collection of pens. About a half-dozen empty black notebooks. Grid paper. Pencils. Four unopened bottles of red. Two eaux de vie. Vieille Prune. The remnants of a life in transit. I felt a strange chill on the back of my neck.

That sense that everything we accumulate – all we pile up, everything and everyone we connect with – is inevitably left behind. None of us avoid this fate. Which is why we must side-step timidity when it comes to the present tense. All we have, in essence, is the here and now.

And all I had – and wanted – at this very moment was Isabelle.

*

We fell into bed the moment I walked through her door. All over each other. Naked in moments. Crashed across the duvet. The four-day respite had built up vast desire. Pulling me in. Spreading her legs to take me deeper. Then closing them. Forcing me even further within. Her groans mounting. My arms encircling her. The aroma of her perfume – something lavender, subtle – wafting into me. My fingers on her nipples. Hearing her breath quicken. The crazed rhythms of our back and forth, back and forth. Her cries mounting. Her hand plunged against her mouth as she let go. Moments later the pressure within me detonating. A sudden explosion that landed like a punch to the head, then cascaded into the deepest sense of release. I fell against a pillow, spent. She turned toward me, her fingers stroking my face.

'*Mon amour.*'

It came out in a whisper. I whispered back:

'*Mon amour.*'

A long, deep kiss. Then she was out of bed, her tall frame shadowed by a candle aglow on her desk. Her red hair astray across her face. The luminosity in her eyes.

A visual miniature that still stays with me: the naked beauty of Isabelle, moments after we had brought each other to a place of rapture. The swaying of her narrow hips as she did fast, practical things for our benefit. Opening a bottle of wine. Finding glasses. Retrieving her pack of Camel Filters, a steel Zippo lighter, a chipped café ashtray.

I understood so little of life then. But I was still able to grasp the wonder of all these simple elements coming together and it engendered something approaching gratitude. For having this perfect moment with this dazzler of a woman about whom I still knew virtually nothing, but with whom I was in bed under an eighteenth-century roof in twentieth-century Paris.

'How was your weekend?'

As soon as it came out of my mouth I regretted the question's banality, its quasi-probing of matters personal. I sensed her shoulders clench. A momentary shudder of disapproval.

'It was just fine. Restful.'

'You went away?'

'To our place in Normandy. Near Deauville. There's a beach, la Manche – the Channel. English weather in France. Beautiful gloom.'

Our place. The first time she had used a plural pronoun to describe her life outside of this tiny, under-the-eaves space.

'You chose it for its gloom?'

'For its beach. For being two hours from Paris. Me, I love the blue of the South. The brilliance of the light. That whiff of Afrique du Nord when you disembark from the train at Marseille Saint-Charles.'

'Why not have a place there?'

'Paris–Marseille is nine hours by train. A world away. Impractical for a weekend out of the city. Also, the family has always had a place in Normandy.'

'Your family?'

'Not at all. The family with means. His is an old family, with deep connections in the military, the upper levels of the Republic and, of course, the financial establishment.'

'And you? No family with money?'

'My parents were both teachers in lycées. Bookish, interesting, self-contained, quietly dissatisfied. My father wanted to write novels. My mother thought she should be a high-level academic. Instead they taught school. Because of that, because of the limitations of *la vie quotidienne*, they became disenchanted with their union together. So they both got involved with other people. Which led to the usual chaos. They divorced. And remarried mirrors of each other. The human need to repeat.'

'Do you have brothers, sisters?'

'An only child.'

'Like me.'

'It's a strange condition, being the one and only by-product of all their years in bed. Tell me why it was so sad for you. Being their only child.'

'I never indicated . . .'

'No need to. It's very much there in the way you carry yourself.'

'I'm that obvious?'

'To a fellow sufferer like me, yes. It is one of several things that I sensed about you that first night in the bookshop: a lonely young man, and not just because he's by himself in Paris. A deeper sort of loneliness. One that he has known, perhaps, since childhood.'

I didn't know what to say. Except:

'And you got that from just our first conversation?'

'Are you offended?'

'Hardly.'

'But your tone. You sound shocked.'

'Shocked that you read me so well so fast.'

She leaned over and kissed me.

'Now tell me why it was so lonely.'

This was the last thing I wanted to recount, lying naked next to her among the contorted sheets. But some voice within me hinted: dodge the subject and you will lose some crucial intimacy between the two of you.

So I told her about Mom and Dad and growing up far too normal in Indiana and knowing that my future was elsewhere . . . especially after my mother's death. She listened in silence. When I finished she slid her arm around me, bringing me closer.

'My world may have been dissimilar to yours. But your childhood – that is familiar territory for me. I, too, lived there, but with a mother as detached as Papa. Entrenched only in herself.'

*

Mid-February. Our fourth week together. New snow. Then a desolate week of rain. I learned a new word: *glauque*. Grim. Bleak. Isabelle had a cold. A constant cough that turned into a baritone hack.

'I must give these up,' she said, stubbing out a Camel Filter into the ashtray balanced on my naked chest. We were in bed. It was 18h00 according to her European clock. Our twice-weekly event. Always five until seven. Always with a three- or four-day interregnum. The rules. Her rules. I never challenged them. Not since that first morning-after phone call, when I over-hinted that waiting four days to see her next struck me as interminable. Her cool response let it be known: *These are the frontiers. Accept them or be gone.*

I accepted them. Fastening my lips anytime I felt an expression of love reaching them. Even though I was just that: in love. Wanting nothing more in the world than her. Thinking: we are ideal. On every level.

She knew this. She got the romantic turmoil swirling within me. She liked it. Because it compounded my passion with her. But once, when I did start to admit the state of my heart – whispering '*Je t'aime*' – she put a finger to my lips and whispered back:

'*Arrête.*'

That was another rule: we could refer to each other as lovers, but we were not 'in love'. Even though in bed it was never sex, it was always making love.

I abided by the rules. I posed few questions about her life. I found out she was translating a novel by an Austrian writer who specialized in what she described as 'fractured narratives'. I glanced often at her crammed bookshelves – the volumes in five languages, so many writers about whom I knew nothing. Big gaps in my limited cultural education that I now wanted to fill.

'I've read so little fiction.'

'Then start now.'

*

The next day, armed with her list, I went to Shakespeare and Company and bought novels by Dreiser and Flaubert and Zola and Sinclair Lewis. Now I had another component to my very open days. I set myself the task of reading at least two novels a week. Isabelle was my literature professor. I learned all about Flaubert's obsessive rewriting of *Madame Bovary* and how it was the first novel that had ever tackled the subject of domestic boredom and the corrosiveness of marriage.

'Most people marry for love,' she said. 'Then they wake up years later and find themselves trapped in the sameness, the listlessness, of long-term conjugality.'

'But of course, that isn't your story.'

A tightening of her lips. I knew my comment would cause this response. I still made it. Because some weeks into our romance – she preferred the word *aventure* (which, I discovered, was one of several French synonyms for 'affair') – I still knew nothing of her life beyond these afternoon rendezvous. Or about her husband. All conversations were steered away from him. The unspoken third party.

'I am talking in generalities,' she said. 'Anyway, one of the great truths about *Madame Bovary* is that Emma is not very bright and fails to recognize at the outset that Charles, the small-town doctor she's marrying by virtual arrangement, is a bore.'

'What's your husband's name?'

A pause. Then:

'Charles.'

*

So now he had a name.

Some days later I discovered his profession: investment banker at one of the financial houses in Paris. Divorced. No children as his ex-wife couldn't conceive. A most elegant fellow: cultured, highly literate, well connected, discreet. He met Isabelle in 1969. She was in her twenties. Writing her dissertation at the Sorbonne. Just ending a relationship with a 'Maoist biker' named Edmond.

'Everything about Edmond was extreme. His politics. His view of sex. His anger at everything established in the world. An interesting year – but his aggression became dangerous. One day I simply decided: no more. Suddenly he became a very little boy. Crying, pleading, begging for another chance. The aggression, the radicalism of his perspective . . . it was all a façade. And neediness is such an unattractive attribute in a man.'

Was she dropping a hint?

'And then, in a radical volte-face, I fell for a man of finance.'

I had just finished going down on her. A post-coital desire to bury my head between her legs. She didn't object. On the contrary, during our last time together she had let me know how, when I moved down on her, she liked the lips parted and stroked with my tongue, how she responded best to a slow, deliberate, up-and-down movement. I was a fast learner. At first, she was a little hesitant about telling me what made her open up. I told her she should tell me all.

40

She taught me not to rush. How to hold back until she had climaxed. The way we had to intuit each other when entwined. The moments when to be full throttle; when to exercise a gentle touch. She asked me about my experience before her. I admitted it was limited. In high school there had been a girlfriend named Rachel who came from a very Baptist family and discovered she was crazy about sex as soon as we had our first experience of it together. 'You know I love you – and the fact that I did it with you means just that.' But we were seventeen. We were a typical Midwestern pubescent couple: sex in the back seat of her soldier brother's Buick. Sex in a six-dollar-a-night motel we discovered across state lines in licentious Illinois. A pregnancy scare. A demand that I commit to her. Me fleeing to the state university in Bloomington, and Rachel ending up at a teachers' college where she found herself 'with child' courtesy of one of her professors. Rachel had a son and became the wife of a man twenty-three years older than her.

'At least I'm not that old,' Isabelle said.

'What's your age?'

'Don't you know that is a forbidden question?'

'Not when we're sleeping together.'

A pause. Her lips tightened. Then:

'I'm thirty-six.'

'You are in no way old.'

'You are being too kind. And now I am changing the subject, fully aware that I stupidly brought up the age difference between us.'

'I like the fact that you are older.'

'I like the fact that you are younger.'

41

'How old is your husband?'

She reached for her cigarettes. And said:

'You still haven't told me about your other lovers.'

'At college I was too busy studying to have a steady girlfriend.'

'But you slept with women during the past four years.'

'Three or four. There was an economics major named Elaine who wanted to get serious with me.'

'But you wanted to flee entrapment?'

'And your husband?'

'What about my husband?'

'His age?'

'Fifty-one.'

'So he's fifteen years older than you . . . and I'm fifteen years younger.'

'Happenstance.'

I learned how they met – at a dinner given by a mutual friend.

'You know the expression *un coup de foudre*? What you Americans call "love at first sight". That was myself and Charles at that initial dinner. A few weeks later he left his wife, found us an apartment.'

'You still love him?'

She scowled at the directness of my question. But still answered it.

'Yes, my love for Charles is still there, still deep.'

'Then why do this?'

'A life needs many rooms, many compartments.'

'Like the one you have with a conveniently single, younger man like myself?'

'Why the angry tone?'

'I never thought of this as a compartment. An arrangement.'

'Nor do I. I was simply explaining that—'

'I am, metaphorically speaking, a room. A place you can enter to get what you want without the messiness of commitment, and then close the door on it.'

'Samuel, please . . .'

'Please *what*? Accept your "rationalist" approach to what we have?'

'And what is it that we have?'

'Love.'

'You are confusing passion with love. Passion is something we create magnificently together. I long for these hours together. For your touch. For feeling your desire, your need for me. As I hope you feel my desire, my need for you.'

'You're everything I have ever wanted.'

'But you know so little about me.'

'What do you mean by that?'

'We have no day-to-day life.'

'Because you keep our times together regulated. Twice a week, two hours, no more.'

'I *am* married. I have a day-to-day life with someone else. A life I do not plan to disrupt. You have never lived with anyone, have you?'

I shook my head, knowing that my inexperience in such matters was about to be held up in front of me; a mirror that would force me to stare back at the petulant, jejune lover who was overstepping many boundaries right now, the principal one being wanting more when I already had so much with

Isabelle. It's the way in most matters intimate. They cannot ever simply be kept to the erotic enjoyment of one another. After a certain juncture they must have greater meaning. The prospect of a future must be attached; passion for passion's sake cannot be enough. I had yet to work out this very human need for commitment and possession. Isabelle was way ahead of me here.

'When you eventually have a domestic relationship, you will see how your life together changes. No matter how deep the love, the quotidian arrives. You wake up next to each other, day in, day out. The lust you once had for each other quietens. Because it loses its newness, its amorous immediacy. And if you have children . . .'

'Why don't you have children?'

'That's a conversation for another time.'

She stubbed out her cigarette, pulled back the duvet, got out of bed, her lithe body – which I now knew so well – illuminated by the flame of the candle on the little table where she ate lunch. She opened the door to the tiny bathroom and removed a simple gray terrycloth robe from a hook within. Slipping into it, she announced:

'I have a reception I need to be at in less than an hour.'

'So you want me to leave?'

'I think we got ourselves in over our heads today,' she said.

'By which you mean I started getting possessive.'

'By which I mean, if you cannot accept that within the limits imposed on this there is much wonderful mutual pleasure to be had together, if you must insist that you "need more", then I have to end this now.'

I blinked. Many times. I studied her face, half turned away from me. Tight, controlled, rational. A voice within me hissed: don't lose all this through the stupidity of possessiveness.

'I'm sorry,' I said.

'Don't be sorry. On a certain level it's touching. Sweet.'

'Let me be direct here: I have no real life outside of this.'

'You are *here*. In Paris, *living* here.'

'And I have you. Twice a week. Which is wonderful.'

'That it is.'

I got out of bed. I came over to her. I put my arms around her, opening her bathrobe. I pulled her close, hard again. She stepped back, closing her robe.

'I don't have time,' she whispered.

'Your event is at seven. It's just six now.'

'And it's taking place in the *huitième*. I will need half an hour to get there on the Métro, and a half-hour beforehand to ready myself.'

'To wash away all trace of me – of us. He'll be there, won't he?'

'By "he", do you mean my husband? Charles? Yes, he will be there. The man getting the award is a long-standing friend.'

'*Why* don't you have children?' I asked, speaking before thinking. The question came out like a shotgun blast.

She rubbed a hand across her eyes. She turned and faced me.

'His name was Cédric. He was born on the thirty-first of December 1973. Those first few weeks were absolute happiness, even the sleepless nights, the exhaustion, the relentlessness. Charles was devoted to him. Being a mother was all I had ever hoped for. Especially after growing up with parents who were uncertain about being parents; who were there but always elsewhere.' She motioned to the cigarettes and her lighter, still on the cascading mess we had made of her bed. I went over and collected both, grabbing my jeans en route. As she lit up, I half dressed.

'You're putting on your clothes because you know what I am about to tell you.'

I grabbed my T-shirt and pulled it over my head. Though she had spoken the truth – I did sense what was coming – I still said nothing. She fixed her eyes on mine. They didn't waver as she said:

'On the night of the twelfth of March 1974, I put Cédric to bed in his crib. I held him as always and whispered how much I loved him. He went to sleep moments later. My husband and I went to bed. We slept straight through the night. When I woke it was almost eight. Charles and I never rose that late, because Cédric was our natural alarm clock. But that morning there was silence. When I entered our baby's room, he was lying there, in his crib, motionless. A small smile on his face. I will never lose sight of that smile, it will always be there until the day I leave this life. Within moments of picking him up, I was screaming. Because he was not breathing. Because he was not responding to my shrieks. Me begging him to answer me. Him not moving whatsoever. Because Cédric was dead.'

Silence. Her eyes didn't move from mine.

'Sudden infant death syndrome. The police, the medical examiner who did the autopsy, the psychiatrist to whom I was sent when I began to plot how to kill myself – which I saw as the only solution to the massive, horrible pain that was drowning me – all the experts told me the same thing: I had done nothing wrong. Sudden infant death syndrome has no rhyme or reason. It was as if the Angel of Death just chose, at random, a healthy child and decided to snuff out its tiny life. Cédric was two months, two weeks, two days when he died. For the first two years after his death I became a virtual recluse. I lost fifteen kilos. Nothing the doctors gave me to sleep lasted for more than three hours. No tranquilizer took away the pain. Charles and I had several serious talks about me being institutionalized for a time. I will not say that there was a day when I turned a corner, when I flipped a mental switch and the agony ended. The agony will never end. But I had no choice but to re-engage with life.'

Part of me knew I should reach out for her hand. But another, more anguished part of me had a question swirling around.

'And since this tragedy—'

She interrupted me.

'Have we been trying for another child?'

That was the moment I expected her to look away. She didn't.

'Not yet. But as soon as you head back to America I am coming off the pill.'

'Charles knows all about this?'

'Charles is my husband. Of course we have discussed this crucial matter. It is what couples do, Sam.'

'Thank you for this *crucial* insight.'

'What's with your petulant tone?'

'Petulant? *Petulant?* Just like a little boy—'

'I didn't say that.'

'But it's how you see me: the naive young man with a degree of sexual prowess. Someone you can see for a few hours here

47

and there, then toss away as soon as you decide you're ready for a new baby.'

'My decision to see you – to have these precious moments with you – has nothing to do with my decision to try for a child again now. After Cédric's death I decided I never wanted another baby because I could not stand the agony of possible loss again. So I went on the pill to ensure I would never get pregnant. Then I changed my mind.'

'Especially as the American kid is coming to the end of his time here.'

'How dare you be so simplistic,' she said, anger now in her voice.

'Simplistic? I've just been your interlude fuck, your "I'm still grieving" fuck. Now to be dismissed as soon as you decide—'

'Where is your empathy, Samuel? Your kindness?'

'You'd never think about having a baby with me.'

She glared at me, wide-eyed.

'Oh, so this is what this temper tantrum is really all about? It should be your sperm . . .'

'I love you—'

'You have no idea what love is, Samuel. Because you still have no idea about life.'

'Whereas your elderly husband . . .'

'He is hardly old. But yes, he is more than twice your age – and a proper, mature adult.'

'Unlike me.'

'Yes, unlike you. Because a real man shows compassion and understanding and selflessness. Charles and I lost a child together, the worst thing a couple can ever cope with. And Charles stood by me as I went through near madness. That's an actual man. Not some sulky adolescent with a limited perspective on the complexities of—'

I reached for my sweater and my jacket. 'I won't take up any more of your time.'

And I walked out the door and down the stairs, not once turning back to see if she was watching me walk out of her life.

*

The next evening, I was on a train to Venice. To economize I didn't buy a second-class couchette or a reserved seat. At Chambery – with dawn outlining the sky – I was informed by a newly boarded elderly couple that I was stretched across their reserved seats. The entire compartment was reserved. So, too, were all the other compartments. The dining car was not yet open – and was beyond my budget anyway. I spent the next long hours in the corridor of this carriage, using my backpack as a backrest. I kept telling myself my exit from Isabelle's life had been entirely justified; that she'd been using me all along. As I came to understand later in life, when we are guilty of a stupid move, a wrong call, we often rewrite the storyline to make it into one we are able to live with. But the more I kept trying to twist the narrative to justify my bad behavior, the more I realized that I was sidestepping the heart of the matter. In an attempt to distract myself, I turned to the novel in my backpack. *Madame Bovary*. Isabelle had been so right about Flaubert. A shape-shifter who broke new literary ground by writing the first novel about domestic boredom. Charles Bovary was a sad, provincial momma's

49

boy. A bore. Isabelle's Charles was a metropolitan man of success. They found love together. They made a child together. Then they'd suffered a sorrow beyond dreams together. And I'd ridden roughshod over her grief. Stupid pride. A lack of emotional nuance that spoke volumes about my immaturity.

The Italian border guards came aboard the train at Ventimiglia. One of the cops cadged a cigarette off me after lowering his entry stamp onto my passport. A plan was hatching in my head. Get off the train here. Get the next train back across the frontier. Return to Paris late that night – but not before getting off the train for an hour in Lyon to call Isabelle and beg forgiveness.

Lyon to Paris was five hours by train. I would be back in the 5th before midnight. I would fall into bed. I would sleep the deep sleep of the repentant, the atoned. When morning arrived I would go to Le Select and loiter without much intent. At 17h00 I would be punching in the door code at 9 rue Bernard Palissy. And back in Isabelle's forgiving arms.

What made me not act on this plan and repair the damage before distance deepened it? As desperate as I was to jump ship and race off to Paris, my knowledge of Isabelle – limited though it was beyond the wondrous contours of her body – told me that this approach would be considered adolescent, needy. Especially as she might have decided, in the wake of yesterday's events, to write me off. And who could blame her?

Venice. Dark chromatic skies. Light insidious rain. Canal lights all tenebrous. A cheap half-star hotel with a bad bed and an alley view, beneath which angry cats copulated much of the night. I admired the baroque aquatic grandeur of the place. I heard Monteverdi sung in San Marco's and thought there might just be a God. Or at least one who enabled such ecstatic music of the spheres. I walked five to six hours a day. A cure for my creeping sadness. I ensured that, outside of ordering food and services, I put myself in no situations where a conversation might be struck up. Further punitive measures, but also a part of me just didn't want to be talking with anyone right now. I booked myself passage on a mail boat bound in four days' time for Alexandria, but which docked after two days at sea in the Athenian port of Piraeus. Before I disappeared into Greece, however, I decided to throw what is known in American football as a Hail Mary pass. An attempt to turn around a lost cause. I went to Western Union and sent a long telegram to Isabelle.

I acted stupidly. I am profoundly sorry, apologize for my thoughtlessness, for hurting you. Say the word and I will come back to Paris. And will not demand anything more than our treasured afternoons together. I am here in Venice until this Friday.

I will understand if you say no — and will not bother you further if that is your response.

I think about you with immense tenderness.

With all my love

I added a PS, saying that if she did want to telegram me back, here was the address of my hotel. After that I could be reached c/o American Express in Athens.

I didn't expect to hear anything from her.

I didn't hear anything from her. My sense of loss deepened. And Venice – that most spectral and sinister and waterlogged of cities – just served to heighten my silent grief.

On my last day there I had to check out of my room before noon. I left my backpack at reception and went to a small café nearby for a cheap pasta lunch. I drank two glasses of wine. I returned to the hotel to collect my bag and then catch a vaporetto to the port. The owner handed me a yellow envelope.

'Just delivered five minutes ago,' he said. 'You are in luck – or not.'

Because, of course, a telegram is always the purveyor of either good news or bad.

I opened the envelope.

Samuel – your message touched me. Whatever about those final hours together please know when you are next in Paris I would be happy to welcome you back to 9 rue Bernard Palissy. In the afternoon, bien sûr. Je t'embrasse, Isabelle

*

In the afternoon.

That was to be our fate. Her way of again telling me: *this is all I can do.* I let that petulant thought drop away. Replacing it with another realization:

She is letting you back in the door.

I pocketed the telegram. I asked the guy behind the desk if he could store my bag for a few more hours. I headed out to the travel agency where I had bought my boat ticket. They allowed me, for a small fee, to trade it in for a second-class train ticket back to Paris that evening. Then I moved on to the post office. I dispatched another telegram.

Back in Paris late tomorrow. Je t'embrasse fort.

Afterwards, I put through a call to my place of residence in Paris. The hotel receptionist told me that my old room was free the following night. I booked it for the next ten nights. Then there was one final bit of personal housekeeping to deal with – finding a TWA office and reserving my flight back to the States some weeks from now. Non-stop from Paris to New York on a 707, then a connecting flight to Minneapolis. My clerkship was imminent, the judge's secretary having written to me c/o American Express in Paris some weeks before I ran away to let me know that she had found me accommodation in a small hotel opposite his chambers; that I would be working a forty-hour week for one hundred dollars, the cost of the hotel being met by his firm, but all else to be covered out of that weekly C-note. How I now wanted to write back: *Fuck your clerkship. I'm staying on the cheap in Paris.* How I knew that canceling at such short notice would be a black mark on my future legal resumé. Instead I sent a telegram back, stating all that she proposed was fine and I was 'looking forward to this excellent opportunity'.

Liar, liar.

But we do what we have to do to meet our obligations in the hope that this will somehow advance us.

The anxiety of freedom.

And I was heading back to all the obligations I had piled high on myself.

But first . . .

The all-night/all-day train to Paris. I bought a couchette. I slept intermittently.

North of Munich I was out of my couchette. A change of trains. Now in a narrow, second-class seat for the run to Paris. The Gare de l'Est in late afternoon. Early spring, pellucid sunlight streaming through the slanted glass roof. I passed two phone boxes. I didn't make the call.

'Monsieur Sam!'

Omar's greeting as I hauled myself and my backpack into the tiny hotel lobby. He even gave me a kiss on each cheek.

'How is life, Omar?'

'The usual. No change.'

My old room. I unpacked, grabbed one of the thin bath towels, wandered down the corridor to the shower and washed away all those hours of travel.

The next morning, the owner of Le Select handed me yesterday's *Herald Tribune* and the phone. As the roulette-wheel dial spun clockwise seven times, my standard breakfast showed up beside me – *citron pressé, croissant, grand crème*. I closed my eyes as the ringing tone commenced. One ring. Two rings, three, four, five, six . . . damn it all, she was out. Seven rings, eight, nine . . .

'*Âllo?*'

She sounded breathless, as if she had just dashed in.

'Isabelle?'

'Sam?'

'Yes, it's me.'

'Our timing worked.'

'Five p.m.?'

'Oh, yes.'

I hid in a movie. I browsed in a bookshop. I tried to tamp down my anxiety; that ongoing fear within me – there since childhood – of being turned away.

I didn't have to consult a notebook for Isabelle's door code. It was engraved within. The door clicked open. I moved across the courtyard. I reached *Escalier C*. I rang the bell next to her name. A buzz. I was in.

'Hello . . .'

Her voice from above. I told myself: *don't run up the stairs*. I ran up the stairs, my heels percussive on the worn wood.

'A man in a hurry.'

Her voice again as I came closer. The spiral of the stairs turning with every floor. Until there I was. Facing her. Her red hair was loose. She smiled. I smiled back. I wanted to throw myself in her arms. Instead I accepted her outstretched hand. She pulled me across the threshold, the door closing behind us. She tossed her cigarette in the kitchen sink, then put her hand behind my head, gathering my hair in her grasp. Pulling me forward, she kissed me with slow deliberation, her free fingers grasping that area of my jeans that was already rigid, desperate to be inside her.

The aroma of Isabelle enveloping me. The longing I'd felt for weeks. The sense: there is no one in the world like her. There is no one I want more. Her burying her head against my chest. A hushed howl as I let go. All equilibrium knocked sideways.

All sense of time and place lost. Until I fell to one side. And she took my hands in her hands. Her eyes aglow. Running her index finger down the contours of my jaw. Letting me cover her face, her eyes, in soft kisses.

*

I told her I wanted to hold her naked. She let me take off her dress. I threw off my own clothes.

She leaned over and kissed me.

'I missed you,' she said. 'More than I thought possible.'

'And I you.'

Again she ran her finger down my face, my arms tightening around her. Moments later we were making love again. No crazed reunion passion this time. Instead: great deliberation. A heightened sense of the intimate that I had not known before. The connection, the complicity . . . this was new territory for me. Especially as Isabelle was responding in kind. Pulling me in deeper. Her eyes locked with mine – as if everything in life was just us right now. As if we'd both found something as immense as it was fleeting. She looked at me:

'That was . . . extraordinary. And rare.'

'I agree – speaking from my limited experience . . .'

'Trust me, what we have here, together, it could never be sustained day in, day out. Which is why I don't want you to fly the Atlantic in – when must you leave?'

'Nine days. But I can come back . . . when I am allowed out.'

'And when I am able to see you. Because I am coming off the pill next week after you're gone. Maybe I will fall pregnant

56

quickly. Maybe not at all. *On verra*. We shall see. I will keep you informed. But you will come back to me, yes?'

I found myself staring out the narrow window just beyond all the books and papers strewn on her desk. I noticed the shadows on the worn roof tiles, the copper glow of dusk in the early, the fact that I was in this tiny apartment at the top of a spindly staircase in the 6th arrondissement of Paris, and I was in bed with this singular, remarkable woman – who was declaring love in a way I didn't fully understand. But did I need to understand everything when it came to this moment entwined together beneath sloping ceiling beams? Had she not just told me everything?

I leaned over and kissed her.

'I want to see you again.'

She closed her eyes, the smallest of smiles on her lips.

'A very good answer, Samuel.'

WE AGREED TO exchange two letters a month. Her idea, her rules. Ones she made right before I returned to the States – to that clerkship in Minneapolis. I hated the idea of saying goodbye to Paris. I dreaded the idea of three months in a midweight, mid-American city. I dreaded leaving Isabelle. She insisted that I go – not just for all sorts of professional commitment reasons (which I understood), but also because she really was seriously intent on getting pregnant.

'If you are here I will want to be with you several times a week. And that will create potential paternity problems. This child – it must be Charles's.'

We were, as always, in bed. Just days before my departure west. The usual post-lovemaking accoutrements: red wine, cigarettes, talk. I had wondered out loud once or twice about perhaps going out for dinner, extending our time together into the evening. This was nixed immediately, Isabelle noting: 'This is our special time together. Here and here alone.' The subtext of that statement being: *Paris is small, Paris talks, and I am intensely private. Which is why we are not going to be seen outside together.* I never again raised the idea of stepping out together in Paris. But I did ask:

'Does Charles have someone else in his life?'

'He does, yes. He doesn't know that I know. But I know.'

'How?'

'The usual ways. Business meetings that go on late. Needing to get to bed early – ergo, no sex – after a rendezvous with his "friend".'

'Do you know who she is?'

'An editor at one of the bigger publishing houses. A German. Very tall. Late thirties. Very much the single woman – desperate for a child.'

'You know a lot.'

'*Paris est tout petit.*'

'As you've indicated before.'

'Charles has been seen with this woman. In Paris and elsewhere. I would hope that he is taking precautions to ensure that Greta does not end up pregnant. But how can I insist on this?'

I fell back against the pillows, smiling. Isabelle nudged me.

'I do not like your all-knowing grin, which seems to imply: *Oh, these French . . .*'

'Well, you do play by different rules.'

'Don't include all my compatriots. There are many among us here who would have no tolerance whatsoever for the arrangement that Charles and I have.'

'But your arrangement is an "unspoken" one.'

'As you will discover, my dearest Samuel, that is the best sort of arrangement. No rules or regulations, no demands, no creation of limits. Nothing said. All understood instinctively.'

'And if he does have a child with her?'

'We will have to negotiate the complexities of all that.'

'But were you to get pregnant by me . . .?'

'I wouldn't allow that to happen.'

'Because Charles would be furious.'

'Because Charles is my husband – and Charles was Cédric's father. And Charles will be the father of our new child, should I get pregnant again.'

'So Charles can have a child with someone else. But you—'

'Let's not go there again, Samuel. This is my choice. And you must respect it. Just as you must understand—'

'I know, I know . . . I am so young, immature.'

'You are a work in progress, Samuel – and nearly thirty years younger than Charles. You don't have children, nor should you at this juncture in your life. Any more than you should have any sense of the ties that bind. And you are a deep romantic – one of the many things I love about you. But if we had a child together . . . a child made from the passion we share . . . would you truly be able to renounce all possibility of contact with him or her? Could you bear to see him or her raised by another father?'

Damn. She knew me better than I did.

I asked:

'Is it wrong to want a child with you?'

She leaned over and kissed me.

'It is a beautiful thought – and one that touches me. But life so often comes down to the confluence of two people's timings. What would you do here? Learn the language? Perhaps find a way of getting a *carte de séjour* and a job? Would you expect me to leave my husband and set up a new life with you, when my only knowledge of you is these afternoons here? Bewitching afternoons. The passion we share when we are in this bed together . . . it is precious. Because it is rare. Lightning in a bottle, so to speak. Unlike a long marriage, in which there is not the exhilaration, the urgency. There is something different, perhaps deeper, perhaps routine. All long-term couples speak in subtext. Ours is different because it is not shaded by contempt. We use subtext to avoid hurting each other. And that, *mon jeune homme*, is love. Perhaps no longer a passionate love. But love nonetheless.'

I knew not to ask more questions.

'I apologize for getting a little possessive there. *Why not me?* and all that.'

A light kiss on the lips from Isabelle.

'We will be happier this way,' she said.

I tried not to seem too clingy on our final afternoon.

'This time tomorrow I will be somewhere in American airspace.'

'And I will be ruing your absence. I will miss you deeply. Tell me you will find a way of getting back to Paris.'

'If I came at Christmas you might be a little child heavy.'

'Christmas would be impossible, pregnancy or no pregnancy. But if you come in the spring . . . I will have a nanny who can allow me to sneak away for two hours and meet you here.'

Spring 1978. A year from now. As if reading my thoughts, she said:

'A year is nothing. Our afternoons . . . they will continue. They will always be part of us.'

Her goodbye.

*

Feeling bereft was a new sentiment for me, not sampled before now. The judge in Minneapolis was a gentleman made of flint: dry, rigorous, cerebral in his concision. I read his need for cogency and modesty in his clerk. I gave him what he demanded. We were on the same Midwestern frequency. He was spare with praise, but having been in the vicinity of a distant father for all my formative years I wasn't unnerved by his stony countenance. Minneapolis in summer was humid and buggy. The hotel was simple, severe. I worked late most nights, frequently typing briefs into the small hours. I ran by the lake most days. On weekends I went to movies and frequented a bar where the beer was always cold, the air conditioning cranked up, and the revolving blues bands were passable. I sidestepped the attention of the barmaid, Lisa, who seemed to know that I was in residence alone around the corner from this agreeable dive and who on two occasions let it be known to me that her truck-driver boyfriend was out of town. I didn't take her up on either offer, as lonely as I was. Because Isabelle continued to loom large.

I finished the clerkship. On my last day the judge had three final words for me:

'You did well.'

And that was the end of our conversation.

I went home to visit my father for the weekend. My stepmother was conveniently out of town.

'Dorothy was so disappointed not to be here,' Dad said. 'But her sister in Muncie needed help choosing furniture for her new apartment. The poor woman is still a spinster at fifty-eight.'

I suspected that Dorothy had arranged this interior-design weekend as a way not to have to spend time with me. Though

I was always correct and circumspect with her, I sensed she knew that I'd never truly warmed to her strict Baptist way of viewing the world. As a result I was relieved that she was elsewhere. It gave me the chance to have time with my dad. As always he expressed pleasure in seeing me. As always he didn't seem to have much to say to me – and became standoffish and uneasy when I tried to initiate a degree of father–son closeness. It wasn't as though there was any antipathy between us. There was just that ongoing lack of connection. Dad listened with patience and a modicum of interest as I gave him a sanitized view of my time in Paris (he would have been horrified to learn that I had been having an affair with a woman who was breaking the seventh commandment). I told him about my work with the judge. He asked me questions about my Harvard Law ambitions. I tried to draw him out on his own life. I got the usual thin answers. I helped him repaint the basement that Dorothy had just remodeled as a rental apartment. We took two long walks in what passes for woodland in Indiana. We ate dinner twice at a steakhouse that was Dad's business local. We managed to fill the awkward silences that crept into our conversation on a regular basis. When he brought me to the airport on Sunday I hugged him goodbye and told him that I loved him.

'Love you too, son,' he replied in a flat voice, empty of real emotion. I boarded the flight. As I flew east, I found myself thinking: so this is how it will always be with a father who, though in no way mean or malevolent, will always keep himself out of emotional reach.

The plane touched down in Boston. I took a taxi across the river to Cambridge. And then . . .

Law School. All that preliminary talk about us being the gifted ones, the chosen ones – it all vanished within hours of our first classes. Fear was instilled in us that initial academic day: the realization, bequeathed to us professor by professor, that we were now fighting for our academic lives. This was going to be social Darwinism according to Ivy League rules.

Criminal law, contracts, civil procedure, torts, legislation, regulation, property. The classes were often Socratic. Brutal in their weaning out of those who couldn't keep up with the rigor, the pressure. The calculus of surviving: absolute focus underscored by the necessity of perseverance. I was called out twice my first week for an ill-informed response to a question tossed at me by my torts professor. 'Are you certain you belong here?' he asked me. There were no smirks or giggles from my fellow students. They all knew their public shaming would come soon enough.

Twelve of my class dropped out within six weeks. One of my classmates took an overdose of sleeping pills after being ridiculed in class three times in a row. The fellow survived, eventually transferring to the Business School. Not a word was ever said about the professor and his sadism. It was just an accepted part of the decor.

I had managed to get a single room in a hall of residence. I went there to sleep, nothing more. Four hours of classes a day. Eight hours of study. The Law School library was open until midnight. It was always full. No one had close friends. We were all too harried, weighted down for that. I forced myself to jog a half-hour a day on a path by the Charles. Autumn in Cambridge was New England wondrous – when I allowed myself to glimpse it. I granted myself one day off a week. Saturday. Then Sunday arrived and I spent nine hours hunched over law books again.

Law school. Sex was not part of the agenda. I missed it. I wanted it. I didn't go looking for it. Too many thoughts of Paris. Unlike many of my classmates, I didn't complain about Harvard's all-consuming nature. I had nothing else in my life.

Isabelle's letters were short, affectionate, with occasional mentions of her translation work and the occasional Parisian anecdote. She always closed with the same two lines:

Thinking of you always, my dearest Samuel.
Je t'embrasse.

In mid-October her second letter of the month ended rather differently:

One important thing I need to tell you, Samuel – three months ago I discovered I am pregnant. The baby is due in mid-March. It is immense news. I am so happy that this blessing – for that is what it truly is – has come my way again. Just as I am also singularly terrified . . . for so many obvious reasons. For the coming months I need to concentrate fully on getting through this pregnancy without complications. So I will be ending our correspondence for now – but with the hope that it will start again once I am assured that all is well with my new child.

I hope you will take this news reasonably, Samuel. I hope you will be happy for me.

Of course, I wrote her back a cordial letter telling her how pleased I was for her; how I hoped this new child would bring her much happiness; how I wished her all the best. Privately, I found myself going through a period of silent despair, of mourning. A sense that – for all her reassurances of a possible future connection – Isabelle was, in fact, bringing our brief, intense story to a close. I wasn't angry at her. Just somewhat lost. And thinking: I have spent the last four months since returning from Paris holding on to the absurd belief that there might just be the prospect of a life together. Romantic hope is often an exercise in sidestepping the actual heart of the matter.

As always, the ferocious Law School workload subsumed me. Work: the only antidote to loss. Or at least that's what I kept telling myself until I walked into a bar not far from Symphony Hall, sat down on a stool and found myself next to a woman named Siobhan. An Irishwoman. From somewhere west and wild called Connemara. Flaming hair, of course. Just finished a law degree early at Trinity College Dublin. At the end of a six-month roam across America. Heading back home to Dublin in a week and a job offer as a solicitor in a leading firm there. We were mirror images of each other's career trajectories – and she was immediately intrigued that I was 'a Harvard Law fella'.

'Now, I've met a few of you Harvard lads,' she told me after the second pint of Guinness, 'and most of you seem to have taken a course in being in love with the aroma of your own self-importance. But you're either rare beacon of modesty or the sort of fucking chancer who uses shyness as a come-on.'

Siobhan could be serious and exacting and riotous. Just as, after a few glasses of whiskey, she could go savage. 'Mental' was the word she used to describe herself in these extravagant states. She was chatty. And lonely. Like myself. I walked her back to the cheap hotel off Copley Square where she'd taken a room. I told her I'd love to see her again and gave her a peck on the cheek as I said goodnight. Her response was to grab the back of my head and put her tongue deep down my throat. A few minutes later we were in her shabby room, pulling each other's clothes off. Siobhan was carnivorous. She tore into my bare back with her nails. She bit my ears in moments of un-bridled fervor. From that night onwards, I spent the days buried in law studies and the nights even more buried in Siobhan. She would thrust and pump and scream as we made love. When she came the eruption was always accompanied by the exclam-ation: 'Jesus fuck!' Keeping up with her erotic program was work. There was an excitement to the sex. It was down and dirty and rough. It had nothing to do with lovemaking. When the chaos ended she would often give me a light punch on the shoulder and tell me:

'Not bad, you.'

Siobhan was smart and funny and hyper-rational. She worked me out fast: the loner streak, the need to connect, the absence of anything resembling familial warmth.

She made this pronouncement on our second night together. That was the night Siobhan pounded on the thin hotel walls with her fist as we made love. It caused the guy in the next room to knock on the door and enquire if we were having a fight.

'Only in me fucking head,' Siobhan shouted through the door, laughing like a loon, handing me a bottle of cheap wine that she'd bought when we were out for dinner and which we'd uncorked before throwing off our clothes. Me being me, I'd pushed the cork back in the bottle right before we fell into bed. Now I watched my mad Irish lover pull the cork out with her teeth and splash wine into the two little glasses left for us on the sink, then hoist herself up onto the sink and pee.

'Can't be bothered throwing my fucking clothes on to use the bog,' she said, since her hotel had shared toilets down the corridor. 'Doesn't bother you now, does it?'

'Not at all,' I said, lighting us two cigarettes, thinking of the wonderful absurdity of this scene. Especially when, moments later, she curled up next to me on the lumpy double bed, clinked her glass against mine and said:

'And now I want to pick your American legal brain about comparative elements of unfair competition and trademark law.'

She did just that, puffing away on a Lucky Strike. Siobhan had quite the analytical mind. She loved what she called 'the dialectics of law', looking upon its drier precepts in the same way that mathematicians I'd met found poetry in calculus. She could talk up a storm on a particular torts case. She was conscious of coming from 'the Wild West', as she referred to her home province of Galway. For all her assurance, she kept referring to herself as a 'culchie' and seemed quite obsessed with making an impact on the Irish legal world.

'I know your heart is elsewhere,' she told me on our third night, sitting in a cheap Italian place in the North End, plates of antipasti on the table in front of us, an empty bottle of house wine about to be replaced with a fresh one.

'Sorry?' I said, bemused by her statement.

'Listen to you. All defensive like. Never play poker, Sam. You've got a tell.'

'There's no one in my life.'

'Yes there fucking is – and if my tone tells you anything, I am hardly reproaching you for that.'

'I never ask you about your life back in Dublin.'

'That has been noted – and somewhat appreciated. But just so you know, there's a fella there who wants to marry me. His name is Kevin. Smart, decent, reasonable – and thinks I am the best thing that has ever crossed his path. So I approve of his good taste. Just as I know I won't be marrying him. Because I can see the boredom already creeping across the threshold. And because part of me wants to be with a bollocks for a while – which crosses you off the list. Not that you are in any way as dull as Kevin tends to be. You're quiet. But in a way that hints at a lot of grief within. And you are in love – but not with me. Not that I expect you to be in love with me. Not that I expect this to last more than this week. In fact, it can't – I am due back in Dublin to take up my post at Hickey, Beauchamp, Kirwan and O'Reilly Solicitors.

'No doubt within the next two years I'll buy a house – because that's a sensible thing to do. No doubt I'll meet a barrister with a bit more zing to him than poor dear Kevin – and will get married and have the big wedding and find myself up the spout. And I will probably go on and have a gaggle of kids – because that's also expected and sort of what I want. Just as I also want to send off a telegram to Hickey, Beauchamp, Kirwan and O'Reilly and tell them to stuff their post, and then fuck off somewhere like Australia for the next three years and get a job pulling beer at a bar on the beach and sleep with surfers, telling myself, *Now this is freedom*, even though I know I'd probably wake up for the fifth fucking time with some fool named Bruce and wonder why the fuck I wasn't back in Dublin making my way in the world.

'Which brings me to the larger question: why do we always want what we fucking don't have? And then when we get what we want we immediately become dissatisfied with what we chased after for so long. And yes, I am being just a tad garrulous, but I know I am going to reject the transient nature of freedom for something more permanent and solid, all the while sensing that I am going to turn around ten years from now and think: another six minutes of boring sex with this now big-gut husband of mine, another fucking morning of school runs – why the fuck am I not in Paris? But what would I do in Paris, anyway?'

'You could learn French.'

'You mean, like you.'

'I've never mentioned learning French.'

'But you told of those months earlier this year you lived in Paris and I know that the woman who still has your heart is French.'

I said nothing. Which, in turn, said everything.

'So, are you going to tell me about her, the way I told you about my Kevin?'

'There's nothing to say, except that it's over.'

'Bullshit. You still hold out hope that you and your beloved will be reunited – even though you've also told yourself it's over.'

I felt my face turning a feverish shade of crimson.

'Am I that much of an open book?' I asked.

'Instinct is everything, lover. From the moment I saw you I knew: no love at home, a broken heart abroad, very driven, very ambitious and very cautious about ever showing your vulnerabilities to anyone . . . especially the woman currently sharing your bed and actually enjoying it.'

I turned away as if I had been slapped. Not because I was angry or offended. Rather because everything she had just said was too damn true.

'You know what I fear?' I finally said.

'Tell me, love.'

'That I am going to make the same compromises that you know you will.'

She leaned over and kissed me.

'Then there's a pair of us in it,' she said.

The new bottle of wine arrived.

'Let's get scuttered and then go back to the room and fuck our brains out. This is only going to last till Monday, when I have to board a flight back to Dublin and my fucking turgid destiny. Not that it would last much longer between us in any case.'

'Why do you think that?'

'Because I need a man I can boss around. And though you are not exactly Mr Macho – of which I approve – you also have a distance to you. You are lonely, but you are not against being alone. Even though, more than anything, you want to connect.

71

But you're also independent. Fiercely so. You don't even understand this part of you as yet. You think your lonely childhood will be redeemed by the love of a good woman. The truth is: even when you find what you think is love, you will be longing for another parallel reality. You will never settle. Your loneliness will always be chasing you. Because it so defines you.'

She sat back after saying all that, filling our two glasses near to the brim. Then she leaned over and grabbed my crotch, kissing me deeply at the same time.

'Don't tell me you're not flattered by my analysis of your malaise. It makes you far more interesting than you think yourself to be.'

'I've never considered myself interesting.'

'There you go. In vino veritas. But let me give you a word of warning: you can, if you so desire, sidestep all the traps I'm going to fall into.'

I lit a cigarette. I sipped my wine.

'I'll keep that in mind,' I said.

'You still haven't told me about the Frenchwoman.'

'There's nothing to say.'

'Because there's everything to say. But that, too, is your taciturn style. The Midwestern closed book. Which I find strangely sexy. But I am strange about most things to do with men.'

The weekend arrived. Siobhan's leave-taking was just days away so she insisted I didn't go near my studies until she boarded that flight Monday night. It meant cutting a day of classes, but I decided I could just about get away with it. We made crazy love twice a day. Her violence in bed had a definitive sensual-aggressive charge. She encouraged me to be violent back. To tear at her skin, to slap her around, to penetrate her in places that I had hitherto thought 'off-limits'. She chided me when I let her know that I had my frontiers; that sodomy and sado-masochism were not arenas of sexual interest for me.

'You're a bit of a timid one, aren't you?' she said.

'It's my Baptist upbringing.'

'I'm a fucking Irish Catholic. And I'm not against my lover slapping me around or penetrating my arse.'

'You have such a romantic way with words.'

'So says the cautious Midwestern boy who doesn't want to get too down and dirty. I mean, how do you know you won't like anal sex until you've tried it?'

'Maybe I just don't want to try it.'

'Because it's a grievous sin according to some holy-roller Sunday-school gobshite who held your spiritual and moral imagination hostage for ten formative fucking years, with the result being—'

'We have very good sex.'

'That's not thanks to the Baptist creep who told you never to put your—'

'Believe it or not, Reverend Childs never gave us children a sermon about such things.'

'But I bet he wore one of those light blue striped suits and a bowtie.'

'You are perceptive.'

'Or I just make up this shite as I go along – and some of it actually turns out to be true.'

The next morning, as I got out of bed to head for the toilet, Siobhan shouted after me:

'I think I've scarred you for life.'

I had been avoiding an inspection of my back in the bathroom mirror for some time. Knowing full well that I would be appalled by the crazed railroad lines of scratches made by Siobhan's ever-sharp nails. Even when I told her the first few times in bed that the way she dug her claws into my back was more than a little painful, it had only made her slash me harder. That stopped me from complaining again. The scratching continued, our ferocity in bed permitting Siobhan to bite and claw and yank hair with increasing abandon. I accepted the violent underside to sex with this future Irish High Court judge; a woman I would run into twenty-seven years later at a big international legal conference in Bern. She had to introduce herself to me, as she'd put on thirty pounds and was suited in gray severity. We exchanged light kisses on both cheeks. I learned about her judgeship and that she was the mother of four children – the oldest of whom was twenty-four. Her husband, Conor – who was with her – was a blocky, bald man; a successful property developer who grew disinterested in me when he discovered I had nothing to say about the game of golf. We didn't have an opportunity to talk much that evening, being seated at different tables. But she did come by after the endless speeches, a glass of wine in hand, a little tipsy, a business card in her free fingers.

'If you ever get to Dublin . . .' she said, slipping the card into my suit pocket.

'You never know. You look well, Siobhan.'

'Stop talking rubbish. I look like the plump matron I always told you I'd become.'

'Don't do that to yourself.'

74

'But I've done all this to myself,' she said, the sweep of her hand following the pronounced curve of her hip. 'Unlike you, who's looked after himself. With one exception: the sadness in your eyes. What's that all about?'

I turned away. I shrugged. I said:

'Life. It's never simple, is it?'

'Which makes what we had – *shared* – all those years ago . . . it was kind of magic in a daft way, wasn't it?'

'Indeed.'

'No more scars on your back?'

'They healed.'

'And the psychic ones?'

'I only have good memories.'

'Liar.'

'I'm speaking the truth. Were your memories of that time together so bad?'

'Hardly. It was the last time I knew freedom . . . or at least allowed myself the illusion of freedom.'

The illusion of freedom . . .

Taking the shirt off in that seedy Boston hotel room in the early winter of 1977, I knew that the scars on my back were severe. Which is why I chose not to look at them. Deciding that in the last days we'd have together, she'd dig her nails even deeper into my skin; knowing that there was an impending finality to all between us; that we would soon go our separate ways; that all this shared sex and waking up next to each other and filling the time together . . . all these fleeting illusions of coupledom . . . they would all vanish as soon as she boarded the plane back to Dublin and her own pre-written destiny.

When Monday morning came she woke me at nine, her mouth between my legs. Instant hardness. She pushed herself atop me, gyrating up and down. Intense slowness. No violence, no wild rage. An elegiac softness to her movements. A sense of quiet farewell. I reached out, letting my fingers stroke that region at the top of her triangle. Rising moans; the measured yet insistent mounting expectation of explosive release. My hands clutching her thighs as she sunk deep onto me. Holding herself there as deep shudders rolled over her. Today a first: her nails did not attack my skin. Today another first: we came together. Falling off me, her body trembled with the aftershocks of her climax. I put my arms around her. She buried her head in my chest. She sobbed for a moment. Then she looked up at me, touched my face.

'This has been happy,' she said. 'And I don't do happy very often.'

Later that day I offered to accompany her to the airport.

'Nah, we're saying goodbye here,' she said, leading us back into the hotel lobby to collect the suitcase she'd left with the bellboy when we had to check out of the room at noon. He now brought it outside and flagged down a taxi. I kissed her. Our last kiss. She stepped away from my embrace, saying:

'Back I go – from the unexpected to the thoroughly expected.'

'Have an interesting life,' I said. 'It's the least we owe ourselves.'

'Shut up,' she said, then kissed me deeply.

As the taxi pulled away from the curb, I waved at the window against which her head was leaning. But she didn't see my final gesture of farewell. Because she was already elsewhere.

*

76

A week or so after Siobhan disappeared from my life I received a letter from Dad informing me that he and Dorothy had decided to spend Christmas with her childhood best friend at her home in Palm Springs. He didn't ask if I wanted to join them for this desert Yuletide holiday. He did say that the house back in Indiana was mine if I 'wanted to return home'. I read that sentence and found myself thinking: what is home these days? Then I checked with the doorman at the Law School Residence Halls and found out that I could stay in my room over the holidays and avail myself of the communal kitchen at the end of the hall. I wrote my father a card saying that I hoped he and Dorothy had an excellent Christmas and that I would be staying in Cambridge. His reply was a return envelope with a $200 check and a note giving me the phone number he could be reached at when out west: *Hope you can buy yourself something nice with this gift. Do call Christmas morning our time. Love, Dad.*

I wrote back, telling him that I had just found a job to keep me occupied over Christmas – and that I truly appreciated the generous gift. I also told him that I loved him. Which indeed I did. Just as I had also come to accept that, while he did have some degree of paternal feelings for me, he was simply incapable of allowing me to come close to him.

My professor of constitutional law – learning by chance that I was flying solo over the holidays – got me a paid research project with a white-shoe Boston law firm. Eight hundred dollars to compare six different ways a major pharmaceutical company could sidestep a lawsuit about a diabetes drug that might have resulted in eight New England patients going into insulin shock.

'Your first proper taste of our talent for sullying our hands with the dirt of large corporations,' the partner at the law firm told me when I entered his office.

Before New Year's Eve I had found an out clause for the pharmaceutical giant; a legalistic dodge that would allow them to sidestep many millions in angry patient claims. The partner was impressed. So, too, was the Swiss suit from the Big Pharma company who was running their northeast operation. He told me that head office in Zurich wanted to offer me a thank-you bonus. An additional one thousand dollars. I accepted. After the meeting I agreed to a drink with the partner, who registered over the second Beefeater martini my deep ambivalence about getting paid so well ($1600 – a fortune in 1977) for doing corporate grubby work. The partner's first name was Prescott. He was married to a woman named Missy. They had two young daughters, Clarissa and Emeline. They lived in a big colonial house in Brookline. Prescott told me, as the second gin-and-vermouth depth charge turned him effusive, that he had married at twenty-five, been a father at twenty-seven, a partner in this firm at twenty-nine, and a father again at thirty-one.

'Two-year intervals seem to be my thing,' he noted as he lit up a Tareyton. 'Just as I only smoke two of these a day – usually with a fortifying cocktail before heading home to my much-admired life.'

Admired by whom? I wanted to ask – but didn't dare.

'So I suppose you'll be doing all this soon?' the partner asked me, stubbing out his second cigarette and lighting up a third one, immediately noting: 'Of course, Missy will sniff my breath as soon as I walk in the door and know that I overstepped the tobacco and booze quotas by one apiece.'

Does she set your limits for cocktails and cigarettes? Is Missy your mommy?

It is astonishing how subversive one's thoughts can become at the bottom of a deep cocktail glass.

'You haven't answered my question,' the partner said, the words ever so slightly slurring.

'There was a question?' I asked.

'Perhaps just an inference about one's evident destiny.'

'Is my destiny that evident?'

'Only if you allow it to be.'

As you did?

I said nothing. The partner continued:

'The truth is, you have a clear analytical talent for contractual law. And for finding the fault lines in the litigious language of the opposition. You have seriously impressed a group of elegant, morally heinous Swiss pharma executives . . . and in the process you've made us look good. Now, having been to Harvard Law myself, I know you have no time to do any extracurricular work during term time. But I am certain I can find you a nicely remunerated summer gig here next year.'

'That sounds promising,' I said, simultaneously thinking, *But I want to spend the bulk of next summer in Paris*, though also wondering if Isabelle, the new mother, would truly want to see me again.

'But I am going to offer you nothing,' the partner said, waving the newly arrived third martini in his hand, 'until you answer my fucking question.'

I smiled, knowing that to do so would be to play to my advantage.

'"So I suppose you'll be doing all this soon?" That question?' 'Precisely.'

'We are all the architects of our own prisons,' I said. 'I haven't decided what mine looks like yet.'

I wanted to tell Isabelle all about this exchange. I wanted to wonder out loud, in print, if I was destining myself to a career trajectory I didn't want. I knew that I did get a certain cognitive kick from the intricacies of law: its forensic nuances and layered interpretations. There was so little that was empirical in law. How you manipulated a narrative to render a judgment in your favor – it was a bit like constructing a novel (not that I had any ambitions in that realm of literary endeavor, or could even begin to imagine how such a dense fictional enterprise was built from the ground up). I also wanted to ask how her pregnancy was progressing; to tell her that she was very much in my thoughts.

Instead I pushed such ideas aside. I told myself once again: this is over. Her last letter to me had said as much. Accept it. And don't dwell on the thought that had come to me repeatedly during my crazed week with Siobhan: how all that mad, ravenous carnality just highlighted the ache I still felt for Isabelle, and how sex with her was never sex. It felt like love . . . even if she could never say that word when it came to us.

Weeks earlier I'd considered just sending her a Christmas card. I decided it best to honor her insistence of no contact.

Law School recommenced a few days after the start of the New Year. It continued to be ascetic, monastic. I continued to bury myself in work. The months passed. Winter gave way to a hint in early April of forthcoming spring. And then, days later, the mercury dived and an out-of-nowhere blizzard slammed into Boston and its environs for thirty-six hours. Three feet of the white stuff descending from above – like a celestial eraser rubbing out all peripheral vision. Outside, movement was limited, nearly impossible. Classes were canceled. Public transport suspended. Those with cars forbidden to take to the roads until the Niagara of snow ended.

On the second day cabin fever began to take hold. I pulled on heavy boots, the one thick sweater I owned, my parka, scarf and gloves. I braved the external world. I was the one and only fool out and about in such extremity. But I reached the Law School. Falling inside – yes, the front door was open – I carried an inch of snow in with me. Snow that began to melt as soon as I connected with the overbearing heat inside. There was a vending machine that sold anemic coffee or hot chocolate or truly miserable tea for a quarter. I opted for the chocolate kick. As the machine urinated light brown liquid into a flimsy plastic cup I decided to check my mailbox, figuring it would be empty.

It wasn't.

One letter awaited me. A French stamp, a Paris 6ème postmark, her distinctive river-flow black calligraphy. My heart skipped several essential beats. I tore at the envelope, my natural inclination toward the inevitable negative outcome making me expect the worst. I scanned the letter, wanting to take in immediately two telltale markers: the opening salutation, the final sign-off. The first was in English:

Dearest Samuel . . .
And she finished with:
Je t'embrasse très fort.
Promising.
In between these two was:

My apologies for the tardiness of this letter. My daughter, Émilie Irène de Monsambert, was born on the seventh day of March 1978. Her entrance into the world was not the easiest of passages. I was in labor for over twelve hours. There was a scare when the umbilical cord was discovered wrapped around her neck. Controlled medical panic followed. An emergency Cesarean. Immediate anesthetic for Maman – which I screamed and shouted against, as I so wanted to be compos mentis for her arrival into this wonderful bordel that is life. But as they were cutting my abdomen open I had to be blacked out of reality for several hours. When I woke I started screaming again. Because I saw that the crib next to my bed was empty. Naturally I assumed the worst and immediately thought: if this child has been taken from me too I am simply not going to be able to go on. But the nurse on duty calmed me down, telling me that I had given birth to a girl and she was in the ICU for 'routine observation' – which again made me think the worst. Though I was absurdly weak, I insisted that I be allowed in to see her. The nurse refused. I screamed some more. My husband – who, as it turned out, had slept in a chair opposite my bed all night and had just stepped out for a cigarette right before I came round – was back in my room, doing his best to calm me down. Saying he'd been to the ICU and all seemed reasonable.

As I told you, we called her Émilie – and she is truly magnificent. She has an aura of calmness and radiance. Of course I am wildly biased. Of course I have the most profound, unconditional love for my extraordinary daughter. Of course I still worry that there may be developmental damage owing to her complicated birth – though the doctors keep reassuring me that all is well. But that is the problem with a past tragedy: it overshadows everything. And you cannot help but wonder if fate will target you again . . . as it did so in the drama surrounding Émilie's arrival in the world. But perhaps that is another offshoot of tragedy: it makes you believe that the veneer of life is not just inherently fragile (which is a near-empirical truth), but that it will crack and swallow you whole at any unforeseen moment.

But I am, by my very nature, a romantic pessimist; one who believes that happiness – if found – has a terrifying transience. And reading this all through again, I apologize for my air of preoccupation. Émilie may emit a sedate glow, but she is currently suffering from colic and for a week I have perhaps slept without interruption for no more than two hours straight. With my blessing Charles has taken to sleeping in the spare bedroom.

And that is my news from Paris. Except to also say:
I am thinking of you – fondly, passionately.

My hot chocolate was cold when I finally remembered that it was awaiting me in the vending machine. Having read and reread Isabelle's letter three times through, I retrieved the watery cocoa, took one sip, then headed out into the arctic afternoon.

Near the Law School, on Brattle Street, was a café that served a *chocolat chaud* spiked with brandy. It did the job – and was simultaneously laced with a certain *nostalgie française*. I grabbed a booth and sipped my alcohol-fueled cocoa and found myself going legal forensic as I went through Isabelle's letter four further times, trying to discern its manifold subtexts. Zeroing in on details about Charles's seeming detachment: the way he was out smoking a cigarette when Isabelle came around from the anesthetic. The fact that they were not sleeping together. Was this hinting at deeper problems afoot between them? Or was that merely wishful thinking on my part? Dumb wishful thinking.

I wrote back to Isabelle, my letter scrawled on lined paper from my torts notebook. I said that I was so pleased for her; that Émilie sounded superb and she should have faith in the doctors when it came to their reassurances that she had come through a complicated birth unscathed . . .

As soon as I wrote that I crumpled up the paper and started anew. Knowing full well that to tell Isabelle not to worry about her daughter would be taken as the height of insensitivity. Best not to be too reassuring in that very American way of ours – eternal optimism at all costs. Best to be sympathetic and tell her that I understood completely why she was still worried about Émilie's ongoing well-being and that I was with her as she negotiated the white nights and anguish of a newborn.

So I went to the Western Union office in Harvard Square and sent her a telegram of congratulations, adding that I had a break after exams (and before starting the internship I was hoping to land) and could come to Paris on May 14 for a week if she said yes.

A week passed. A telegram arrived.

See you at 9 rue Bernard Palissy on 15 May at 17h00. The door code remains the same. Je t'embrasse fort – Isabelle.

*

Paris.

I was back in Paris.

And Paris made me happy.

Omar was on duty at the hotel front desk. He came around to give me a hug and a kiss on each cheek.

'Same coat!' he said.

'How is life?' I asked him.

'Oh, you know – same old, same old. But some things change. This time I've upgraded you to something a little better.'

The room was exactly the same old pleasant dump I'd happily loitered in all those months ago, only this time on the top floor with a view not of an alleyway but the rooftops of the 5th arrondissement. It had a small balcony. It took five minutes to unpack. I stepped out onto the tiny lip of concrete with its chipped railing perched on the sixth floor. I saw the Jardin des Plantes – a dense green space – in the near distance. I peered down on cafés and cinemas, a low-lying fog and street lights suffusing Paris in a brumous glow. I tipped Omar twenty francs and asked if he could bring me up a tisane to help me sleep. I bummed a cigarette – suddenly wanting a smoke after months of abstinence. You could still smoke in lectures and on one floor of the Law School library, not to mention in the hall of residence where I currently parked my body at night. But I'd been a good boy and had put cigarettes out of my life since becoming a law student. Now back in Paris – one of the great spiritual homes of smoking – God how I wanted a cigarette again. Omar offered me one of his Camel Filters and a light. I stood on the balcony and sucked down hard on it. The initial wooziness gave way to a nicotine calm. The balm of the dangerous. Paris and cigarettes. Isabelle and cigarettes. How I wanted her now.

The same bad stand-up toilet arrangements. The same tiny adjoining shower. Breakfast at my old local café. The proprietor behind the bar nodded to me when I came in. Not as if to say, *so where have you been all these months?* Rather, as if I had been elsewhere for the weekend. I took a stool at the bar. Without asking, he brought before me *un citron pressé, un croissant, un grand crème* and Saturday's *International Herald Tribune*. I ate my breakfast and read the two-day-old paper and tried to tamp down my unease. Expectation – especially that which has built up over many months – is a rabbit hole; a maze without egress. All I could do was show up at the arranged time and see what the landscape between us would be.

It was one of those insidious days in Paris when a chilled light rain refuses to blow away; when the greyness is all-encompassing; when you find yourself thinking: I am living in perpetual mildew. I looked at my copy of *Pariscope*. I found a cinema open on the rue des Écoles in an hour. I hid there until 4.30 p.m., by which time Emil Jannings was a broken man – an academic undone by his love for the unattainable Marlene Dietrich and falling apart in 1920s Berlin. The rain outside had relented. I walked down backstreets to the Théâtre de l'Odéon. Then I turned into the rue de Rennes and down the narrow side street that was Bernard Palissy.

There were new books in the office windows of Les Éditions de Minuit. The same plain uniform covers. The same severe authorial photographs, indicating: non-user-friendly literature published here. I punched in the door code. *Click.* I walked into the courtyard. I headed straight toward *Escalier C.* Her name – the third buzzer from the top. I pressed it down. Silence. I waited a good thirty seconds. I pressed it again. Silence. *Oh shit.* I wanted to light up a steadying cigarette. Instead I held down the bell one last time. For a good ten seconds. Silence. I lit up that cigarette. I told myself: so this is how it has panned out. Stood up in a Paris courtyard. No doubt a crisis of some sort or another that has kept her from meeting our rendezvous. Or the realization that what we once had – as limited in its timescale as it was – was now untenable in the wake of her daughter's recent arrival in the world.

The door sounded into life. I jumped. I was being summoned inside. I dropped my cigarette. I grabbed the door handle, yanking it open just before the buzzing stopped.

'Hello . . .'

Her voice at the top of the stairs. I threw prudence aside. I began to charge upwards, remembering every twist and turn of this staircase. When I reached the final landing, my arms were open, ready to encircle Isabelle. But the first sight of her threw me. Standing in the doorway as always, a cigarette in hand (as always), a sad smile on her face (as always), and the look of someone who had not slept in weeks, maybe months. Deep crescent moons beneath her eyes. Her freckled skin beyond pale – the hue of chalk dust. Her countenance shell-shocked, dejected. But most disconcerting was the severe loss of weight. Isabelle had always been lithe. Now she looked like the victim of some desperate plague or famine. She was emaciated, gaunt, the sense of fatigue immense. She saw how taken aback I was by her changed state. Nonetheless I pulled her toward me, clutching her tightly.

'Not too hard,' she whispered. 'I might break.'

I loosened my arm. I held her gently by her shoulders. I leaned forward and kissed her on the lips. Hers remained closed. I pulled back. I looked at her with care.

'What's happened?'

'Come inside.'

I followed her into the studio. My eyes went wide as I saw the state of her desk. Once orderly, systematic. But now awash in crumpled notes and brimming ashtrays, unwashed espresso cups, three half-empty wine bottles, manuscripts, papers cascading onto the floor. Dishes were piled up in her tiny sink, the bed unmade, the sheets not changed for weeks, the entire, once immaculate studio now showing all the signs not just of domestic neglect, but of all the evident disorder within.

Isabelle watched me take this all in. She reached for my hand. I let her thread her fingers in mine.

'If you want to flee now I will understand.'

I pulled her toward me again. But now she recoiled, her entire body tightening up as if she couldn't bear any proximity to me whatsoever. She went and sat down on the sofa, stubbing out her cigarette in a whiskey glass with around fifteen dead butts in it. She lit up another Camel Filter. I glimpsed a slight tremble in her hands.

'So . . .' I said finally.

She closed her eyes, a small smile accompanied by a sob. Then: 'I was going to send you a telegram last week . . .'

'Saying?'

'Don't come. That it's all too hard for me right now.'

'Tell me . . .'

'My doctor calls it the baby blues. Something that hits bad mothers who don't deserve children.'

She put her face in her hands and started crying uncontrollably. Now I did join her on the sofa. Now she did accept my arms around her as she buried her head in my left shoulder and let go. I held her for a good five minutes – it was as if she had been carrying around all this grief for a very long time and only now could let go. When she finally subsided she jumped up and disappeared into the bathroom.

My brain was reeling. It was clear to me that whatever had overtaken Isabelle right now was out of her control; that she was prey to forces dark and virulent.

When she emerged from the bathroom a few minutes later her eyes remained red from crying, but new makeup had been applied and her hair brushed and tied back.

I held out my hand to her. 'I am so sorry things are so hard right now.'

She stayed where she was.

'And I am so sorry that you have traveled the Atlantic at great time and expense to confront this *bordel*. And most of all the disaster that is me.'

'Why is this a disaster?'

'Because as much as I want you right now, the idea of you or any man touching me . . .'

'I don't have to touch you if that's impossible right now.'

'But you want to touch me, yes?'

I had to stop myself from smiling.

'Of course I want to be all over you. Deep inside you. But if that can't be . . .'

She buried her face in her hands.

'I am such a *catastrophe*.'

'Don't say that – when this is out of your control.'

'You don't know the details, the facts.'

'Tell me.'

'They are too difficult to relate . . .'

'I won't judge you.'

'Everyone's judging me. *Everyone*.'

'Why?'

A long pause. She took two deep drags on her cigarette.

'According to my doctor, when you have the "baby blues" you are prone to craziness; to doing things that you never thought possible.'

'Such as?'

'Being unable to sleep for days and days – not because your beautiful daughter is keeping you awake, but because strange voices have come into your head. Voices that whisper doubt and guilt and calamity in your inner ear. Voices that suggest the worst things imaginable. And then, sometime later, you find yourself staring down at your sleeping child – the child you have dreamed of having, the child who will help alleviate all the monstrous pain you have been carrying with you – and thinking: *maybe I should kill you and kill myself.* And then you are running down to your kitchen, horrified by the voice you've just heard suggesting such atrocious things. And once there, falling to your knees and slamming your head against the kitchen tiles in an attempt to shut out those terrible voices.'

'When did this happen to you?'

'It happened several times the first month after Émilie's birth. My husband then discovered me trying to give myself a skull fracture. He rushed me to a hospital. I was admitted to the psychiatric ward. When I was still showing all the signs of this craziness – and also crying out for my daughter – Charles gave them permission for me to undergo shock treatment. I only learned of this minutes before they brought me to the operating theater for this "procedure". I screamed and shouted and begged them not to go through with it, but the doctors were insistent that it was the best solution for this problem. You can't imagine what it's like being strapped to a gurney and a hard rubber bar placed between your teeth to avoid you biting down on your tongue and electrodes strapped to your head and then—'

She turned away. I wanted to reach out for her, but she was curled up in a corner of the sofa, deliberately out of my reach.

'How many of these "treatments" did you receive?' I finally asked.

'Three.'

'And . . .?'

'They helped. I had them all over the course of twelve days. I was evaluated closely. The doctors were pleased with my progress. They put me on some pills to help me sleep and control my moods. Charles had already hired a maternity nurse. Now she was there to supervise me with Émilie. Imagine the disgrace of that – longing for a new daughter and then having to have someone there to protect her from you.'

'But clearly this was not you . . .'

'That's not what Charles's family thought. It's the problem with old money – they expect impeccable behavior at all costs. And if you dare to go deranged . . . It is the biggest failure of character imaginable. My mother-in-law visited me in hospital wearing Chanel and regarded me as if I was a street urchin who had been shoved into her life. And her voice! "My poor son told us of the incident in the kitchen. Imagine trying to smash your head open on Italian marble. Most disappointing, Isabelle. God knows having a child is not a simple matter, my dear. I know these things can go a little wrong. I know a bit about the baby blues. But you have turned it all into an opera by Wagner. Your very own *Götterdämmerung*."'

'So, did Charles do better than his mother?' I asked.

'Don't be catty.'

'Not intended.'

'Yes it was. And I understand why. Yes, Charles was *corrective* – I think that's the right word – when it came to his mother, even though, truth be told, he's still intimidated by that little martinet. No doubt she is telling her son: "I warned you about marrying someone beneath us."'

'Surely Charles doesn't think that.'

'I would hope not, but although he might say something along the lines of: "Now, Maman, that is a little extreme," there is no way he would ever put the bitch in her place. Or risk offending her by seriously defending his wife in the face of her dismissive, offensive comments. That would breach all sorts of noblesse oblige protocols – and the fact that French aristos are as clannish as the Mafia when it comes to the family. And listen to me ranting like an angry adolescent . . .'

'You are hardly that.'

'That is exactly what I am according to Madame de Monsambert and her entire clan.'

'Well, they are stupid and small and very wrong.'

She reached over and touched my face.

'You sound so American.'

'Is that a problem?'

'Hardly. On the contrary, it is most refreshing. You are far too nice to me.'

'Because you are far too hard on yourself. And also because you have clearly been through hell.'

She finished her cigarette, immediately igniting another. She could see my eyes widen at her ferocious cigarette intake, which was far more extreme than when we had last been together, when she was just a two-cigarette-an-hour smoker. Now it was one cigarette after another. She saw my concern. She interpreted it as a reproach.

'You aren't going to go all health fascist on me and start quoting American medical research on cigarettes and lung cancer?'

'Why should I do that when you clearly know it already?'

'Touché,' she said, cracking open her Zippo and lighting up the new cigarette already between her lips. 'If I didn't have cigarettes I think I would have already thrown myself under a Métro train. Thoughts of Émilie stopped me. Thoughts of you stopped me.'

I took that in, trying not to look too surprised . . . or too pleased. I failed.

'You shouldn't play cards, Samuel. You show your hand too easily.'

'I never thought—'

'What? That I have what you Americans like to call "feelings" for you? Perhaps deeper feelings than you can imagine. And ones which have intensified profoundly during this long absence.'

I wanted to tell her about the immense loneliness of the past months; the quiet agony of being apart from her. Instead, I took her face in my hands. And said:

'You are beautiful.'

'Liar. I weigh nothing, I look like a skeleton, a phantom. Haggard and—'

I kissed her. Lightly on the lips. She resisted.

'How can you want someone so horrible?'

'You are everything I want.'

I kissed her again. Tears were falling down her cheeks.

'I cannot do this.'

Another kiss. This time she did not try to struggle against me, but her face was even more awash with tears.

'I don't deserve this, you—'

'Shut up,' I whispered and pulled her closer.

For a good five minutes I held her tightly against me as she wept unbridled. It was more than unnerving, the manner in which she came apart, her cries so loud, so savage, that I feared a knock on the door and the arrival of a spooked neighbor, wondering out loud what torment was being enacted in this tiny studio apartment. I had never witnessed such wild grief. Some instinct within warned me against saying a comforting word – because Isabelle was beyond comfort right now. I just held onto her as tightly as I could as this vast spasm of grief overwhelmed her. When she eventually subsided, lifting her head from my shoulder, she whispered:

'Please don't look at me. I am so ugly.'

'You are beautiful.'

'Shut your eyes and imagine me beautiful.'

I did just that. Then I opened my eyes. She was gone. I heard the shower start.

A sudden wave of exhaustion flattened me. Delayed jet lag. The insane rigors of the past term. The storm and stress of the past hour. The torment encircling Isabelle. I staggered to my feet. I climbed into the unmade bed, its linens rank, unchanged for weeks.

Lights out.

At least, I didn't remember falling asleep.

But I did clearly remember the unnerving instant when I jolted awake and found myself alone in the silent studio. There was that surreal first moment when I found myself wondering: *where am I?* Then my memory assembled those last minutes with Isabelle before she stormed off into the bathroom and I was sideswiped by all the drama and transatlantic time changes. And now? Now it was . . . when? And what was I doing here and where was my love and . . .?

I sat upright. I reached for the cord running down from the spotlight floor lamp at the side of the bed. A bulb sputtered into life, flickering madly like a firefly in the swansong of its brief life. But there was enough illumination to see that, according to my watch, it was 4.06 a.m. *Merde, merde, merde.* I had passed out for almost ten hours. I stood up and went toward the bathroom, the bulb burning out just as I hit the light. I peed. I opened the tiny shower and found soap and shampoo. I washed myself down with the small hose. I dried off. I came back into the darkened room and turned on a desk light and found a note. And a key. I read:

My Samuel:
I am not surprised you passed out after my performance this afternoon. Had I been you I wouldn't have fled just the apartment, but the country too. I cannot apologize enough for the extreme nature of my comportment. I could plead 'baby blues' or what the doctors call a 'nervous breakdown'. But I would rather take responsibility for my actions without excuse. Your kindness, your decency, your patience . . . thank you.

When you fell asleep I couldn't bear the idea of waking you up and shooing you out into the Paris night at the moment I had to leave for Émilie. So I decided to leave you in peace . . . and leave you a key. When you wake up there is a small espresso machine and good Italian coffee awaiting you on the hotplate in the kitchen. Take this key and please lock up. And if you

can bear to be in my company again, I will be back here at
17h00.

I discovered something tonight: mon jeune homme has
become a wonderful man.

Je t'embrasse très fort
Isabelle

I read the letter twice. The part of me that always needs re-assurance – the child who craved to be told he was a 'good boy' by parents who were critical and distant – found her words like a balm, consoling. But I also found myself thinking: this is love, I saw not just her grief but her immense loneliness. Loneliness that – for all the differences in our respective lives – mirrored my own. This husband of hers had clearly not given her the support she needed as she negotiated that dark wood after the birth of their daughter. Though he might not have been as direct about it as his fiendish maman, silently he was nonethe-less as critical as that shrew of a woman. And he had allowed Isabelle to feel that she was deficient as a woman and as a mother because of her descent into temporary madness – even though he surely knew that she was dealing with psychic forces beyond her control.

How I wanted to save her from such desperately judgmental and unfair people. I was willing now to put everything on hold and be with her in Paris. Or, if she too was now seeing that ours was a love that would be transformative, perhaps she might be willing to roll the big dice and come to Cambridge with Émilie, and we could raise her as our daughter and I would finish my law studies and then . . .

And then . . .

That was the kicker.

And then . . .

A happy life lived by one and all. Love eternal sworn daily. The bliss of domesticity radiating through our home. Émilie growing up bilingual. Isabelle translating manuscripts, me finishing law school and becoming so fluent in French that I immediately land a partnership in a major Anglo-French law firm. Then, at the start of the 1980s, we have a child together and . . .

I found a packet of cigarettes on Isabelle's desk. I fished one out and lit up. I found my underwear, jeans and T-shirt and got myself dressed. I found the espresso maker and the packet of highly aromatic coffee and made a small pot. I had slept deeply for the first time in weeks. Sitting down with my cup of espresso, I sipped it between further drags on my cigarette and thought back to my little fantasia on a theme of a proper life with Isabelle . . . imagining telling her, in the middle of her crisis, that she would be so much happier if she upped sticks and journeyed across the Atlantic for life with a poor law student in a tiny garret in Cambridge, Massachusetts. I knew enough now of my beloved to realize she would never step away from a certain level of what she had once called 'bourgeois comfort'.

And with this realization came a moment of pre-sunrise clarity: back away from the dream that we could ever have anything but those afternoon hours together. Isabelle had been telling me this in her own quiet, firm, sensual way from the outset, but, I understood now, a significant part of me hadn't wanted to see what was directly in front of me. I'd kept telling myself: *in the end she will see that the only possible road to happiness involves voyaging down that garlanded path with me . . .*

What drivel.

No. Let's not get too hard on ourselves here. Love can send you into a fictive trance, rich in manifold possibilities. Love can also apply the brakes on such reveries in a truly harsh way. So much so that you find yourself thrown against the windscreen looking out on that panorama of hope known as *the future*.

Ah, the future. When you are smitten it is impossible to consider just the here and now. There must be forward-looking deliberation of your life together. To be a couple is to be endlessly obsessed with the future.

But to be with Isabelle meant being grounded in the absolute present. With the knowledge that the future would be exactly as life was now. Even in the midst of storm and stress and a huge upheaval in one of our lives. This was my moment of predawn clarity, after ten hours of seamless sleep, over a second espresso and a follow-up cigarette: the recognition that I could no longer dream about a life with Isabelle. This was life with Isabelle – and it would not budge beyond its already calibrated limitations.

There was a sadness underscoring this comprehension . . . and a strange liberation as well. No need for future monogamy or emotional fidelity or believing she was 'the one'. Yet there was a subtext to this acceptance of freedom. Knowing that were she to say yes to my scenario – to a future of real life together – I would embrace fidelity with a vengeance. In the knowledge that she was, verily, 'the one' . . . although Isabelle would have recoiled at being categorized in such a way.

'Never again tell me I am the love of your life,' she'd informed me a few weeks into our romance last year when I had indeed made that pronouncement. 'It sets up the worst sort of expectation. It dooms a couple – because the bar has been raised far too high.'

So there it was: the one who wouldn't be the one but who wanted me to be the one when I was in her city and could accept the five-to-seven window of *oneness*.

Having just constructed that less than nimble sentence in my head, I could not help but smile. Then I glanced around the studio and felt terrible that Isabelle – who liked controlled disorder on her desk and cleanliness everywhere in this small space – had decided that her internal chaos would be imposed on this space to which she escaped for a few hours every day. At her apartment, a nanny and a cleaner were no doubt keeping a lid on her turbulence – if, that is, she had allowed it to spill out at home. But here she was giving full rein to chaos theory. Seen again in the thin light of night, I knew immediately that a gesture needed to be made. And with time on my hands, and an instinctive desire to render order out of bedlam, I immediately went over to the sink and looked into the cabinet below to find a few garbage bags and a modest collection of cleaning supplies. Before starting, I opened the tiny fridge and discovered a small glass pot of plain yoghurt, still not toxic according to the date printed on its silver foil cover. In a cabinet I discovered a few squares of dark chocolate and wolfed them down. It had been over fifteen hours since I had seen food and I was hungry. I made a final pot of coffee. It snapped me further awake. Then I went to work – beginning with the pile of dishes in the sink. Within twenty minutes all were washed and dried and put away. I emptied ashtrays. I cleaned out all the rotting fruit in the fridge and a collection of vegetables in the cupboard that were beginning to resemble a penicillin culture. I found an all-purpose spray and a rag that wasn't too dirty and attacked all the surfaces around the apartment. I upended into a black plastic sack three bins piled high with papers. I picked up all the spilled manuscript pages from the floor around her desk. I repaginated them. I tidied up all the other documents on her desk. I cleared dust off from her manual typewriter. I found a mop and bucket and washed down the tiles in the kitchen and bathroom. I found an old vacuum cleaner – it looked like something my grandmother used back in the day, but it still did the job. Once the debris from the carpets was sucked up into that ancient machine I stripped the bed and grabbed the towels from the bathroom, first using them to clean the sink and the shower stall. I found a bottle of bleach and a brush and scrubbed out the toilet.

When I finally looked at my watch it was nearly 6 a.m. I shoved the linens and towels into a plastic bag. I saw a laundry basket in the corner between the bed and the desk. It was piled high with Isabelle's dirty underwear, two pairs of jeans, one white and one black shirt, all of which I also dumped into the plastic bag. I grabbed my black pea jacket, pocketed the key and headed out into the morning. Darkness still enveloped the streets. A light, insidious rain. I walked fast with the bag of laundry down the empty prospects of the boulevard Saint-Germain toward the Métro at Mabillon. Lighting a cigarette once inside a carriage heading east. Disembarking at Jussieu. The five-minute walk to Le Select. The patron noting that this was the first sighting of me at such an early juncture of the morning. The usual breakfast. The usual day-old paper. More cigarettes. And then, at seven, a quick trip to the laundry next door. The old woman who ran it – Romanian, I thought; she'd washed my clothes weekly last year – told me that, yes, she could have everything washed and folded according to darks and lights by 15 h 00 that afternoon, but if I wanted the shirts hand-washed and ironed it would be an additional fifteen francs each. I relieved myself of the bag and went back to my room. I got into sweat clothes and a pair of sneakers that I'd treated myself to a few weeks before my trip to Paris and headed off at a light canter into the Jardin des Plantes, where I circumnavigated the park.

After collecting the laundry at three I stopped at a nearby florist and bought a bunch of lilies. I was back at Isabelle's studio half an hour later. I was wondering if she had arrived before me; if I was going to walk in and find her wide-eyed at the transformation I had made of the disorder of her studio. But it was empty. I unpacked the laundry, remaking the bed and hanging up towels now fluffy and smelling of lavender detergent. I put all her folded clothes and the two ironed shirts on the sofa. I found a vase, filled it with water, used scissors to shorten the stems of the lilies and organized the flowers in the simple glass container, placing it on the café table where she often ate lunch. Then I made a list of things that she needed – toilet paper, kitchen paper, dishwashing liquid, more coffee, more cleaning supplies – and left the apartment, locking it behind me.

There was a shop up on the rue de Rennes that had everything I was seeking.

At five, as I mounted the stairs of *Escalier C* of 9 rue Bernard Palissy, I heard a woman – her voice hinting at someone in the middle passage of life – on the second floor shouting repeatedly:

'*Tu ne peux pas me faire ça . . . tu ne peux pas me faire ça.*'

I loitered by her door for a moment, awaiting the opposing party's retort. But there was no reply. Just silence. Followed by:

'*Tu ne peux pas me faire ça . . . tu ne peux pas me faire ça.*'

And silence again.

I mounted the stairs, expecting to hear Isabelle's usual melodic 'Hello' cascading down toward me.

'Hi there,' I shouted as I turned the compressed corners of the staircase.

Silence.

When I reached her door I found it open. But she was not, as usual, standing in its frame. Rather she was at her desk, a cigarette on the go, the manuscript I'd tidied now strewn every-where, several pages to the left of her typewriter. She was pounding the keys as I entered. She did not look up at me.

'Good afternoon,' she said, typing away. 'Please put the key I gave you on the table and then please leave.'

'What?' I said, thinking: *she didn't just say what I heard her just say.*

'The key on the table . . . and shut the door behind you.'

I walked over toward the desk.

'I didn't say you could come in.'

'I'm coming in.'

'No, you're not.'

I returned to the door, the Midwestern boy in me not wanting to transgress.

'I don't understand.'

'Don't you?'

'Have I done something wrong?'

She stopped typing and finally looked up at me.

'I thought you were my lover, not my maid.'

'That's what this is about?'

'How dare you decide to tidy me up.'

'Tidy you up? I just thought—'

'She's crazy, she's mad, and she's turned into a slovenly disaster . . .'

'Did you sleep last night?'

'So you are now saying I look ugly?'

'Did you sleep last night?'

'Stop trying to change the subject.'

'I was trying to help. Just thought you could—'

'*What?* Use a little imposed anal-retentive American order on the disorder of my life?'

She was shouting. I stood there, the bag of cleaning supplies cradled in my arms, blindsided by a fury I didn't understand. Only that it was clear the dark stuff had enveloped her again.

'How bad was it?' I asked. 'Is Émilie OK?'

Now she was on her feet.

'You dare imply that I am endangering my daughter again!'

'Isabelle, my love—'

'I am not your fucking love!'

And then, out of nowhere, she hurled the ashtray on her desk at me. Cigarette butts went flying as it made its trajectory across her studio. I jumped out of the way as it hit her kitchen shelves, smashing into a row of glasses, shattering them all. I stared wide-eyed at Isabelle, rage, hatred in her face. I dropped the bag. I ran. Charging straight down the stairs. Pushing through the door into the courtyard. Racing across its cobbled confines. Through the narrow entry corridor. Out into the tiny street. A fast right turn. I was about to charge directly into the rue de Rennes when a taxi braked and the driver began to scream at me and I suddenly realized that I had almost run right into the oncoming afternoon traffic. A cop on the street grabbed me by my jacket collar, yanking me back onto the sidewalk just as the taxi driver jumped out of his car, hectoring me.

A steady rain was falling. Besides being emotionally concussed I was also drenched. I hurried to the boulevard Saint-Germain, my head down. I did something I never do in Paris. I jumped in a taxi. Once inside I huddled in a corner of the back seat, shaking and crying, the driver glancing at me in the rear-view mirror, disconcerted by my instability, my tears.

When we reached the hotel Omar looked at me as I hurried past him.

'Monsieur Sam?' he said.

I just shook my head and headed upstairs to my room. Once there I stripped off my jacket, my clothes, grabbing my bathrobe. I fell onto the bed, clutching a pillow as a substitute for the woman I should be holding right now in a bed across town. A woman who just turned on me in the most sudden, ferocious way. What had I done to deserve all that? What kind of trespass had I committed by daring to clean her apartment? Had I breached her privacy? Did no good deed in life go unpunished? Was I guilty of naivety?

A few minutes later, there was a knock on the door.

'Monsieur Sam, please let me in.'

Omar.

I forced myself up. I opened the door. Omar was there with a tray.

'What has happened to you?' he asked.

'Nothing bad. Just heartache.'

'That is always bad. I have brought you a tisane to help you relax. And a small Calvados.'

'You are too kind.'

'You had me worried.'

'I'll be fine,' I lied.

Omar came in and settled the tray on the tiny table that also served as my desk.

'Let the tisane steep for another five minutes,' he said. 'It might help you sleep.'

Having woken at four that morning and having made the fatal error of daring to clean up Isabelle's studio – an act interpreted as a major piece of manipulative gamesmanship for reasons I still couldn't fathom – a wave of fatigue was now slamming down on me again, just as it had yesterday evening in the wake of the melodrama with Isabelle.

'You are a very good man, Omar,' I said.

'So are you,' he said. 'Don't let anyone tell you otherwise.'

But they do, they do, I felt like saying but didn't, because self-pity was something that my dad had always stamped down on and I assiduously avoided, as I did consider it pointless and self-defeating.

'I just need sleep,' I said, proffering a ten-franc note.

Omar put up his hand.

'It's on the house.'

'But this is for you,' I said.

'No need, but thank you. Call if you need anything else.'

He left me alone. I sipped the Calvados, appreciating the apple-brandy burn, the way it tamped down the anxiety of the hour. I steadied myself further with a cigarette and the thought that the mental torment that had seized Isabelle had made her act in a totally out-of-body way. Or, at least, that was what I wanted to believe. The other part of my brain – the prosecuting attorney's voice within – encouraged me to consider whether she had shown me that pathological side of her persona before – the one full of ongoing rage and moments of violence. I wanted to believe otherwise . . . to tell myself again that she'd been possessed by a post-natal madness and I should not believe that I was now seeing her dark subtext.

I sipped some more of the Calva, sucking down the cigarette, trying to keep anger and sadness and profound disappointment at bay, and failing on all fronts. I turned to the tisane. It tasted minty and medicinal. I found myself thinking: I am back in Paris and going to bed, for the second night running, at a time usually reserved for seven-year-olds. My body clock was not simply off, it was skewed. I finished the tisane and decided to stretch out on the bed and take a siesta, telling myself to set my little travel alarm clock for 9 p.m., figuring I could go out for dinner nearby, then head to the rue des Lombards and find my way into a jazz joint's late set. I lay back on the bed. I shut my eyes, wanting to black out the last few hours. Sleep was instantaneous; a knockout punch. And then, out of nowhere, there was pounding on the door.

'Monsieur Sam, Monsieur Sam . . .'

Not Omar's voice. Rather that of Tarak, the other Turkish night man. The room was pitch-dark. My wind-up clock gave off a cheap glow: 3.13 a.m. *Merde. Merde. Merde.* Another precious Parisian night squandered on trauma sleep. I switched on the bedside light.

'Monsieur Sam, Monsieur Sam . . .'

'Coming, coming . . .'

'You have a visitor.'

'Me?' I said, wanting to add, *But I know no one here.*

Except . . .

'A woman?' I asked.

He nodded, adding:

'I told her – it is the middle of the night, he is probably upstairs asleep. But she was insistent. Told me to tell you she has a taxi waiting.'

'A taxi?'

'That is what she said.'

'Can't she come up?'

'She has a cab waiting.'

'Why?'

Tarak just shrugged, adding:

'She actually handed me a hundred francs when I told her I couldn't wake you. And she gave me this.'

One of her elegant ivory envelopes. Her calligraphy in black fountain-pen ink across the front: *Samuel*. Inside:

Mon amour:
If you can somehow forgive my insanity and this middle-of-the-night intrusion, I am awaiting you downstairs. Please give me a chance to give you the most passionate of apologies.

It took me about three seconds of deliberation to say:
'Tell her I will be right down.'
Tarak smiled his approval.
'Very good, monsieur.'
Two minutes later, I walked down the six flights of stairs to the lobby. And there she was, her red hair loose around her shoulders, her face drawn, eyes red, a black raincoat belted around her ever-decreasing frame, a lit cigarette between her fingers. Hearing my approaching footsteps she turned and moved quickly toward me, taking my face in her hands, kissing me with great deliberation on the lips and whispering:
'I don't deserve your decency.'
'Why the taxi?'
'We are going to Bernard Palissy.'
'But we could go upstairs.'
'Bernard Palissy . . . *c'est nous.*'
'Are you sure about that?'
'You hate me now, don't you?'
'Hardly. I'm just . . .'

I could have finished the sentence with many a word: worried, fearful, scared, uncertain, ambivalent. But Isabelle leaned her forehead against mine and said:

'Is forgiveness possible?'

'What did you tell your husband?'

'He is away . . . with his woman. I told the night nurse guarding over Émilie that I couldn't sleep and was going to my office to work and would be back in the late morning. She was fine with that, as the nanny comes in at nine.'

'But maybe the apartment is too tidy. Or maybe, having tried to brain me with an ashtray . . .'

She forced her forehead even harder against mine, her hands firmly gripping my shoulders. Telling me:

'I will understand if you walk away from me now. But it will kill me, my love. Kill me, because I am not well. Because I had to stop myself this afternoon from throwing myself out of my studio window. Because I don't deserve Émilie, I don't deserve you. Because Charles and his family are right: I am a failure as a mother and as a woman. And I have now so failed you.'

She didn't move her head away from mine as she whispered all that. I felt her tears on my face. I felt the gauntness of her body and could almost discern the waves of distress coursing through her. Now it was my turn to pull her closer. Saying:

'Let's get in that cab.'

We said nothing in the ten minutes it took for the driver to negotiate the dark, empty streets. Isabelle lay her head against my shoulder, my arm around her, her fingers grasping my spare hand. When we reached the front door, she punched in the code, took my hand and led me through the courtyard and up the corkscrew staircase. She kept her fingers in mine all the way to her front door, as if to emphasize she was now cognizant of the fact that she had done something potentially deal-breaking, irreparable . . . and that she did not want to let me go. When she opened her studio door I noticed immediately that all the shattered glasses had been swept away. So, too, the cigarette butts and ash and the ashtray shards.

'I cleaned up the mess I made,' she said, pulling me toward her. 'That will never happen again.'

'It's behind us,' I lied.

'No, it's not,' she said, stroking my face. 'It happened – and I have to live with the consequences of what I did, how I ridiculed your goodness and tried to hurt you. How—'

'Enough,' I said, kissing her deeply while thinking: this is the first time she hasn't been the one to say stop when the conversation gets too effusive. Moments later she was pulling off my jacket, my sweater, her hands undoing my belt. I was simultaneously unbuttoning her shirt, my lips grazing her neck, my free hand raising her skirt. We had our clothes off quickly. We fell backwards onto the bed. She pulled me into her immediately. Wrapping her legs around me. Whispering to me to be as gentle as possible. Letting me push downwards and then not moving as I touched the deepest depths within her. Every time I was about to start a back and forth motion she tightened her legs even more profoundly around me. Saying:

'Don't move. Don't ever move. Because I am not letting you go.'

But move she did. Slow, almost imperceptible upward thrusts while keeping me rigid and still within. The effect was almost hallucinatory. The most gradual, slow, intense movements while we were locked as close as could be – her eyes all but boring into me, the longing, the need, the desire there. And the mounting convulsion that overtook her first, causing her to bury her face in my naked shoulder and bite down on me. I muffled a howl. Exploding moments after. Sideswiped by the intensity of it all – augmented by the crazed tension of the day and that cocktail of need, distress and a dash of new-found ambivalence all churning within.

'*Je t'aime*,' she said as we held each other tightly.

'*Je t'aime*,' I repeated back – only this time there was an unspoken question mark underscoring this declaration. Did Isabelle sense that? Is that why she sat up and found cigarettes and the studio's second ashtray and asked if I might like an eau de vie – *une mirabelle*? Or wine? Having been in bed since six surely I must be hungry? There was cheese and a baguette that she had only bought in the late afternoon. Could she prepare a plate for me?

'That would be nice,' I said. 'And yes to the wine, please.'

My tone was, as always, quiet, polite. But I could also sense a telling detachment on my part; a sense of not knowing what to make of the woman now walking naked toward the kitchen, the single side lamp by the sofa (turned on by Isabelle when we came in) providing oblique illumination, making this all seem enigmatic, illusory. Or, at least, that's how I was reading the strands of light criss-crossing my lover's narrow hips, swaying as she walked, making me want her again . . . even as another part of me wondered: might this all be undone now?

'Be careful of your feet,' I said, moments before they connected with the kitchen tiles.

'How right you are,' she said, backing away and opening the bathroom door, slipping her feet into sandals while also putting on a robe. 'You think of everything.'

'You cutting your feet is about the last thing either of us needs to cope with right now.'

'Especially as you are thinking of vanishing into the distance.'

'I never said I was going to do that.'

'But you are thinking it.'

'I am thinking . . . I am very happy that you are in a better place now.'

Isabelle rolled her eyes and favored me with a smile caught somewhere between amusement and wistfulness.

'I admire your diplomatic skills, Samuel – but I can always scent when doubt has entered the room. And who can blame you for brimming with doubt right now, after a hefty glass ashtray was aimed at you.'

'It was thrown in anger by someone not themselves because of an illness. And I didn't even have to sidestep its path – so, yes, it was hurled, but not at me.'

I stood up and put on my underwear and T-shirt. Isabelle looked spooked.

'You're not leaving, are you?'

'Hardly. I just thought it was better to eat semi-dressed rather than nude.'

'Oh good,' she said. 'I'll have everything ready in just a few minutes.'

I used this time to duck into the bathroom and wash off the long siesta and all that passionate entanglement with a fast shower.

As I used the hose and a bar of soap to lather up my skin I replayed that last exchange in my head.

'You're not leaving, are you?'

Strange, isn't it, how the balance of power in a couple can change in an instant. And though this shift was now predicated on a moment of violent anger, the truth is: it's less about the incident itself than the way it alters your world view. Before the ashtray was hurled I was desperate for a life with Isabelle, obsessively thinking: I have found the ideal beautiful Parisian intellectual of my dreams – and one who puts up with my early-twenties American naivety. If only I could convince her away from her well-heeled, deeply establishment husband and everything that his *grand bourgeois* life represents.

But now what I saw was that she feared losing me. Did that give me a sense of one-upmanship, of power? Hardly. I wanted no power over Isabelle. On the contrary, I just wanted life with Isabelle. All this past year I had awaited the letter telling me that, on reflection, our little arrangement would have to cease, for a plethora of logical reasons: geographical distance, a new-found fidelity for her husband, the birth of her child making her recommit herself utterly to the family project, my immaturity, the fact that she had found another Samuel, but one who conveniently lived full-time in Paris. If she decided to jettison me, how would I ever meet another Isabelle de Monsambert again?

But now . . . broken glass/shattered illusions? A facile metaphor. I had seen her in a desperate place. I had no knowledge of her baby-blues condition. I had – I realized – no real knowledge of Isabelle outside this room. But she had come and found me. She had ventured into my half-star hotel in the middle of the night. And she had just told me she loved me. A day ago such a declaration would have been like a proclamation from above – radiant optimism filling my world and all that.

Love when declared after a desperate misstep – it's the hardest love to embrace. And yet the last thing I wanted right now was to have the few days left to us before my puddle-jump return to Boston shaded by ambivalence, doubt. Or to have those relationship discussions that are a one-way ticket into shared despair. It was the middle of a Parisian May night. Disaster had been averted by her bravery in showing up and getting me out of my lumpy bed. We had just made love in a way that spoke volumes about the passionate complicity we felt for each other. Was it not best to act as if the melodrama of the late afternoon was now firmly in the past tense; and, for the time remaining until my departure on Sunday, there was nothing more to say about all that had transpired? We had this moment. And a few more to come before the week ran out and I had to return to the responsibilities with which I had chosen to fill my life. Isabelle was on the other side of this flimsy door. I wanted all that she represented – for the next few days at least.

*

Later that night, as we worked our way through a bottle of Saint-Émilion, she told me:

'Had I thrown the ashtray at Charles he would have had me committed again.'

'He sent you to the psych ward?'

She nodded.

'And he really agreed to the electric shock treatments?'

A long, deep drag on her cigarette, a glance down at the table.

'He signed the necessary forms, yes.'

'Do you hate him for that?'

'I was in a bad place. I could not make a rational decision – or at least that's what they told me. I didn't want such an extreme treatment. It made me lose my memory, equilibrium, for over two weeks. But it did restore a degree of sanity to me. Just as the medication they subsequently had me on curtailed the mad urges within. But then I stopped the medication.'

'Why?'

'Because though it quelled the eruptions, it also deadened me. I couldn't work, write, feel. My entire body felt tranquilized; my brain encased in cotton wool. I had no physical desire whatsoever – not that Charles was in any way indicating that he wanted passionate engagement with me, as he had his Hun for that endeavor. But my lover was crossing the Atlantic. I wanted to remember what it was like to want and be wanted. To have you deep inside me. To dig my nails into your back and feel you explode within. Things I had missed for months. Things that – even with the tranquilizers – I was desperate to feel again. So a few days before you arrived I went off the pills.'

'Was that wise?'

'Clearly not! But bless your understatement. Actually it was an insane thing to do – as I found out several hours ago. I called my doctor after the incident. He told me that instead of taking the two tablets he prescribed three times a day, I should now just try one tablet thrice. I asked if I could get away with just a half-tablet. He told me it was risky – and I really don't want

116

to have to return for more electroshock horrors. But I am determined, for as long as you are here this week, to stick to that low dosage. I need to feel you. I need to *feel*.'

'Won't this all eventually blow off, like a bad storm?'

'So they tell me. But I want to leave this subject behind us as well. It's Wednesday morning. We have just until Friday evening together. And then you will disappear.'

'Not for ever.'

'But for a significant amount of time.'

'I could change all that.'

'No you couldn't. And nor could I. Anyway, my mother told me once that at the outset of their romance, my father made a big statement: "Ours is love eternal." The reality – especially as I remember it – was a very long descent into disaffection. An atrophy that clouded their lives and completely colored my childhood and adolescence.'

'Tell me more,' I said, pouring out wine.

'I spoke of this in the past.'

'Only in the most limited sort of way. Tell me more.'

'But we don't have much time.'

'You have to leave this morning when?'

'By ten, ten thirty at the latest.'

I checked my watch.

'Then we have six hours.'

'But it's a sad story. Because most marriages are sad.'

'As I have never been married, and as my father was aloof and my very decent mother was affectionate in her own modest way – put it this way, I'm still craving love.'

'So am I,' she said, putting her fingers through my hair.

117

Silence as that shared declaration hung between us. Then:

'Is an aspect of love talking intimately until sunrise?' I asked.

'At least until sunrise.'

'Then tell me your story. I want to know it all.'

*

Talking until sunrise. Emerging light cascading across the rooftops beyond. Night waking up. The bottle of Saint-Émilion nearly empty. The ashtray full – and Isabelle, in full flow of softly articulate divulgence, lighting cigarette off cigarette as she talked about being thirteen, coming home early from school with terrible early period pains, and finding a man, half naked, emerging from the parental bedroom.

'He was a little flabby and had an absurd moustache – very popular at that era. One of my mother's colleagues at the lycée where she taught. He was rather amused by my embarrassment at seeing him coming out in his underwear – they were light blue boxers with polka dots . . . very silly. The man smiled at me and said: "Shall I tell Maman you're home early?"

'Then he ducked back into the bedroom. I could hear low voices in fast, perturbed conversation. Maman finally emerged, clearly just back in her clothes, her hair and makeup all astray, castigating me for coming home early. I tried to explain about my period pains. She sent me to my room. I remember curling up on the bed, crying from the cramps that had taken me over and from the confusion swirling around my head. Around fifteen minutes later Maman arrived with aspirin and a cold compress. She told me to take the pills and then lie face up in my bed while she applied the compress to my forehead and sat by me and asked me to forget about what I'd just seen, and to promise that I would never tell Papa about Maman's "friend". And she said:

'"One day you too will be married and you will learn that, as Alexandre Dumas once noted, the chains of marriage are indeed very heavy and you sometimes need other people to help you lift them." I had no idea what she was talking about – only that myself and Maman now had a secret. And Maman assured me that I would never come across such a scene again.'

Then, stubbing out a cigarette, she noted:

'Funny how we repeat so much from our past. Maman never finished her doctorate. Nor did I. Maman married in the belief that she would have eternal passion. So did I – even though I also knew that, having won me, Charles would revert to his *grand bourgeois* ways. And just like Maman – who died of emphysema last year at the age of sixty-six – I too would have my own *"jardin secret"*. It was Charles – who has his own *garçonnière* near his office in the *huitième* – who bought for me the studio in which he and I began our story when he was still married. This allowed me to eventually carry on my own adventures while he carried on his. So we, in turn, replicated his first marriage, even after telling ourselves that our marriage would be . . . yes, I will repeat myself again . . . *la passion eternelle*.'

I asked her if our little arrangement was a repetition of earlier affairs she'd had. She touched my face, then leaned over and kissed me.

'Are you asking me if I am some scarlet woman – some character out of Colette? Like Léa in her novel *Chéri* – the older courtesan with a predilection for younger men?'

'You're hardly a courtesan.'

'I am surprised you know the word.'

'My vocabulary extends beyond matters legal. But you're not answering my question.'

'You should never ask a woman about her past lovers. And if a woman begins to start telling you in great detail about her former men, you should immediately think about being with someone else.'

'You don't have to answer the question then.'

'Thank you. But know this: outside of a small adventure that lasted *quinze jours* around the time I found out about Charles's first mistress, you are my only lover. And you are still in my life more than a year after our first encounter. And I told you, *je t'aime*. Does that not provide you with enough answers?'

We fell back into bed thereafter. Again our lovemaking was initially quiet, gradual, deliberate, wanting to prolong our increasing intensity. I had my eyes focused on her throughout. Watching her absorbed in the purity of passion. Vehement concentration in the movement of our bodies, in the way we were locked together, rocking as one, so together yet also each in our own separate spheres. I saw her eyes opening, shutting, her hands everywhere over me. The way she would change our rhythm or let me shift our position. Pulling her on top of me. My two hands grasping her thighs as I pushed upwards. Seeing her above me, her eyes tightly shut, her face veering between pleasurable contortion and rising abandon. And I couldn't help thinking: intimacy of this sort is so desired, so craved, because it is also so rare.

'If I saw you day in, day out, our life would change,' Isabelle said later as she lay across my chest.

'Only if we let it,' I said. 'The trick is to keep passion kindled.'

'I love your naivety, *mon jeune homme*. Your belief in all those wonderful quixotic ideals about a couple. If you want to maintain such fantasies – and they are lovely ones – never live with anyone, never have children, and definitely never make it all legal by getting married. But you will do all that, just as I did all that – because it is not just what is expected of us, but what we tell ourselves we want.'

'But love with someone you consider—'

'*The one and only? The love of my life? My soulmate?* I particularly find that last one the most questionable. We think we have found the ideal partner for this difficult journey that is life . . . and then we discover that what we want at a certain juncture is no longer what we once craved. Needs change. So, too, does your perception of the other . . . just as the person to whom you swore undying love has their own questions about you. Am I sounding like someone whose illusions have been shattered? Hardly. Because I entered into marriage with Charles very much in love but knowing that marriage is also a social contract with many subsidiary clauses and much fine print. Especially when the family to which you have spliced yourself has a decidedly eighteenth-century vision of the world: everyone has their place according to long-standing decrees and dictums. We still know love and the occasional moment of passion. But not like this, not like us. Which is why you cannot leave in four days.'

'Hold me captive then,' I said.

'Would you like that?'

'By all means. Take away my passport. Keep me locked away here. Your love slave – allowed out for fresh air and pastis.'

'There is no fresh air in Paris. Pastis is something you should drink in Marseille. And smart love slaves become bored quickly. And flee.'

'I will come back.'

She pinned down my shoulders, hard, her face tightening.

'Do you love me, Samuel?'

'Absolutely.'

'Even after what you've seen this week?'

'Especially after what I've seen this week. If I told you you are everything I have ever wanted . . .'

'I would say: I will remain everything you have ever wanted as long as you never do "life" with me. Which is why it will break my heart when I say goodbye to you in two days – and why I want you to go. Because it will make you come back to me.'

*

Isabelle left at ten that morning. We were back in bed at five. She was up and dressed and following me out the door at seven. We returned to bed at (no surprise) five the next afternoon. Our time together overran thirty minutes. Isabelle left at seven thirty. As we walked down the stairs, I asked: 'As tomorrow is our last time together for many months, could we possibly go out to dinner?'

She quoted me Jacques Prévert, a writer of note in the 1950s, who had once noted: *Paris est tout petit.*

'If we choose a restaurant around here I will be spotted with you.'

'Let's eat in some outer arrondissement. Do you know anyone in the *dix-neuvième*?'

'I've never been to the *dix-neuvième*.'

'Then let's go discover it ourselves.'

'But there's nothing there.'

'How do you know that if you've never been there?'

'The same way I can discern that Antarctica is nothing but snow and ice without ever having been there. I still couldn't go, owing to the fact that this weekend I must join Charles for a family thing in Normandy. Which means that we must leave with Émilie and the nanny by 6 p.m. So, could we meet at three?'

'Do I have any choice?'

'Don't take it that way.'

'Why not? I have this one week here. You could have made an excuse, saying that you couldn't go away this one weekend, and have had another two days with me. I know what you are going to say: this is the way it works between us. *Un cinq à sept.* So I accept that. Just as I have accepted everything else this week.'

'That's not fair.'

'Actually, that's very fair. Because I have been completely fair and empathetic and understanding as you negotiate this terrible business. I am not asking you for a quid pro quo. Still, you make it very clear to me that I am an addendum to your life.'

'You know that's not true. I have declared so much to you in the last few days. And I thought you had come to accept our arrangement.'

'I have clearly accepted it. But you make all the rules, Isabelle. When I can see you, when I can't. You can decide to drop in on me in the middle of the night to beg forgiveness. And I give it to you. And come here with you. Everything you want from me, you get. I ask so little of you. Surely you could have told your rich husband: this weekend I need to stay in Paris. But let me guess – there is some big get-together in the family chateau in Normandy, and as the wife of an aristo banker, appearances must be kept up, even if your husband and his horrendous mother did have you committed to a psych ward—'

'Whatever you want to say about his mother, it was Charles who got me to that hospital and sanctioned the shock treatments for my own betterment – and for Émilie's protection. But he did not have me committed. He did not keep me from my daughter. And though he hasn't been effusive with his empathy, he has not turned his back on me, which, given his background, is extraordinary. No doubt you don't want to hear this. Because that would make Charles complex, nuanced – not the one-dimensional, arrogant, cold, authoritarian cliché you would like him to be. Because that allows you to feel like the tragic hero, rejected by his beloved for the older sugar daddy.'

'Well you have certainly shown your hand,' I said. 'So why don't I just leave you to your happy life and your passionate husband and your—'

She reached for my hand. I pulled away, all troubled petulance. She grabbed my fingers and yanked me back to bed.

'I told you before you came that the weekends are impossible,' Isabelle said. 'Trust me, I would much prefer to be in bed with you on Saturday afternoon than taking a damp walk with my sister-in-law, an interior decorator whose aesthetic vision is still rooted in the Versailles of Louis XIV. But there it is. I have not promised you one thing and then changed course. You know the limits . . . just as I also know that you will continue to rail against them until you yourself fall in love.'

'I *am* in love.'

She leaned over and kissed me.

'As am I . . . And now I have to get home. Until tomorrow . . .'

*

Tomorrow . . . Friday. Three p.m. *Quinze heures* in her language. Slashing rain. The third day straight of grim inclemency. I had spent the morning as I had spent the previous evening: killing time in an upscale way. Cafés. Bookshops. Cafés. Museums. Cafés. A cinema. Cafés. Paris was being drenched. I was feeling turmoil sweeping over me again. The evaporation of possibilities; the non-negotiable departure back to Boston at 09h30 on Sunday. The return to law-school asperity the following morning. An educational system to which I would be indentured for the next two and a bit years before I scrambled to pass my Bar Exam and get a foothold in some corporate legal hierarchy, making partner by the age of thirty being the usual goal. Part of me wondered: why not get the degree and then do something Peace Corps and steamily tropical for a few years? A stint tutoring in Upper Volta. Or working on some water-reclamation project in Papua New Guinea. Passing reveries – and ones I knew I would not act upon. Even though – as I had told Isabelle that afternoon in bed – I realized that I had the flexibility of choice as long as I didn't entrap myself with the strictures of responsibility.

'Your vocabulary, your use of language . . . they are becoming so rich,' Isabelle told me as we lay in a post-coital sprawl across her bed, and I found myself thinking that we had under ninety minutes before she would have to head off for her familial weekend beneath gray Deauville skies (or, at least, I wanted them to be as gray and soggy as Paris had been since my arrival). Twice while we were making love I had seen Isabelle gazing deeply up at me then turning away. Looking preoccupied and cheerless.

'Am I making you melancholic, forlorn?' I'd asked.

'Why do you ask?'

'Because you look so disconsolate.'

That was when she complimented me on my improved vocabulary, asking me if all the legal documents I was reading had made me up my semantical game.

'Legalese is dry, hyper-detailed,' I said. 'But one of its few benefits is its lexicon. Sometimes I think discovering new words is my way of staying sane amidst the banality of so much that I have to absorb.'

'The translator in me approves. My father used to tell me, "Always be learning . . . even if it is something as simple as a new phrase, a place name you've never encountered before, a street happened upon for the first time."'

'I think it's called curiosity.'

'Give me four synonyms in English for "curiosity".'

'Is this a test?'

126

'Could be. Go on – four English synonyms that I might be able to use.'

'Concern, interest, intrusiveness, snoopiness.'

'That covers the spectrum from positive to negative.'

'Don't most words? Even benign ones like "good" are loaded with subtext: positive, pleasing, reputable, superior, *recherché*.'

'And what are the synonyms for "distance"?'

'Paris . . . Boston.'

'I see a world view forming here.'

'I see too much time browsing a thesaurus out of boredom and loneliness.'

'Why are you lonely?'

'Because you are here in Paris – far away from me.'

'Find someone there then.'

'I told you already: I have no time for "someone there".'

'Not even for sex?'

'That too takes work.'

'Not that much work.'

'You'd be surprised. Sex is more transactional in America.'

'I am sure that at a university as worldly as yours you can find someone who is just into the idea of sex for the sake of sex.'

'But that is not this, us.'

'Which is why it would be just sex.'

'If I were to suggest that you were to visit me in Boston . . .'

'And leave my Émilie behind? Not a chance.'

'Say you brought her with you?'

'And also had a nanny accompany me so she could look after my daughter while you and I made love?'

'We could look after her ourselves.'

'But that would mean having her in the bedroom while we . . .'

'Doesn't she sleep in the bedroom you share with Charles?'

'Charles is my husband; Charles is her father.'

'And she is just months old and wouldn't exactly know who was sharing the bed with Mom—'

'Stop this now. It will not be happening. Any more than I will be seeing you outside of Paris. Outside of this studio. Outside of the hours of the late afternoon. We have been dancing around this issue incessantly all week. I fear losing you from my life. The other day, after the ashtray incident, I thought: *he will walk out and I will never see him again.* It crushed me. But when you press me to make more of this, I pull away.'

'Asking if you could visit me is hardly a demand to leave your husband. It is just letting you know that I hope it isn't months before we see each other again. Please don't accuse me of over-playing my hand here when the truth is I accept the situation.'

I pushed up as deeply as I could within her, bringing her head down to face mine. I could feel her tighten and contract. I kissed her fiercely, pushing up even harder. I was full of lust and longing and sadness with just a touch of anger underscoring it all. I whispered:

'The big question here is: what do you want?'

Her response was to bear down on me, thrusting and thrusting until she came with a muffled shriek, me following moments later. A long silence followed. Then she said:

'Years, decades from now you will look back on these moments in this bed and think: there was a time I could come twice in one hour.'

'So speaks the woman with the fifty-year-old husband.'

'You would have to say that.'

'Because you were, in your own way, making the comparison.'

Another silence.

'You still haven't answered my question,' I said. 'What do you want?'

She sat up and lit a cigarette.

'The older you get the more you will begin to realize: what you want changes all the time. Which is why it is a question without a single answer. We all say, "I want this, I want that, I want you." The truth is, we haven't a clue.'

'So . . . you want me?'

'Absolutely.'

'And yet you don't want me.'

'Oh, I want you. But not to the exclusion of the life I have created for myself – as flawed as that life may be on certain levels.'

'So, you want that life and you don't want that life.'

'That's it exactly. And that is why life is a farce, yet an absolutely crucial one. Because it is the only farce you will ever have.'

*

An hour later we left the apartment. It was precisely 5 p.m. Isabelle wanted to be home in twenty minutes and in the car with her husband and daughter before 6 p.m. All going well, she would be turning the key in her chateau in Normandy by 9 p.m.

'And what will you do tonight, my love?' she asked as we loitered for a moment in the narrow corridor between the court-yard and the front door.

I just shrugged and resisted the temptation to say: 'Certainly not walk into a chateau, like you.' But petulance always leaves a terrible aftertaste – and robs you of a dignified veneer. Best to play the man who can handle sending his impassioned lover back to her spouse and child.

I reached for her hand. I wanted to take her in my arms now and devour her against the mailboxes in the corridor. But when I tried to pull her toward me, she stiffened.

'We had our goodbye upstairs,' she said. 'Down here someone I know from Les Éditions de Minuit might walk into the building and see us.'

'And appearances must be maintained at all costs.'

She dropped my hand.

'You know that is exactly how things are.'

'Yes, I know – and accept – that.'

I took her hand again. She squeezed it tight.

'I do not like the idea of saying goodbye to you,' she said.

'But that's what we do.'

'You will come back this summer?'

'After the internship in New York finishes . . . yes, I can find a week or two before I have to be back at school. I suppose you will be gone all of August?'

'That is how it works here.'

'Well then . . . *on verra*.'

'You have to come back,' she whispered.

'*On verra*.'

'Stop being so existential.'

'Just realistic,' I said. 'I want to come back. But . . . *on verra*.'

She leaned over and kissed me lightly on the lips. As she turned towards the door I began to follow her.

'Let me leave first,' she said.

'Just in case Charles has spies outside the door?'

'Just in case I run into somebody I know. And we shouldn't be talking of such things now. Especially when, the moment I walk out of that door, the ache for you will start.'

'Because you have decided that you can't have me.'

'Because I have decided there is no getting around one's destiny.'

'And what, pray tell, is your destiny?'

'To know that I need to send you back to your American life, your American reality, while also knowing I will long for you daily . . . and will fear you getting wise and finding someone else and dropping me.'

'That's what's known as a contradiction,' I said.

'We are all contradictions. Which is why love is so impossible, and so necessary.'

'To try to still the contradictions within?'

Another light kiss on my lips.

'Precisely, my love,' she said, then added: 'But all those contradictions within . . . they are never truly stilled, are they?'

A fast glance at her watch.

'Time has run out,' she said. 'For now.'

'*On verra*.'

'*Je t'aime*.'

131

And before waiting to hear if I was going to answer with a similar declaration of love, she was gone.

*

Three weeks after my return I received a card from Isabelle:

I was translating a poem by Pablo Neruda today about the ethereal nature of matters carnal and having the most profound erotic thoughts of you. Might I entice you over for a week this summer? I think of you, of us, and sigh with longing. Je t'embrasse très, très fort – Ton Isabelle

Ton Isabelle. Your Isabelle.
I wrote back:

The erotic thoughts are shared ones. I came across a quote from Nietzsche: 'It is amazing how a small idea can take over an entire life.' Indeed. I am interning in New York this summer. I work until August 18th and could be in Paris the next morning. I must return to Cambridge on August 29th as I start classes again two days later. Might you be able to somehow find a way of getting to Paris for that final August week? I hope so. I long for you too.

Two weeks later another card from Isabelle:

Book your ticket. I will be in Paris 20 August, mon jeune homme que j'adore.

I wrote back:

I will be at 9 rue Bernard Palissy at 17h00 le 20 août.

That was late June. Eight weeks later – days before my arrival – I had no choice but to send the following telegram:

With regret I must cancel my visit to you. Something momentous has happened. Love.

Three

LOVE.

Actual love.

Proper love.

Mutual.

Reciprocated.

With no strings . . . for the moment anyway.

Love.

Was I seeking it?

Aren't we all?

Love.

I finished my telegram to Isabelle with that one word: *Love*. Knowing it could be taken both ways. A sign-off – yet one not followed by my name. A deliberate omission. Because I was also making a declaration. And one that let it be known: I will no longer crave a life with you . . . because I have found one elsewhere.

Love.

The next day, at the law firm where I was interning in New York, a telegram arrived from Paris in reply:

Enigmas always have a revealing subtext. I presume you are canceling because you have fallen long and hard for someone. But do not want to announce it directly to me. If you have found love I am genuinely happy for you. Just as I hope this

will not be a permanent shutting of the door. You know where
to find me. Je t'embrasse . . .

I didn't reply. No need. And yes, I will admit that a small part
of me was pleased to make the enigma a little passive-aggressive.
Returning to the States after those complex days in Paris, I'd
dug into my internship, trying to muffle the disquiet within.
And though we'd exchanged the occasional postcard or letter –
and made plans for our late-August rendezvous – part of me
kept thinking: this is a one-way ticket to nowhere. And I so
want and merit more.

I want more.

Have you ever thought how the trajectory of your intimate
life is so dictated by that statement: the need for something
beyond what you now have? The belief that there must be a
better version of the love you are chasing; a bulwark against all
the uncertainties of life?

So, yes . . . I wanted more. And yes . . . part of me was
silently angry at Isabelle for not being able to give me more.
*I love you and I am now going home to my husband, the father
of my much-wanted child* is never the best of results for the lover
left wandering the night streets. And yet, conversely, it could
rightfully be argued that I'd bought into this romantic set-up.
So why rail against rules I didn't like but still accepted?

Herein was the dilemma that I had been grappling with
since my return from Paris: even in the midst of edgy subtext
and a flash of high drama, the sense of absolute passion never
left the room. But the room was one we occupied for a few

end-of-the-working-day hours. It was divorced from all things quotidian – which is what made it both exceptional and outside of the shared life I told myself I wanted to find.

I had started many letters – letters crumpled and tossed through the air into the nearest can – in which I wrote various versions of the same grumble: that while she was everything, and I might on one level be crazily entwined with her, she remained permanently just out of reach. Truth be told, that cut too deep. But, as I reasoned after I punched out on my typewriter each new variation, she knew this. And me writing it would not change her mindset, her carefully argued reasons for staying in the domestic decor she had constructed for herself. So in their place I dispatched a series of pleasant, chatty updates about my life – always with expressions of erotic yearning thrown in, and the fact that the end of August was just weeks away. Her letters were coolly loquacious, and let me know that life had stabilized; that Émilie was wonderful and Charles was 'just fine'. She also wrote:

And yes, I keep thinking about you inside of me – and I find myself wanting to jump on a plane to Boston or New York, but I know that is impossible with Émilie so young. How I wish I could convince you to find time to get over here for a few days as soon as your exams are finished.

But she knew I had accepted an internship at Larsson, Steinhardt & Shulman. It began the Monday after my finals, and that was a non-negotiable start date. It was a prestigious gig – they were a leading white-shoe firm. The summer job paid very nicely: seven hundred and fifty dollars a week. I'd found a bedroom in the Morningside Heights apartment of a couple of Columbia Law students. My roommates also worked twelve-hour days. The guy whose room I was letting was spending the next three months at the Supreme Court. At Larsson, Steinhardt & Shulman I was assigned to Mel Shulman, the oldest partner and someone who relished 'a good contentious contract'. His specialty was litigation with a sideline in 'the nasty, internecine aspect of trusts and estates'. There was something decidedly old school and non-flashy about Mel Shulman. I was given a cubicle next to his office. I relished finding the structural weakness, the erroneous construct in a seemingly immaculate document . . . or that subtextural component of a will that gave our client some wiggle room when it came to challenging what Mr Shulman called 'inheritance manipulation'. The work was highly detailed and exacting. I took to its rigors. I prepared detailed memos for Mr Shulman on all that he had me investigate. He encouraged me to function like a legalistic detective – 'exacting but also creative in your forensics'. He seemed pleased with my work.

'When you finish Harvard you have an immediate home here,' he told me a few weeks into the summer. I thanked him and had no problem putting in ten- to twelve-hour days. I also insisted on getting back to the apartment most nights by nine and getting out of my suit and heading out again in shorts and a work shirt to explore the jazz joints, small cinemas and dive bars of the Upper West Side.

Around my third week into the job I was browsing through the *Village Voice* as I ate a lone Japanese dinner at a small joint on 116th Street and noticed that a screening of a Raymond

Chandler double feature was on at the New Yorker cinema down on 88th Street and Broadway. It was a Friday night. I had the weekend ahead of me – and I'd actually left the office that evening at the reasonable hour of six, so I would be well in time for the start of the first film at 7.45 p.m. In my shoulder bag I had a sweatshirt as a defense against air conditioning as well as a packet of Gauloises from a carton I'd bought at a fancy tobacco shop on Madison Avenue in the 50s. I finished my tempura. I caught the subway back south to 86th Street. The New Yorker was a wonderful old picture palace with an art deco marquee, a raffishly down-at-heel interior and a balcony where you could smoke. A double feature was always three bucks – and tonight they were showing *Murder, My Sweet* with Dick Powell and *The Glass Key*: two cinematic rarities from the Chandler canon. The place was half empty. I took a seat right in the front row of the balcony. I lit up a Gauloise and opened my copy of that day's *New York Times*. I heard a voice behind me:

'A man who smokes Gauloises and doesn't wear dark glasses indoors.'

I turned around and found myself facing a woman about my age. Chestnut hair, hazel eyes, a smart smile, beautiful in a quiet, understated way. I smiled back.

'Would you like one of my Frenchies?' I asked.

'According to my dad – a proud deranged veteran of the United States Marine Corps – a Frenchie was soldier shorthand for a condom.'

'Now, my dad was also a damaged Marine – but being a strict Baptist from Indiana he never had sex during the war.'

'He clearly had it once thereafter.'

'Maybe twice.'

'You sure?'

'Well, I am an only child.'

'The thick plottens.'

The lights went down.

'Thanks for the Frenchie,' she said, touching my shoulder ever so lightly.

Murder, My Sweet was wildly dated; a B-movie film noir and a terrific feast of bad acting. I did follow the plot, but I was more preoccupied with that rapid-fire exchange.

'Well it sure as hell isn't *The Big Sleep*,' my neighbor announced as the credits rolled.

'Very little is,' I said as the lights came up.

'So, a fellow film buff?' she asked.

'When time allows.'

'And when it doesn't?'

'I am buried in law books.'

'There are worse things to be buried in.'

'Such as?'

'Embalming. Undertaking. Cost accountancy. Actuarial analysis. Being a proctologist. Mind if I steal another of your Frenchies?'

'Only if you tell me your name.'

'Rebecca. And yours?'

'Sam.'

'Sam, with your smart French cigarettes. Let me guess: you buy them in Paris, where you were for a few months before returning home to do the safe American thing.'

'Thank you for reducing me to a cultural cliché.'

'Didn't George Orwell note that all clichés are fundamentally true?'

'Nice citation. And let me guess: you went to Sarah Lawrence or Hampshire or one of those other edgy, arty colleges, and you work somewhere very literary and far too smart like the *Paris Review* or the *New York Review of Books*.'

The lights were dimming for the next film.

'I'm a lawyer.'

And that was the actual truth – as I learned afterwards in a dive bar she took me to on Broadway and 83rd Street. Rebecca Wilkinson had grown up in Nebraska, the daughter of a literature professor who'd ended up exiled from New England at the state university. Her mother was a well-regarded regional poet who'd had a major mental meltdown ten years ago when Rebecca was just edging into adolescence and she'd been in and out of institutions since then.

'Dad drinks, Mom breaks down, I was their only child. I fled.'

New York was always her dream. Her way out of the provinces and familial despair. Her Moscow. She got a scholarship to Barnard. She did absurdly well there. She got a scholarship to Columbia Law. She was offered five different associateships on graduating with a variety of white-shoe firms. She chose to join Millbank, Ritter & Cage, where they mixed high-level corporate clients with a considerable amount of socially conscious pro bono work.

'As I am just in my first year there, none of the interesting death-penalty work – or prosecuting crackers for institutional racism in Alabama – has landed on my desk. Learning the corporate ropes and all that. And accepting their money. You know the deal: play their game as an associate for the next eight years, build up your client list, bill many hours to show that you are a rainmaker, then make partner by your mid-thirties and start deciding what you want to do with your life.'

'What do you want to do with your life?'

'Turn into the great crusading defense attorney of my time. Free condemned men and women from miscarriages of justice. Uncover major corporate malfeasance. Stick it to the man. Meet the man of my life and have a couple of kids, but still insist on a full and fantastic career. Maybe take a sabbatical for six months and live in Paris. Like you did. Should I suddenly announce to my employers that I want to run off with you to Paris for six months . . . *au revoir* my future partnership. But perhaps I should sidestep all that potential security. And live on the rue— name a street in Paris.'

'Rue Bernard Palissy.'

'Describe it to me: its look, dimensions, its buildings and shops, the neighborhood . . .'

I tried to do so, without hinting at anything personal about the place. Her response:

'So the woman you were in love with lives there?'

'Did I say anything about love?' I asked.

'You don't have to.'

'I'm that transparent?'

A slight shrug, another of her ironic smiles.

'How serious is it?'

'It was an arrangement. A passionate arrangement.'

'Was? So it's over?'

'It's over,' I said, simultaneously thinking: have I just uttered a half-truth, a lie? Or, perhaps, an aspiration: to find a way around the quiet ache that encased most thoughts of Isabelle. Sitting opposite Rebecca – whom I'd spoken to now for around thirty minutes – was I already plotting an emotional escape route? Do we often fall in love because the timing is right and because we want to balm the wounds of a passion that has not turned out the way we wanted it to turn out, even though – as experience was beginning to teach me – when it comes to matters of the heart, the narrative always skews away from that which you once envisaged?

'Truly over?' Rebecca asked.

'When is anything like that truly over?'

'I can't argue with that.'

We sat drinking in that bar until two in the morning – the conversation flowing forth with an ease and an interaction that was both bracing and arousing. Never underestimate the erotic charge from very smart talk with someone to whom you've taken an immediate fancy and from whom you are getting commensurate sentiments. She hinted that she'd just ended something important.

'I've walked down the same side of the street as you have,' she said. 'Speaking for myself, it's a one-way ticket to severe heartburn. But like you I'm going to say nothing about it . . . for the moment anyway. Except that it is in the recent past, and I am not going there again.'

I found out that she lived on the Upper East Side – 'the vanilla ice cream part of town, but I have an amazing deal, and actually the neighborhood still has a bit of old New York texture to it.

Maybe I'll invite you over sometime . . . If, that is, you want to continue the conversation, see where it brings us?'

'Yes, I'd like that very much.'

'Will you not feel it deeply unromantic if we have the Japanese moment and I give you a business card?'

'*Kanpai*,' I said, using the one and only word of Japanese I knew.

She took out a pen and wrote a number on the back.

'Here's my home phone. I have the requisite New York answering service in case I'm not home. And I share a secretary with five other associates at work.'

'No doubt if you are out a message will find its way to you.'

'If, that is, you deign to call me.'

'Am I giving you any indication I won't do that?'

'You haven't offered me your number yet.'

'Because I was waiting for you to finish giving me your numbers.'

'So you say.'

'Why are you sounding so doubtful?'

'Too much disappointment.'

'I'll try not to disappoint you.'

'That's what they all say.'

'I'm not all of them.'

'How do you say "we'll see" in French?'

'*On verra.*'

'I like the sound of that. Did your friend on the rue Bernard whatever-it-was-called use that expression a lot?'

'Yes, she did.' I could have added: it was her preferred pronouncement, her world view – and as such, one that she used all the time.

'*On verra*,' Rebecca said, trying out the expression again. 'It has a lovely musicality. And it is so French. Will you take me to Paris?'

'Don't you think we should have dinner first?'

'Touché. I'm still waiting for your phone number.'

I wrote down the main switchboard number at Larsson, Steinhardt & Shulman. I explained that the receptionist was rather old school and didn't like taking calls or messages for summer interns. And the phone at the apartment where I was subletting a room had no answering service.

'I'll deal with the Stalinist receptionist at your law firm. Now put me in a cab . . . And as it's Saturday night tomorrow and I don't think we need to play that "need to wait forty-eight hours to not show too much interest" game, why don't you tell me where we are meeting for dinner, and then I will suggest the 11 p.m. session at the Village Vanguard. Do you know Bill Evans?'

'Not really.'

'A huge gap in your education. Name a restaurant. Cheap and cheerful works for me.'

I mentioned Asti's, a little joint on 12th Street – not far from the Vanguard. 'Eight tomorrow?'

'I like a fellow Midwesterner who rejects the idea of dinner being a 5.30 p.m. event. It's a date. Now put me in a taxi. I need sleep.'

Outside the dive bar I hailed a speeding yellow cab. It braked in that 'stop on a dime' manner that seems to be kamikaze second nature to all New York drivers.

Rebecca pulled me close and gave me a light, direct kiss right on the lips.

'Let me try out my very bad French,' she said, her arms around my neck.

'Go ahead,' I said, kissing her back.

'*Je suis ton destin.*'

And then with a final kiss she was gone.

I walked the thirty blocks back to my sublet, replaying all that had just happened.

I am your destiny.

As I headed north up Broadway, I kept thinking: you decide at the last minute to go to a film-noir double feature, you decide to sit in the front row of the balcony, you choose a certain seat, you light up a pretentious French cigarette, and you discover a most loquacious, droll woman behind you. Also alone. Also – as it turns out – single . . .

Is this what is meant by happenstance: the accidental, the unforeseen, the random music of circumstance and chance that might just send everything in your life down a wholly new path?

And why, all the way home, did I find myself thinking: she is the woman I have been looking for? Because it was true? Because I wanted it to be true? Even though I still knew absolutely nothing about her . . .

We had dinner the next night. We talked even more non-stop. We went to the 11 p.m. Bill Evans session at the Vanguard – and I was so knocked sideways by his brilliance that we stayed for the 1 a.m. set. Hitting the streets at almost two thirty in the morning, Rebecca took me by my shirt and said:

'With the exception of those two sublime hours of piano, we have talked non-stop since 8 p.m. And everything that has passed between us has been nothing short of pretty damn wondrous. Shall we now vanish *chez moi*?'

There was much I could have said at that juncture – especially about Rebecca's more than upfront style; the fact that she clearly liked to be in control. But I was smitten in that way men become smitten when desired. Flattery will get you just about everywhere with a guy. Add this to smart conversation with a woman who was super bright, lovely and who made me laugh – and it was clear that it was easy to fall for her. Especially as she was my age, available and as desirous of a serious connection as I was.

'Let's vanish,' I said, taking her in my arms and giving her our first deep kiss.

Her apartment was in a walk-up on East 85th Street between Lexington and Third. Small. Indifferently decorated. Almost sterile. But rigorously organized. Neat. She saw me taking it all in, sizing it up.

'Don't judge a book by its cover,' she said, pulling me toward her.

'Am I that transparent?'

'Absolutely. I see all.'

And we fell into bed.

We had both been drinking for about six hours straight. Which meant that our first time making love was the wrong side of sloppy; a decided lack of heat between us. Blowsy passion that lasted minutes before Rebecca fell off me with an ambivalent semi-groan. When I next came round it was late morning. I smelled coffee. Rebecca emerged out of her tiny alcove kitchen naked, an espresso pot and two cups dangling from her hands.

'Morning,' she said, her voice thick with morning-after be-fuddlement. 'I sense we need Italian caffeine.'

'I sense that too.'

She sat down next to me on the bed. We drank the entire pot of coffee and then I pulled her back into bed. We had hangover sex. Seriously fatigued sex – yet still underscored by the need to prove something to each other. Who once said that the history of all intimate relationships is written in the first week; that all the signs of things to come emerge in those first days? But thanks to the impulse of wanting love you tend to sidestep certain self-evident truths and embrace the amorous headiness of it all.

Not that making love with Rebecca was catastrophic. Or, to go to the opposite end of the room, banal. Nor was it lacking in intensity. Rebecca had told me over dinner the previous night that she'd been captain of the Barnard lacrosse team; that she liked sports for their 'competitive robustness'.

Competitive robustness.

That just about summed up sex with Rebecca. It was turbu-lent, boisterous, sometimes wild, sometimes just rough and ready. But unlike Siobhan – who was almost carnivorous – I sensed deep need and an equally intense loneliness and I responded immediately to her ferocity. Because it mirrored all the solitude I felt too.

Whereas with Isabelle there was a long, inherently sensual arc to our lovemaking – restrained, exploratory, building to some-thing quietly ecstatic – here it was rock and roll, but with a whiff of grasping sadness informing the way Rebecca buried her face in my shoulder as she let go and sobbed for a few quiet moments.

When I whispered, 'Anything I can do?' her response (when considered retrospectively) was most telling:

'Never let me go . . . even if I get out of hand.'

'Why would you get out of hand?'

'Because I am my own worst enemy.'

'That sounds ominous.'

She stroked my face.

'Not if you figure out how to handle me.'

That was also very Rebecca: no attempt to hide the bad stuff. *Take it or leave it.*

I found such directness intoxicating. Part of me wanted to match her need with my own; I told myself that together we could somehow quell the remoteness within. All this crazed certainty so fast. But that, too, was love. The rush toward absolute belief that she was everything I was looking for; that, after just a few hours, we had stumbled into something extraordinary together.

In the coming weeks we spent virtually every night in her apartment – so much so that I eventually gave notice on my sublet and moved what little I had into her tiny place.

Things I learned quickly about Rebecca:

She loved sex first thing in the morning without fail – and even if I'd been up late working she would nudge me awake and want instant, fast rapture. Just as she was also keen on lovemaking at least three early evenings a week when she came home from the office and needed 'a sexual antidote to all the banality of the day'.

She was as rigorously organized about her life as she was about sex. She approved of the way I adapted to her mania for everything being in its place: hanging up the bathroom towels in a certain way; ensuring that all wine glasses were lined up according to size; that the magazines fanned out on her coffee table remained in the correct order.

Despite this need for domestic regulation – about which she could easily send herself up – she had a wonderfully decadent side. A 'Let's go to four films this weekend . . .' or 'Let's hit three jazz gigs until four in the morning . . .' or 'Let's dive-bar-crawl on the Lower East Side' side. Just as she also loved haunting bookshops and brought me to her preferred jazz record shops up near Columbia and down on Waverly Place.

That was another deep, instant attraction: she had embraced her status as uber adopted New Yorker with intense relish. Yet she saw herself as a bohemian, hating anything to do with social climbing. She was obsessed with all aspects of social justice – was already trying to get herself attached to a gay-rights case that would challenge New York State law on inheritance tax for homosexual couples of common-law marriage standing. And she was appalled by the Supreme Court's decision to back the death penalty and was *passionately* determined to lead the legal fight against its injustices.

Passion. Her preferred word. She had a vast passion for so much. Especially – as she told me most days – *me.*

I was the best thing that had ever happened to her; the man she had always dreamed of meeting. We talked about how to sidestep all the evident temptations of partnership; how, perhaps, in time we would set up our own alternative firm: young, super-smart, progressive, forward-looking, championing lost causes. Oh the plans we had after just a few fast weeks together . . .

Rebecca said that having children was something she absolutely wanted, but that we would raise them below 14th Street and sidestep all the suburban temptations that so many couples were still succumbing to. But we would wait three or four years – until Rebecca was thirty – before having kids . . . By which time we'd have our law office up and running, beholden to no corporate substructure but our own; determined to do professional and personal life in a wholly original and independent way.

Plans, plans.

Rebecca loved plans.

Because Rebecca needed order. Because everything about her life prior to her arrival in New York was about disorder, her two academic parents having decided to 'live in an eternal commune' when it came to domestic life and raising their child.

'My parents loved chaos. My mother worked in our attic, a tiny study that looked like it hadn't been cleaned for five years, refusing to have a dishwasher, telling me from the age of seven onwards that if I wanted clean, pressed clothes I should learn to wash and iron them myself. Dad was worse, even more disordered. I don't think they ever bought any new clothes for about ten years. "Wear it until it falls apart" was their credo. Grow vegetables in the garden and live off them. Become obsessed with creating your very own compost heap. Use old newspapers as a substitute for toilet paper – because why harm trees by wiping your ass with them? Turning up their ashram-influenced noses against anything reeking of money . . .'

'But clearly,' I said, 'all their social-justice stuff rubbed off on you.'

'Absolutely. But it also made me need to live with a high degree of organization and to like nice things around me. This apartment – it's a sublet. And I hate its sterility. But I put seven thousand dollars aside last year. I want another ten in my account by New Year's Day. And I have fifteen grand in a bank in Omaha: my heritage from my grandfather. Put it all together and I can buy myself half of a two-bedroom apartment in the West Village. I have the place already picked out. Right off University Place and 11th Street. With fifty percent financing, the mortgage and the maintenance come out to around $524 a month. But I'm going to be on $80k next year. My parents were always telling their alternative friends: "Rebecca's rebelling against us by embracing corporate law with all the high financial trimmings . . ." Do you think I talk far too much about money and how it can work for me?'

I found myself laughing, telling Rebecca:

'As someone who was raised in the most austere, boring household in Indiana – and there is a prize for that honor – I am very happy to embrace the good life with you.'

Plans, plans. Two months into our romance and we were already looking to the future. How we would take it in turns to commute every weekend between New York and Boston. How I would accept the associateship offered by Larsson, Steinhardt & Shulman and would move permanently to the city – and into Rebecca's soon-to-be-purchased co-op a year from June. And how I would, in the short term, cancel my proposed upcoming trip to Paris at the end of the month.

Love.

We agreed that secrets had no basis between us; that we always had to ensure clarity and absolute honesty between us. Which is why Rebecca told me all about the fifty-year-old partner in another law firm, Stephen Maidstone, with whom she'd had a very intense affair for almost a year . . . and which had ended when his wife discovered all.

To say that Rebecca had been overinvested in this older fellow was to engage in understatement (as she herself also admitted).

'Steve told me that I was the love of his life.'

'Did you think the same thing about him?'

'You mean because I have told you that you are the love of my life?'

'Perhaps . . .'

'Steve was astonishing. Totally corporate and conservative when you saw him. But wild in private.'

Did I want to be hearing this? I wondered quietly to myself as she waxed lyrical about this board member of the Scarsdale Gold Club, a man who had few cultural interests, who rarely read anything outside of law documents, yet who became (in Rebecca's eyes) Henry Miller once he discarded his Brooks Brothers suit and tie on the floor of this very same apartment where we now lay naked across her narrow double bed.

'I know it all sounds absurd: becoming so bound up with a man for whom an actuarial chart was erotic literature, and on whom I developed a stupid fixation . . . Which I now see was some fucked-up Daddy Transference thing – lashing out at my rejecting hippie father by investing myself utterly in the ultimate button-down.'

I sidestepped talking about my own recent past. To speak about that life in Paris would be to undermine so much I truly wanted not to corrupt. Especially if I articulated the real sadness I was feeling at certain key moments.

And yes, I asked myself how could I be in love with Rebecca when I was somewhere silently preoccupied with Isabelle . . . even though I knew Rebecca was the woman I should be falling in love with. Because she was evidently, on so many levels, the better choice – if you somehow think that we choose the moment to fall in love. And here I was being legal/analytical again, yet also telling myself: this is the woman I was destined to meet . . . and with whom a future is actually possible.

Reading that last paragraph back to myself, I cannot help but be amazed by my immense certainty; my decision after just a few weeks that I should buy into the romantic program that Rebecca was constructing for us, but which (truth be told) I was also complicit in building. Yes, part of me might have thought: all this is happening so quickly. And yes, I am aiding and abetting its *grande vitesse*. Because I had convinced myself that I so wanted it; that it was the absolutely right destiny for me.

Was I deliberately not looking at all that was in front of me? But outside of her slight control-freakdom – of which she was wittily cognizant – I couldn't really see anything that was sending out dire warning signals along the lines of 'Abandon All Hope Ye Who Enter Here'. Yes, there was the fact that the sex, though always robust, never edged into the sensual, but she liked it and wanted it regularly. We couldn't believe our luck otherwise: the way we buoyed each other up and seemed to understand when support was so desperately needed. We seemed to cohabit well in her small space, and understood that neither of us liked to be crowded. We talked endlessly. And God how we both wanted this connection to succeed; how we felt it would calm and even alleviate so many of the doubts and fears within.

In the spirit of full disclosure, I finally told her everything about Isabelle. To her credit Rebecca wasn't judgmental. Nor did she express outright jealousy. But she did want to know how deeply I felt for 'this semi-accessible Parisian of your dreams'. Unlike me – who had pressed her only for little details about her lover – Rebecca wanted to know all: how it started, our season of trysts, the months of longing, the compromised return in the midst of Isabelle's 'baby blues'. And she even let it be known that if I did want to go to Paris and see her she wasn't going to stand in my way . . . but she couldn't promise that she would be waiting for me when I came back.

'That's not to say I will definitely throw you overboard. I just can't say how I will feel if you do decide that she is the destiny you want to chase. But I will respect your choice.'

I canceled the trip after this, sending that telegram to Isabelle, telling myself that I was making the right decision . . . that I had found someone amazing and should stop chasing after someone who would never truly commit to me, and with whom any future was geographically impossible. Part of me convinced myself: this is all for the absolute best. And in her telegram to me she wished me well, doing so with the elegance and detachment that were so much part of her world view.

I couldn't get a refund on the plane ticket. Rebecca commiserated and scrambled to find a vacation alternative for us. Within twenty-four hours we'd agreed to spend the time in upstate New York – renting a cabin deep in the Adirondacks. We brought books, wine, boots for hiking, swimsuits for diving into the cool waters of glacial lakes. We shut ourselves away from the world for ten days straight. The cabin was simple, basic, seriously isolated. Twice during our week and a half there we got into our rented car and drove half an hour to the closest country shop and stocked up on food. We made love twice a day. We slept monumentally long hours. We read. We had periods when blocks of time would pass and little in the way of conversation was exchanged between us – and there was never a sense that the silence was indicative of anything more than being comfortable enough with each other not to speak. Just as there were stretches when we could not stop talking to each other; when I marveled just how we never ran out of interest in each other; how the conversation was always so charged; how we truly got each other.

Did I rue the lost week in Paris? Of course. I longed for life away from American predictability. I wanted to have breakfast in Le Select, haunt little cinemas, and climb the forty-eight steps up to Isabelle's 'under the eaves' refuge to find her, a cigarette in her fingers, her desire for me so pronounced.

But we all edit such coming attractions to remove the thorny stuff that undermines the pristine version of things we like to project in that screening room between our ears. Such as the fact that every night at seven I would be back by myself wandering the city, forlorn and trying, unsuccessfully, not to imagine Isabelle at home with her husband and daughter. I held on to that image every time I felt a stab of longing for Paris.

Instead, I looked out at the Elysian wonder of the Adirondacks, and gazed at Rebecca on the hammock stretched between two trees, deep into the new John Updike, and found myself thinking: this is good.

After ten days Rebecca drove me across the back roads of upstate New York into the more northern quarters of New England, then down to Cambridge. I reopened my dorm room and was informed by my girlfriend that I really did need to invest in a proper queen-size bed if we were going to do this commuting relationship thing for the next twenty-one months.

The next day we went to a furniture shop in Porter Square and chose a rather substantial bed with a mahogany headboard and a serious mattress.

'Our first proper bed,' Rebecca said after I handed over a check for $335.

Every other weekend for the next nine months, Rebecca shared that bed with me. Just as I was in her bed in Yorkville all the other weekends. I got adept at studying manically on the Greyhound bus I hopped twice a month at 3.35 p.m. after my last Friday class, cramming madly on the 6.46 p.m. return bus on Sunday. Rebecca would arrive on the Amtrak train that shunted into Boston South Station just minutes into Saturday morning, giving us two nights together before she too headed back to her professional world on the 5.15 p.m. Sunday service. The days apart suited us well. The pleasure of seeing each other after five days apart was immense. A rhythm developed. Two days of passion and shared pleasures, then back to our own worlds. As a trunk call between New York and Boston was still costly, we'd arrange for a time every day when Rebecca would call me from her office, ringing the communal phone on my dorm floor.

Law school was even more intensive the second year. I had no life outside of classes and study and my weekends with Rebecca. She, in turn, was getting increasingly frustrated with the amount of white-shoe case work she was handling, but when she closed on her co-op right before Christmas she did note, with a high sense of irony and resignation, that 'I have traded professional latitude for my own small entrée into the New York real-estate market' (a very nice two-bedroom apartment on the eighth floor of an apartment building off Washington Square Park).

We spent most of Christmas that year moving her in – and buying furniture with her Christmas bonus. It was Rebecca who was the design obsessive, deciding she wanted a subdued Danish Modern look. She had a great eye and a need to get all the interior-decor details exactly right. Over the New Year's Day weekend, I agreed to fly out with her to Omaha. Arctic cold, flat, empty terrain, a city in post-industrial decline, and two parents who were wearing their aging hippiedom reasonably well, and who were welcoming in a detached way. Their house was indeed communal chaos – as if any sense of orderliness was a conformist offense. I tried to discern if they were still close as a couple or simply rubbing along in their own crunchy granola way. Still, this 'meet the parents' event went reasonably.

To be in a couple – especially one in the early years of its journey – is to tell yourself that you will be remarkable together; the exception to all the usual romantic rules that seem to come into play whenever the quotidian begins to assert itself.

For the next year and a half, even though she had the far more luxurious place, Rebecca insisted on coming north to Boston twice a month. Because, again, we were a couple and we both had to show commitment by traveling back and forth to each other.

Eighteen months. A set of second-year finals. Another summer gig at Larsson, Steinhardt & Shulman. A two-week hiking vacation in Montana. My final year in law school. Graduation. A job at Larsson, Steinhardt & Shulman. I moved into Rebecca's apartment. And when she discussed the idea of marriage – of setting a date and all that, but having something non-traditional – of course I said yes. Why? The word 'certainty' came to mind – even though it also tantalized and vexed me.

We set our marriage date for December 21, 1980: half a year hence.

I was now slotting into life. All the boxes ticked. And telling myself: you're happy.

And still in contact with Isabelle.

*

I did reply to her telegram in the wake of my cancelation of the August week:

> *Thank you for your generosity and affection. You will always be in my thoughts. Je t'embrasse – Sam*

Months went by. Then, in October, a letter showed up.

My dearest Sam

Late autumn in Paris. Encroaching darkness. And I am missing you.

My news is minimal. Émilie sleeps through the night. She smiles constantly. Everyone tells me she has a most happy countenance. I concur. But in my grimmer moments I wonder: how long will she hold that eternal smile once the realities of life begin to crowd in? And when she discovers at school just how mean other girls can be?

But, as I said, those are my depressive episodes. Of which there are fewer. Thanks to more electricity to the brain. I tipped into the shadows a few weeks after you left. The terrible infanticidal thoughts came back. Charles found me in our kitchen in the middle of one night, banging my head again on our floor in an attempt to silence the crazed pathological voices within. I was institutionalized for four weeks. I was subjected to even more intense electroshock therapy. I lost short-term memory for over a month. I was allowed to convalesce. I found myself longing for you with an intensity that, in part, had to do with the after-effects of the treatment . . . but which was also a true yearning for everything about you, about us.

Which is why I was so expectantly counting down the days until August and your arrival and being back in your arms.

And then your telegram arrived.

Am I jealous of this woman you are now with?

Absolutely.

Do I feel as if I have lost someone for whom I still have deep, genuine love?

Absolutely.

Am I being a bit excessive here . . . what you Americans call 'heart on your sleeve'?

Absolutely.

But there it is.

Cards on the table . . . as you Yankees also say.

And more cards on the table – though you haven't come out and said exactly what is going on . . . Who she is, how serious is it (though you canceling the trip to Paris tells all)? I have been wrapped in the most profound regret since I opened the telegram and realized: he has been grabbed (as I always knew you would be).

I don't know what else to say. Except: I don't blame you for giving up on me. Because I gave you no hope. Because – and I see this now – I am stuck in my own confinement, more a luxurious cul-de-sac than a prison. And yes, I am writing this far too late in my study at home, many doors closed to ensure that Charles does not hear me typing. And when I finish writing I am putting it in an envelope without reading it and writing your address and grabbing my coat and heading out to the nearest letter box and posting it before I have a chance to reread it and change my mind.

Je t'aime . . . and please do not tell me anything in reply about her. Even though I want to know everything.

And if you change your mind and can somehow come to Paris . . .

Was I just a little thrown by this letter?

To use her recent word of choice:

Absolutely.

Did I wonder: discovering that I had bumped into love, was Isabelle now having a touch of buyer's remorse because I was now out of reach?

Had I been still single and burning for her, would the balance of power have been different? Would she have kept me comfortably distanced and needy? Or had my shift in circumstance suddenly pointed up the continuity of her own circumstances, her own choices?

And then there was the whole way her letter played with my own sense of involvement with Rebecca. I knew it was absurd to think of this in the simplistic sense of either/or. But for the first time Isabelle was hinting at wanting something beyond our afternoons. But that, too, I sensed, was tied up in the fact that I was no longer available. And though part of me felt this intense and desperate yearning for her, the more rational part of my brain cautioned: you, too, are reacting to that which is out of reach and has always been so.

Naturally I said nothing to Rebecca about this letter. And when she came up to visit me a few days later and we fell quickly into bed, and the sex was as intensive and fast as ever, I found myself envisaging Isabelle . . . and the way that making love with her – whether it was languid or expedited – always had an erotic charge and density that was simply not there with Rebecca.

But what was there with Rebecca was complicity. A sense of being able to construct the edifice of a life together, our shared references that required no translation.

We long for what we can't have, and simultaneously wonder if what we do have – and which brings us so much that we have always wanted – is too easy.

Follow that trajectory of twisted logic – a hall of contradictory mirrors – and you end up bereft on all fronts. Chasing love as an elusive reverie rather than something serious and stable.

Of course, Rebecca asked me if I had ever heard back from Isabelle after I canceled going to Paris.

I told her about the telegram in which she had expressed sadness but wished me well.

'Did you feel sadness when you read that?' she asked.

'Don't we all feel a degree of sadness at the end of something, even if we know that, at heart, it's not best for our emotional health? But it's behind me.'

I was lying.

Because when is anything that was intimate and significant and caused you to lose sleep ever truly behind you?

*

I never said a word to Rebecca about that extraordinary letter received from Paris in the early autumn. As she never asked me if I had ever heard from Isabelle again, I didn't feel as if I was trading in falsehoods. Nor did I say anything when, around two weeks after receiving her letter, I decided that a reply was overdue and necessary.

I wrote:

Dear Isabelle
Well you certainly gave me a lot to think about . . . as you always do.

At the outset let me say just how sorry I am that you had to go through a further dose of hell. I can't imagine the horror of it all, let alone having to endure the treatment prescribed. I am so relieved to read that the worst seems to be over — and would never have sent such a short telegram had I known. Just as I must say: from all that you have continued to describe, you clearly have a very good man in Charles. And one who, most tellingly, is kind to you — and deeply understanding. As — from what you've told me — you too have been there for him. I hope it doesn't sound disingenuous of me to say: you are lucky to have each other.

Which brings me to your letter, your declaration of love. When in the past I made such declarations, you told me to not harm myself with a proclamation that could not be reciprocated . . . that I was presumptuous to think all along that this love was indeed reciprocated and deeply shared.

And now there it is on the table . . . and I feel just a bit conflicted. Because her name is Rebecca. She is a very brilliant and funny and beautiful woman. She is of my generation and is a highly qualified lawyer. She lives in New York. She tells me I am all she has ever wanted. And — truth be told — I cannot make such an overriding declaration. Because you are all that I have ever wanted. But you remain — even now — out of reach. Would you really drop everything, pick up Émilie and start a life with me here? We have discussed this before. You yourself have noted in your letter that you live in a well-upholstered dead end. I would hardly call it that. And yes, there was a moment some months ago when, had you proposed what you propose now, I would have committed utterly to you. But what I also know from my relatively limited experience of life – and from the past few months with Rebecca – is that we have no idea what a true intimate existence with someone is until we've lived it. I was unable – for many reasons – to discover that with you. And that is not a reproach – just the truth of the matter. With Rebecca, we commute, but we see each other every weekend. As such we have begun the process of a life together.

Reading all this back I find myself wondering: are so many major junctures in life all about timing? We talk about destiny, true love. I felt that with you. Overwhelmingly. Coupled with bad timing.

And now . . .

I apologize for being direct about Rebecca. You asked not to know. But it's better that you know: she is my future. Did I want that future with you? Bien sûr. But . . .

Timing. Timing.

And yes: je t'aime . . . but not in any futur proche way.

I am always your friend.

Was this a cruel letter? Was there a degree of payback for being told that everything I envisaged with Isabelle was just out of reach? Was I allowing a sense of dominance to underscore all this? Now I have someone important in my life . . . someone who truly wants me . . . and who has not pushed me away for a pre-existing life. And now, finally, you have seen just what you have sidestepped. And as much as I still want you, you come with too much in the way of accompanying valises.

Whereas with Rebecca the road is open, clear, not strewn with so much detritus.

Or at least that's what I was telling myself now.

There was a long silence from Paris after this letter. Months of silence. Not a word. I was buried in work, in my weekends with Rebecca. Intriguing how, in the wake of a definitive letter, we all want some sort of validation that there is still a door open; that things aren't irreparable, even though you've engineered them that way.

I am always your friend.

Considered retrospectively, the most crushing thing you can tell a one-time lover is that you now just want to be pals, killing it for all sorts of self-justifying reasons. You think you have considerable power when you make such a declaration; when you remove the possibility of a return to intimacy. Even if you convince yourself that this decision is for the best, you find yourself ruing the fact that a door has been slammed shut. And you have to take responsibility for that loud action – even though you will endlessly try to convince yourself that the other party has played a role in this leave-taking . . . that you've done something so extreme because they have offered you no other solution, or because you are certain that such drastic action is in your best interests.

But unless the other party is seriously deranged – or having such a negative impact on your life as to cause you psychic damage – downgrading a love affair to a friendship is always tinged with regret. And also underscored by an underlying question: why do we spend so much of our lives burning romantic bridges? As Isabelle had said to me all along: there is no need to be definitive, *case closed*, about such things. Especially as life should be lived according to the more open existential principle of: *on verra*. We'll see.

So although I wasn't surprised that there was no reply, a tinge of disappointment lingered. Only once did Rebecca ask me if I was still in touch with my 'Parisienne inamorata'. I told her that I had written Isabelle about my new life and that things were, as a result, over between us. Rebecca smiled and kissed me and whispered 'Thank you' in my ear. Competition eliminated. She had me totally to herself – and that was where I too wanted to be.

Somewhere atop a mountain in Montana that summer – waking before dawn in a small cabin way up in a northwestern corner of the Bitterroot Range – I had a disquieting moment of minor revelation. Rebecca was still deeply asleep. I dressed quietly, stepping outside to watch night wake up. A hint of luminous haze dimming the celestial fireworks of the stars above. Then a dot in the epicenter of the sky. One that began to expand like a cartographically drawn white line demarcating the eternal horizon. Moments later, like a two-way curtain being lifted, the line opened upwards, downwards. The epic grandeur of the vertiginous Rockies enveloped me; a horizon of such raw, primal beauty that I blinked and felt tears.

I looked out at the vista enveloping me. Prehistoric. Snow-dappled (even in late August). Craggy in its immense contours. Then I thought of my beloved in bed last night, working her way through a tricky law judgment, a legal pad on her knees, taking copious notes, telling me we'd make love in the morning. That quote of Nietzsche's about a little idea taking over an entire life came back to me. So, too, the realization: when it came to choosing between the great pleasures of the flesh and the technical heft of the law . . . well, she was, shall we say, divided.

Hours later – after we'd had our ten minutes of mid-morning passion – we took a long hike into the great wide open, the trail turning narrow, tricky. Standing on the edge of a cliff face, staring out at all that primordial vastness, Rebecca took my hand and began to exclaim:

> *In this broad earth of ours,*
> *Amid the measureless grossness and the slag,*
> *Enclosed and safe within its central heart,*
> *Nestles the seed perfection.*

Then she told me she had just been quoting Walt Whitman.

Rebecca: intensely literate. Intensely well informed. Intensely cultured. Yet also possessing a rigidity when it came to wanting life to play out the way she felt it should – and getting just a little compulsive when the trajectory of things did not follow her master plan. And when a bit too much alcohol was involved. I began to notice a certain tendency towards obstinacy – which, on two recent occasions, had spilled over into a whiff of anger.

'Are you suggesting that I was snappy with that waitress?' she'd asked me on the way home from a late set at the Vanguard one night.

'You just tend to get a little tetchy after the third Manhattan.'

'I can easily handle three cocktails. What I can't handle is rudeness.'

'All she said was "You seem in an awful hurry tonight" when you kept waving for the check.'

'You agree with her that I'm Ms Impatient?'

'Sweetheart—'

'Don't sweetheart me . . .'

She broke free of me, charging angrily up the street. Part of me wanted to chase after her. Part of me was completely thrown by this outburst. But then, moments later, she came running back to me, contriteness itself. Putting her arms around me. Shame in her eyes. Saying:

'That was shitty of me.'

And she assured me that this outburst was a one-off. What she called 'in vino stupidus'. In turn I assured her the incident was behind us.

Weeks, months passed. There were no further boozy flare-ups from Rebecca. I continued to live on a New York–Boston trajectory. Silence from Paris. I had slowly come to accept that my letter had truly put the kibosh on everything; that I had killed it all. And that knowledge was bittersweet. There was sadness that contact had been lost; that I had ended things so conclusively. Relief that I was now free of much doubt and could end my conflicted dance between the woman who so wanted me and the woman who kept me hanging on. Especially as it is an integral part of human nature to long for that which is just out of reach.

And then, out of nowhere, a telegram arrived. A knock on my door from the doorman at our hall of residence.

'Western Union for you,' the guy shouted. 'You there?'

'I'm here,' I said back.

Whoosh. The sound of an envelope sliding under a door, gliding along the parquet and landing not far from my feet. A telegram at 7.46 a.m. is never a sign of good things to come. I figured my father had left this life and one of his crabby sisters (there were four, all grim) had dispatched me a message about his 'passing' (a word I already despised as it sidestepped the reality of death). So I took a deep breath and opened the yellow envelope, reading the short, upper-case message:

In Boston for three days. Can you meet me at the Ritz-Carlton tomorrow 1 p.m.? Thinking of you. Many kisses – Isabelle

Disbelief was my initial reaction. Disbelief and shocked bemusement.

Isabelle in Boston? Absurd. She never left France – bar an occasional non-Normandy holiday somewhere Italian.

Isabelle *in Boston*?

I read through her telegram many times, trying to seek significance in every cadence of its construction, concluding that she was playing a gambit here. But one where her intentions were clear – a rendezvous at a hotel, *many kisses* – and she knew the denouement she wanted. She was offering me the chance not to see her, to close the door permanently by refusing to cross the River Charles to make the appointment, yet she was simultaneously daring me into seeing her. To not resist temptation. To enter the same arena in which she had played when involved with me in Paris: the clandestine. She knew I was involved. She knew it was serious. She knew I had broken things off for all those reasons. And yet here she was, in this city, *my city*, letting me know that things were not over between us . . . if, that is, I would meet her tomorrow at 1 p.m. at Boston's most upscale hotel.

Part of me wanted to wire back immediately: No thanks.

Part of me wanted to do nothing and let the opportunity pass.

Part of me wanted to let Rebecca in on all this – thereby demonstrating my immense loyalty to her and my self-restraint. A big part of me immediately dismissed this idea as one propelled by fear and guilt, even though, as yet, I had nothing to be guilty about. But as much as I loved and needed Rebecca, there was another part of me that knew if I told her about this telegram, this invitation to recommence, the Pandora's-box effect would spring into play.

I knew it would cause much storm and stress within, and why land her with all that? An ex – if I could even classify Isabelle as that, as we were never formally a couple – had contacted me, wanting a meeting, wanting more. To share that would be to pass on my own conflicted thoughts to the woman I loved. Silence was the smarter option.

And a big part of me knew a great truth, articulated by a law professor: 'As I used to tell clients: a secret shared is no longer a secret.'

I would like to say that I had a long night of the soul about whether I should/should not see Isabelle. Actually the decision came to me quickly and in camera . . . privately, while taking an early-winter run along the banks of the Charles.

It would be wrong of me not to see Isabelle while she was here in Boston. We'd had an important intimate connection. It was now behind us. Not to show up would be both immature and an insult to the pleasure we had given each other; the passion and intense familiarity we'd shared. But I would go to the rendezvous clear about one thing: I would not be crossing the line of intimacy with her. I would not betray what I had with Rebecca to reconnect with an afternoon fantasy that had never had a future. I now had a future with someone. I was no longer alone in the world. I would not risk that whatsoever.

So I went to the Western Union office on Harvard Square and paid one dollar ninety-five to have the following missive dispatched across the river.

Happy to meet you for lunch tomorrow at the Ritz at 1 p.m. Best wishes – Samuel.

As formal and pleasant and cold as a business RSVP. She had put her cards on the table. I'd just shown her mine.

That night, around eleven, just when I was about to surrender to sleep, the phone rang. Rebecca. She was in one of her strained moods when everything from the professional day had piled atop her, she was spouting bile about work colleagues and a client who was a total sleaze, 'and I've had about two glasses of wine too many and I have the worst fucking period pains right now, and I really am fucking fed up with everything tonight, and why the fuck do you put up with such a mess like me, and . . .'

I reassured her we were good; that we would be together at the end of the week, but that maybe four glasses of wine in rapid nighttime succession wasn't the best antidote to a tough day . . .

'Are you accusing me of drinking my despair away?'

'You're in despair?'

'I don't know.'

'You're only thinking that way because you're a little world-weary tonight. And another thing: you're hardly a mess.'

'Why are you calling me that?'

'Because you called yourself that a moment ago.'

'Did I?'

Oh God . . .

'All will be fine, my love.'

'Why do I always feel like you have to be giving me a fucking pep talk?' she asked, boozed-up anger underscoring her comment. I was a little thrown by her tone and the vehemence undercutting it.

'Sweetheart,' I said, 'I think it best if we speak tomorrow when you are in a better place.'

'What the fuck do you mean by that?' she asked, the anger now well above the surface.

'Good night,' I said, putting down the phone. It immediately started ringing again. Instinct told me not to answer it. Instead I followed its cord to the wall socket and quickly unplugged it. I sat down on my bed. I put my head in my hands. I found myself thinking: that was truly terrible . . . and was it an indication of matters hidden, a side to her kept out of my line of vision until now?

I slept badly. When I woke shortly before sunrise I plugged the phone back in. As I made myself a cup of instant coffee on the little hotplate I'd installed in the room, the phone began to ring. I checked my watch: 6.47 a.m. This time I answered it.

'I haven't slept – because I have been on this phone since the moment you hung on me, trying to call you back.'

Rebecca sounded hushed, deeply unsettled.

'I unplugged the phone,' I said, adding: 'And I slept badly too.'

I heard a sob on the other end of the line. Then:

'I won't blame you if you want to end things between us after my appalling performance.'

'What got into you?'

'A bottle of wine got into me. I overdid it because the day had been such a shit show.'

'But I've seen you with a bottle of wine in you before and things didn't turn nasty.'

'I know, I know.'

Another sob. Then:

'If you leave me I'll die.'

'That's just a little extreme, Becca.'

My affectionate name for her – and used at this moment as a form of reassurance.

Another sob.

'I am so, so sorry.'

'OK.'

'You're too good. I don't deserve you. I love you, Sam.'

'And I you.'

But I was still going to meet Isabelle at 1 p.m.

I decided to dress appropriately for the Ritz. Last summer Rebecca had taken me shopping at Brooks Brothers for an all-season suit. Dark blue. Pinstripes, wide lapels. She'd also insisted that I buy three pale blue shirts and a striped tie, telling me at the time that if I wanted to play the corporate legal game I had to dress in the uniform demanded.

Why was I wearing this now? In part because the Ritz back then had a rigorously enforced jacket-and-tie dress code in their bar and restaurant. But also to let Isabelle know: forget the faux-bohemian look I sported back in Paris . . . I am a lawyer (or just about) now. If pressed, I would tell her that my girlfriend had chosen these clothes for me – and I felt very at ease in them (which, truth be told, was a semi-truth).

It was a chilly December morning. I took the Red Line across the river to Park Street. With a little time to kill I walked across the Common and the Public Gardens as light snow began to cascade down. It did nothing to quell the fretfulness, the angst, ricocheting within me.

I arrived five minutes ahead of the agreed time. But she was there already. In a corner booth. A cigarette on the go. A notebook and a fountain pen and some manuscript pages spread out in front of her. She was wearing a simple black turtleneck and a black leather skirt. I noticed that she had lost the gauntness that had characterized her in the aftermath of her depression. Her red hair was loose. She didn't see me enter, which allowed me to halt about ten feet from her and take her in. Her poise, her subdued beauty. The extraordinary radiance that had grabbed my attention in that boulevard Saint-Germain bookshop where we first met. I felt something rise up in me that was still as extraordinary as it was now disquieting: love.

She glanced away from her papers. She saw me taking her in. I walked toward her. She held out her hands. I took them.

She gripped my hands tighter as I pulled her toward me and gave her a kiss on each cheek – *à la française*. I locked my fingers in hers.

'It is so good to see you,' she whispered.

We sat down. She reached for my hand again. I took hers. A moment of silence when we just looked at each other. I momentarily recovered.

'What brings you to Boston?' I asked.

'My husband. He is speaking at a banking conference being held over two days here. We are just in Boston for four nights. I do not like leaving Émilie for long . . .'

'And how is Émilie?'

'In her second year now. The love of my life.'

'I'm happy for you. And happy to see that you seem in a better place.'

She reached for her packet of cigarettes. She offered me one. I accepted.

'A proper French cigarette,' I said, my head buzzing.

'I have been trying to reduce my intake,' she said. 'I fail constantly.'

'We all have our ways of making it through the night.'

'What's yours, Samuel?'

'Work.'

'Your studies go well?'

'I cannot believe they will be over in a few months. And then I will be a working man.'

'And tell me, how is your beloved?' Her tone was pleasantness itself. Rancor-free.

'Rebecca is just fine. She is due here on Friday.'

'Then it is fortunate we are leaving tomorrow evening.'

'Why did you contact me yesterday?'

'You mean, why not when I arrived on Sunday afternoon? Because your last letter was rather definitive and I was afraid that if I approached you, you would tell me to go away – or not respond at all.'

'But then . . .'

'But then, yesterday morning I took a long walk around Harvard Square. Across the beautiful campus. Past the Law School. Hoping against hope that our paths would cross. Which was, I know, an absurd reverie. But one that spoke to many longings within. That's when I saw a Western Union office and decided to try my luck with a telegram.'

She took my hand and said:

'Samuel. What if I was willing to chance life with you here in the States?'

'Are you serious?'

'I wouldn't speak about such things if I wasn't serious.'

'And what are you proposing? To arrive here with Émilie, to move into my student room, all two hundred square feet of it—'

'I was thinking New York. When you finish in a few months. We could rent an apartment. And yes, Émilie would be with me. But you would be working. And I have friends who work for the Alliance Française there and who have told me I could teach part-time. I'm telling you: I am willing to try a life with you.'

'And what has made you decide now to "try" a completely new life with me?'

176

She met my gaze.

'Fear.'

'Of what?'

'Of not taking a risk. Of playing it absolutely safe. Of waking up ten years from now in deeper middle age and finding myself thinking: why didn't I act on what my heart was always telling me I must do?'

Long silence. This was what part of me so wanted. Yet part of me was terrified of it. Because I was trying to imagine whether I could handle such a life. Living with this woman suddenly no longer in her plush Parisian comfort zone. Setting up life with me in a small apartment. Moving in with a child. And then – and yes, I was thinking fast now – if I did want a baby with Isabelle . . . And yes, part of me wanted children, theoretically anyway, though not immediately . . . But if I did want that child, Isabelle was thirty-eight now . . . that child would have to be made soon. Did I really want to weigh myself down with all those responsibilities so immediately? To place myself in a corner from which there would be little easy escape?

Her hand tightened around mine. I didn't pull away. I stared straight at her. Again thinking: she is beyond beautiful. And here she is now telling me everything I longed to hear for years – and how often does that ever happen in life? But I kept thinking about Rebecca. How I knew what I was getting into with her. How much we shared on so many levels. How all this from Isabelle struck me as too sudden, too precipitous. But how I was also so tempted by it all. I said:

'You've given me a lot to think about.'

'Don't think. Act. Starting now. The room upstairs is free.'

I shut my eyes, telling myself: you should not cross that line. If you walk away now you will carry with you much regret. And if you go upstairs with her you will also walk away with much regret.

What is loyalty? Can it be fractured in a moment? Will mine to Rebecca be shattered after I get into bed with Isabelle? And how will I face the woman I have told I love – and whom I do indeed love – in just two days?

Or was I thinking too much here? Teasing out the arguments on both sides of the aisle. Trying to rationalize what I wanted to do in the face of what convention told me I shouldn't do.

'I want you, Samuel. I know that now. But that is a decision for another day. We are, instead, right in the middle of the here and now. Come upstairs with me.'

Were this a religious tract this would be the moment of satanic temptation. Or, conversely, the Pauline conversion on the road to Damascus. A major moral decision. A primordial choice.

Everyone looks for subtext at critical moments like this one. *I went down this dark path of relationship betrayal because . . .* (fill in the self-justifications). Or: *I stopped myself from much-desired sex beyond the bonds of my primary relationship because I knew . . .* (fill in all the obvious self-congratulatory Boy Scout platitudes).

The truth is: either choice will bring you some degree of regret and possible grief. We're told we have to commit, to dedicate, to be true to one and one alone. Just as we want that from the person with whom we have decided to build a life. But if we

178

are honest with ourselves we are all immensely torn and conflicted . . . especially when it comes to matters intimate.

And in that instant I decided: if I shut the door on an afternoon with Isabelle, what would I gain in exchange . . . except ongoing ruefulness at having sidestepped an essential moment of passion?

She knew what I was thinking. She leaned over and whispered to me:

'Freedom is the hardest thing to bear.'

Reaching into her bag, she took out a key and pushed it across the small table between us.

'Room 706,' she said, and then I watched her narrow hips sway against the tightness of her leather skirt as she crossed the bar and entered the main lobby of the hotel.

I glanced at my watch. The snow was now swirling outside. I thought: she wants a life with me. All that I have desired I now have within reach. Even though I also knew: all that she just proposed is scaring the shit out of me. How can it be that once we have what we always thought we wanted we become fearful of actually having to live out the life that will accompany the alleged fulfillment of our dreams?

I stood up.

The elevator operator wore one of those 1930s blue uniforms with a stiff little cap that made him look like a refugee from the Albanian navy. He noticed the room key in my hand and took me to the seventh floor without question. Room 706 was at the end of the corridor. I knocked on the door. From the other side came her voice:

'It's open!'

I walked in. The heavy red velvet blinds were closed. All lights dimmed. A candle illuminating the room. A massive bed. A red velvet bedspread. Half pulled down. Isabelle. Naked. Her hair spread around her.

'Hurry,' she said.

I was throwing my suit jacket to the floor, kicking off my heavy black shoes, losing the pinstriped pants, the stiff shirt and tie, my boxer shorts. Falling into Isabelle's arms. Her body warm. Her legs immediately around me. Pushing me down on the mattress. Her mouth deep against mine. Her legs spread over me. Her hand guiding me in as she whispered:

'I want you immediately.'

And she had me immediately, her body exploding with a shudder as she bore down on me. Me slipping deep into her. Her immediate groans as I grasped her legs and pushed upwards. Holding still as she rocked back and forth, her groans growing in volume. I raised myself up to kiss her, my hands deep in her luxuriant hair. Now moving up and down in tandem with her. Her pleasure rising. How well we knew each other in such an intimate way. What immense complicity between us. Making love in this deeply entwined way was the ultimate form of communication.

As she came, shudders racing through her, she pulled my hand away from her clitoris and bit down on my index finger. Before taking my face in her hands and looking as deeply into my eyes as anyone has done.

'*Je t'adore,*' she whispered.

'*Je t'adore,*' I said back.

I was so conscious of the warmth enveloping us. The contours within her. How she varied the way she pulled me in and out of her. Moving with my own rhythms.

I lost track of time. I buried all thoughts of life beyond this room, this bed. I held back for as long as I could manage. And then, all at once, everything exploded. I found myself collapsed against her shoulder, an after-shudder overtaking me, a sob catching in my throat.

Almost immediately Isabelle put her face up against mine, her eyes wild with the passion of the moment.

'Us,' she said. 'Us.'

I stared straight into her eyes. We held this gaze for minutes, not wanting to lose the intensity of the regard with which we viewed each other. And I couldn't help but think: there are moments when all the densities and complexities that shadow you momentarily fall away and you discover the euphoria of rapture. When the connection is so simple yet profound and overwhelming in its erotic magnitude.

Afterwards we said nothing for a very long time. Our arms tight around each other, awash in all the heat generated together. And without uttering a word the sadness began to seep in between us. All this communal passion, all this wonder – and the unspoken acknowledgment that it was never like this with anyone else – undercut by the realization: tomorrow she disappears back across the Atlantic. With her husband. To her immensely civilized life in the City of Light. The day after, Rebecca would take the late train from New York and we would drink a glass or two of red wine together and then get into bed and pleasure each other in a few minutes and sleep well into the next morning and get up and discuss where we'd have breakfast and whether we could score last-minute student seats for the Boston Symphony Orchestra. And we'd have a nice brunch somewhere. And haunt bookshops. And take in an old film at the Brattle or the Orson Welles. And cross the Charles. And eat something in Chinatown. And hear Ozawa conduct Boston's fantastic symphony orchestra. And return to my room and the big bed we bought together and make love again and be asleep fifteen minutes later, and I would tell myself: what a lovely, refined day we had. And what a lovely, refined woman she is, and reassure myself that I was making the right choice.

'I don't want to let you go,' Isabelle said.

'That's always been my line,' I said.

'Now it is mine too.'

Her right index finger traced its way along the contours of my face.

'Can you spend the afternoon here?'

'I have a seminar at 4 p.m. – and it's one which I cannot get out of, unless I want to get into the bad books of my professor.'

'Work is work.'

'But I could come back here tomorrow at twelve noon.'

'We have to be out of the room then.'

'Come to me then.'

'Charles has arranged for someone to take us up to Salem, to see where the witches were tried and burned.'

'Cancel it and come to my room.'

'There's also a final lunch which I just can't get out of. Trust me, ever since you confirmed that you could meet me today,

182

I have quietly explored ways out. But Charles has let me know: I have to be there. He rarely asks me to do anything.'

'Could you come over tonight?'

'We're going to Symphony Hall at eight, part of the conference program. Charles is rushing from the airport to be there – and I have to play the wife before that at the pre-concert reception.'

Silence as the reality hit me: this was my one and only time with Isabelle.

As always she was seeing behind my eyes.

'I never really thought you wanted to see me again.'

'Part of me didn't . . . because it hurt too much. Knowing that you were out of reach.'

'And now I'm not.'

'But you are still not available tonight or tomorrow.'

'And you haven't made a decision yet. Nor am I mad enough to expect you to. I know this is huge. For both of us. As such . . . time, reflection, thought . . .'

Why did I think: *Or, actually, let's rip up the rule book and be imprudent? Let's run with the crazy, wondrous possibility of a future together?*

But this was accompanied by a concurrent thought:

Show me your real commitment by getting out of one of your wifely obligations tomorrow. Show me your changed loyalty to me . . .

'If only I could see you again while you are here,' I said.

Isabelle stiffened. She got the subtext immediately.

'And if you can't, you are going to think: she is not really that committed to us?'

'I didn't say that.'

'But it's implied.'

'What's implied is: I love you. And this came out of the proverbial blue. And it's all fantastic and vertiginous. And I want you more than anything.'

'Then you have me. Just not tonight or tomorrow. Say the word and I am here.'

I tightened my arms around her.

'The world has just been turned upside down.'

It was now almost two thirty. I needed an hour to travel back across the city to Cambridge, get home and change out of my suit and walk the ten minutes from the residence hall to my seminar.

'We have half an hour,' I announced.

'I have an idea how we are going to spend it.'

For the time remaining we did not take our eyes off each other, bar the moments when the pleasure became extreme and she snapped her eyes shut and held onto me with a desire and a need that I had felt in the past, but that was now underscored by all that had been declared. When she came she buried her head in my shoulder and began to sob.

'It will be so terrible getting into this bed without you tonight.'

'Come to me late. My place is ten minutes by taxi from Symphony Hall, just across the bridge.'

'Charles and I have a rule. We never do anything to embarrass the other person.'

'But if you are planning to leave him . . .'

'I have too much respect for him to tell him here. When he is in a swirl of business and needs to focus and show his immaculate public face to the world. This can all wait until Paris. Besides, we never discuss my lovers.'

Lovers. The use of the plural. A subject we'd rarely confronted before – because I didn't want to go to that corner of the street where jealousy shows its green eyes.

But now . . .

Now I heard myself saying:

'And in the time since we've been apart, since you've gotten through the depression, has there been someone else?'

She reached for the cigarettes on the table by the bed. I had clearly asked the wrong question.

'Why is that relevant here?'

'So you have been seeing someone.'

'So have you.'

'But there's a difference here. You're married, I'm not. I wanted you. I couldn't have you. Because you *are* married. So I naturally was susceptible to someone else's romantic interest.'

She lit her cigarette, taking a ferocious drag on it.

'Do not play the naive young man, Samuel. We all have needs. Sex is a crucial one. As you know. And sex for the sake of sex is different from sex as an expression of love. What you and I have is love. As this afternoon showed yet again.'

A long silence. I suddenly felt a strange rush of guilt sideswipe me. Guilt augmented by massive confusion. Isabelle had just told me she was sharing a bed with someone else while I was elsewhere. Would it be just a matter of time before she found a man in New York after setting up a life with me? Was she telling me: all these declarations of love are predicated on the understanding that fidelity is a movable feast? And there is an inherent inevitability that the desire for you and you alone will go south?

'I have to get back,' I said, getting out of bed and gathering up my clothes.

'Now you're angry,' she said.

'Just trying to process—'

'Process! Process! You and your ultra-American need for answers! Trying to figure out any of this – the mysteries of the flesh, of desire, of what it means to be a couple and how it has its immensities and its profound limitations. You want clarity in the midst of human contradiction. You will just find more incongruities. And the sooner you understand that, the faster you will fathom that fidelity to oneself means you can properly give love to others.'

'Fidelity means just that: being true to someone else to whom you've promised steadfastness. Which I wasn't this afternoon.'

'But were you true to yourself?'

The bedside phone began to ring. Isabelle reached for it, answered it, heard who was on the other line and was immediately deep into the call.

'*Oui, chéri. Dis-moi. Comment je peux t'aider?*'

Him. Charles.

I finished dressing. I found a notepad on the other bedside table and wrote: *Please join me tonight. Here is my address. Here is the phone number for the concierge downstairs. He takes messages. I will await you after your concert. Je t'aime.*

Isabelle watched me write the note, then leave the pad face down on the bed. I checked my watch: 3.05 p.m. I truly had to dash. Isabelle was still deep in conversation with her husband, dealing with something he urgently needed; she was writing down many details on her own hotel pad. I tapped my watch, hinting that my departure was imminent. She raised her free hand in a gesture of desperation . . . she simply couldn't get off the line. I came over to her. I put my left hand in her luxurious red hair. I pulled her toward me, forcing her to pull the phone away as I enveloped her mouth in a massive kiss. She responded for about ten seconds, then heard the voice of her husband on the phone asking:

'*Chérie, t'es là?*'

That was her cue to pull away from me and return to the man on the end of the line.

'*Oui, mon amour . . .*'

I stood still. Wondering what to do next besides leave.

Again Isabelle made a gesture as if to say: circumstances beyond my control. Then she mouthed three words: *je t'aime*.

I acknowledged the words with a nod. I left.

Four hours later, returning to my room drained after the seminar and the events of the day, I found a telegram awaiting me, pushed under my door.

My love: so sorry to be otherwise engaged when you had to leave. I just cannot come tonight. Impossible. But what is possible is all that I promised you earlier. Please write me in Paris to tell me yes and we will begin to make major plans. Je t'aime.

I saw that the telegram had been sent from a Western Union office on Boylston Street, not far from the hotel. Isabelle was covering her tracks, not having this missive of love sent from the Ritz on her husband's dime.

A ferociously cold night and, after a hiatus, snow was now falling again. Before I left my room, dressed to resist the cold, the local NPR station on my transistor radio said there was a very good chance that, if the snow continued, the airport might be closed tomorrow. My romantic-expectation meter jumped into the red zone. Isabelle's flight would be grounded. The concert canceled. She would call me or send a telegram. She would make an excuse to go out for a few hours. Tomorrow we would be sprawled across my big bed. I would have time on Friday before Rebecca arrived to change the sheets and practice the art of compartmentalization. Or, if after another few hours in Isabelle's arms I was convinced that this was truly the destiny I had to follow, I would tell all to Rebecca and withstand her rage and ferocious reproaches and accept that I was a low life who didn't know the wonderful narrative he was throwing away with a wonderful woman who would be very much there for him no matter what. She would say I was chasing after something that was only meant to be in the arena of two-hour bursts of clandestine passion. She would say that I would last three weeks of domestic life with my French fantasy and her very real child, and when I was simultaneously trying to make my way in a law firm and having to deal with broken sleep on account of a child not my own – 'Well, the shine will come off your romantic shit very damn fast, Mr Adolescent.' She would say that I was turning my back on a New York life already in place for me and a woman who understood my quirks and faults, as I did hers; who might not be a wild-eyed sensualist but who liked sex and gave herself to me every night – perhaps fast, but never with disinterest. A woman from my world, speaking my language, who got me.

Yes, indeed . . . chase after the fantasy of the unobtainable; a woman who kept you at bay, who has now suddenly changed her trajectory, possibly on a whim. Or maybe with the hangover of that unnerving depression she'd just weathered. And do you have any idea whatsoever what day-to-day life with her will become? Unlike with Rebecca, whom you've been quasi-living with and with whom you cohabit very nicely.

No, go on, throw it all away for the dream of what, until now, you just couldn't have. Shoot yourself in the foot with a machine gun, pausing twice to reload . . .

This entire reverie danced through my head in the time it took me to zip up my down jacket and wrap a scarf around my neck. A moment of uneasy truth. Making me sit down on the bed and grip its box spring, as if this symbol of conjugality with Rebecca was ballast in the midst of a great many illusions.

As I pushed myself back onto my feet and out into the New England night frost, I found myself thinking: so, you were actually able to see the immense worth and value of what you have with Rebecca thanks to that much-longed-for final afternoon with Isabelle. And yes, this is how I would compartmentalize what had happened (self-justification alert here): going back to bed with Isabelle had convinced me of the rightness of now committing myself completely to Rebecca.

How classically American: virtue arriving in the wake of transgression. Redemption courtesy of a truly guilty conscience.

Anxiety is the dizziness of freedom.

That phrase again.

It haunted me much of that night.

Just as I also told myself:

There is freedom in stability. The certainty inherent in knowing exactly what you are getting into and why.

But do we ever know what we are truly getting into? The trajectory of the story we are entering when we make the choice that sends our life down a path not predestined? Even though the very nature of becoming a couple is believing that together you can invest in that future where happiness is possible.

Again, I slept badly that night. Boston was indeed completely closed down the next morning as snow continued to fall. All flights were grounded, classes canceled. I spent the day revising an essay and preparing case studies. I spent the day awaiting a phone call that might change the plan of action I was about to trigger. Or a telegram. Or her arrival on my doorstep that would have signaled . . .

What sign did I really need here?

I'd already convinced myself of the best course of action. I'd thought it through. As so many of us do – telling ourselves that our thought processes are the right ones, when most of the time they are simply attempts to quell the fear within.

Still, I later came to wonder what the outcome might have been had Isabelle made that call on that snow-bound afternoon. Or walked the few paces to the Arlington T stop and changed trains at Park Street and emerged at Harvard Square and found her way to my room. Action sends you one way. Inaction another. But in the end we ourselves make choices in the wake of the choices of others. Just as they make choices based on the signals we send them. Or not.

So I waited out the day. And nothing came my way.

I slept badly again.

The next morning, I bought at the Coop a postcard of T.S. Eliot. Beneath a photo of the great poet in later life there was a quote from his poem 'The Hollow Men':

> *Between the motion*
> *And the act*
> *Falls the Shadow.*

On the other side I wrote Isabelle's address in Paris. And this message:

I am marrying Rebecca. Je t'aime . . .

Two contradictory thoughts in one sentence.

Isn't this how we play such things so much of the time? Even if often we keep them out of everyone else's line of sight?

I bought an airmail stamp. I dropped the card in a postbox. I knew that, this time, a permanent silence would follow.

I was wrong about that.

I did indeed hear again from Isabelle.

Seven years later.

Four

Seven years.

I finished law school.

I moved to New York.

I took up residence in Rebecca's apartment.

I joined the firm of Larsson, Steinhardt & Shulman.

My father died. Pancreatic cancer. As high speed and as ruthless a death as the one suffered by my mother. We'd had little to do with each other for years. He'd maintained his benign distance from me – with, I was sure, the encouragement of my stepmother Dorothy. I accepted this neutral estrangement, but still kept him abreast of my life – a letter twice a month. He wrote back without fail – and his tone was friendly, informative, distant. We had an annual weekend visit to his house in Indiana when Dorothy was out of town. Dorothy called me the morning after the cancer took his life, saying he had gone fast. I didn't buy this statement – and could have demanded to know from my stepmother why she'd left it too late to tell me he'd had so little time among us. I decided not to engage in that conversation. I flew to Indiana. I sat with his cold body as it lay in an open coffin in the local funeral home. I went to the funeral and maintained my composure when the Baptist minister spoke about how my father had been an exemplary dad to me and so proud of my accomplishments. I bit down hard on my lip as I watched his coffin lowered into the Midwestern earth. Halfway back to Indianapolis and the airport in my rental car, I pulled over to the side of that empty two-lane blacktop and stepped out into fields of corn and leaned against the bonnet of this borrowed Ford hatchback and cried for several minutes like the lost child I truly felt myself to be. Then I climbed back in behind the wheel and drove off. Thinking: we so often weep for what should have been, and for the sad story now over, whose trajectory can no longer be changed.

Two months after my father passed into the eternal shadows, Rebecca and I were married.

She wanted a traditional wedding, albeit on the small side. We had exactly that style of wedding with one hundred guests. We went on a honeymoon to the Amalfi coast. Epic. Ancient. Vistas of pure grandeur. A proper break from the world. Lovemaking twice a day. Lovely ease together. Three final days in Rome. I wanted to move there on the spot.

'Does it remind you of Paris?' Rebecca asked as we strolled hand in hand through Trastevere.

'I would love to show you Paris,' I said.

'Let's wait a few years,' Rebecca said.

I became a New Yorker. I loved being a New Yorker. The city's manic rhythms, its edginess, the way high and low life existed at such close quarters, its splendidly arrogant belief that it was its own city-state somewhat beyond the sensibility of the rest of the country . . . I embraced it all. Like Rebecca, I wasn't interested in playing that social-climbing 'Importance of Being Fabulous' New York game. When the weekend arrived we haunted small cinemas, small theaters, jazz joints, bookshops. We also had a growing circle of friends – largely young professional couples like ourselves, many of whom were having children and were resisting the white-flight temptation of a move to the burbs. We often spoke about how, when we finally did have kids, we too would stay put in Manhattan's mean streets. The well-manicured, white-bread world of Westchester and Connecticut would never be our domestic destiny.

Our marriage was going just fine – because we were both so ferociously busy and stretched that weekday life seemed like a perpetual time-and-motion study. We were beyond focused and driven, in keeping not just with our legal worlds but with the tenor of our hyper-competitive times. Sex between Monday and Friday became a rare event. At the weekends we did manage at least one morning and one evening of intimacy – which, even when I tried to slow it down, didn't extend beyond the usual quarter of an hour. 'You want too many frills,' Rebecca would complain when I attempted to argue that we didn't have to be time-efficient about making love. 'I like it short and sharp – and let's face it, I do make you come like a high-speed train. And last week, when I was beyond stressed, I still agreed to fuck you on Tuesday night and Friday morning . . . and that dawn fuck was after four hours of sleep.'

I told myself: ignore exchanges like this one. When we were able to detach from the *Sturm und Drang* of legal life – the need to bill hefty hours, the need to find new clients, to network with ceaseless regularity, to win at all costs – we did find solace in culture and in each other. Rebecca knew for around a year that her star was falling at her firm. Especially after a case went very wrong for her. An open-and-shut case of criminal negligence against some prep-school kid who killed his girlfriend while driving drunk. Her parents were suing his exceedingly rich family for millions. But the kid's lawyer uncovered the fact that the girl – an eighteen-year-old named Samantha – had been arrested herself for driving while intoxicated ten days before this fatal accident. It seems that her dad – a Wall Street big deal – had got the charges dropped through a discreet exchange of funds with the arresting cops in Mount Kisco (a very wealthy suburban enclave less than an hour north of the city). The kid's lawyer used this detail mercilessly during the hearing, arguing that the girl walked herself into all sorts of trouble . . . including getting into her drunken boyfriend's car. The judge threw the case out. Though her father was culpable for not telling Rebecca about this incident, she was still accused of incompetence by her firm's elders. They all indicated that she hadn't been forensic enough when researching the case and had now put their practice in a bad light. And they informed her that any chance of her being made partner was now beyond the realm of possibility.

I was (I hope) a most supportive husband when Rebecca went into a tailspin after this sizeable setback. Just eighteen months earlier she'd been so certain of getting the partnership that she now descended into what could best be described as Kübler-Ross's five stages of grief – denial being, at first, the biggest of them all. When reality bit and she found that getting a new job in her mid-thirties was going to be a tricky proposition in the ultra-competitive New York legal world, where a perceived failure truly counted against you, she began to get into the 'rage' part of the cycle. As I was the person closest to her – and as I had been fast-tracked into partnership at my firm – there was a period (it lasted about eight months) when she had these blow-ups. Not that she said terrible shit directly about me. But about everybody else. And her disappointments

195

in life. How she too was a brilliant lawyer and it was just not fucking fair that I got promoted and she didn't. Of course I agreed completely with her. Just as I made discreet enquiries and pulled a few behind-the-scene strings and got her directed to another firm – smaller, less hefty in its metropolitan import, but still bespoke, with a strong social-justice record. I sensed, from what I knew of the partners, that they would find Rebecca to be a good fit. There was only one problem: the position was not a partnership one. Rebecca was less than pleased by this – especially as she thought the firm was exactly up her progressive street. When I encouraged her to accept the job and wait and see how everything played out she blew up at me, telling me that she'd found out I'd been greasing the wheels to get her this job and why was I playing her fucking father – even though he was an impossible fucking hippie – and . . .

The night after this blow-up I was working absurdly late in the office, dealing with the case of an elderly woman who had been removed from her son's estate in the weeks before his death (at the age of sixty) from lymphoma. His wife had been behind this deed and I was still trying to find an angle in the rewritten will (and the correspondence between the wife and her late husband's attorney, all of which I had subpoenaed) to create the sort of legal leverage that would get this Lady Macbeth to give my client some sort of just settlement (especially as she was crowding ninety and in need of money to see out her final years). As the clock approached midnight I decided that it really was time to head home. I stood up. I went into the large bathroom off my office. I relieved myself and splashed water on my face. I caught sight of myself in the mirror.

A thirty-something lawyer in a suit. Still youngish. A few fatigue lines around the eyes. No gray hair. No serious thickening around the gut, but I really needed to get to the gym five times a week. Which truly meant getting up at 5.30 a.m., considering the twelve- to sixteen-hour days that were now part of the deal. There was a momentary stab of searing regret. Isabelle. Paris. What could have been. And the life that I'd constructed for myself.

As I told Rebecca, 'One of the many things I love about my work is the way I discover that human behavior surpasses the "stranger than fiction" test on a daily basis.'

'Loving your work,' Rebecca replied tonelessly, exhausted after another difficult day on her hopeless-cause case. 'What a luxury. I love so very little right now.'

'That viewpoint will change,' I told her. 'And I hope you do know how loved you are.'

'Loved by a man who, unlike me, has just fast-tracked to partner. The trusts and estates genius. The legal guru when it comes to the mess of others.'

Tonight I found a mess closer to home. The remains of a Chinese takeout dinner not just spread out across our dining table, but hurled against our off-white walls. Along with a big red stain: the aftermath of a wine glass being projectiled against the same surface. There were sizeable Jackson Pollock-like crimson drips amidst the remains of the stir-fried something also adhering to the surface. There was loud rock and roll blaring from the FM tuner on our hi-fi system. And there was Rebecca passed out on the floor, an empty bottle of very good Margaux lying next to a further half-empty one of Pauillac. Rebecca had her mouth open. It was wet with wine and vomit, a small puddle of both near her head. She was still dressed in her work clothes, her skirt hiked up high, her white blouse and her jacket also covered in all that she had regurgitated. I rushed down to her, making certain she was still breathing, still alive. She groaned when I all but slapped her cheeks, her eyes jumping open in drunken, toxic shock.

I went into action. I got Rebecca to her feet. I carried her into the bathroom. I positioned her on the toilet in such a way that she couldn't slip off the seat. I got her undressed. I ran water into the now plugged sink. I walked her over. I told her: 'I am about to put your face into the sink . . . don't panic.' She still struggled and roared as I did this, words not coming out of her inebriated mouth. I cleaned off her face. I dried it with a towel, I carried her into the bedroom and slid her into pajamas and under the covers. Then I spent the next hour sweeping up shards of glass and using a bucket of hot soapy water to clean the wall and floor, to bring order to chaos. Thinking back on that early morning in Isabelle's apartment, cleaning up her mess. Trying not to get too spooked by the extremes of her post-natal depression. Wanting to do good. Fearing the possibility of impending loss. Using the act of extreme tidying-up then and now as a way of tamping down my anxiety.

The wine stain on our living-room wall was not at all easy to remove. It needed much 'elbow grease' – but I became obsessed with getting it thoroughly lifted, stripping down to my T-shirt and boxer shorts to avoid damaging my suit. When all was reasonable again I took a very hot shower and poured off the remaining glass or two of Pauillac 1979 from the bottle Rebecca had yet to finish. Then I sat slumped in an armchair, thinking: this is one bad portent of things to come.

Our sofa had a pull-out bed. I opened it up and crashed for four hours, then got up and went back into our bedroom. Rebecca was still passed out across our bed, breathing heavily but not showing any signs of possible medical trouble. I showered and dressed for work, drank a great deal of coffee and left a note: *Call me . . . I love you.* But as I walked to my office a terrible question took hold of me: were we doomed as a couple?

The call came around noon that day. Rebecca didn't sound just profoundly hungover, but also deeply shell-shocked.

'Did I do something stupid?'

'You mean you don't remember hurling Szechuan something and a wine glass at the wall before vomiting and passing out on the floor?'

A long sob at the other end of the line.

'I am such a fuck-up.'

'You are just your own worst enemy. What happened?'

'One of the partners called me into his office at the end of the working day and told me that my belligerence around the firm had been unsettling everyone. And it had been decided at a meeting that afternoon to let me go immediately – on full pay until the end of the year . . . when I was going to have to leave anyway.'

'And this was a reason to drink yourself stupid and do splatter painting on our wall with very good wine and a Happy Valley takeout?'

'I'll get help.'

'That's up to you.'

199

'You won't leave me, will you?'

'Can we talk more about this later?' I asked.

'There's nothing to say. Except: I am so profoundly sorry.'

That night when I got home, Rebecca all but threw me into bed. I allowed myself to be ravaged. Afterwards she buried her face into my naked shoulder and said: 'That booze craziness will never happen again.'

Rebecca made good on her promise. Giving me no excuse to think about heading to the door marked 'Exit' . . . at least not for that craziness. As it was another one-off incident, I wasn't going to go all Twelve Steps on her. Or start making sanctimonious threats. When Rebecca wasn't engulfed in one of her black dogs, when the toxic stress that was always adjacent to her (like some dangerous neighbor) didn't threaten to overwhelm her, she was such an engaged, smart, clever woman. To her credit she started talking to a therapist. She began to run three miles a day. She restricted her drinking to two glasses of wine a day. She landed a new associateship, accepting that it was another non-partnership position but also one that, barring any mess-ups on her part, she could keep indefinitely. I told her she should keep looking out for other positions that might lead to the tenure she'd once so craved. But now, in the wake of being let go and having that huge Margaux-fueled meltdown, she had stopped being obsessed with the big P of Partnership. Especially as she had now decided that the time was right for her to fall pregnant.

Part of me had always wanted to be a father. Had Isabelle allowed me, I would have had a child with her – because I was gripped by the romantic notion that a baby is the ultimate expression of love between a couple. And also because I knew I would always be shadowed by a father who, due to his own sad complexities, just wasn't present for me. So yes, there was more than a touch of 'I can do better' in this desire to become a father, to silently show the man who spent much of my life politely sidestepping me that, unlike him, I could be engaged and truly loving as a dad. Though the responsibility of being a parent was just a bit terrifying, that other part of me – the lawyer who wanted to find solutions to the disorder we make of things; who still believed in the possibility of redemption in the wake of unhappiness, of personal chaos – also felt that having a child might actually reawaken the proper love Rebecca and I had once shared . . . and which recently had been subsumed by the pressure of careers and the underlying competitive tension between us.

I won the case for the elderly woman – garnering her over $3 million from her late son's estate. I also stopped a pre-emptive raid by an uncle and aunt on a $30 million trust for two children orphaned when their parents' light aircraft crashed coming into Nantucket. Our firm did very well indeed out of both cases. I was on a winning streak – but was also following my mentor Mel Shulman's advice and not playing the cock of the walk at work or elsewhere.

'Although I sense it's not your style,' Mr Shulman told me after I got the fund raid thrown out of court, 'always remember a key rule of life: never fall in love with the aroma of your own perfume. Success is a fragile veneer.'

It was the 1980s: an era of absurd conspicuous consumption and extreme material success. I was now earning serious money –

and saw many colleagues and certain of our friends becoming unduly excessive on the flash-the-cash front. I went the other direction. Mr Prudent. Mr Circumspect. Mr Quiet – and someone who billed more hours than anyone else in the firm.

'Why do I need to work?' Rebecca announced one night at a dinner party with friends of hers from Columbia Law. 'When genius here is making $400k a year and is still happy to live in our modest co-op – even if he did pay off our mortgage with his big Christmas bonus last year.'

'Twelve hundred square feet in a prime West Village location is hardly modest,' I said.

'But we could still afford something bigger,' Rebecca said, breaking her two-glasses-of-wine rule that night and suddenly bringing an ongoing domestic tension into a public arena.

'This is not the time or place.'

'Oops, am I sounding like the frustrated junior partner – sorry, associate . . . you're the partner – in this marriage?'

'Not now, sweetheart,' I said, gripping her hand rather hard under the table and glancing very deliberately at her now empty fourth glass of wine.

In the cab back home she fell silent when I told her:

'That did not look at all good. And it's really "your own worst enemy" stuff.'

'Maybe you should marry someone else. Maybe we should stop trying for a child. Maybe I am not at your level anymore.'

'Maybe you should start thinking about talking to your therapist about your drinking.'

'Oh, please. This is one or two glasses of wine over the limit. And I'm hardly operating heavy farm equipment. Or driving kids to school. And this is the first time I've had just a little too much since the last meltdown . . . which was six months ago, right?'

'I don't like our dirty linen washed in public.'

'Oh, we have dirty linen?'

'Every couple has dirty linen.'

'And what are you saying – that I just showed everyone ours with the shit stains?'

Silence. I couldn't believe what I had just heard. Nor could the cabbie, who shook his head slowly. Rebecca saw this and didn't like it.

'Since when do you have an opinion about any of this?' she demanded of him.

'Ignore her,' I told him.

'As he ignores me.'

'That's bullshit and you know it,' I said, my voice suddenly loud . . . and as I was someone who never expressed anger loudly, Rebecca actually cringed.

Conversation closed for the night.

Early the next afternoon, my secretary handed me a letter that had just arrived that morning. Seeing the postmark *Paris 6ème* and that ever-identifiable black ink etched by a fountain pen, I felt a surge of longing and deep anxiousness.

My dear Samuel
It has been an age. We need, I sense, to be back in touch – to have the lines of communication between us opened again. You are too important to me to have vanished behind a wall of silence.

My news – since it has been seven years since our last encounter in Boston. I am still with Charles. We are, as always, reasonable. Émilie is now quite the young lady, a great reader and she has great aplomb, even when dealing with the little monsters in her school who give her such grief (little girls are truly horrible to each other – as I all too well remember). I so admire her spirit and her optimism – and will do everything humanly possible to maintain her positive perspective. But as we both know, life has this ability to disappoint and dismay the longer one travels through its strange parade.

On which note . . . I will be very un-French here and speak directly: in the wake of you saying no to my romantic proposal in Boston I went into a tailspin for about a year. Especially as I knew after the fact that not meeting you chez toi was a fatal mistake. Life has these moments where others send us a signal that asks us to show our true hand. You did that after that afternoon in bed at the Ritz. I knew you were torn. I knew you had your petite amie. I sensed you were uncertain which way to turn. I wanted so much to flee after the concert and be naked with you in your bed. Would it have been impossible for me to do that? It might have raised one of Charles's considerably bushy eyebrows. But I probably could have done it. Why didn't I? That is a larger question I still can't fully answer. Isn't the biggest mystery in life oneself? You want this, but you do that . . . knowing it will probably cost you what you want. Perhaps I couldn't hint in front of my husband that there was someone important in my life, even though he'd been very open with me about his affair. Perhaps part of me was terrified of actually crossing that frontier of no return with you. I really was ready to come to New York with Émilie – but when you asked me (in, I sensed, a subconscious way) to show you that I was serious about taking that (for me) vast step and leaving Charles and everything so well upholstered and secure about my life . . . of course I hesitated. Had you persisted and insisted I make good on my declaration about starting a life with you in Manhattan might I have jumped in your direction? Truthfully, I don't know. I want to believe that I would have . . . but I am not as courageous as I wish I was.

So, yes, I entered into a period of despair afterwards. I knew you were getting married. I knew you would be true to your wife – especially after stepping out on her that one time with me. Just as I knew that geography would now truly separate us. I had lost you – and I didn't have to. And I wondered for a long time afterwards: would a post-concert taxi ride across the Charles River have changed the trajectory of everything to do with my life? Did I dodge an opportunity – knowing that it was one I should have embraced on the spot? Did I make the wrong choice? Although I did appreciate your Christmas card some months later I chose not to reply to it largely because I was hurt . . . even though I realize I hurt myself. Just as I know I was paying for those years when it was clear that I was never going to leave Charles and you were living in hope. Absurd, isn't it? We both want the same thing – each other. And it wasn't just our timing that was off . . . it was also a failure of my nerve. And now you are married. And me . . .?

I was seeing someone during the last two years. A journalist. An arrangement much like the one we had. A man my age.

Interesting, but also married. And intensely possessive. Was it love? Not really. It filled a gap in my life. But it wasn't you. And it wasn't the passion we shared; the complicity between us. And I ended it because he wanted too much – and he couldn't accept my boundaries.

What is the point of this letter? An apology for not crossing over to you on a snowy night – and thereby convincing you that I was serious about building a life with you. Belated best wishes for your marriage – with the genuine hope that you are happy. And a reopening of the door, I suppose.

I am thinking of you – and hoping life is reasonable. Because, I have come to discover, 'reasonable' is actually a good aspiration.

Je t'embrasse,

Ton Isabelle

I reread the letter several times over. No mention of her work. No mention of much to do with her marriage (as always). Clear delight with her daughter. An undercurrent of that quiet bleakness that underscored so much with Isabelle. I knew that melancholy was part of her internal equation. But it was one that never expressed itself directly. In the past, during those rare moments when she acknowledged that she lived with a certain ongoing private gloom, she noted that this was a component of her métier. Most of her professional life on her own, in her head, with the texts waiting to be turned into another language.

I put the letter aside, knowing that an immediate response would not be one marked by clarity. Some months later, things thought through, I took a sheet of typing paper from my desk and threaded it into the IBM golf ball on my desk. I hit the on button. I typed fast with two key-dancing index fingers:

Dearest Isabelle

A thought struck me reading your letter: we share a similar belief in the flawed nature of life. Which doesn't mean that we are miserable or pessimists. Just realists. And when you have a realistic perspective on the nature of just about everything . . . well, isn't that the starting point for melancholy? Which, unbeknown to those who don't suffer from it, isn't an affliction bound up in dejection, despondency, distress, dolefulness (to do a thesaurus riff). Nor is it a choice. Rather it is a state of mind, located somewhere between a condition and predilection . . . and one predicated on the belief: accept the hopelessness and don't think that there is some Holy Grail of happiness that awakes you. It's all muddle. You have to do the best amidst the muddle. But don't expect me to wear a perma-smile at the same time.

Your letter touched me hugely. And the fact that you announced that the door is still open . . . that was a true wrench for me. For obvious reasons. Marriage and all that. And more news: Rebecca is pregnant.

Where can we truly go from here, my wonderful Isabelle?

Yes, the much-worked-for child – we had been trying with immense diligence and constancy – was now en route. Rebecca was elated. She wanted motherhood. And when, month after month, fertility hadn't arrived, the sense of personal failure had been coupled with a growing fear: maybe we weren't going to do this naturally. Maybe one of us had a problem. Maybe the whole grim bevy of fertility tests and IVF treatments awaited us. Most of all, maybe Rebecca wasn't capable of having a child.

This had been her biggest fear; the ever-increasing nightmare. And one that underscored so many feelings of inadequacy that spoke to the central issues in her psyche. The day she came home from her ob-gyn with the official thumbs up – yes, she was definitely going to have a baby – the sense of relief had been trumped by triumph. For all the occasional jibes and competitive stresses – and despite her occasional moments of ugly intoxication – ours was a marriage with a strong sense of shared purpose. Or, at least, that's what I told myself whenever middle-of-the-night doubts started to creep in. And so I felt an immense stab of love for Rebecca when, on my arrival home from work, she came running into my arms, tears cascading down her face as she told me the big news: it had happened. We were going to become parents. I was relieved, elated, and just a little overwhelmed by the thought: becoming a father meant assuming an immense, lifelong responsibility. And one I wanted to do so well.

Rebecca being Rebecca, she became beyond expert in all things prenatal. Just as she was determined that the entire pregnancy and birth would come off without a hitch. Not a drop of alcohol now passed her lips – even when, during the final trimester, her doctor told her a glass of red wine now and then might indeed be a welcome relief from the dietary hair shirt she was wearing. She must have read two dozen books on the subject and attended prenatal yoga classes, which she told me kept her 'chakras centered' and also allowed her to 'find release from all the inevitable catastrophic scenarios I play out in my head'. Even though there was no indication of a troubled pregnancy or potential complications she swore off sex for the entire length of time she was carrying our child. I patiently tried to convince her that there was no need to take such an extreme approach. But Rebecca was adamant, throwing up manifold excuses about not wanting to take any risks whatsoever, and how it was only eight months.

I bit the chastity bullet. Not wanting any external problems – and also having vowed to myself never to transgress again as I had with Isabelle in Boston – I resisted all the possibilities on display everywhere I turned in New York. Just as I turned down a business trip to Paris because the temptation to see Isabelle would be overwhelming. The fact that the only response I'd had from Isabelle had been one of her simple white cards with a one-line message – *I wish you and your wife much happiness on the forthcoming birth of your first child* – indicated that she wanted no further contact. I took the hint. I kept my head down. I was the supportive spouse and father-to-be at home. Meanwhile, there was work: the best refuge from larger 4 a.m. questions you know you should be asking yourself but decide it's best to sidestep . . . for the moment anyway.

*

Our son, Ethan Caleb, was born in New York Hospital on January 15, 1988. His mother gave birth without the benefit of anesthetic. Trust me, this was her call, not mine. I tried to argue her out of such an extreme eighteenth-century approach to childbirth, saying that if she was going in for a root canal surely she would accept Novocain in her gums. But Rebecca was adamant that having an epidural or some other form of pain relief would not just 'lessen the experience' but also endanger the baby. The attending obstetrician told her that this was medically illogical, that her baby would probably be happier emerging into the world from a mother who wasn't in extreme pain (as she most definitely would be). Rebecca being Rebecca, she refused all agony relief. I was, of course, present for the birth and horrified by the sound effects produced by Rebecca in the throes of natal torment. Horrified because the pain was so monumental and monstrous and utterly unnecessary. Ethan arrived into the world accompanied by suffering. Rebecca was so traumatized by all that she had endured that she was initially too weak to hold her baby. I did that almost immediately after the cord was cut and one of the nurses wrapped him in a white terry blanket immediately dappled in blood. Ethan was inconsolable. When I asked one of the nurses if I wasn't holding him properly, or was doing anything to cause him such distress, she glanced over at Rebecca to make certain she was out of earshot (she had collapsed into an exhausted semi-sleep), then whispered to me:

'It always happens when the mother refuses the needle. The child emerges distressed because the mother's so distressed. But he will calm down and forget it all ever happened this way.'

As I drew my son close to me for the first time I was both overwhelmed and fearful. Could I do this right? The immensity of fatherhood was daunting. So, too, was the overwhelming love I felt for him. I wanted to tell him: 'Sorry about the difficult arrival into life. I promise to make it all better from this point on.'

Rebecca herself also 'moved on' from the trauma of the birth as she threw herself into motherhood with hyper-intensity. She wouldn't hear of any outside help. She moved into the second bedroom – which, of course, we'd turned into a nursery to deal with the broken nights and to ensure that I slept. I offered to deal with the weekends – when I could afford to be tired and share the *nuit blanche* burdens. But she was absolutely determined to do all this herself – even if she was surviving on little sleep and fighting exhaustion. She also announced after six weeks – when she was due back at her law firm – that she wanted to take a further leave of absence to have 'more important early home time' with Ethan. The firm agreed – as long as it was unpaid. I supported her decision, but privately wondered if her need to immerse herself 24/7 into the life of our newborn son was dangerously overstepping the parental commitment mark. I knew that by going down this line of thought I was negotiating complex terrain. I would be challenging her huge maternal impulse. But I was observing an ever-increasing aberrant streak emerging – she was literally day and night with Ethan, taking to sleeping in his room on a camp bed she installed there for herself. When I tried to bring this matter up with her – to hint with calculated gentleness that she didn't need to be Mommy non-stop – her reaction was one of accusatory anger: 'Are you telling me I shouldn't be doing this role perfectly?' I pointed out that there was no need to even consider the idea of perfection when it came to motherhood; that, as I was discovering (when Rebecca allowed me time with our son), being a parent for the first time was a grand improvisation and one you learned on the job.

'I am very happy to do the broken nights on the weekends,' I repeated to her. 'I am very happy to come home and babysit if you want to go out and see friends, a film, a play. And we really should get a babysitter and go out ourselves one night.'

'And leave him alone with someone else? What an insane thought. Tell me you are just talking crazy here.'

Her tone edged into fury. I backed off.

Sex did finally come back into the marital picture. Around ten weeks after the birth, she let me back within her again. I could sense that she was half ardent, half elsewhere. I said nothing. I was just happy to be making love again with Rebecca. It became a rationed-out experience – maybe twice a week and even more accelerated. 'Let's get each other off and be done with it.' I should have insisted that we talk about our strange new quick-fire intimacy – and the fact that to Rebecca everything was *Ethan, Ethan, Ethan* – as I knew this was getting truly unhealthy. I kept my head down. I burrowed even deeper into work. I was superficially accepting of Rebecca's *idée fixe*. I dodged any opportunities to express my concerns – because, from recent experience, I could see that such comments would lead to an uncomfortable confrontation. And I just didn't want to go there right now.

Nearly nine months after Ethan's arrival in our lives Rebecca had a meeting with the partners at her firm. They agreed to take her back. She agreed with me to find a day nanny for Ethan – and she ran the job interviews with the rigor of the CIA choosing their undercover agents in Eastern Europe. We interviewed several prospective nannies and agreed together to hire Rosa, an outgoing, clearly capable Dominican woman in her mid-thirties. We instantly thought that she was good news – and I privately liked the fact that she'd immediately sized up Rebecca's anxiety about returning to work and knew how to tamp it down. Once she was back being a lawyer, Rebecca still called Rosa every hour on the hour. To her credit Rosa was fantastically patient with her chief employer – though often quietly dropped a comment to me ('Your wife must not fret so much about Ethan – the more relaxed she is the more relaxed he will be') that signaled she was finding Rebecca just a touch overbearing. Still, a working rhythm did develop between them. In turn, our personal life had a regularity to it. Rebecca began sleeping back in our bed all night. One night a week she went out. One night a week we would have what Rebecca dubbed our 'date night' and we would head out for dinner and something cultural, with sex to follow.

I began to take French lessons three times a week. A young woman from Lyon named Danielle. Late twenties. It worked well. I was (in her words) an attentive and scrupulous pupil. Just as she was a rigorous teacher. We met every Monday, Wednesday and Thursday at 6 p.m. in my office – though if work called me away she was very flexible about rescheduling. I told her at the outset about living in Paris and wanting to actually get my French to a reasonable level of fluency. I worked hard. I did homework. I never mentioned to Rebecca that I was intensively learning French. I sensed she might think: he's still not over the woman in Paris and this is his way of remaining tangentially connected to her. Which, on a certain level, might have been the truth. Best to say nothing and keep my French vocabulary books at the office – and to rush home after the lesson and have the evening with Ethan.

I was home five nights a week with my son. I did negotiate one night out every Friday with a new friend – David Kennicott, a journalist with the *Wall Street Journal*, recently divorced, badly wounded by the process. My time out with David became a safety valve. He too was a father – with a seven-year-old daughter named Polly who was now living in an East 70s townhouse with Mommy and her new fellow. David was dating and bumping into considerable craziness and wondering if he was giving off a 'trouble is my business' vibe. David was also super-shrewd and funny and very appreciative of whiskey and cigarettes (which he smoked non-stop) and tenor saxophonists (he played in a part-time band . . . not badly at all). He was happy with the once-a-week hang-out. We circulated through the jazz clubs of the city. We had considerable mutual trust and I was able to talk about the unaddressed difficult contours of my marriage and how I was concerned about addressing these issues directly with my wife as we had found a certain reasonable equilibrium together – yet one which I knew might fracture in a heartbeat. David had come over to the apartment once for Sunday brunch and genuinely liked Rebecca, though when I pushed him later he admitted that he could see her anxiety about being the perfect mother. He counseled me to keep the status quo for now and to be pleased with the fact that everything was just about stable between us.

'A new child creates an entirely new dynamic in the life of a couple. And it can turn into a vast pressure point. Be pleased that, for the moment, her mania has calmed down a bit and you are going through all the marital motions – sex, the weekly night out, no fights over "you're not doing your share" and all that predictable shit. Just hope that nothing critical comes along to upset the apple cart. A crisis might expose all the fissures in a dangerous way.'

Direct words – but David was direct about such matters.

Prescient words as well. And ones that came back to me weeks later when Rebecca called me at the office to say that she was working late and that she'd asked Rosa to stay on with Ethan. I was supposed to be meeting David for our jazz and bourbon night out. I offered to cancel it. It had been a hugely intense period for me – two weeks straight without a day off, two vast cases to deal with. Rebecca insisted I go out, have a little down time. Rosa would stay on until 10 p.m. and as it was the weekend tomorrow she wouldn't have to be in early the next morning.

'I know she could use the overtime as well,' she said.

So out I went on my evening with David. He brought along a friend – a young playwright named Phoebe Rossant. I found her edgy, funny, even more vulnerable than David, and initially rather supercilious toward me . . . especially as I showed up from court in my usual somber Brooks Brothers suit. When she learned I spent my days dealing with trusts and estates she made a few initial jibes about me being in the 'funereal' part of the law. But I steered the conversation into a discussion of what I called our new Gilded Age – and got her talking about the inherent problems of trying to get edgy, funny family dramas with a decided feminist edge on in a world where the talk was of buying a big loft in Tribeca. And how, amongst our generation of Young Urban Professionals, the talk was all are you 'summering' out in the Hamptons? How much is your stock portfolio worth? How many Armani suits do you have in your closet?

'How many do you have?' she asked, her tone arch.

'No Armani,' I said. 'No designer stuff whatsoever. Off-the-peg suits. I own three.'

'And he changes into a leather jacket and black jeans when he goes out to hear jazz,' David added.

'A man of conflicted identities.'

I shrugged, saying:

'Like you I deal in narrative. Like you I am a student of people's infinite capacity to make life difficult for themselves and others. Like you I spin stories. And as you also well know, money and sex are not just the two tectonic plates in our culture – in fact, in just about all cultures – but the central motivations behind most personal melodramas.'

Phoebe turned to David and said:

'So why have you been hiding this guy from me for all this time?'

I didn't know what to say in reply. What I thought was: she's wonderful . . . and there's an immediate connection between us.

Was that the moment when so many of my accumulating doubts about the marriage – all the post-natal compulsions and control-freak dramas of the last year – psychically caught up with me, rendering me interested in someone else for the first time since that moment, many years ago now, when I left the Ritz in Boston in the snow, wondering if our impending marriage was the wisest of moves? I'd vowed then not to cross the infidelity line again. I was now a father.

Things with Rebecca weren't romantic, but they were stable. And stability was crucial for Ethan's future. We are all told that marriage is work. But marriage is an infernal compromise. Bar that one exception – before vows were exchanged – I had been faithful. I had been constant. I had been patient. I had been supportive – even when part of me thought: I am very alone in all this. Because my wife had been living with a demon from the moment her career stalled. And I had been in denial about so much to do with the increasing fragility of our coupledom, burrowing into work, playing the yes-man to Rebecca's disorders, always doing what I do best when it comes to a personal confrontation: dodging the argument, sidestepping impending crises, being relieved when we got through another day without a major melodrama. Otherwise it was all work. And I couldn't help but wonder: was I so obsessed with winning on the legal front because I felt so lost at home?

I saw Phoebe glance at the wedding ring on my left hand. The second time she did so I instinctively bundled it up into a fist, as if trying to deny its existence. She saw that and smiled. She reached into her backpack and pulled out a notebook and a pen and scribbled down a number and her name.

'So, I have to head out. But I want you to call me.'

She tore out the page and pushed it over to me.

'If you want to visit the set of our crime and punishment show, that can be arranged. But I'd far prefer it if you'd buy me a beer.'

'I'd like to continue the conversation,' I said, half wanting to, half knowing: *under no circumstances should you complicate your life* . . . while, the bad-boy voice in my head was whispering to me: *of course you should complicate your life.*

Phoebe leaned down and gave me a light kiss directly on the lips, whispering into my ear:

'I am going to expect that call.'

After she left David lightly punched me on the arm and said:

'You dog. You waltz in and immediately win the ever aloof Phoebe.'

'I was hardly trying to do that.'

'Which is why it worked.'

'But I wasn't trying to "work" anything.'

'But you did, without question, give off a distressed vibe.'

'Oh please.'

'She saw you covering your wedding ring. I saw that too. She sensed immediately: this is an interesting man in an unhappy domestic situation.'

'I'm flattered . . . and I am doing nothing about it. Life at home isn't that bad at all.'

'But is it really good?'

I dodged an answer, saying that it was late and I had to be home. When I got there I found my wife up, looking panicked. She had our son in her arms.

'When I got home just before ten, Rosa told me that Ethan vomited several times tonight and was listless. She thinks he's just picked up some bug. What worries me is that vomiting and listlessness are the telltale signs of meningitis.'

'But does he have a rash or has he had seizures or anything like that? Let me see. Can I hold him?'

Ethan did feel feverish. And he seemed to be in a deep sleep. When I tried to rouse him he didn't respond to my voice or to any of the increasingly firm taps I applied to his body.

'Are you sure there are no rashes anywhere?' I asked.

'I looked him over everywhere.'

At that moment I lifted one of his tiny legs and checked the undersides of his feet. Rebecca was right by my side and when she saw what I saw she let out a sharp, 'Oh fuck, no . . .' Because there, on the sole of his foot, were red and brown pinprick marks; a rash that was already beginning to blister.

'Did you see this before?' I asked Rebecca, trying to keep my anxiety in check.

'Of course I didn't fucking see it. Do you think I'd just fucking sit here knowing my son has meningitis?'

'That wasn't an accusation. But we have to leave for the ER now.'

In a crisis, as I came to discover over the years, my voice always went quiet. Preternaturally so. With Ethan in my arms I started moving toward our front door.

'I'm holding him!' Rebecca shouted, grabbing a blanket to protect him against the air conditioning that would be everywhere but the autumn streets outside. I didn't argue. I handed our son to her. I steered us all out the door, into the elevator, and into the first taxi I could hail on the street. Our nearest hospital, St Vincent's, had a reputation for being an urban zoo. Better to do a taxi dash across town to the New York Hospital, where Ethan was born and which was an oasis of Upper East Side calm. The ER there was busy at almost eleven on a Friday night. But the moment I told the receptionist that we thought our nine-month-old son had meningitis, she picked up a phone, made a fast call and had us in with the resident pediatrician and two nurses within minutes. The doctor confirmed that Ethan did have all the telltale signs of either bacterial or viral meningitis – and told us he was ordering blood cultures and a spinal tap immediately. Rebecca looked like she was about to go into free fall.

'If I'd only seen this . . .' she wailed.

'When did you first see the rash?' Dr Hutheesing asked.

'Half an hour ago,' I said.

'I was with him an hour before my husband got home. There was nothing there. Believe me, I checked him everywhere.'

'Oh I believe you, ma'am,' Dr Hutheesing said. 'The rash can show up out of nowhere. You did the right thing bringing him in immediately. Don't blame yourself.'

'You should have stopped me from working late,' Rebecca said loudly, yet largely directed at herself.

Hutheesing put a hand on Rebecca's shoulder.

'There is nothing you could have done to stop this. How and why meningitis attacks a child—'

'I could have stopped it!'

This came out as a howl. Hutheesing exchanged a glance with me. Rebecca saw this.

'See! See! The two of you are blaming me!'

Hutheesing now whispered into the ear of one of the attending nurses, then turned to Rebecca and said:

'Ma'am, my colleague here is going to bring you to a room where you can lie down. And if you need something to help you stay calm . . .'

'Don't you fucking patronize me.'

'Rebecca, that is no way to—'

'You all know it's my fault, don't you?'

'You have to keep quiet, ma'am,' the nurse said, her arm now around my wife, not in a reassuring way, but as a form of restraint. 'Now let's get you settled in somewhere where you can get some rest . . .'

'I am not leaving you with my baby. I am not—'

She started struggling against the nurse's grip. A second nurse – another woman, less physically imposing but undoubtedly as strong as her colleague – was now gripping Rebecca on her other side. She was surrounded, trapped. But she still began to fight like hell, screaming abuse, obscenities, completely out of control. Hutheesing looked over at me, his eyes asking, 'Are you OK if we subdue her?' I nodded my assent. The restraints on Rebecca made her fight more. Her violence was beyond alarming. Hutheesing calmly went over to a tray of medication. He found a vial of something and a hypodermic needle. He told one of the nurses to roll up Rebecca's sleeve. This made my wife struggle even more.

'Aren't you going to fucking save me?' she cried at me.

'Ethan is the issue here,' I said, standing over the small gurney on which my son had been placed, beyond frightened by the thought: my son might not survive all this.

'Hold her tight,' Hutheesing told his colleagues as the needle went in. Moments later Rebecca's violent convulsions subsided. Hutheesing whispered something further to one of the nurses. Her associate let go of Rebecca, who now seemed to be in a state of walking sleep. The first nurse returned a moment later with a wheelchair. Rebecca was positioned in the seat and wheeled off, Hutheesing explaining to me that he was admitting her to the psych ward for 'observation'. He asked me if she had shown 'signs of obsessive compulsion' in the past. I nodded.

'She clearly needs help. But more tellingly, so does your son.'

Then, signaling to another nurse, he informed me that Ethan was going to be immediately whisked up to the pediatric ICU and that he was ordering a lumbar puncture to collect cerebro-spinal fluid (CSF), explaining that when meningitis hits, the CSF often shows a severe dip in glucose levels along with an increased white blood cell count and dangerously heightened protein levels.

'Can there be long-term effects?' I asked.

'I won't sweeten an already difficult pill and say you shouldn't worry about such things right now. But the truth is: yes, there definitely can be future complications. However, the fact that you got Ethan to us straight away – that your wife hadn't seen the rash an hour before you did – can only help matters. Anyway, it is going to take several hours before we know anything. I would go home and get some rest. Give the receptionist your phone number and we will call as soon as—'

'I'd rather stay here,' I said.

'I'm sure you would. But we will know nothing until tomorrow morning. Why sleep all night sitting up in a plastic chair, espe-cially when your presence here will change nothing? Your wife is in crisis. Your son needs one parent in a reasonable place. Please go home, sir. Could I give you something to help you sleep?'

I shook my head. I asked the doctor if I could stay by Ethan as he underwent all those terrible tests. Hutheesing shook his head.

'Go home now, sir. Give us your phone number. We will call you as soon as we have news.'

I didn't want to leave, but the doctor was ordering me to go. Perhaps he was right – I needed rest to deal with whatever lay ahead.

'Will he get through it?' I asked.

The doctor hesitated before saying:

'The next forty-eight hours are critical.'

I found a pay phone in the waiting room. I called David. No answer. I left him a brief voicemail, just asking him to call me urgently. I went home. I sat by the phone sipping Scotch for two hours. I called the hospital. I spoke with the nurse in the pediatric intensive care unit. No change in Ethan's condition. I got undressed. I climbed into bed. I tried to sleep. Not possible. I called the PICU again. Nothing new to report on Ethan – and the nurse told me that if I'd give her my number she'd get Dr Hutheesing to ring me as soon as he arrived at 8.30 a.m. I thanked her and still set a clock. The knowledge that the doctor would call allowed me to pass out for a few hours. The alarm went off at 8.30 a.m. Dr Hutheesing phoned at 8.36. He informed me that he had good news: Ethan's condition had stabilized, that he was out of mortal danger – but that he was concerned about 'one or two long-term issues'. When I pushed him on this point he said that he didn't want to discuss anything until he met me face to face. I asked about Rebecca. She too was 'stable', but there'd been a scene earlier when she woke up and insisted on visiting Ethan in the PICU. The nurse had said she would have to wait until the attending pediatrician arrived and Rebecca had blown up and tried to flee the psych ward ('Not an easy thing

223

to accomplish, seeing that it's in permanent lockdown'), then had to be restrained and sedated again. I put my head in my hands and said that I would be at the hospital within the hour.

Ethan stayed in the pediatric corner of the ICU for almost ten days. During this time Dr Clarke – the resident on duty there – confirmed that they were concerned that, though he was now free of the virus, in the long term the meningitis might have affected his hearing, his sense of balance, his kidneys and his liver.

'Because he's a baby we can't say for sure if the damage is severe, permanent, minor or even non-existent. We've run some basic tests and I am concerned about his hearing. But time will tell. I am sorry I can't be more definitive about all this. At least he has pulled through. Meningitis can so often go the other way.'

This news was kept from Rebecca until she came home. I became an obsessive, reading everything I could find on meningitis, using contacts to put me in touch with two leading experts on the illness. I found out all its terrible possible side effects. The experts confirmed what Dr Clarke kept telling me: given Ethan's very young age it was still too early to assess the severity of the damage.

Rebecca was released on the same day that the doctors allowed me to bring Ethan back home from the hospital. She kept repeating out loud that she was to blame for our son's illness; that had she not been out working late that night . . . I tried to convince her that this was crazy thinking; that a virus is a virus and nothing she could have done would have prevented it from blindsiding our beautiful son. She then turned on me, saying that if I too had been home that night . . . And yes, that did cause an attack of massive guilt. Because I too had been beating myself up ever since Ethan fell ill, telling myself that had I not been out flirting with another woman, had I been at the apartment a crucial hour or two earlier . . .

Rosa, who was back working on a full-time basis, stepped in here, letting Rebecca know that neither of us was responsible for anything that had gone down, and that she was beating herself up unnecessarily. Rebecca's response to this was to threaten to fire Rosa. I stepped in and told Rosa to simply ignore her unhinged rhetoric. However, when we brought Ethan to our pediatrician the following week – Dr Ellingham having been fully briefed by the team at the New York Hospital – Rebecca went into near free fall when he told us that he wanted Ethan's hearing and sense of balance rigorously tested as he was worried about possible deafness. Ellingham also informed my wife that she needed clinical help urgently – especially when he found out that she had abandoned the mood-control medication she'd been put on when admitted to the hospital.

On the way home in the taxi I asked Rebecca why she'd given up on the Valium that had kept her stable for the past ten days.

'Because I don't deserve stability. Because I don't deserve mental pain relief.'

She did, at my insistence, begin to talk to a new therapist – who in turn also asked that she see a psychiatrist as it was clear that she needed pharmacological help. Back she went on Valium – and for several months she did stabilize. Which was fortunate, as during this time we were given some profoundly difficult news: as a result of the meningitis Ethan was 75 percent deaf. To say that we were both knocked sideways by this news would be to engage in understatement. We were devastated. We went to three leading ENT specialists. The one we chose to work with was a no-bullshit German woman named Dr Helga Cerf – who ran all sorts of tests and was exactingly thorough in her analysis of all that had befallen Ethan's hearing.

'In my estimation the situation is difficult. There is still some minor eardrum function. There is still some reverberative effect in his inner ear. Alas, meningitis attacks the nervous system, resulting in sensorineural hearing loss. As Ethan is not even a year old – and we cannot yet gauge completely how he responds to aural stimulation – what we can determine at this point is that, as you have been previously told, he has probably lost three-quarters of his normal hearing capability.

'Will this mean we can treat it with advanced hearing aids? Will he need to be taught sign language as a form of communication? Will he be able to master speech and communicate in a normal verbal way? I so wish I could give you definitive answers. I am going to recommend that – with your permission – we attempt at even this early stage of development to implant very small hearing devices in his ears to see if these will make an early difference and allow him to absorb sounds and voices – all absolutely crucial for his development. We will continue to monitor the situation very closely – and will take all the appropriate steps necessary to try to ensure that Ethan overcomes this disability.'

When we got home that afternoon, after putting Ethan to sleep in his cot Rebecca went into the bathroom, locked the door and proceeded to scream and shout for the better part of a half-hour. She would not let me in. She would not respond to my desperate attempts to get her to emerge. Eventually I decided to let her expunge all the grief inside her – and shouted over her agony that I was going out to take a walk.

I headed to a local bar, Chumley's. I ordered a beer and a shot of Irish. I lit up a cigarette. I put my face in my hands. I stopped myself from coming undone in public, but I did sense I was very near the edge of stress and exhaustion. For days I had tried to keep at bay the terribleness of what had befallen Ethan, us – and the obsessive thought that I had not been able to protect him. Now I was discovering just what it meant to come face to face with life's tragic underside. Outside of losing my mother and dealing with a permanently detached father, I had not really known much in the way of difficulty in life, no great catastrophes. No terrible injuries suffered by anyone important in my life.

Until now.

Is tragedy the price we pay for being here? The truth is: there are catastrophes in life where you are complicit. Show me a divorce where it's all down to the bad behavior of one party. Where there are not competing narratives about what went wrong and why. But then there are the bad winds of happenstance; of immense misfortune landing directly in the epicenter of your life. And for a parent there is no greater distress or horror than something befalling your child. I was now the father of a child with a disability. And I knew that this hard, desperate fact was one that would shape the entire trajectory of my life from this moment on.

Rebecca talked with her therapist three times a week. We could afford it – and it did seem to stabilize her for a time. She announced that she wanted to give up her job and look after Ethan full-time. I convinced her to keep Rosa on as a second pair of hands (and, though I wouldn't say it, as a safety valve if she went into another tailspin). We could afford Rosa as well. Just as we could afford the best medical treatment for Ethan. He did have those micro hearing aids surgically installed in his ears. Rebecca kept saying that they made a world of difference. I didn't contradict her, but from my own attempts to speak loudly to him, to clap my hands near his ears, it was clear that Ethan wasn't responding at all well to noise. Rosa quietly agreed with me: my son seemed locked in a silent world. We regularly returned with him to see Dr Cerf. She counseled patience – to wait and see if, in time, the hearing aids coupled with his physical development would improve the situation. Explaining to us that it was still too early after the harm wrought by meningitis to fully assess the extent and permanence of the aural damage. Rebecca bought a proper single bed that fitted in a corner of the nursery – and that is where she began to sleep every night of the week. Our sex life ceased. Even though I didn't argue with my wife's need to be by Ethan's side, I did hint on several occasions that the lack of intimacy was not doing us any good; that a marriage without sex was one heading into troubled waters.

'Our child has been damaged in a permanent way – and all you can think about is getting off?'

'It's not about "getting off". I can do that myself. It's about that essential component of being a couple . . .'

'I know many functional marriages where sex is a thing of the past.'

'And they are largely people in late middle age where contempt is seething below the surface.'

'You'd be surprised.'

'Why can't we find time even just once a week to have an intimate moment with each other?'

'Because I have larger concerns now – and because I feel about as sexual as a toilet seat.'

'Nice metaphor.'

'Live with it.'

'We need that connection, Rebecca.'

'It's how it is,' she said, sounding definitive. And she refused to talk further on the matter.

Despair is an arena most of us find ourselves in at some juncture during the course of the narrative called our life. Like tragedy, this was new terrain for me. Melancholia – as Isabelle had once analyzed – was that below-surface condition that I kept out of public sight, but which was still very much a defining part of me. But despair was new terrain. I would try to spend at least an hour a day during the working week playing with my son, and was with him the majority of every weekend. Ethan was just becoming a toddler. Someone who smiled rarely and who seemed locked in and barely responded to the sound of my voice. I held on to those moments when shouting something seemed to get his attention. But it had to be a proper shout – and even then I sensed that he was just hearing a distant vibration, even when I was sitting close to him. Dr Cerf encouraged us to speak as loudly as we could to Ethan – though only in concentrated doses so as not to overwhelm him. But the glimmers of hope were fleeting ones. And I was feeling the increasing pull of the black dog on my psyche: the sense that I was becoming submerged by a creeping sense of hopelessness that was absolutely anathema to my 'can do – there is a solution to all this' persona.

As someone who had struggled with serious depression after his divorce, David saw all the telltale signs of my increasing despair. He insisted I start talking to his own therapist, an ex-Jesuit named Patrick Keogh who had his office in the mid 50s, who was as rigorous as he was humane – and who had me challenge much to do with my cold upbringing, my now toxic marriage and my longing for love. Naturally I told him all about Isabelle and how I thought that I had lost something fundamental in me when I'd pushed her away. His reply was:

'But if someone is expressing ongoing ambivalence about being with you and then does an immediate volte-face, of course you are going to be in considerable doubt and turmoil. Stop beating yourself up and thinking you were the cause of all this. Isabelle lost you as well.'

As for Rebecca, he warned me that it sounded as if she was in the throes of bipolar behavior and that I needed to protect myself and Ethan if she got out of control. From all I had described, I was going to have to either put up with her mad mood swings and aberrations or move on – taking Ethan with me.

Some months into our weekly sessions I came in and sat down on his mid-century sofa and told Patrick that I had started an affair. Patrick asked me about her. I told him she was a play-wright, brilliant and passionate.

230

'Are you in love?' he asked me.

'I could be,' I said. 'She tells me she is. She also tells me that she is terrified of getting hurt; that an involvement with a married man is usually a one-way ticket to misfortune.'

'Unless the love is reciprocal, and you want to build a future together.'

'It's too early to tell.'

'Of course it is. And how are you handling the complexities of all this – if, that is, it is complex for you?'

'You know better than anyone now about my relationship with guilt. I always blamed myself for my parents' distance from me. I always felt that I was doing something that was keeping Isabelle at bay. And yes, part of me feels terrible about the betrayal of Rebecca. But she in turn has informed me that, for the foreseeable future, our sexual life is dead. That's been hard for me to bear.'

The affair had started tentatively. One evening when I couldn't sleep I'd sent Phoebe a long letter saying that, yes, this was an-out-of-the-blue communiqué months after we'd first met and much had transpired since then. I'd then outlined all that had happened with Ethan and the downward spiral of my marriage. I apologized for being direct, for sharing a great deal of bad stuff with her. I then added one final line, saying if she ever wanted to meet up for a drink I'd be very pleased to buy us a round or two of martinis.

How did I feel writing this letter on my very new Apple computer at three in the morning while my wife and child slept in the next room? Yes, there was some unease, a sense I was dabbling in something potentially combustible. And there was also an edgy excitement. And – dare I admit it – a curious undercurrent of hope.

I did not print out this letter and fax it until the next day when I got to the office. Had I sent it from home Rebecca might have discovered the number on the regular weekly printout of all faxes sent, which I saw her scrutinize with interest. I had always known that she had a certain jealous streak. And though in the past I'd always reassured her that I would not break the seventh commandment, ever since she had withdrawn from sex I could sense that she was now hyper-conscious of my movements: whom I was meeting and where, what faxes were being sent from our home machine. I once made the mistake of pointing out to her the strange counterpoint of her increasing suspicion about my fidelity at a time when she was refusing to make love with me. Her response:

'Then go sleep with someone else.'

'Do you mean that?' I asked.

'You're a free man.'

I was pretty sure this was anger talking and not what she truly thought. Still, something extraordinary had arisen out of her fury – her booming voice had caused Ethan to shudder a bit.

'Did you see that?' I asked, excited that our son was responding to sound . . . even if it was thanks to his parents' furious exchange.

'As long as I yell at you our boy gives us an indication that he can feel the bad vibes between us.'

'There is no need for bad vibes.'

'So we should be celebrating our wonderful fucking life?'

'Ethan has the best medical care going. He will get the best educational care going. He will learn sign language. He will learn to talk after a fashion – and in time maybe he will be able to talk well. Just as he will perhaps, in time and with certain medical procedures and advancements, regain some hearing.'

'Aren't you Mr Fucking Pollyanna. This is a disaster. We are a disaster. And you should go fuck some other woman because you're never fucking me again – because I fucking hate you. And the reason I fucking hate you is because the night he got the virus you told me it was OK for me to work late. Had I been here—'

'Will you stop this insanity?'

'Insanity? *Insanity?* I am living in hell and you call it insanity—'

'You're boozing again, aren't you?'

'Oh fuck off.'

'Vodka. That's your poison. Stoli. No smell on the breath – and you keep the bottles on the ledge outside the bathroom window.'

'You're a fucking fantasist.'

At which point she stormed out of the room and into the bathroom. I gave pursuit but she slammed and barred the door behind me. I was suddenly enraged. I screamed at her to open the door. I rattled its handle. I began to force the door.

'Go on, break it the fuck down,' she yelled from within.

I started throwing my entire weight against the door.

'Too late, asshole,' she shouted, throwing the door open just as I started a second assault against it. I fell in on top of her, knocking us both against the sink. At which point she lashed out and caught my neck with her nails.

'Fuck!' I screamed.

She lashed out again, but I managed to grab her hand.

'Go on, fucking break it!' she screamed. 'And let me get a million off you in the divorce.'

I pushed her away, grabbing a towel to staunch the blood. I saw the bathroom window thrown open. I staggered over and checked the window sill. Empty. I stared down into the alleyway eight stories below. I was sure there was a smashed bottle in the courtyard but from this height I could see nothing. I turned and pushed by her, walking into our bedroom, throwing some clothes and toiletries into a bag, marching out the door. And thinking thereafter – as I was in the corridor outside our apartment, awaiting the elevator down to the liberation of the outside world – what insanity this all was. Domestic chaos. And I was leaving my son with a crazy woman.

I turned on my heel. I pulled out my keys and walked back into our apartment. I informed my wife: let's forget all that happened. She just shrugged, holding our son in her arms, looking beyond spent. I relieved her of Ethan. At first she wouldn't let him go. But I quietly told her that what she needed more than anything now was sleep. She finally let me take our son in my arms and went to the cot in the nursery on which she now slept all nights. Half an hour later, when I was sure she was truly passed out, I crept into the nursery and settled Ethan into his crib. Then I went into our bedroom, where I shook out one of the sleeping pills that my doctor had prescribed. It took longer than usual that night – I was staring up at our bedroom ceiling as if it was the cosmos waiting to swallow me. Eventually it shut me down for a few hours. The next thing I knew my wife was next to me in bed, dressed in pajamas, but with her arms very much around me, sobbing into my shoulder, telling me how much she loved me, how sorry she was for lashing out the way she had. I held her and assured her all was well (which was anything but the truth – but there are fragile moments with fragile people where telling the truth is counterproductive). She kissed me deeply. But when I responded in kind she pushed me away. Saying:

'I'm not ready.'

When I got to the office that morning there was a fax from Phoebe awaiting me:

Dear Sam

Reading your letter was vertiginous in the way that other people's bad news is vertiginous and also vicarious . . . because it has you wondering: is the veneer of life that fragile? Of course it had me reflecting on so much, most of all your evident perseverance and resilience. Though I am childless – my first and (to date) only husband never wanted them – I have nieces and nephews (five altogether – I am the family failure when it comes to fecundity), including one who has Down's syndrome, a fact that ended my brother's marriage, so I have seen what a child's disability does to a couple. Just as I also sense from your letter that you are grappling with some very major questions about your relationship right now . . . if you will excuse me for being direct. And I also know that, yes, I would very much like to have that drink with you soon.

Courage.

My very best

Phoebe

A few days later, I told Rebecca that I would be out with a bunch of fellow lawyers that night. She'd been having another bad morning when I left – Ethan had been up half the night. I'd heard his strangled screams at 4 a.m. and had headed immediately into the nursery, but when I'd asked if I could take over and let her crash in the marital bed while I dealt with him, she'd again been adamant that she would handle it all.

'Anyway, don't you have a big day in court and an attorney dinner thing tonight?'

'It's still not fair on you.'

'Stop sounding so fucking altruistic and Mr Humane. I know you can't stand any of this—'

'Let's not go there.'

'Because then you would, what, rip me a new asshole?'

She came very close to me as she said this. Though vodka is the choice of many a serious alcoholic because it carries little smell, I could still discern distilled potato fumes on her breath . . . plus Rebecca would veer into a rage whenever smashed. And I was pretty certain she was smashed now. I sidestepped her, finished tying my tie, grabbed my suit jacket and headed for the bathroom. Once inside I bolted the door, went to the window and opened it, feeling out on the ledge until my hand found a bottle. I brought it inside. A liter of Stolichnaya, two-thirds empty. The forensic part of my brain found myself wondering why, having been challenged before about her booze hiding place (which also kept the vodka nicely chilled), she decided to keep storing it there? Was this an act of defiance, a non-verbal fuck-you to me? And an acknowledgment that, yes, she was drinking in such a serious way that she had to keep it clandestine?

I came back into the living room. Rebecca was slumped on the sofa, passed out. I checked my watch: 7.48 a.m. Rosa would be here in just under forty-five minutes. I looked in on Ethan in his crib. Still asleep. I made more coffee. I decided I would call my secretary when she arrived at 8.30 a.m. and ask her to have my associate bring all the many documents we needed to the court and I would meet him directly there. I sipped my coffee and watched my sad alcoholic wife snoring deeply on our couch. Rosa arrived. She took in the scene – and the fact that Rebecca's somnolence was caused by something other than exhaustion. I motioned for her to follow me into the kitchen. But before that she and I both went back into the nursery to check that Ethan had not woken up. Assured that he remained asleep, we headed to the kitchen, closing the door behind us. I poured Rosa a mug of coffee and came straight out with it:

'Have you been aware that my wife has a serious problem with alcohol?'

Rosa shook her head.

That's when I told her about Rebecca's drinking, her booze-fueled rages, the vodka bottles on the bathroom window ledge. She was shocked – and said that she'd never seen Rebecca intoxicated, though frequently she would come out of the bathroom with a big glass of what she'd presumed to be water and would go into the master bedroom and have an afternoon nap. Might that glass of clear liquid have contained vodka?

'Honestly, I would know if she'd been drinking. Maybe she's just doing it in a way to keep herself topped up all day – and then occasionally goes over the edge? With your permission I will try to check the bottle of vodka on the window ledge during the day to see what sort of level it goes down to – or if it's replaced.'

'Does she take a nap most days?'

'Indeed she does.'

'Can you see about checking the glass afterwards – to see if it is full of vodka? And I presume she does go out for a walk or for her appointments with her therapist or psychiatrist. When she does so, can you scour the apartment to see if she has a stash of vodka bottles somewhere?'

'All this makes me very uncomfortable, sir. But I do understand that Ethan's well-being and security are at stake here.'

'Indeed they are. And I will make it up to you, Rosa. A nice bonus.'

'There's no need, sir.'

'Yes, there is. And can you babysit tonight – even with Rebecca here?'

'Of course, sir.'

This entire conversation – and the ugly scene with Rebecca that preceded it – flooded my head as Phoebe locked her fingers with mine. Was I using the incident that morning (and everything else recently) as a form of self-justification for the line I was about to cross? Absolutely. Just as I told myself: when someone stops having sex with you – more specifically, the person with whom you have agreed to build a life, to have and to hold, forsaking all others and so on and so forth – there are two choices: suffer in silence and revert to onanism (as so many people do), or seek passionate solace elsewhere.

'You don't have to get home fast, do you?' Phoebe asked.

'She will be asleep in the baby's room when I return, but I've ensured our nanny is babysitting tonight.'

That was my way of letting Phoebe know: my marriage is in a deeply bad place. Her fingers tightened around mine.

'Let's get out of here,' she whispered.

What struck me so forcibly about making love with Phoebe for the first time was how needy she was, how vulnerable, how desperate for a passionate connection. How she gave so much yet was also uneasy about giving so much – because it left her open to the danger of further harm. Is that an increasing preoccupation after life has knocked you about and lovers have brought you disappointment? You size up your romantic failings and assess your feast of losses and also find yourself thinking: I am responsible for so much of how this entire scenario has panned out? Is that when you find yourself caught between need and caution? Not that Phoebe was cautious in bed. Her ardor was ferocious, all-encompassing, a touch of *life and death* to it all. It was intoxicating – and I responded in kind. But it also signaled: this was not just going to be a *cinq à sept*. It was going to take on significant import . . . if we let it.

When you feel lost amid the toxic cloud of despair – especially one triggered by a relationship you have no choice but to return to nightly and which you now know is doing you psychic harm – the idea of being found is exhilarating. *Someone to watch over me* and all that. Phoebe, as I came to learn, was desperate for a life together. I was desperate for a refuge from the ongoing psychodrama of home life. I sensed from the outset – though never articulated it – that these two disparate needs might lead to a difficult reckoning down the line.

But initially we were just engrossed in the wonder of having connected, of not being alone – yet also being circumscribed by the parameters that are implicit in a love affair where one of the parties is legally spliced to someone else.

Still, for many months we simply reveled in the time we had together. I soon had a key to her apartment: a compact one-bedroom place in Chelsea. I kept a change of clothes there. Two nights during the work week I would get to her place by six. I arranged for Rosa to stay on those evenings as well, telling Rebecca that I wanted her to have time out with friends on the nights I had to work late (and thereby ensuring that Ethan wasn't left alone with his mother while I was elsewhere). As soon as I walked into Phoebe's apartment we'd instantly fall into bed. Our lovemaking was never rushed, never hurried, and always intense, with an edge of ravenous yearning that under-scored the fact that we could not have each other on a normal daily basis; that we had to be surreptitious, never out in the open. But that, in turn, gave it all an immense avidity; a force-fulness that was heady.

And then, when we fell out of bed an hour later, I would change into what became known between us as my 'downtown disguise' and we'd head out into the New York night. We used the time with brilliant intensity. When you only have five hours together twice a week there is a magic to this window of wondrous opportunity. Phoebe insisted early on that this arrangement suited her perfectly. She frequently wrote late. She was under commission for about four episodes a year of her television series – which gave her enough to pay her way in life and even have a holiday or two. Her actual stage plays had all been performed in small theaters. Prestigious, not lucrative. She often fretted that if the producers decided on a writers clear-out and took on new talent – as they did every other year or so – she would find herself without her essential source of income.

Being with Phoebe was never banal. When Rebecca decided to visit a college friend named Barbara in Santa Barbara for a week with Ethan, I insisted on Rosa accompanying her and arranged all the flights, telling Rebecca this would allow her to have proper time with Barbara without having to worry about looking after Ethan non-stop. Rebecca knew that I really wanted Rosa there to ensure that Ethan was out of danger if she tipped back over into serious drinking.

With Rebecca away, Phoebe and I had a full seven days together. I would check on our answerphone at the apartment by phoning in every few hours during the evening just to see if there was a message from Rebecca. There usually was – and I was able to phone her back from Phoebe's using a code on her touchphone to hide the number. One evening Rebecca asked me why our own number was not being displayed on the phone at her friend's, and why the number didn't show when she put in the code for a callback. I had an answer ready – I had decided to disable that facility on our phone as I was having to deal with a potential new client on the West Coast who often worked late and I didn't want him to have our home number.

'You really know how to cover your tracks, don't you?' Rebecca said.

Steady now. Show no anxiety, no fear that she might be on to you.

'By which you mean . . .?' I asked.

'You tell me.'

'Tell you what?'

'Her name.'

'Whose name?'

'The woman you're seeing.'

'I'm seeing someone?'

'That's my supposition.'

'A wrong supposition.'

'We'll see about that,' she said.

'Why don't you worry about larger realities – like Ethan's next appointment with Dr Cerf? I spent an hour on the phone with her yesterday. She has many thoughts about educational possibilities we can pursue—'

'Congratulations – you win the Father of the Year Award. But I'm the one who's with our son day in, day out. You don't think I'm up to speed on his developmental progress? You who only see him for an hour every evening.'

'I'm around all but two nights a week. Just like you.'

'But on those two nights you're with your mistress.'

'I work those nights.'

'Yeah, right. You hate me because I won't fuck you anymore.'

'Have you been drinking again?'

Click. Rebecca had slammed down the phone.

I took this call on the extension in Phoebe's kitchen. But she'd been in the living room, looking over a draft of a new episode at her desk. Though I'd tried to keep my voice low

I knew that if it was too low and whispery Rebecca would get even more suspicious. However, if I spoke normally Phoebe would hear the gist of this unfortunate exchange. Which, of course, she did.

'A shot of something?'

'I didn't want you to hear all that.'

'I did. What's your poison?'

'Scotch works.'

'To quote that great jazz standard: "How long has this been going on?"'

'You mean, between us?'

'That's what I mean.'

'You know the answer to that question.'

'So do you.'

'Four months.'

'Four extraordinary months. I'm as happy as I have ever been.'

'Me too.'

'Even happier than your time in Paris?'

'I haven't talked very much about all that.'

'Which leads me to believe that it was as serious as they come.'

'There are chapters. That one is closed.'

Even though the truth was my last written words to Isabelle had indicated there could be no future between us, the acute sense of loss was always there . . . albeit carefully hidden from view.

'And this chapter?' Phoebe asked.

'We are still just four months into it.'

'But if I were to ask you now: Rebecca or me?'

Pause. I knew that anything I said could be taken down and used against me.

'Does it have to be either/or?' I asked.

'You're answering a question with a question.'

'Because you have posed a Gordian knot of a question.'

'Try an answer.'

I shut my eyes, then opened them and reached for her packet of cigarettes.

'If I could leave her, I'd go. But there is Ethan. As you know, he has a disability. As I have told you, his mother is an alcoholic. The fact that I have a full-time nanny at Rebecca's side. Say I did win custody of my son. A child who will spend years needing rehabilitative care at home and at special schools here in the city. Would you really want to become his surrogate mother?'

Phoebe fell silent. Clearly thrown by the question.

Finally:

'I want a child of my own – preferably by you. A baby I will feel move and kick and grow within me, who will come out of me with considerable pain – even with modern anesthetics – and will cause me sleepless nights and will worry me ceaselessly and to whom I will give unconditional love. And – cards on the table – I want this child now. I'm thirty-seven. My biological clock is about to run out. If I wait a year or two, the chances of me being able to conceive will only diminish further. So I find myself in now-or-never territory. And in love with you. And knowing that what I am telling you tonight probably puts you under a massive amount of pressure. But I think we could do this wonderfully together. There's a chance here that doesn't come along often. And . . .'

She fell silent, reaching for her cigarettes. I put my arm around her.

'I have to get Ethan away from my wife. That comes first and foremost. If you think you could handle having him live with us . . .'

I could sense the hesitancy within her as she fired up a Marlboro Light, falling silent, searching for a response. Eventually saying:

'Can I meet him?'

'I think that can be arranged.'

'But if I say yes to Ethan living with us . . .?'

'Yes, I will give you the baby you want.'

She gripped my hand hard, her eyes misting up. But there was nothing celebratory about this moment; rather, a hint of melancholy. For evident reasons. We had just made a sort of Faustian bargain with each other – a maternity trade-off. And one I knew might be the source of much future tension. I kissed her on the head. I said:

'I know I am coming with considerable baggage.'

'I think I can handle that.'

Rebecca came home two days later. Ethan looked wan and fatigued. This worried me. As did Rebecca's evident exhaustion. She said he had been having crazed broken nights: 'Howling at the moon, unable to stop.' She'd called Dr Cerf, who told her that as he was now over eighteen months and far more cognizant of life around him, our son was probably now reacting to the silent world in which he lived.

'Why didn't you call me and tell me about this – and your consultation with Dr Cerf?'

'Because you were elsewhere all week.'

'Bullshit. I was here.'

'Bullshit back to you. Ramon – the evening doorman – told me yesterday when I got back that he hadn't seen you all week.'

'Just like that he came out with that statement?'

'Hardly. I asked him if he'd seen you around. He said, "I thought your husband was away with you. He hasn't been here any of the nights I've been on."'

'His mistake.'

'More bullshit. I called our maid Juanita. Asked her to change the sheets before I came home. She came by the apartment yesterday, then called me to say that the bed looked like it hadn't been slept in.'

'I changed the sheets myself when I had a night sweat.'

'Why did you have a night sweat?'

'Because I am married to an angry alcoholic. Which is just a little stressful – even when you are three thousand miles away. And because I found your stash of vodka.'

'How could you have been searching for vodka all week when you were off somewhere fucking your girlfriend?'

'I was here – and as I had time on my hands I burrowed around your closet and found that suitcase in the back where you keep half a dozen bottles of Stoli.'

Actually it was Rosa who had found the stash and told me about it, meeting me at the apartment the day before she accompanied Rebecca and Ethan to the West Coast. She was a little ashamed of burrowing around in one of her employer's closets. She said nothing when I brought out a camera and took photos of the suitcase, the vodka stash, its position in

246

the closet, or when I entered the bathroom and climbed up on the closed toilet seat to open the window and take a photo of the half-empty Stoli bottle on the window sill. I had promised Rosa I wouldn't tell Rebecca that she had helped me uncover evidence of her severe alcoholism. Just as I promised to keep her on as Ethan's nanny when I gained sole custody of my son and moved us out of the apartment that Rebecca had bought over a decade ago – and which she deserved to keep in the divorce.

'You're bluffing,' Rebecca said now.

'I have photographs.'

'You're bluffing.'

'Photographs are evidence.'

'You could have planted all that evidence in an attempt to—'

'Think what you like.'

'You're divorcing me, aren't you?'

'This is a hateful situation.'

'If you think you can get custody of Ethan . . .'

'The courts will decide that.'

'And they will also know a thing or two about you.'

'Such as?'

'You'll see. And don't think you can paint me as a lush. Because out on the West Coast something happened. I met someone.'

It took me a moment to digest this.

'Who exactly?'

'Jesus.'

'Oh please . . .'

'It's the truth.'

'And where did you meet Jesus?'

'In the YMCA in Santa Barbara.'

'Jesus hangs out there?'

'I was at an AA meeting.'

'And what brought this about?'

'My friend Barbara convinced me to go.'

'Because you were smashed.'

'Because I needed help.'

'So now you know why I insisted on Rosa traveling with you. Because I was worried that you might be drunk again while in care of Ethan.'

'Stop compiling evidence. Because I have evidence of my own. Phoebe Rossant. Lives at 333 West 26th Street, apartment 2B. You've been seeing her for sixteen weeks, two days. You met her through your friend David who writes for the *Journal*. You both like drinking at Chumley's and book shopping at the Strand.'

'And how do you know all this?' I said, trying to keep my alarm and rage in check.

'The old-fashioned way: a private detective.'

'Jesus Christ – was that necessary?'

'Absolutely – since it gave me the evidence I need to proceed with the divorce and sue for custody of Ethan.'

'Such grounds might be mitigated by your alcoholism . . .'

'What proof of that do you have besides unopened bottles of vodka and my new-found sobriety thanks to Alcoholics Anonymous?'

'You think you are going to win this courtesy of a few days without Stoli and some talk about the loving forgiveness of Jesus?'

'See you in court, counselor – and I want your cheating ass out of this apartment tonight.'

'Fuck you,' I said.

'You're not sleeping here.'

'We'll see about that.'

I went into the bedroom. Our bedroom. Where for months I had slept alone. I sat down on the bed. The same bed where we made Ethan. Where we had pledged love to each other. Where we had given each other fast bursts of pleasure. Where we used to talk late into the night, our arms around each other, a sense of complicity and a shared future shielding us. Was this the moment when the point of no return had been crossed? My lawyer's brain whirled. I reached for my address book in my jacket pocket. I called Gordon Collins, the divorce expert in our firm. Always upbeat – as befitted a fellow who liked to be called Gordy, and who dealt daily with the crazed dance that is called marital breakdown – Gordy was at home and certainly didn't mind hearing from me. When I told him what was going down here he whistled loudly and said:

'Fear not. We'll limit the damage. How do you feel about leaving your son alone with her? I know she's talking AA and being born again, but did you smell booze on her?'

'I'm afraid she struck me as truly sober and very righteous.'

'Ex-alkies always are – especially when they've made the acquaintance of their Lord and Savior. Do you think your lady friend would take you in tonight?'

'I have no idea if she is at home.'

'If she is, and she is opening the door to you, then go. If not, find a hotel. Now here's another thing – insist that you have time with your son this weekend. I know you are, without question, an ultra-responsible dad, but now that we are in a divorce landscape we immediately need to start showing that you want shared responsibilities for your son. Especially in light of his disabilities. No doubt, if she's on day eight of Twelve Step heaven, Rebecca is definitely going to want to hit an AA meeting tomorrow to keep the good sobriety vibrations going. Tell her you'll take Ethan for the two hours while she's out. Just two further ground rules. As much as you may hate her right now, be rigorously polite, but also firm if she gets arrogant and bossy. Know that she will threaten you with all sorts of terrible consequences. Opening gambits in a divorce are always games of intimidation. Do not be cowed by their absurdities. My job is to beat back their extravagant demands and make them see sense. The other ground rule: write nothing, leave no outraged messages on her answerphone, make no threats whatsoever. Call your lady friend. Or call a hotel. Pack a bag. Insist that you babysit Junior tomorrow while she is out doing the higher-power detox. Then get the hell out of there . . . and call me tomorrow.'

Before hanging up, I thanked Gordy for the witty repartee at a dark moment.

'Well, we won't allow Madame to ruin you. And at the same time we won't let you get too gloomy.'

After hanging up I immediately called Phoebe. Luck was with me. She picked up on the third ring. I gave her the large-print edition of all that had gone down. And I asked if she could put up with me moving in for a while.

'Get over here now.'

I found a suitcase. And a suit bag. I packed up a week's worth of clothes in fifteen minutes. Then I grabbed my top coat and placed everything by the front door. I walked into the nursery. Ethan was continuing to cry uncontrollably, despite Rebecca cradling him.

'He's having a bad day,' I said.

'It's been a week of bad days. But today is especially bad. He clearly senses the violent psychic waves between us.'

'Stop going new age on me.'

'Children feel adult vibrations. Especially a deaf child. And he hears all the anger between us.'

'But *violence*?'

'Emotional violence' she said. Like you accusing me of hoarding vodka.'

'OK, those photos I took of your bottle stash were complete set-ups. And the reason you're now a new-found AA convert has nothing to do with drink problems. You're just researching a one-woman show on Dorothy Parker.'

'You're mixing me up with your playwright. To whose arms I presume you will flee now.'

'Because you're kicking me out.'

'Stay then.'

'Do you mean that?'

'No.'

'Fine. We're clear on that then. Are you planning to go to AA meetings this weekend?'

'What business is that of yours?'

'When you go I'd like to babysit Ethan.'

'And disappear with him off somewhere? No way.'

'You know that wouldn't happen.'

'You're a lawyer, Sam. Someone who always needs to win, always needs to be right. And I know now that you won't stop until you've won full custody of Ethan.'

'That is not my intention.'

'Even more bullshit.'

'I have a right to see my son.'

'So you say.'

'That is the law. Unless there is danger to the child's life. As in: a parent having a substance abuse problem.'

'See you in court, counselor.'

'Can I have the name and number of your lawyer?' I asked.

'Why? So you can call him up and see who has the bigger dick?'

As Gordy told me: don't rise to the bait. So I just pulled out my pocket notebook and pen and handed it to her.

'Your lawyer's name and number, please.'

When I saw her lips purse I knew she was sizing up whether or not she could tell me to fuck off. Or whether she too was wondering if by telling me I couldn't see Ethan she might be crossing a legal line and it might, in time, rebound on her. I stopped myself from saying something like 'Let's be civil about this, Rebecca,' because that might have provoked her into greater defiance. So I just stood there and held the silence until she scribbled out a name and number.

'Thank you,' I said. And I left.

That night in bed Phoebe asked me:

'Diaphragm in or out?'

'You still haven't met Ethan.'

'I'm at the height of my cycle the week after next. It wouldn't be dangerous now without it.'

I hesitated. She saw this.

'You are uncertain,' she said.

'I want you to meet Ethan.'

'Because you are uncertain.'

'Because I want you to meet Ethan.'

'And also because you are torn up by the end of your marriage.'

'Are you surprised?'

'Unfortunately not.'

'As all this went down around three hours ago, as it was an eleven-year relationship, and as there is a child's welfare at stake – a child with "special needs", to use that expression I detest—'

'Fine, fine, fine. I know I am being deeply self-centered. I know I am thinking about me and me alone, as every man before you has told me.'

'I'm not saying that here. I'm just being—'

'Prudent. Because you don't know if you want a child with me. And who can blame you, given all you are dealing with right now. And given that I am genuinely afraid of taking on a deaf child. Not because I don't think I can handle it. I know I can handle it. But I fear how much work it will be and how it could impact my experience of raising my own child. So, all I can say now is, of course I will meet Ethan, and all that I said to you the other day – about wanting a baby with you – still profoundly holds true. But . . .'

Silence. A long one. Then Phoebe got out of bed, crossed over to her chest of drawers, opened the top shelf, removed the large plastic case in which she kept her diaphragm and a tube of spermicidal jelly. She disappeared into the bathroom, returning five minutes later saying:

'I'm nice and safe for you now.'

The next day, Gordy rang Phoebe's phone in the late morning (with her permission I'd given him her number). She'd just left for a Saturday-morning brunch with a producer. Gordy had some disquieting news. According to Rebecca's lawyer, his client had become seriously obstinate and was refusing to grant me access to my son.

'She is, if I may say so, borderline schizo. Even her own lawyer – who I know from an earlier case – has been trying to get her to see sense. But she is convinced that if she lets you have access to Ethan you will disappear with him.'

'Where to? Guatemala?'

'Some flight of fancy like that, yes. Give me a few days to get this round of new-separation fisticuffs behind you and we will get you your access.'

I certainly needed a bit of comradely counsel right now. I called David. He was at home, free jazz blaring in the background. I told him I had a small crisis on my hands.

And then he mentioned a place in Union Square where we could meet for brunch in thirty minutes.

David, as always, was a great listener. And highly cunning/ calculating. Telling me that he'd wager money on the probability that Rebecca had met a guy at AA – a fellow alky, 'probably not as educated and classy as she is, but who can see that she needs a guru, a male defender, so he'll be moving in on her romantically, with a view to helping her-asset strip you and profit from your bad divorce.' While on the subject of Phoebe . . . 'well, she's wondrous, but the biological imperative is there now. Do you want to fulfill it and hem yourself in further? Maybe yes, maybe no. Maybe you go both ways. But know this: once you commit, you are tethered to two children with two different women for decades to come. With Ethan, you will be looking after him for as long as you are sentient. If you have a baby with Phoebe, you get to pay the last tuition check when you are well into your fifties. Your call, sir. Phoebe is rather spectacular. But five years down the road you might think: I am in the deepest cul-de-sac imaginable . . . and, like all dead ends, it will be one of your own making.'

My client Jeff Swarbeck was in a far darker place, given that the Feds were accusing his California business partner, Dan Montgomery, of using embezzled funds to create a trust in the names of his own children and Jeff's. My client was certainly aware of the trust and had contributed to it as a form of tax minimization, but he was unaware that Montgomery had used illegally garnered funds to enhance it. Now there was a criminal case pending – and the California DA was certain that Jeff had been in on the embezzlement and was threatening him with jail time. I had no choice but to head to LA. My secretary arranged all the flights and the accommodation. During a long week in the City of Angels I met with the prosecutors, who offered my client a deal: plead guilty and he'd only serve ten years. I showed them a cavalcade of evidence that Jeff was the innocent party here. The DA pushed home the point that, when sharing a trust with his business partner, he should have been aware of where all the money was coming from. *The hand of one is the hand of all.* Over the course of two very long negotiations I got the DA to agree that, in exchange for turning state's evidence against his business partner, all charges against Jeff would be dropped.

Case closed. I returned to my hotel. I called my client and informed him that, as long as he was smart and cooperated with the authorities, he was out of danger of being incarcerated. Jeff agreed to do all that was asked of him by the District Attorney. He thanked me. I went to the minibar and opened a split of red wine. I drank it down. I caught a glimpse of myself in the mirror of this overblown five-star hotel. Immediately I was transported back to that half-star hotel in Paris, to my twenty-one-year-old self looking at his half-shaved reflection in a cracked glass and thinking: welcome to *la vie de bohème*. Whereas now I existed within the concrete, frequently grubby, avaricious reality of adult life. And there was not an ounce of poetry in any of it.

Later that evening, I recounted this introspective moment to Phoebe. Her reply down the transcontinental phone line was:

'So give it all up and vanish off to Paris. Make your way back to your Isabelle and sell your suits and find that beneath-the-eaves single room where you can write free-form verse and develop a taste for absinthe.'

'All right, all right, I know I am engaging in romantic cliché.'

'Which we all need. Look at me, grinding out upscale pulp television drama for the mass market. I am fortunate to be doing so. Fortunate to be making a living by my pen. But I want to be a great playwright, not some small-screen hack for hire. Maybe that will happen, maybe it won't. Maybe twenty years down the road, when I am almost sixty, I will accept that disappointment is part of the equation of life. Because we are all, on a certain level, disappointed. Aren't we?'

'Perhaps that's one of the reasons most of us have the strong urge to reproduce. Because we secretly hope the next generation will do it better the next time around. On which note . . .'

'Let's not go there tonight, sweetheart. Like you I've had a long, long day – and I need to fall into bed and black out thoughts of life in the future tense.'

'We'll talk tomorrow then.'

'No – we'll talk Monday, as I have accepted an invitation from a college friend to spend the weekend with her up in Rhode Island. Jayne has just gotten divorced and is headmistress of a not-bad girls' boarding school in Barrington. I'm going to jump on the train up there tomorrow afternoon and spend a few days walking on the beach and drinking too much Chardonnay with my very sardonic Jean Brodie-esque friend, emptying my head of everything.'

'Lucky you.'

'It's hardly a three-month Tibetan retreat, but I hope to return to Manhattan madness moderately refreshed on Monday.'

'I miss you.'

'I'm pleased to hear it. A transcontinental kiss to you.'

During these days away I spoke to Rosa daily, getting an update on Ethan and discovering that Rebecca was indeed attending daily AA meetings and had asked one of the doormen to take away all the vodka and wine stashed around the house. Shortly after ending the call I phoned Phoebe at home, figuring that as it was now Monday afternoon she must be back from coastal New England. But I got her answering machine . . . on which I left the following message:

'My love, you are in my thoughts constantly. And yes, a few days away does clarify so much. If you want a child with me, I want a child with you. My lawyer says that, at best, I might end up with shared custody of Ethan. Which means that it will not be the non-stop care you were so worried might impinge on our own child. I will always do everything for Ethan, always be there for him. Just as I will always be there for you and the child we have together. My love for you is vast, limitless.'

Ah, the cascading language of amorous affection – which contains so many aspirations for a future together. We cannot function within the enigma of love without hope. It is the essential underpinning of the entire enterprise.

At the end of my message I reminded Phoebe of my phone and fax numbers here (in case romantic whimsy made her want to write me) and told her I would be home and back in her arms in a few short days.

Then I rang David to have a catch-up schmooze. Only I didn't get David, as one of his colleagues at the paper picked up his phone and informed me that my friend had decided to take a last-minute trip to Rome over the weekend and would be back next Monday.

The next day, I had a breakfast meeting at eight thirty. I woke up to the arrival of room-service breakfast and the waiter handing me a sealed envelope, saying a fax had arrived late last night and had been slipped under my door while I slept. As he arranged dishes and utensils and a coffee pot on the table he rolled on, I opened the envelope and was puzzled to see a handwritten letter on notepaper from the Hotel Raffaello, Via Urbano 3/5, 00184 Roma.

And then I recognized the penmanship.

Dear Sam

I phoned home last night to check messages on my answerphone and found yours. I decided it was imperative to write you immediately and come clean about something that erupted out of nowhere last week and has changed the course of everything for me.

I am not going to couch this news in the language of self-justification or over-explanation. Just the basic hard facts:

I am in Rome with David. We are in love. We are now a couple. If you are thinking: this is all crazy fast – especially as we have known each other as friends for years – well, as you well know, when it comes to matters of the human heart we are hostages to happenstance and the mystery called ourselves.

I'm sorry.

Phoebe.

I didn't crumple up the paper. I didn't let this faxed letter tumble to the ground as I absorbed this hard new reality, I didn't challenge her volte-face. I knew the reasons behind it; her motivations behind this news. And how damn obtuse and perplexing we all were. How you never truly knew anyone. And how the loss of serious love, that hypothetical future of craved-for happiness – even if you don't have an actual, clear understanding of what that means to you – is a wound that is never truly cauterized.

I glanced at myself in the hotel mirror. An ironic thought amidst this terrible moment – when I did feel truly lost – sideswiped me:

Midlife was nigh.

Five

DIVORCE: A DRAMA that inevitably turns into a melodrama.

Divorce: the end of love, the beginning of hate (if the process turns toxic – which it usually does) and the discovery that hate is also an expression of love gone wrong.

Divorce: an arena where money is a huge subject of contention because it serves as a means by which to mete out punishment in the wake of love gone wrong and the alleged betrayal of vows once spoken – though truth be told, infidelity takes many forms and is not rooted only in the physical.

Divorce: where even if you win materially you still lose. Unless, of course, this legal ending of a legally binding domestic contract is an escape clause from havoc, violence, abuse.

'Now, as there were no incidents of a physically or psychologically unpleasant nature between you, as you have a child with special needs who must come top of your priorities, I suggest that we try to make this process as streamlined and as simple as possible – and try to reach an accord without running up astronomic costs.'

That was Gordy, sitting opposite Marc Judson – the short, edgy, quick-talking lawyer who was representing Rebecca. She was seated next to him. Dressed in a conservative dark blue dress, her hair pulled back, a single gold crucifix around her neck. It was six months after our separation, we were in a conference room at Judson's office, and her lawyer was talking about her conversion to Catholicism and how it had 'transformed her'. Just as he was also explaining her need for vast sums per month for alimony and child-support payments on top of all the costs of the special-needs education that Ethan would require. I made a point of staring directly at Rebecca as Gordy articulated his contempt for her domestic budget, which he had before him, and which included twice-weekly therapeutic cleansing massages (to maintain her sobriety), a personal trainer and three sessions a week with her shrink.

'This budget is beyond surreal,' Gordy told the other side, informing them that no divorce judge would approve such a financial proposal, especially given the reckless past histories of his client and her new inamorato.

'My client entered AA voluntarily, which in itself shows a powerful need to change the trajectory of her life. But she was never intoxicated or incapacitated whilst caring for her son before that. And my client only began to drink after your client – a man so wrapped up in his career that he could only spend perhaps three or four hours with his son every week – began an affair with a woman who wanted a new family with him.'

I tensed so much when this accusation was hurled at me that Gordy had to put a very steadying hand on my arm, silently informing me that any eruption at this juncture would be playing right into their hands. So I remained silent – and found myself now being stared down by Rebecca, a huge, triumphant smile on her face.

All this accusatory ping-pong was costing each side more than three hundred dollars an hour – and as Rebecca had no income to speak of, the judge at the preliminary hearing informed Gordy that his client was going to be responsible for her legal costs.

'That's like buying bullets for my fucking assassin,' I told Gordy afterwards.

'Welcome to Divorce 1990 – American style,' he said. 'It gives them some leverage, but we'll have some too. It will still all come down to one issue, though: how angry and vengeful your ex decides to be. You stay smart. Never once contemplate trying to win this. You just want to come out in reasonable shape. That will be the victory.'

As it turned out Rebecca was seriously angry. At least I did get to have my son to myself every other weekend and two nights during the week. I found a nanny who also had experience of working with deaf children. Ethan was now at that moment when most children begin to properly articulate words. Jessica – a twenty-six-year-old African American woman – started working in a very basic way with Ethan to teach him how to sign. She had trained as a teacher specializing in disabilities, but quickly realized that in today's post-Reagan world, where education cuts were biting everywhere and teachers were profoundly underpaid, being a specialized nanny was a far more lucrative form of endeavor – 'By which I mean that I can pay the rent and have a modestly reasonable standard of living.'

In the wake of everything falling apart, I'd rented an apartment in the West 20s – furnished indifferently, but with a separate bedroom for my son. After working with him for several weeks Jessica reported that Ethan was responding well to learning sign language. She agreed to tutor me in signing and also suggested that she take over when he was at home with his mother. I agreed and called Rebecca, stating that I would pay for her to have

Jessica too. Her response was to hang up on me. Some weeks later, during one of the many ongoing negotiations between the two sides, Gordy did get Judson to see sense on the issue of this very gifted teacher working daily with our son – especially as I was paying for it.

'She wants to spend you into submission,' Gordy said when Judson informed him they would accept twenty grand a month plus all educational expenses until Ethan turned twenty-one. The point of such tactics was to destabilize me, as this was half my annual income that she was demanding. Though Gordy kept reassuring me a deal would eventually be struck, that this would not carry on indefinitely, that I should follow my lawyer's instincts here and not allow myself to be overwhelmed by it all, I was indeed overwhelmed by it all. Especially in the wake of Phoebe dropping me for my best friend . . . I suddenly found myself in emotional free fall, knowing on a certain level that I was the architect of so much of this and wondering what would have happened if I had accepted Isabelle's offer of a life together in New York. Would we too be divorcing now? Would I be having to pay for her displacement to the States? Was I some class of disaster area when it came to romantic choices? Gordy reassured me that everyone with a degree of self-awareness going through a divorce posed such questions of themselves. And that I really could not blame myself for Rebecca's drinking or Phoebe's decision to run off with my best friend.

'The cards just fell the way they fell,' he said.

Thanks for the haiku, counselor. The truth was: I knew from the outset about Rebecca's rigidity and her need for everything to be in its place, so why hadn't I sensed that, when the inevitable tough stuff came our way (as it does in all relationships), her inflexibility and her rage might find expression in extreme behavior? Just as I had known about David's long-standing desire for Phoebe, and that Phoebe herself was very clear that my son's disability was as much of a concern for her as her own ever-slowing biological clock. I never talked to Gordy about the despair I sank into after receiving Phoebe's fax from Rome. The sleeplessness, the desolation, the sense of failure. I began to lose weight. I began to lose cases. The senior partner, Geoff Mitchell, told me that I was one of the firm's biggest assets, citing my amazing ten-year run of victory after legal victory. But three high-profile litigations had gone the wrong way. They all knew that I was going through a horrendous divorce. They also 'sensed' (their way of indicating they had all the details) that I had 'other personal problems'. And so they wanted to propose that I take a break from trial work; that I consider taking on a more senior managerial role and perhaps consider running one of our offices elsewhere for a while.

'We know you did some time in Paris and you are nearly fluent in the language. Say we were to offer to put you in charge of our Paris office?'

This meeting came the day after Gordy informed me that the best deal we could cut with the 'other side' was $15k per month, but with Rebecca covering half the costs of Jessica's tutoring and with the agreement that this sum would be fixed until Ethan turned eighteen.

'Consider how, in just five years, you are going to consider this sum to be reasonable—'

'There is nothing reasonable about any of this.'

'That is indeed true. And I won't do the "hell hath no fury" line. We all pay a price for love and the loss thereof. Yours is psychic and fiscal. So be it. The other side knows that we are soon going to begin deducting their legal costs from the final settlement – because she is not being reasonable. And because if this does end up back in court, God fucking forbid, a judge will see that she's been unnecessarily destructive. It cuts both ways. I have a client right now whose wife left him for a tennis pro – a kid fifteen years his junior. The man is hell-bent on vengeance. But as I told him, vengeance is drinking poison and hoping the other person will die.'

But Rebecca was still bound up with the idea of revenge. Her lawyer told her to back off – that it was absurd to chase after a small increment on top of what was already a generous settlement, and that it could blow up in her face. She did finally approve of Jessica as a tutor. Ethan was responding more and more to the early signing lessons. Jessica told us that, as long as we continued to insist on intensive, three-hour-a-day, one-on-one tutorials for Ethan, she could have our boy properly signing by the age of six.

Of course Jessica informed us of this separately, as there were no lines of communication between us. The lawyers did the talking. When Gordy broached the idea of Ethan having six sessions a week with Jessica, my ex's lawyer informed us:

'Our client is wondering if your client, being a single man now, might be sleeping with his son's teacher.'

Gordy politely told Marc Judson to go fuck himself. Just as he told me not to rise to the bait; that my ex was clearly trying to play the provocateur. Gordy's solution to this problem was a simple one: he informed the other side that if Rebecca didn't agree to and totally facilitate the six-day-a-week tutoring sessions for Ethan – all of which would be paid for by me – we would move in court to have her become fully responsible financially for Ethan's private teacher and to be responsible for finding a teacher of the same caliber as Jessica.

Rebecca backed down. We cut a deal. It was one Rebecca was still not happy with because – though lucrative for her – it did not hobble me. Money is money. People who say they are not driven by money are almost always lying. Though there are those among us obsessed by the highly warped sexuality of money, the rest of humanity is simply tortured, on a sliding scale of agony, by the subject; how (on a certain uncomfortable but absolutely true level) money is the way we keep score in life, becoming a benchmark that helps shape our world view. Money is also revenge for being the kid picked on in school, the guy who never got the girls, the wronged spouse, who, having lost spousal fidelity, now wants to wreak havoc through financial pain. That was Rebecca. But final terms were eventually hammered out; a deal I could live with. Life stabilized into a rhythm of five days of non-stop work and two days of non-stop Ethan. On the two weekends a month when Ethan was with his mother, I worked. The brilliant Jessica did the agreed three hours a day tutoring with Ethan. I took signing lessons. I accelerated my French lessons. I subsumed myself in things I needed to be doing for Ethan's well-being, my future in France, my work. It allowed me some mental breathing space amidst the constant residual pain.

Shortly thereafter I also heard that Phoebe had given birth to a seven-pound, two-ounce son they named Henry. (Who bestows on a kid that prematurely middle-aged first name?) I sent a short note of congratulation – which, in turn, resulted in a short communiqué back from David. It was the first time I had heard from him since they'd run off with each other. He thanked me for reaching out, for the touching welcome-to-the-world note for Henry, and for being *so gracious about everything. Perhaps we can meet for a Scotch or three soon?*

My response was: silence.

On the day that I learned how to say 'I love you' to Ethan with a gestural manipulation of my fingers I decided to accept the transfer to France – with the proviso that the firm flew me over two weekends a month to see my son. They agreed. After being knocked to the mat, after staggering up again and fighting back, after finally ending the war so that, although you know there will still be skirmishes ahead, the big battle is behind you . . . what else can you do but try to vote with your feet, move on to the next phase of your ongoing story?

Or, in my case, pick up another story long since dropped – though, when Paris was first proposed to me, my first silent thought was:

Only this time without Isabelle.

Which was, in fact, my way of saying to myself:

Only with Isabelle.

*

I arrived in Paris in early winter. My firm had a company apartment it maintained in the 8ème, not far from its offices. The place was pretty much faceless, a bland, modestly sized two-bedroom spread, its decor very international-hotel-room nothing. And the 8ème was all business: offices and upscale shops and overpriced residences for the global monied brigade. A sense of faux luxury and complete transience. I didn't care. I quickly made the apartment my own. Books. A stereo. Jazz and classical CDs bought in quirky shops in the 5ème and 6ème. A few film posters framed and hung on the bare beige walls. A decent espresso maker. My typewriter and notebooks and pens spread out on the desk. And a new-found, serious need for cigarettes to stave off the melancholy within – and the fact that I was missing my son non-stop. I found the work running our Paris office – two junior lawyers, an administrative/secretarial staff of five – straightforward. No big cases like those in the States. One Kuwaiti oil man based in Paris and fighting extradition to New York on a tax fraud rap. Otherwise, clients with international residency issues. Clients with company taxation issues. Or copyright issues. Or trust and estate issues that crossed international boundaries. Or . . .

You get the point. Upscale paperwork. Nothing at all riveting about any of this. But I wasn't complaining. I was getting paid the same as I had been as a partner in New York for about half the workload and none of the professional high pressure. My colleagues were efficient, conscientious, largely pleased to be working in a well-run but not overly stressed corporate-law environment. I was given an 'international transfer allowance' from the firm.

I had put back on ten of the pounds I had lost during my recent cavalcade of calamity. I was not overweight. But not fit. And looking a tad chunky. I still had all my hair. My face, though lined around the eyes, wasn't as ravaged by all the recent personal chaos as it could have been. During my first week in the city I was dispatched to a doctor in the quartier for the required company check-up. He was a bored, well-dressed Lebanese man named Huthwa. He told me after doing all the usual things doctors do in a check-up that I was about four kilos over my ideal weight, that my lack of sleep was worrying (and he put me on a pill that did knock me out, but which he warned should only be taken in the short term, as I could develop a serious dependency), and that I was crazy to be smoking a packet of cigarettes a day.

'My advice is: stop immediately. Quit while you are ahead and all that. But if that is not possible, then give yourself a date no more than twelve months from now to end your dependency on them completely. You are not in bad shape otherwise. The sleep problem should be regularized by the pills. But you need to find a way off them eventually as well. Dependency is something we all have a considerable amount of in life.'

A Lebanese doctor as philosopher king. For his air of perpetual ennui, I sensed a fellow sufferer in Dr Huthwa. Just as I also found myself thinking: dependence on the romantic other is something I need to distance myself from for a while.

I also made a professional decision: I would become as quietly detached as possible from my work. By which I meant, when I was in my suit in the office I would be as rigorous as always. If I needed to take a client out to dinner or to travel down to Geneva or Lausanne on business (we handled a few lucrative tax exiles in Switzerland) I would do whatever was required and would do it well. And then I would go back to my apartment and change into my jeans and leather jacket and grab the Métro across the Seine and . . . float. The ambition impulse – that very American need to validate myself through the ethos of *achieve, achieve, achieve* – had left the room. It was parked in another part of my psyche for the immediate future. Though immaculate and consummately competent at the office, internally I was detached. No one saw this, no one knew my immense ambivalence, except myself. As soon as 19h00 arrived, I was gone. Home five minutes later on foot. Out the door in a non-suit identical minutes later. Out for an evening of floating. The usual time-filling preoccupations: cinema, jazz, bookshops, cafés. But I so feared more rejection at this juncture that I held off contacting Isabelle.

The despair hit in waves. I missed Ethan, but had my two-weekends-a-month travel deal with the firm: they even allowed me to use an apartment they maintained in the West 50s for my paternal visits. It was agreed between Gordy and the other side that Jessica would join us for the three days I was in town. Just as I had my secretary in Paris research the matter and find me, through contacts at the embassy, an expatriate American woman with a hearing-impaired daughter who was fluent in signing and gave me three hours of lessons a week. I found a French tutor with whom I had an hour's lesson a day, paid for by the firm. I kept busy on the self-improvement front. I filled my evenings on the cultural front. I continued to smoke a pack of Camel Filters a day. I walked incessantly. Several kilometers every night – especially when the pills didn't work and sleep wouldn't overtake me and I tried to read, tried to work, but instead found myself dressed and on the darkened streets, no direction in mind, adrift with insomnia and the need to perambulate.

One night, three weeks after my arrival, I jolted awake somewhere before three and decided: *take the risk, roll the emotional dice*. So I grabbed a piece of office stationery I had at home. I reached for a pen. I wrote:

Dear Isabelle
I am living in Paris. Have been here for almost a month. Here for at least five years. If you can bear to see me can I please buy you lunch? If you don't think that's possible, no need to send me any message. C'est entendu.
Je t'embrasse
Sam.
PS I am up late and will drop this off by hand in your mailbox – if, that is, the door code hasn't changed.

I put the letter into an envelope. I wrote *Isabelle* on the front. I grabbed my coat. Thirty minutes later I was standing in front of 9 rue Bernard Palissy. Empty streets. The occasional late-night drunk. New novels in the window of Les Éditions de Minuit – all in the same uniform covers as before. Her front door: the same scuffed dark brown door I had faced so many times in the past. All these years on I remembered the code: A8523. *Click*. It opened. Some things never change. Her mailbox was on the right. I stepped into the little courtyard. A light, frigid rain was now falling. I looked up in the direction of the top two windows on the right, just below the eaves. Her windows. Dark. Not that I expected to find her here . . . though, of course, that hope was there. The rain picked up velocity. I turned on my heel. I fled. I found a taxi on the rue de Rennes. I was home fifteen minutes later. I threw off my clothes. I fell back into bed. Sleep came to me this time – perhaps because, after all these weeks, I had finally gotten up the courage to contact her.

I was up three hours later. I packed a bag. After four weeks here I was returning to New York that evening. I collapsed on the plane, sleeping for six of the eight hours, thinking: I will be up half the night tonight. Still, it didn't matter. I was excited to see my son. When I reached the apartment on West 57th Street between 8th and 9th Avenues – another of my firm's early-nothing executive suites that was going to be my monthly New York base for the next five years – Jessica was already installed, with Ethan asleep in the spare bedroom.

Ethan was so lost to the world that when I crouched down by his bed and kissed his head he groaned a little, then turned over and showed me his back.

'That's some welcome,' Jessica said.

I found myself smiling, whispering:

'Does he know I am coming?'

'Yes,' she said. 'And I told him before he went to bed tonight that he could expect to find you in the big bed in the next room when he woke up. So don't be surprised if you get an early-morning wake-up call.'

'You explained all that to him by signing?'

'You don't have to whisper.'

That reality hit me hard. Even though it was the reality I had been living with ever since the meningitis rendered the world of sound beyond his comprehension. But the very fact that in my tired, jet-lagged state I had forgotten there was no need to whisper near his bed out of fear of rousing him from sleep . . . that knowledge pierced me. Seeing this, Jessica said:

'He really is a bright little guy and is making great progress.'

I kissed my son on the head and looked over at Jessica.

'Hello, Jessica!' I signed. 'You are doing such a great job with my son.'

She signed back:

'That's because he is such a smart boy. And he's started forming full sentences with his hands. Just yesterday when I showed him that photo of you he immediately signed back to me: "Daddy!"'

Maybe it was the lateness of the hour – almost five in the morning according to my body clock. Maybe it was the weeks of sleeplessness – and the fact that I was still struggling with the loss of family life with Ethan and still smarting from the way Phoebe had jettisoned me. Whatever the trigger, I felt tears running down my face. The ache of separation had been enormous.

I checked in on my son twice more before falling into bed. Four hours later I felt someone tugging my hair. My eyes opened and met Ethan's. Still looking half asleep, he was trying to make words but coming out with discordant sounds, then fluttering his hands and signing: 'Daddy!' Then: 'Welcome!' I grabbed him in my arms and held him close to me. He put his arms around my neck and mimicked me holding him. Then he took hold of his ears with both of his tiny hands and giggled.

'I've so missed you,' I signed him.

He smiled back. Did he understand what I just said? I signed further:

'Are you hungry?'

Now he nodded and pulled me by the hand out of bed and into the kitchen, pointing to where there was a box of cereal – Coco Pops – on a shelf. I brought it down. He signaled that he wanted the box. I handed it to him. He opened it and started eating the cereal with his hand. I signaled: 'Let me put it in a bowl for you.' He again looked puzzled, and held onto the box protectively, howling a little bit when I indicated he should part with it. I signaled for him to stop the crying. I explained through gestures that I was just going to have him pour the cereal into a bowl for himself, then took a carton of milk from the fridge and also showed him how to pour it on his cereal (stopping him before he drowned it). But when he reached into the bowl with his fingers there was an awkward moment when I signaled he had to go to the drawer next to the kitchen sink. He took out a spoon, then he sat down and ate the cereal.

Doing all this with my son I felt a stab of guilt – for missing so much of the day-to-day business of watching him grow and develop. And I could see that he very much wanted and needed his father with him. I was relieved that Rebecca had gotten him potty-trained and that Jessica had done amazing work to date on the signing front. His language was limited, but he could communicate certain basic things thanks to signing. Over the course of the weekend – as we went to the Central Park Zoo and the dinosaur hall at the Museum of Natural History (the T-Rex startled and delighted him) and went shopping for toys at FAO Schwarz (which, of course, he adored) – I felt a wave of delight that had been absent from my life for months, years. My own recent important relationships might now lie in tatters. I might stare in the mirror and see myself as the corporate suit I'd vowed never to become, on a career path I'd nevertheless simultaneously chased with a vengeance. I might wonder out loud at all the compromises and 'selling myself short' decisions I'd made. I might wonder why I hadn't spent six months crossing South-East Asia with a backpack or vanishing into Patagonia. Or trekking across my own country, which I'd promised for years I would do. Divorce had got in the way of that one. I made excuses for all the other missed opportunities. And now here I was, a man making more money than 99 percent of the inhabitants on this planet and finding that – after tax and alimony and child support and all of Ethan's educational needs – I had just about enough to maintain a pleasant lifestyle for myself. But I still owned nothing in the way of property, Rebecca having got the apartment that she originally bought (and on which I had paid the mortgage) outright in the divorce. I was, on the surface, a man of considerable metro-politan success with nothing to show for it, and unable to walk away from it all and start anew – because of the divorce ties that bind.

The weekend passed far too quickly. When Jessica showed up Sunday afternoon to take Ethan back to his mother's I found myself clutching my son so hard that he struggled against my grip and looked at me with bewilderment. Until he saw the tears on my face. His response: he took my ears in his little hands and pulled them, giggling, clearly wanting me to lose the emotion and laugh with him. Which I did. But I had to let him go. He accepted Jessica's hand as she walked him to his pushchair. As they left the apartment his hand shot up and he signed: 'Daddy!'

Afterwards I sat on the sofa for a very long time. Thinking: my son is the one antidote to the pervasive melancholy that shadows my days. And unlike with everyone else to whom I had looked for love and who had pulled back at certain critical moments, my love for Ethan would be, without question, an unconditional one. Unrestricted. Unlimited. Unequivocal.

A car service showed up half an hour later to take me to JFK and the flight back across the Atlantic. I made it to Kennedy ninety minutes before my flight. Air France was on time: an event of seismic significance. The return transatlantic haul is always propelled by tailwinds, getting you there an hour faster. I was at my apartment by ten, showered and suited and in my office thirty minutes later. My secretary, Monique, brought me coffee. She watched me shuffle through the morning mail, looking, looking. She smiled tightly when I reached a square white envelope, my name and address written in telltale black fountain-pen ink. She excused herself, giving me the space to open the envelope and pull out that simple white card I had encountered many times in the past. With the following message on it:

Dearest Samuel
I always sensed you would come to Paris for longer than a few weeks. I am pleased. The past is the past. And the present is . . .
we now occupy the same city. As such: no to lunch. Yes to you

visiting me. Would this Tuesday work? 17h00? You know the address. You know the code.

Je t'embrasse très, très fort.

Isabelle.

*

Isabelle knew nothing about my years of private French lessons. Because we'd had little communication since that moment of madness in Boston. She knew nothing of my life. Nor I of hers. I wrote to her in English because we'd always communicated that way, and I didn't want to immediately provoke questions in her mind about why I was now so far advanced in her language. Perhaps thereby provoking other advanced questions in her mind: had there been another Frenchwoman in my life since we were last together?

I got away from the office at 16h45. Paris traffic, rain lashing . . . the taxi's progress was slow. I had the driver drop me at the corner of Palissy and the rue de Rennes. I dashed down the street, my trench coat pulled tight around me, no time to put up my umbrella. I punched in the door code, charged down the corridor, through the courtyard toward *Escalier C.* Hitting her bell. My hair was now sodden. The buzzer sounded. I pushed the door open. Her voice from above:

'Hello . . .'

I climbed the steps rapidly. Thinking how I'd charged up them twelve years ago – and was now not exactly winded, but a little more sluggish than before. She was awaiting me in the doorway. She had changed. She had not changed. Her skin remained translucent. Fine lines around her eyes. Her red hair still flaming, albeit lightly streaked with gray. She was wearing – as before – a long flowing skirt and a black turtleneck against the winter afternoon. She had always been super-thin. Now she was of normal size – which made her seem less brittle. And she was wearing large circular horn-rimmed glasses. She reached for me.

'*Mon jeune homme.*'

'*Tu es si belle,*' I said, taking her in my arms.

She put a finger to my lips.

'Say no more,' she whispered, then enveloped me in a vast, deep kiss.

We were out of our clothes in moments.

'I am so fat,' she whispered to me as we fell onto her bed and she opened her legs and wrapped them around me.

'*Tu n'es pas grosse. Tu es magnifique.*'

'Liar. My wonderful, handsome liar.'

'I am hardly handsome.'

'Liar.'

She pulled herself atop me, sliding me deep within her. Letting out a vast groan. We moved slowly, with great deliberateness. Our eyes never once leaving each other – as if a gap of all these years meant that we wanted to hold this mutual gaze out of fear of losing it again. Her new shapeliness may have been a source of distress to her – a sign of time's inescapable forward momentum and the way our bodies lose the tight elasticity of youth. But I loved the feel of this less pinched, more voluptuous Isabelle coupled with the intensity of the regard in which she held me. We took our time. No need to cross the finish line in a rush. None of the frantic eroticism that characterized our initial encounters. Now there was quiet, deliberate fusion. And a sense, as she slumped against me afterwards, that the long absence had been, for both of us, an unexpressed agony . . . one which functioned like a dull ache that neither of us (in our very disparate lives on either side of the Atlantic) could ever acknowledge during all the years apart.

'How I missed us,' she said, her head pressed against my shoulder.

'*Moi aussi. Tu as été avec moi tout ce temps . . . même si—*'

She put a finger to my lips again.

'So, *mon jeune homme* has been perfecting his French in my absence.'

'*Parce que je voudrais te parler dans ta langue maternelle.*'

'And I am profoundly impressed by your progress. I presume it was also with the thought that perhaps you might return . . .'

'*Je n'ai jamais prévu le fait que j'allais vraiment revenir à Paris pour vivre ici . . .*'

'Your French is superb. And your teacher has done wonders with your accent. Far less American than before. But you know me to be a woman of certain routines, certain methodologies. As such, we meet here in the afternoons. And our language together is English.'

'But why can't we *mélange* the two?'

'Because I fell in love with you in English. I remain in love with you in English.'

'So no flexibility on the language or anything else?'

'Now that you are living in Paris . . . now that my personal circumstances are somewhat changed . . . maybe there can be flexibility on when we can see each other.'

'You're no longer married to Charles?'

'I will always be married to Charles until the day one of us dies. But he is now sixty-five. Not ancient . . . but he has had some serious health issues over the past three or four years. Diabetes. Hypertension. The side effects of an adult life playing high-level money games and never considering the benefits of exercise. Mind you, I managed to stay thin until recently courtesy of that very Parisian female diet of cigarettes and red wine.'

'I love your body the way it is now. I too am heavier.'

'There! You have admitted it. I am a fat woman.'

'Oh, please. You are—'

'What? *Shapely? Well rounded? Zaftig?* All those male synonyms designed to soften the fact that you, Madame, are larger than you once were.'

'You've forgotten *Rubenesque . . .*'

She lightly slapped me across the hand, like a teacher censoring mischievous behavior.

'*T'es atroce.*'

'*Donc, on parle en français!*'

'Absolutely not. But we will open that wine you brought. And smoke a cigarette. Unless of course you have sworn off them.'

'I did that during my marriage. Since my divorce I am back on them with a vengeance.'

'Bravo. I approve. Even if, after decades of smoking, I wonder when the gods will decide: you have got away with this for far too long. The day of reckoning is now nigh.'

'I had a grandmother who smoked two packs a day and lived well into her eighties. Mind you, she prided herself on being a mean Baptist bitch.'

'And not that I know about such things, but I presume that being a Baptist and a bitch aren't automatically synonymous?'

'It was when it came to Granny and her church cronies.'

'I should still quit,' she said.

'Then quit.'

'But I cannot envisage a life without cigarettes. They are my ballast amidst the instability of everything else.'

'Have things been bad?'

'Get the wine and cigarettes, my love, and we'll trade war stories. By the way, there is a hanger in the wardrobe if you want to ensure your very beautiful suit falls out so you can head off to your next appointment uncreased.'

'I don't have a next appointment – but I will take you up on the offer of a hanger.'

I got out of bed, opened the wardrobe, noted how few clothes Isabelle continued to store here. I found a hanger. I placed it on a chair, then picked up my trousers, meticulously lined up the two legs, placed them over the hanger's wooden crossbar, and then hung my dress shirt followed by my jacket on its main frame. I picked up my tie, folded it neatly and stored it in the inside breast pocket. Then I placed my lawyerly uniform into the wardrobe.

'Most impressive,' Isabelle said. 'If all else fails you will have a remarkable career ahead of you as a valet.'

'Very funny. Is the corkscrew in the same place?'

'Nothing changes here – except the fact that I have gotten progressively messier with extended age.'

'I hadn't noticed,' I said.

'Liar.'

Actually that was the truth. I had walked in. We'd fallen into each other's arms. Into bed. Into the throes of quiet, profound passion. So it was only now that I saw the extent of Isabelle's new-found sense of disorder. She had always been messy. But now there were clothes strewn everywhere, three brimming ashtrays, even more alpine piles of paper and manuscripts and new additions to her library, dishes and a coffee pot needing soapy attention in the sink . . .

'I remember one of the few times – in fact the only time you slept here – and how self-righteous and furious I became at you for daring to tidy up my chaos. I was most unfair – and I knew you decided then and there that's why you could never imagine *un domicile conjugal* with me.'

'That wasn't the reason I didn't take up your offer to move in together in New York with Émilie.'

I returned to the bed with wine, glasses, cigarettes.

'What was the reason? Love for your future lawyer wife?'

'That was part of it. Fear too.'

Isabelle took this admission quietly.

'I understand that concept. So often we walk away from potentially wonderful things out of fear of getting hurt. I too have been guilty of that with you. In fact, I started that trend between us.'

'Looking at it retrospectively, I knew I was walking into a mistake.'

'"Life can only be understood backwards but it must be lived forwards." – Kierkegaard. Was it that bad between you?'

I extracted the cork from the wine. I poured out two glasses and said:

'If I start telling you about it all it could take a little time.'

'I want to know as much as you want to tell me.'

We lit up cigarettes. I started talking. She only interrupted me when I came to something truly terrible in the story. Ethan's meningitis and subsequent deafness and Rebecca's descent into alcoholism totally shocked her – but in a very hushed, Isabelle way. When I finished she put her arms around me and stared into my eyes for a very long time.

'When you walked in here tonight my first thought was: beautiful suit, air of success, and a man consumed by sadness. My Samuel: depressed. Even the way we made love, it was beautiful, but it was also underscored by a sense, for me, that you are so lonely, so desperate for comfort. Now I know why. And I just want to say: what a horrible series of adversities you've had to face.'

'Thank you for not using that desperately American word "challenges".'

'That is indeed a terrible word. But what you've had to cope with – actual tragedy.'

'Ethan is not tragic. The truth is, I've never completely known what I want. With the exception of you.'

'I wouldn't be too certain of that – otherwise you would have whisked me and Émilie off to New York.'

'But my great worry was, had I definitively said yes, had I thrown Rebecca overboard for you, I truly didn't know if you would actually have come.'

A long silence. Isabelle sipped her wine. Then she said:

'I don't know the answer to that question.'

'Maybe my fear of you changing your mind resulted from the way you applied certain absolute rules to all of this. Which, of course, I understood and respected.'

'Perhaps you understand me better than I understand myself. Perhaps I might have balked at bringing myself and Émilie to New York, considering just how profoundly French I am and how I very much wanted Émilie to be brought up in the system here.'

'And how is Émilie?' I asked, noting to myself that she had only mentioned her in passing this evening.

'My twelve-year-old daughter has her dark moments.'

'How dark?'

'That's a story I will tell you another time. One long terrible tale is enough for both of us to absorb this first afternoon back together. For now she is finding her way without too much drama at an excellent lycée. Which is fantastic. But she is a fragile soul. And I fear that one small but telling problem could send her back into the vortex.'

Now it was my turn to take her hand. Now it was her turn to turn away.

She whispered:

'I don't want to come back to this subject for a while. Yes, I will talk about Émilie. What is going on with her at school, her few friends, what she's reading and watching in the cinema: the simple, normal things I'll discuss. But the dark recesses of her mania – if I bring it up again it will be because it has raised its head again and has become insufferable.'

'I'm so sorry.'

'As I am for you.'

'When I last saw you, you told me that you loved me.'

'Indeed I did,' she said. 'As I still do.'

'As I do you.'

We caught each other's eye for the briefest of complicit moments, then looked away. Oh how we knew . . . and oh how scared we were of that knowledge. I pulled her toward me. I kissed her deeply.

'I am so glad I am here. Now. With you.'

'As I am with you. And now . . . now I must get dressed and go home.'

*

We began to see each other three times a week. The usual *cinq à sept* rules. I didn't push them. I didn't ask for greater flexibility. Because given what she had already intimated, it would eventually arrive. For several months we would have the Monday, Wednesday, Thursday trysts – unless I was out of town or business impinged on our time together. This was the big change in the dynamic between us – the fact that now my professional schedule dictated so much. Émilie was at the lycée until 5 p.m. most days and had many after-school activities, not to mention a housekeeper who was there to cook something for her or play older-sister surrogate until Isabelle came home.

'Émilie is at that age where she considers Maman to be some sort of psychic jailer, or at best an embarrassing nuisance. Especially as she suffers from clinical depression, which is being treated by mild pharmacology and regular sessions with a very good therapist. So she is very happy not to have me waiting for her at home three days a week. Just as she would begin to complain of neglect if I was not home right after *dix-neuf heures*. And she is very much a daddy's girl – she adores her father and currently prefers his company to my own. The fact that Charles is somewhat housebound now – it suits her perfectly. Not that she wants to be around him all the time either. But the fact that he is adjacent, in a nearby room . . . that is comforting for her. And we are both happy to do anything within reason that comforts Émilie.'

Isabelle wanted to know everything about Ethan's developmental progress – how he was expanding his repertoire of sign language, the manner in which he constructed relationships with others, would we dare to find him a kindergarten with non-deaf children, and when would he visit Paris? I had a near-daily phone call with Jessica. Gordy being Gordy, he pulled off the coup of getting me an extra four days' custody per month and convinced the younger partners (i.e. those below the age of fifty-five) to show humanity and allow me to spend two weekends and one full week per month in New York with my son – as well as pay for the flights and accommodation. There was, of course, a trade-off: I was expected to be a high-level consultant and active participant in all the big trusts and estates cases the firm was now handling in record numbers.

Meanwhile those days every month with Ethan were the most keenly awaited events in my calendar. According to Jessica, he would count the days until my next visit. 'Daddy's here!' was his greeting to me when he woke early on those Saturday mornings twice a month at the company apartment, when he came into the bedroom to discover that I had arrived late the previous night while he was sleeping. I continued with the twice-weekly signing tutorials in Paris – so my own ability to communicate with Ethan continued to improve. As Jessica told me:

'I am intent on treating him as normally as possible. He will start learning to read at five like any other child, and math will follow. The big challenge will be socialization. Getting him to play with other children. I have been on to Rebecca about this. Finding kids his own age he can play with. She is still very bound up with things like AA and her church, Our Lady of Pompeii, which does have an elementary school attached to it and is a mixture of nuns and lay staff. According to her, the nuns would love to have Ethan among them but fear how well he would integrate with the other children. I have asked her to see if we could make an appointment with Sr Moreno – the boss of the school.'

'Surely there are other elementary schools around which he could attend with you as his shadow?'

'I will certainly start as his shadow, but will train someone else to take over. And I will continue to do all the after-school tutoring and one Friday night a month when you come in from Paris.'

I tried to communicate with Rebecca about the school issue. I faxed her, suggesting that we have a sit-down conversation about the whole subject and research it all together and then decide on the best options for Ethan in the city. Especially as surely we both wanted to integrate Ethan with other non-deaf children as quickly as possible.

Rebecca's answer to my fax was: silence.

Back in Paris, Isabelle was outraged by my ex's lack of dialogue with me over our son's educational future.

'You Americans are absurd when it comes to divorce. Fidelity is breached and it doesn't matter that your ex was drinking herself into a stupor before this. You slept with someone else and you must be made to pay permanently for your transgression against her. And now that she has found her faith, now that she is all pious and Catholic, she can play the self-righteous card against you. Even though you are covering all of Ethan's costs and being the more committed parent.'

This conversation took place over dinner – yes we were eating out together (!) – at a small, *branché* Japanese restaurant opposite 9 rue Bernard Palissy. I had just returned from New York. As promised, I brought back photos (developed at a twenty-four-hour pharmacy right before I left) as Isabelle was now insisting that I take a new set of Ethan every time I visited him so she could monitor his development. She also wanted to know exactly what preschool books Jessica was using, and even made a trip down the boulevard Saint-Germain to the American University in Paris to use their library and research elementary schools in New York. She came back to me with five suggestions, including contact details and the name of the head teacher. She was also furious when Rebecca blocked the idea of Ethan spending a month with me in Paris that coming summer, saying that this was more angry revenge on her part.

'She has lost you. She has lost her career. She is not happy. And she is turning all her rage on you – because that is how mediocre people operate. And she is using your son and money as the only two weapons she can wield against you. It is pathetic.'

This was one of those moments – over dinner, her fingers touching mine to make a point, to reassure – when I found myself thinking: we truly are a couple. Her protectiveness toward me, her interest in Ethan, her desire for me to teach her basic signing so she could communicate with him in a basic way when he finally came to Paris . . . it was all wonderful to see. But she had her own roadblocks too. I asked on several early occasions when I could meet Émilie. She was quietly adamant that, because of her fragility and her attachment to her father, she could not be introduced to me.

'Even if I told her that you were just my friend, she would be suspicious. And she might turn angry and feel alienated. Best to leave it as it is for the moment.'

I also suggested on several occasions that Isabelle join me for one of my weekends in New York. But she was very reluctant to leave Paris even for a few days out of fear that Émilie might take a turn toward the dark side in her absence. I quietly tried to argue that, in the six months since we'd been back together, her daughter had shown no signs of strain. And it would be a fantastic opportunity for Isabelle to meet Ethan and begin to establish a rapport with him. But she was adamant about staying in Paris.

'I know it sounds lame and pathetic and even provincial . . . but I am not someone who is happy traveling. I have claustrophobia in planes. I can just about deal with an hour locked up in that pressurized tube. Nothing beyond that. And I feel out of control. Which I am. The only reason I agreed to the Boston trip was the fanciful idea that I might be able to meet up with you. But I needed far too many Valium to get through both ways across the Atlantic. And I've not been on many flights since.'

'But if I came with you . . . if I was seated right next to you . . .'

'It won't work. I tried once more with Charles for a holiday to Cape Town five years ago. When we reached the airport here in Paris I had a panic attack. So bad that Charles had to get medical help for me. I ended up in the infirmary at the airport. Charles – who had a business meeting in Cape Town – wanted to cancel the entire trip. But I insisted he go . . . and spend the remaining ten days we'd planned together at the luxury hotel he'd booked near the Cape of Good Hope. Of course I knew that he flew his mistress of the moment down two days later. Could I blame him? So if you want to fly your mistress to New York in place of me . . .'

'I am no longer married, so I have no mistress. And I have no other woman in my life because I am with you.'

'You should have someone else – because I am mentally so unreliable.'

'Because you can't get on a transatlantic flight . . .?'

'Because I am a woman in serious midlife, who has come to the same studio apartment every day for almost twenty-five years, and who has worked quietly on my translations, stayed married to the same quiet, decent man, and spent quiet, decent weekends at the same family retreat in Normandy, a month a year at my brother-in-law's spread in the Var, and the usual nights out at the cinema, the concert hall, the opera. I have never wanted materially for anything. I have a wonderful daughter who I am afraid will go off the deep end and destroy our lives in the process. I have you – and that makes me deeply happy. So why can I never get beyond the thought that I have short-changed myself in life? That I have stood still when I should have had a far more adventurous existence. Too much quiet desperation . . . of which I am the complete architect.'

I slid my fingers through hers.

'I myself have these thoughts regularly. But until Ethan is eighteen I am financially tethered to his mother. Not that I am complaining. But if I were to say to you, let's uproot everything and move to Tahiti—'

'I would say no. Not just because I am certain that the tropics become endlessly boring – especially the Francophone tropics – but especially because of Émilie. But even if Émilie was a grown-up and completely stable, self-reliant, totally independent . . . I would still say no.'

'Why?'

'Because at my advanced age I now finally know a few things about myself. I am a coward—'

'Oh please . . .'

'It is the absolute truth. I play safe all the time. I have restricted myself completely. Am I unhappy about this? Should I have been to sixty countries by now like a few intrepid souls I know? Honestly, I am limited. I accept that. My life has turned out this way – all through my own choice. Do I sound melancholic? Of course. Am I melancholic by choice? I sense so. Is that melancholy rooted in my inadequacy? No doubt. Am I going to do anything to change that? Outside of my love for you . . . no.'

But she had now articulated for me what I'd quietly known all along: my love for her was underscored by the knowledge that she would never really leave Paris. Her inability to get on a long-distance flight was also telling. Once I returned to New York, then what? And yet . . . and yet . . . we were now together three nights a week. Our desire for each other remained vast. We never knew a minute of conversational boredom together. She pushed books on me. And films. As I pushed jazz on her.

And at the end of these magical hours together she went home to her infirm husband and fragile daughter. Even if Charles died tomorrow I doubted if she'd suddenly agree to live with me. Because this was the reality we had constructed for each other. Even though it was Isabelle who initially imposed all the rules, I was as complicit in its construction as she was. As well as going along with it, I now understood that I had used it as my strange ideal: the love that wasn't a marriage or another form of cohabitation. A connection as deep and profound as any I had experienced, yet also on another, equal level . . . transitory. Yes, we were a couple of sorts now: who, like just about everyone out there, had suffered and were on a first-name basis with the gods of Disappointment and Heartache. Yes, that added to the acuteness of our passion – that desperate need to connect and be lost within one another. And yet we also got to walk away from it. We were now, at last, joined in the same city. We had not just our afternoons, but a few nights as well. We had a certain hard-won stability.

Time moved forward and the stability held. Winter became summer. I joined Ethan in the States, renting a house on the

Maine coast for a month. I was back in Paris right after my son started kindergarten at the Little Red School House in Greenwich Village. (His mother had given up her idea of parochial school when the nun-in-chief at Our Lady of Pompeii finally informed her that 'I do feel we cannot serve Little Ethan's special needs here.') He had a full-time shadow – a graduate student in education at Columbia named Clara Flouton. His progress in this normal educational environment was not a straightforward one. He had a tantrum the first week. He smashed up a classmate's building blocks out of frustration. We (myself, Clara and his mother) were cautioned on two occasions by the head teacher that, as important as it was to the school to have a student like Ethan among them, if he continued to lash out he would not be able to stay much longer.

Rebecca phoned me and suggested a round-table meeting with Jessica (who was still tutoring Ethan after school) and Clara at her apartment. Rebecca had lost considerable weight – not that she was ever chunky – and was going gray. She wore a gray wool blouse, a somewhat darker gray wool skirt. She had the pinched severity of a premature widow in some particularly frigid corner of New England. But she ran the meeting well – and it was agreed at the end that Ethan join us. He looked around at the four people who were responsible for his future and ran and buried his head in my lap, grabbing his mother's hand simultaneously. I held him as Jessica and Clara signed rapidly at him that if he wanted to stay at this school he had to be a very good boy. Ethan began to sob. I held him, then picked him up and brought him over to his mother, signing to him that we both loved him and would be always united for him. He accepted his mother's open arms. The breach between us was hardly going to be repaired in one of those redemptive moments (replete with the requisite hugging and growth) so beloved of Hollywood. When the meeting ended Ethan insisted that I put him to bed. He found his favorite book of the moment – *Where the Wild Things Are* – and with Jessica in attendance and casting a sharp, critical eye on my technique, I managed to do an improvised signing of Maurice Sendak's text that Ethan adored. Rebecca stuck her head in as I read the last pages, which Ethan turned whenever I tapped the book.

'Well done,' she said as I finished, her tone neither harsh nor reconciliatory.

'Thank you,' I said.

She just nodded and departed the room. Which was my cue to leave.

Back in Paris, life continued to follow a reasonable rhythm. I had my work. Isabelle had her work. Without a word of explanation ever spoken between us, Monique took charge of my schedule to ensure that the majority of my *cinq à sept* engagements could be met. I frequently did professional dinners afterwards. Isabelle shied away from being my *compagne* for these events, rightfully noting that law and finance were small worlds and, out of respect for Charles, she could not be seen playing the role of wife to me. Going to the opera or a concert at the Théâtre des Champs-Élysées was less tricky – even though we did frequently run into certain of her friends and acquaintances. I was always intro-duced as 'my American lawyer friend Samuel', the very phrasing of this statement meant to indicate the *amitié* between us and maintain a veneer of propriety – though as Isabelle noted, they all knew that there must be some sort of other story going on between us.

'So let me get all this social nuance straight,' I said. 'You can be seen with your lover at a performance of *Norma*. But you cannot accompany him to a business dinner because that would indicate serious intent between us?'

'The problem is I would be there with the spouses of your colleagues. I would be assuming the role of the spouse. Impossible, given Charles's standing here – even in retirement.'

Time propelled onwards. Émilie was in rigorous academic training for *le bac*, the result of which determined the future course of your educational life. I still hadn't met her – and didn't push the point. I continued to constantly fly the Atlantic to see my son. Ethan was starting to adjust reasonably to school. He even had a friend – a classmate named Pam Casper, who, without knowing a thing about signing, had worked out how to communicate by pointing and making him read her lips (a new skill that Clara and Jessica were adding to the signing). I maintained my three nights a week with Isabelle. I expanded our business base at the Paris office – and my bottom-line, profit-obsessed partners back in New York were pleased with the upward tick in corporate gain. I received a substantial bonus that year. I banked it, deciding that, as I was paying no rent right now, why buy something in Paris, especially as Ethan's immediate destiny would determine where I ended up next?

There are moments in life – rare ones – where you find yourself free of high drama. Or serious grief. Or the terrible *merde* of others. The next three or so years were a stretch of time when all the cards dealt in my direction were playable ones. Ditto for Isabelle. It was the late 1990s. The Cold War was eight years over. Clinton was in the White House. His sexual stupidities aside – 'Why didn't he find himself a more mature mistress and not some inexperienced adolescent?' was Isabelle's trenchant comment when the insane impeachment proceedings were launched against him – it was a moment of peace and plenty.

One Monday morning I arrived at our office to discover a faxed directive from the firm's 'chief of communications' back in New York, directing us to 'transition' to doing the majority of 'non-binding' correspondence by email. In addition to being told we should now adapt to this newfangled 'online' world, he also informed us that he wanted all partners and associates to have a mobile phone by the end of the year. I did as demanded – even though the cellphone was still a new concept in Paris. Isabelle was dismissive of all electronic communication, saying it was a fad that would pass us by; that the actual letter would never vanish. The thought that we could carry an apparatus that would allow us to be contactable at all times filled her with horror. But within a year she too was online and had a simple black flip phone – specifically because Émilie wanted one. And Émilie – having taken two years off to knock around the world on Daddy's dime and try to write a novel about her adventures in Nepal, Thailand, Cambodia, Laos, Vietnam and nine months as a jillaroo on a cattle station in North Queensland – was now in her final year at university. She had done very well in the bac, so she was studying politics at Sciences Po. We'd finally met – a mere ten years after my move to Paris. Isabelle had arranged seats for a celebrated dance company from Germany – Pina Bausch – at the Théâtre du Châtelet. I was going to be introduced simply as 'Maman's friend'. I had seen many photographs of Émilie over the years.

I was thrown by the discovery that I was looking at a twenty-something version of Isabelle – with the same flaming red hair and intensity and throwaway beauty that never called attention to itself. We arranged to meet for a drink before the performance, with dinner to follow. Isabelle was delayed by traffic. Émilie looked me over with care as I approached her in the café, first addressing me in English. Once I established my fluency in French she was all talk, asking me at length if I thought the Republicans had a chance to recapture the White House in 2000 and would Saddam Hussein remain a neutered autocrat in Iraq or would his territorial ambitions grow again? She told me she was about to start an intensive Arabic course this summer and that she was now seriously thinking about a future in the diplomatic corps – 'though Papa has told me that if I want to go into international finance he would pave the way. Being Maman's "friend", you must know Papa?'

'Not at all. We travel in different circles.'

Émilie smiled tightly. And changed the subject. Isabelle arrived. I observed the mother/daughter dynamic. Isabelle was a little too attentive and clearly overprotective, fussing over Émilie dressing so lightly on an evening that had turned cold and asking her if the heating in her studio flat off the rue Mouffetard had been fixed.

'I am certain that Monsieur would prefer if we weren't dealing in such banalities right now.'

'Monsieur Sam is a parent as well,' Isabelle said. 'And as you will discover when you are a parent—'

'I will never be a parent,' Émilie said, sounding definitive and more than a bit peeved at her mother's comment.

'I said that as well once upon a time . . . when my hair wasn't so gray and I was as lithe as you are.'

My lawyerly training – always consider any public statement for its attendant import – stopped me from saying something spousal and reassuring like 'You are still lithe,' though that wasn't the truth. Like myself, Isabelle was now fuller. Not heavy, but not 'lithe'. And gray. And starting to get lined. And still smoking two cigarettes an hour. She would, in bed, tease me about the small paunch I'd developed – even though I was trying to maintain a modicum of cardiovascular competence and physical shape with a morning workout five days a week. Isabelle had also mocked this new fitness regime:

'That is your American side emerging again: the belief you can disrupt *la forza del destino* and the onslaught of time.'

'Haven't you worked out,' I said, running my index finger up from the small of her back, my lips periodically touching the nape of her neck, 'that we Americans love the illusion of control, the belief that "We can beat this death thing"?'

'It's one of the more exhausting aspects of your culture: the way you think you can fix so much.'

'Myself included?'

'There's just a shadow of that there. France has otherwise corrupted you.'

I'd put my hands into her ever-luxuriant hair, my teeth caressing her neck – something that she always reacted to with extreme pleasure.

'You've corrupted me,' I said.

But now, when Isabelle acknowledged that 'I said that as well once upon a time . . . when my hair wasn't so gray and I was as thin as you are,' did Émilie notice how I rolled my eyes – thereby indicating in an unspoken way that this was hardly the first time I had heard her mother turn rueful about her increasing shapeliness and the silver streaks in the once electric red hair? Which made it pretty damn obvious that I was a 'friend' with a certain intimate knowledge? To her credit, Émilie said nothing – and Isabelle, having seen me make that amused gesture after her comment, probably sensed that the proverbial cat was out of the proverbial bag. I changed the subject, bringing up the thought that Chirac might go down as a far more accomplished master of French centrism and stability than previously suspected. Émilie attacked my point of view on the spot, saying:

'I never knew my mother was seeing an American conservative.'

'I admit to the American part of that description, not the rest.'

We thereafter had a smart, sharp political exchange – not angry or heavily doctrinal, but punchy and informed. I was impressed. Many hours later, after the edgy modern dance and the rather classic dinner, as I was getting Isabelle and her daughter into a taxi, I gave Émilie the requisite kiss on each cheek. During which she whispered to me:

'I approve of you.'

When I recounted this to her mother two days later in bed, it was Isabelle's turn to roll her eyes and tell me:

'About three or four years ago she worked out that Charles and I both have other rooms in our lives. She is of the age now where she is beginning to understand that the intimate life is always complex, if not complicated.'

I again extended my tenure at the Paris office without much argument from my fellow partners. I continued to make our one European outpost profitable. I ran a lean operation, though one where I insisted on reasonable pay rises for our seven employees every two or so years. I was rewarded for such success and prudence with a substantial bonus every December, which continued to be deposited in my bank account in New York. My banker – on my monthly visits to the city – called me in and asked me what I was planning to do with these accumulating funds.

'Buy a house for myself and Ethan to live in when that moment arises.' Yes, I was always plotting his escape from his mother – even though I did try to be absolutely scrupulous when it came to anything I had to say to Ethan about Rebecca. But he was now crowding twelve and he himself began to shyly mention, on occasion, the complexities of life with Mom. Like her rigid Catholic piety (not that he signed me that word). And the way she insisted that he go to church with her every Sunday – an experience he found something akin to the Seventh Circle of Hell (not that he referenced Dante either). He liked his mom when she dropped that inflexible part of herself and was engaged and happy to be with him; when her demons weren't running the show.

Or at least, that was my take on all Ethan reported to me.

As befitted this new emerging age of digital communication, Ethan now had a laptop – and was shown by Jessica how to plug the phone cord into the socket on the wall and do dial-up and then write an email to Dad in Paris – which his father could then respond to as soon as he too was online. Ethan was now a tall, rangy boy, fluent in signing, well versed in lip-reading, and increasingly confident with the written word. When I was on the other side of the pond he would write me one email every morning (arriving in my early afternoon), one again at night (which would be awaiting me when I woke up the next day). The previous summer – after years of legal back and forth – Rebecca had finally relented and agreed that he could spend mid-July to mid-August with me in Paris. I brought Clara over as his minder for the first fortnight as I was working until our office (and most of Paris itself) closed down for the last month of summer.

One of the many intriguing aspects of Ethan's deafness was how it made him hyper-aware on so many other levels. Such as: even though he couldn't hear anyone's voice, although the world was, on one level, permanently silenced for him, once in Paris he wasn't thrown by the fact that everything was in another language (though the discovery that he couldn't read French-speaking lips was disconcerting). He was wide-eyed during that first visit to Paris. I could see him adjusting to the epic nature of the place, its sweep and grandeur, its distance and its neighborhood intimacy. He got to know the boulangerie where we bought the pain au chocolat he loved every morning. He was fascinated by the Métro. He went on a boat trip down the Seine with Isabelle while I worked – and reported to me thereafter that 'Isabelle is very nice'. But he truly adored Émilie, who took him out to see the marionettes in the Jardin du Luxembourg and also actually did take him up the Eiffel Tower and to the zoo in the Bois de Boulogne – all those touristic Parisian things that I had always sidestepped but which meant everything to my twelve-year-old son.

'Can I live here?' he asked when I had to bring him back to New York at the end of the summer.

'Would you like that?'

'I'd like us to live together . . . with Mom.'

I wasn't surprised or thrown by this statement. Just saddened by it. Because I knew that I was going to disappoint my son by informing him that such a possibility was not going to happen; that though he would always have a mother and a father who cared passionately about him, his parents were never going to get back together again. When I finally did explain that to him – that, alas, there was no chance of a reconciliation between us – he responded:

'Maybe you and Mom will fall in love again.'

I chose my next words with care.

'That is a lovely idea, Ethan, but usually that is not what happens when people decide it is better to live apart. Still, we have a nice situation now. And look at how brilliantly you are doing in school. Clara and Jessica think you are ace.'

'But Mom's sometimes sad.'

'That's not your fault, Ethan. If someone else is sad it is their responsibility to make things better for themselves. Even if the situation is a difficult one.'

'But I want a happy ending, Dad.'

I could only think: don't we all?

But this was not the moment for irony. Instead I said:

'You and I are happy together, Ethan.'

'Will that ever change? Will the happiness go away?'

'Between you and me? Never.'

'But happiness can go away, can't it?'

I decided not to sweeten the pill.

'Yes it can,' I said.

And a few months later happiness did just that.

Six

WHEN THINGS FALL apart, the center truly does not hold. Life can have an absolute veneer of relative stability. Of calm assuredness. Smooth sailing and all that. And then something goes seriously askew, the veneer is shown to be eggshell thin, and all comes asunder with a speed that leaves you thinking: there are no certainties in life. Only the desperate music of happenstance.

The year 2001 dawned in Paris to a light dusting of snow. Ethan had returned to New York two days before, having spent Christmas with me. It was the first time he had flown solo on a flight, though I'd arranged through Air France that he'd be accompanied on and off the plane by a member of their staff. Ethan was almost thirteen and had informed me that he wanted to do a transatlantic voyage solo. I'd asked Clara and Jessica for their counsel. They both felt he was ready. And his mother – by email – also expressed no objections. I'd collected him at Charles de Gaulle on 22 December; I saw him off eight days later, watching as an airline employee (who'd been briefed about Ethan's deafness) put an 'unaccompanied minor' packet around his neck after we'd checked in his bag. Then we'd all walked to the security gates, Ethan's hand tight in mine.

'Two weeks?' he asked, his signing so fluent, so second nature to him. Just like his lip-reading. Despite many medical consultations and one hospital intervention three years earlier – when one ENT surgeon held out the slight possibility that a newfangled hearing device in his inner-ear canal might allow him to begin to discern sounds (the procedure proved singularly unsuccessful) – there was clearly no hope that Ethan would ever have a chance of experiencing the world of sound like the rest of us. After the surgery I'd had to explain to my son that the procedure had not yielded the result that we'd all hoped for; that his situation would never change; but that he was nonetheless doing brilliantly and would continue to live an amazing life.

But I am closed off from so much, he wrote later in an email to me. *No music. No words or sounds in a movie, from you and Mom, from everyone else in the world. And everyone tells me how brave and amazing I am – but I am so alone in all this. And I know I will be even more so as I get older.*

'You will always have me,' I said to him during a text conversation the next day.

'Not always.'

'For a long time to come.'

'Mom says everything's fragile.'

'Mom has a bleak way of looking at things.'

'That's why she's so happy being a Catholic.'

I found myself laughing and marveling at how much my son had worked out the nuances of those closest to him.

This year, over Christmas, Isabelle insisted on taking Ethan to see *The Nutcracker* at the Théâtre des Champs-Élysées. When he asked me to ask Isabelle how he would understand it without the music, Isabelle spoke to him in English:

'I will try to tap the Tchaikovsky score in your hand as we watch it.'

306

Which is exactly what she did. When she brought him back to my apartment late that evening – she'd decided that this was going to be her night out alone with Ethan – my son told me: 'I followed the music perfectly thanks to Isabelle.'

Émilie had spent Christmas with her parents in Normandy. She had been twice rejected for the diplomatic corps. Since finishing at Sciences Po she'd been hooked up with a would-be writer named Eric de Saint-Bris and she was beyond smitten with him. Émilie's depressive vulnerability came to the fore on many occasions and it turned out that Eric was not the gem she thought he was. With the urging of her mother and her shrink she'd finally broken things off with the bum a few days before Christmas – after he'd turned on her in a booze- and coke-filled rage at a Christmas party and called her a variety of horrible names and actually attempted to slap her. Fortunately, several people had stepped in and Émilie ran home to the family apartment, woke Isabelle and Charles and sought shelter with them for several days. Her parents counseled staying on with Papa at the family retreat after Christmas to recuperate from all the unfortunate drama that this rotten faux scribe had brought down upon her. But she assured them that a few days in the snow-crusted terrain around Talloires with some close university friends would be the perfect way to start the New Year. Her parents, with reluctance, watched her set off back to Paris on December 27, before heading on to the high terrain of eastern France.

She never got there, having been contacted again by Eric while passing through Paris. He begged her to give him another chance. He told her she was the love of his life, that he was so repentant for his vile past deeds toward her. Being vulnerable and needy and depressive, she bought into his bullshit. And on New Year's Day I received a phone call at my apartment just after dawn. Isabelle sounded as though she was on the verge of delirium. During a drunken argument with her toxic boyfriend the previous night while crossing the Pont Neuf, the shit had lashed out at Émilie. She became so hysterical that she suddenly ran from him and threw herself off the bridge. The fall was twenty meters. She landed with a thud on the edge of the river bank, then rolled into the water and started to be swept down the Seine. The gods were with her. A police launch, patrolling the river on this most crazed of nights, was moored nearby. One of the cops dived into the Seine and managed to stop her from going under in the rush of the river. His colleagues winched them both back onto the launch and an already summoned ambulance on the bank whisked her off to the nearest hospital, where they also treated the extraordinarily brave policeman for hypothermia.

I listened to all this with early-morning horror. Especially when Isabelle informed me that Émilie had landed on her back, crushing two vertebrae in her spine and taking a considerable amount of water into her lungs.

'She may be paralyzed. She may have brain damage!' she shrieked into the phone.

I asked for the name of the hospital.

'No, no, no – you can't be seen here with me.'

'Fuck that. I'm coming.'

'Charles is here. And he is falling apart.'

'Isabelle, please let me help in some way—'

Click. The phone went dead.

Though I phoned and texted her just about every hour on the hour, I heard nothing further from her for more than thirty-six hours. I knew from Isabelle's silence that, having informed me of the monstrous business that had befallen her daughter, she was letting me know: don't crowd me as I deal with this nightmare. But as we entered the third morning of silence I began to think: how are we a couple if she shuts me out at a moment as critical as this one?

Then I got a text: *This has turned from bad to diabolical. I will explain later.*

No further message.

I made a mistake. I called right back and got her voicemail. Told her that we needed to speak; that I was desperate to know what was going on; that I was here to help . . . *and please, please, let me be here for you.*

I was stressed. I was fearful. I was not sleeping. I was angry at being shut out of her life. I should have stepped back, counted to ten. But I also felt pushed away. Marginalized. It is not pretty to acknowledge such feelings. We all want to be super-altruistic at a nightmarish moment for someone with whom we share a life. But did I ever really share a life with Isabelle? Was it an illusion with which I was engaged? Was she now letting me know: when it comes to family, *my family*, you are permanently on the outside of all this?

In the wake of that over-needy message I sent a subsequent text: *Apologies. Worried for you, for Émilie. I love you.*

Her response:

Silence.

Until five days later. January 8, 2001. A text:

I am in a position to see you now. BP tomorrow? 17h00?

I texted back:

I will be there. I love you.

Her reply:

No reply.

I showed up at the studio on time. Not a minute late. Door code. The quick traverse across the courtyard. Her buzzer. The requisite electronic *brzzz* of the door opening. A thought struck me: it was many years since I'd moved to Paris. My French was pretty damn fluent – albeit with an American accent. And Isabelle still would converse with me only in English. And she had never given me a key to the apartment. Just as she would never sleep at mine and had steadfastly refused all offers of a holiday together away from Paris ever since I'd started calling this city home.

We see what we want to see in life. Especially with those with whom we are allegedly creating a future. Until the future is no longer a tenable construct. At which point we acknowledge that we have been living in a realm outside of evident verities. That ever-anguished realm called hope.

I mounted the many stairs spiraling upwards to the garret. Why did I feel as though I was mounting a scaffold from which there was going to be only one final exit? When I reached the top floor the door was open. But Isabelle was not, as always, standing in its frame, awaiting me with evident desire. Rather she was at her desk, a cigarette on the go, staring out at the grimy window in front of her, looking beyond bereft.

I approached her. When I tried to put my hand on her shoulder she recoiled – as if I had poked her with a cattle prod.

'Please sit over on the sofa, Samuel. This will not take long.'

But I still tried to engage her physically. To thread my fingers in hers. She pulled away.

'Are you serious?' she said, the anger right out in the open.

'Do you think I'm after sex?'

'I think you don't realize how seriously you have alienated me.'

'How is Émilie?'

'She will be in a wheelchair for at least a year. But the neurologists believe she escaped paralysis by centimeters – and that after many years of physiotherapy she may be able to walk again without support.'

'At least it's not paralysis.'

'Thank you for such an American equivocation. A never-ending disaster downgraded to a mere disaster – and, in your view, a cause for celebration. *Not as bad as we thought. And not an absolute tragedy, because over here we don't believe in tragedy. We just think: something went wrong.*'

She made that last statement with a faux-American accent. I grabbed one of the chrome café chairs, sat down and reached into my jacket pocket to pull out cigarettes and a Zippo. This was one of those occasions best negotiated with a cigarette.

'And the water in her lungs?'

'No brain damage – but she was kept in a medically induced coma for five days after they pumped her lungs clean of the Seine water.'

'I'm sorry.'

'Oh, and Charles – beyond overcome by what his much worshipped daughter did to herself – had a heart attack two nights ago. Not a big one. He'll probably be out of hospital in a few more days. Nonetheless, the sort of incident that serves as a reminder: mortality for my husband is nigh. Thankfully not tomorrow, but probably within five to ten years. Imagine how that must feel . . . how it *will* feel. Knowing that there are just five to ten more Christmases ahead. Charles will need ongoing attention now. So too my daughter. Charles and I spoke last night. Mentally he was all here. Shaken. Thrown. A bit frightened . . . but also cognizant that it didn't come calling for him this time; that he had been gifted a bit more time among us. And he made a proposal. One which I accepted. That we all leave Paris. The house is there in Normandy. It is spacious. Enough room for the three of us to have our own small realms, yet still be together under one roof. Émilie is going to need twenty-four-hour nursing for a while and a team to literally get her back on her feet. There's a rather good rehabilitation hospital nearby. We can get specialist doctors and physios to help her. Charles will be in a quiet environment; a place for him to detach from the pursuit of Mammon as well as every available skirt going.'

'And you?' I said.

'I will be Mother Superior: the woman in charge of this rest home.'

'All the time?'

She nodded. Adding:

'I can hear the disapproval through your silence: throwing my metropolitan life away. Becoming an upscale nursemaid. Most of all, giving up my American lover, whom I did adore until he got jealous of my family's immense recent misfortunes.'

'I haven't said a damn word.'

'Nor have you needed to. Your silent petulance has been noted. You had to send me, what, a message every hour on the hour in the wake of me telling you my wonderful Émilie had broken her back and nearly drowned.'

'I did so because I was genuinely scared for Émilie.'

'And scared that what is happening *would* happen . . . that I would choose my husband and daughter over you. Which is exactly what I am doing.'

'You are unfairly putting this all on me.'

'Your message—'

'I apologized immediately for being over the top.'

'It distressed me enormously. This pressure to be there for you—'

'That is not true. I called many times at first because I wanted to help, to be there for *you* . . .'

'Because you needed to think: I am her other half.'

'I *am* your other half.'

'*Tangentially.* And you've always known that. And I've made it ever clear to you. For years. Decades. My love for you . . . it is always there. But when you impinge on—'

'This is hardly impinging. I know you've been through a monstrous time. I just wanted to help . . .'

'And you now think I am picking on you.'

'Yes, I do. But you are angry and full of grief and sorrow – and love is often about turning on the person who is there for you, as unfair as that might be.'

'How noble of you. How chivalrous.'

'You don't have to blow this all up, Isabelle. You don't have to decimate—'

313

'If I am leaving Paris . . .'

'You're selling this studio and your *appartement familial*?'

Pause. She reached for her packet of cigarettes, lighting one.

'Not yet.'

'So, in truth, you may be based in Normandy, but—'

'"Truth" is a flexible construct. For the foreseeable future I will be caring for my daughter and husband in Normandy. For the foreseeable future . . . I am stopping this.'

'With just cause?'

'Had you handled this better . . .'

'I did not handle this *badly*. You are looking for an excuse.'

Pause.

'Perhaps I am. Perhaps I am being very unfair to you. Perhaps I am using you as a whipping boy. Or perhaps this entire terrible sequence of events has shown me where my priorities are.'

'When you say "the foreseeable future" . . .'

'See! See! You are holding out hope.'

'By all means go off with your daughter and husband. Focus your entire attention on them. But surely you don't want to stop what we have? Which does not impinge—'

'You think it doesn't impinge? You think I am not emotionally weighed down by knowing I love you, but also have this life that I cannot lose?'

'No one is asking you to lose that life. Step back, please.'

'Émilie's terrible "accident", Charles's heart attack . . . they are both telling me I stepped back too far from everything.'

'Don't be so precipitous. Take some time to let all this terrible-ness settle.'

'The ever-reasonable lawyer. You don't understand: this has to end for me. No more divided loyalties, divided heart.'

'All I'm asking is—'

'I know what you are asking. And I am telling you: no. We are finished. You might not agree with my logic, but you have to accept it. Because there it is. And now you have to leave.'

Why had I always carried with me the wistful speculation: one day it will end this way? To know that because it was not complete, it would never be totally right. But what is right and what is complete when it comes to the disarray to be found in the human heart? I had no answers to that question. Nor could I counter Isabelle's vehemence this afternoon. For her the decision was made; a Manichean choice – and one that, for her own current stability, she had to adhere to. Was she using this harsh decision to break us up as a way of mitigating the guilt she felt right now? I sensed that – but to articulate it in front of her was asking for an even deeper rupture. One thing I knew for certain about Isabelle: any attempts to tell her what you thought she was thinking would be met by a vehement defense of her own position, not to mention exasperation that you dared to think that you actually knew her mind.

So I stood up. I put out my cigarette. I came over to kiss her goodbye.

She accepted my lips on each cheek. Her way of letting me know: we are done here. I left. But not before saying:

'The door is always open.'

Silence.

One more try.

'My love for you will not go away.'

Now she swiveled in her chair, showing me her back. The conversation was closed.

As it remained for years to come.

*

Bad news is dirty tidal water. It washes in, but instead of washing cleanly back out to sea, it leaves residue, muck. And like overly polluted waters, it keeps depositing more slime on your shores.

I kept this rupture to myself. Until I was back on my next trip to New York and Ethan asked me when he would see Isabelle again. That's when I explained about Émilie being ill, and that Isabelle and I were taking a break from each other, and there was a very good chance that we would not be getting back together again. Ethan was wide-eyed.

'I'll never see her again?'

'I don't know.'

'You and Mom break up. And now you and Isabelle break up.'

I wanted to explain that it wasn't me doing the breaking up. But I also didn't want to sound defensive. Or: *it was all her fault*. Unless there is violence or immense psychological nastiness, there is never one party at fault. And the terrible music of chance can blow a couple right off course.

Some months after Isabelle told me it was over – and indeed disappeared completely from the city – I received a middle of the night phone call in Paris. It was Jessica, calling me at 9 p.m. New York time. Ethan had texted her an hour earlier, begging her to get to the apartment as soon as possible. He'd found his mother face down in a puddle of her own vomit, a bottle of vodka by her side. It turned out she'd started drinking again. Ethan was attending the Dalton on the Upper East Side and adept at taking the subway to and from school every day. He'd been invited to a friend's apartment after school and the mother of the classmate insisted on putting him into a prepaid taxi back home around 8 p.m. Which is when he'd walked in and found his mother. Being smart he ran downstairs and found the doorman, who called 911 and also (at Ethan's insistence) Jessica. The ambulance arrived before his tutor. Rebecca was taken off to Bellevue, where her stomach was pumped out and she was dispatched to the psych ward for observation. Jessica agreed to stay with Ethan for that night. I was on a flight to New York the next morning. Ethan was traumatized by discovering his mother in such a state.

'Don't make me live with her again,' he pleaded.

According to the doctors at Bellevue, Rebecca had the beginnings of cirrhosis of the liver. The damage, though worrying, had yet to hit the point of no return. Social services had now been called in. Rebecca was immediately regarded as a danger to herself and, most tellingly, to her son. I stepped in, assuring everyone that Ethan would now be residing with me. I asked for a meeting with the managing partner at our firm and explained all. To her credit, Rebecca also stepped in, asking me to see her. I arranged an appointment in a special secure visitors' room in the psych ward. A hospital guard was with us during our entire thirty-minute conversation.

'Is this necessary?' I asked when he showed up before Rebecca was brought in. The guy – chunky, Hispanic, with a serious Queens accent – replied:

'If, by your question, you mean: do I got to be here while you see one of our patients—'

'My ex-wife.'

'She's still one of our patients. And yeah, I got to be here. Don't worry – anything you say to her is your own business, and I won't be repeating it to nobody. But you can't be alone with her – just in case she does something not smart. That's the rules.'

Rebecca showed up a few minutes later, accompanied by a very large, formidable-looking nurse who had a tight grip on one of her arms. She nodded to the security guard as she handed Rebecca over to his care. My ex-wife was wearing a yellow jump-suit – similar to those I imagined prisoners wore in the city's desperate jails.

'You've got thirty minutes, sir,' the nurse informed me after patting down Rebecca and ensuring that she wasn't carrying any contraband.

'They think I'm packing heat,' Rebecca said to me. I smiled. My ex-wife still did have flashes of the dry wit that I'd so loved early on.

'Jokes like that don't work here, ma'am,' the guard said, pointing her toward the metal chair opposite mine.

'So I gather he's going to be here throughout,' I said to her. 'But he won't take notes. How are you doing?'

'Oh you know: everything's coming up roses.'

'I'm sorry.'

'Why? I'm the fuck-up here. I've just handed you the biggest cudgel imaginable with which to hit me over the head.'

'I don't plan to do that.'

'But you plan to take Ethan away from me.'

'I didn't say that.'

'After what I pulled I know what any court would do.'

'No one wants to go legal here. They said your liver is in throes of early cirrhosis.'

'They told me that too. And yes, I have been going to AA meetings here at the hospital.'

'That's convenient.'

'Such cynicism.'

'Irony.'

'I know that I am in a no-win situation; that you hold all the cards now.'

'We just want to do what's best for Ethan. I've talked to my partners at the firm. I can come back to New York. Pretty much within the month. Jessica and I spoke this morning. She can work something out with her husband, have them move into the apartment until I'm back.'

Silence. She reached for the plastic water jug on the table and poured herself a paper cup of the tepid liquid, draining it in one go.

'A social worker spent an hour with me yesterday, told me about this residential program upstate, near Albany. Six months of drying out and therapy and simple communal living. It costs, but with the money I get from you each month I could pay my way. Which I want to do. And you could take over the apartment. Buy it from me. Move in. Make certain that Ethan doesn't have the jolt of changing places in the middle of the school year. By the time I have finished my six months we can discuss what happens next. Where I'll live next.'

'That's a lovely offer.'

'It's a practical offer. And it's the best outcome at the moment for Ethan, wouldn't you agree?'

'Indeed I would,' I said.

Within four weeks I had hired a replacement to take over running the French office. To her credit Rebecca asked to meet with Ethan – under the supervision of Jessica – and apologized for that terrible meltdown and drinking herself into a near coma. She also cleared out all her clothes from the bedroom, putting them in storage before I moved back in.

And that is how I found myself saying goodbye to Paris.

I arrived in New York in early summer. Ten days before my departure I sent an email to Isabelle, telling her I was returning to New York and explaining the reasons. I also enquired about the health of Émilie and Charles and indicated that if, months on from the break-up, she was ready to see me again (especially with me leaving town) I would very much like that . . . if, that was, she found herself back in Paris.

Four days later I got this reply:

Dear Samuel
You are a wonderful father – so good on you for returning to New York and rescuing Ethan from a very bad situation. Émilie makes progress. Charles is stable. I won't be able to see you before you leave.
Je t'embrasse
Isabelle

I didn't push further. I packed my bag. I flew the Atlantic. I moved in with Ethan. I picked up life again at the firm in

New York. I handled a handful of new cases. I did receive an email from Isabelle enquiring if we had been directly affected by the unspeakable events of September 11, 2001. Ethan was just at school and I was heading to a meeting downtown when the planes hit and the world shifted course. I did write her a rather long email describing the mad terror of that truly fateful day, and the fact that I lost two legal associates who were at a meeting in the second tower, and how for months afterwards my son had broken nights, waking up and crying for me and asking if planes would crash into our building or the building where I worked. Isabelle's reply – on one of her white cards – was a polite, but impersonal one: *How horrible for you. I am with you all. Courage . . .*

I took the hint. I buried myself in work. I was there for Ethan. He had friends. He negotiated Manhattan with aplomb. He started to focus academically – and let it be known to me that he was planning to chase after acceptance at a mainstream college. He even had the grades to aim relatively high. His desire to transcend his disability was an ongoing marvel – though if I ever mentioned how courageous I thought he was his reaction was typically adolescent: 'Stop the praise, Dad.'

Time, time, time. It's inexorable. I had girlfriends. I assiduously avoided any woman in her mid- to late thirties who was desperate for a child. I thought I was in love with a psychoanalyst named Natalie until she began to reveal a cavalcade of compulsions and neuroses that became hard to bear. Especially her need to detail her sex life with the many men she'd been involved with before I'd shown up in her life. When I told her that I was finding it difficult to hear about her affair with a seventy-year-old fellow shrink when she was a mere forty-year-old – and how the fellow had the hardest body imaginable and 'was as wild as they come in bed' – I did say to her:

'Don't you know how alienating these stories are?'

'Why – because you're jealous?'

'Because you come out sounding like an adolescent who finally got to sleep with Daddy.'

There was a clever reporter on *New York* magazine whom I saw for around three months . . . until she told me that she honestly couldn't handle Ethan's deafness. 'I will always feel inadequate around it – and it will serve as a constant reminder that I left it too late to have children.' There was a French professor at Columbia who loved that I was bilingual and my Greenwich Village apartment and late evenings at the Vanguard and the good rapport we had in bed, but who told me after a few weeks that her ex in France had asked to be let back into her life – 'and I know he's the man destined for me.' Then there was a German United Nations lawyer, Julianna: tall, elegant, hyper-cosmopolitan, and very warm with Ethan . . . until she started revealing an authoritarian streak, insisting that my habit of heading out to cinemas and theaters and jazz clubs didn't chime with her preference for evenings at home after work with a good book.

'And you, Samuel, are going to have to stop thinking that at your age you can keep careening around the city like a young man in his twenties with no responsibilities.'

To which I thought: *I don't think so.*

Ethan was accepted by one of New York State's better universities – Stony Brook on Long Island – where they had

322

excellent support for students with hearing impairments. I did tell him when he was applying to colleges that if wanted to go to NYU we were just around the corner from it all. But he rightfully knew that the moment had come to get away from home. So Stony Brook it was. And on the last Saturday in August I rented a car and drove him the two hours out to the campus. I met his roommate, Frank – another city kid, from Brooklyn, full of attitude, but cool with having a deaf roommate – who insisted on helping my son find his way in those daunting first days of college life. After unpacking him and helping him set up his corner of the dorm room and going to a boring campus lunch for new students and their families, I had that wrenching moment of having to say goodbye to him. Ethan could register my sadness at having to let him now fend for himself in this way station between adolescence and adult life.

'I will be just fine,' he signed to me. 'Because you've taught me how to be fine.'

'You've taught me that too,' I said.

'You going to take Mom out for dinner?'

Indeed, Rebecca had shown up earlier that day as well, driving herself down from her home in Albany where she lived with her new husband, Fred, a senior civil servant in the New York State Department of Corrections whom she'd met in AA. She herself had gotten back into law and was a public defender working for Legal Aid. I'd not had the pleasure of meeting Fred. Ethan had – and called him 'a little old and dry, but Mom seems happy. And he's a big Catholic like she is . . . so I guess it kind of works.'

I didn't quote this comment back to Rebecca as we settled into the seafood joint I found for us not far from the campus. It was our first proper meal together in years. We were both very much on our guard. I could see her lips tighten when I asked for a glass of Sauvignon Blanc to go with the dozen oysters I'd ordered – and I could sense that, like so many reformed alcoholics, she so wanted just one drink. I tried to maintain a poker face when she blessed herself before beginning to eat. We made conversation – largely about Ethan and what spectacular progress he had made, and how (as I noted) we had both played key roles in bringing him to this juncture in time, when he was starting a mainstream college and doing so with the minimum of outside help.

'You did all the big organizational stuff,' Rebecca said. 'Finding the tutors, chasing down every educational and medical avenue to help him.'

'And you were there raising him.'

'Because you fled from me and my drinking – and who can blame you.'

'Past tense. Are things good with you now?'

'As in, have I fallen off the wagon?'

'As in, are you happy?'

'What's "happy"?'

'Good question.'

'I have a reasonable life now. Fred is a nice man. Albany is actually an interesting city. We have a subscription to the orchestra, to the local regional theater. We like to hike. My work has its interests – and God, this is sounding so banal. But honestly . . . life is fine. Not where I saw myself when I left

Columbia Law, but fine. Still I often wonder: had the meningitis not taken away our son's hearing—'

'Don't go there, please,' I said. 'What happened, happened. We dealt with it.'

'Or in my case, didn't deal with it.'

'You dealt with it fine.'

'Stop being nice.'

'Stop being hard on yourself.'

'The deafness pulled us apart.'

'It contributed,' I said. 'However . . .'

'I always knew your heart was somewhat elsewhere.'

Pause. I sipped my wine.

'I never regretted for a moment being with you. I loved you.'

'But she was the woman you wanted to be with . . . and couldn't.'

'Past tense.'

'Is it? Really? You were back with her all those years in Paris. And now?'

'Now she is with the husband she never left and the fragile, infirm daughter who depends on her.'

'So you are in touch?'

'Not really.'

'And you mourn her absence all the time?'

I shook my head. Rebecca smiled. Not a sardonic smile. One of quiet commiseration.

'It's all right, Sam. She was always there. From the moment I found myself falling for you I knew you were conflicted. I still went for you – and got you. I know there was a moment when you could have jumped to her. But you chose me. Which, retrospectively speaking, might have been a mistake. And here we are, all these messy years later, and she is still your great passion, your great story. Especially because you both had other lives elsewhere. We want what we can't have. We have what we soon discover we might not want. It's the way so much of all this works. Love. The great pursuit. The great anguish. The great ongoing dream. You still dream of love, don't you?'

Another sip of my wine. Then:

'Of course.'

'Any prospects on the horizon?'

I just shrugged.

'So there is someone who has your attention?'

'How do you know that?'

'Because you were my husband. And because, unlike me, you are still a romantic.'

I smiled.

'Guilty as charged,' I said.

'Oh come on,' Rebecca said, 'you can tell me about her.'

'Not yet,' I said.

There were reasons why I still classified Lorrie Williams as 'not yet'. We'd met while standing in line at the Vanguard. She was with two friends. I was alone. She noticed I was reading *DownBeat*. She asked me if I was a musician. We got talking.

'Are you always alone when listening to jazz?' she asked.

I explained that I was divorced, that I had a son about to start college, that I was single.

'As in just out of something – or am I being too curious, too forward?'

Julianna was two months behind me. So I said:

'Yeah, recently single . . . but not with any hangover effects.'

'I like that. Nice turn of phrase. I'm divorced and recently single too, though the divorce came five years ago.'

'Kids?'

'Didn't want them, or at least not with him.'

'And thereafter . . .?'

'Biologically too late. And the wrong guy again.'

The doors for the 11 p.m. set opened. She told me her name. I told her mine. She introduced me to her two women friends – both around her age. Both with wedding bands. They asked if I would like to join their table. I found out that one of the women – her name was Joan – was celebrating her birthday that night, and that they had all been together at college years ago. I said that I didn't want to gatecrash their evening – but did ask Lorrie if we could exchange phone numbers. She scribbled hers in my notebook, as I did in hers.

Several times during the gig that night – Cedar Walton and his trio – I saw Lorrie looking over at me and then she gave me a simple, telling nod, acknowledging that she saw me looking at her. I waited the requisite forty-eight hours, then phoned and we arranged to meet. She proposed a trip to the East Village to see some 1960s experimental American cinema at the Anthology Film Archives. I sensed this was a test. She taught film studies at The New School. I showed up dressed downtown. She liked that. She liked that I knew my stuff on the director (Stan Brakhage – a search engine tells all). She liked the fact that we went to a small Mexican joint afterwards and talked non-stop until midnight. I put her in a taxi home and handed the driver a $20 and told him that the fare was on me. Before he drove off she gave me a fast, light kiss on the lips and said:

'A cool evening.'

So too were the next three evenings out. Talk, talk and more talk. We found out much about each other; a quiet but growing sense of connection underscored by the hesitancy that comes from too much recent romantic disappointment and the desire to sidestep hurt yet again. And yet, and yet . . . late on that fourth date, a Saturday night, falling out of a bar at almost one in the morning, she linked her fingers with mine and said:

'And now I really would like you to invite me up to your apartment.'

The sex was cautious, a little tentative. Lorrie admitted that, after her last break-up, she'd not been with anyone for almost a year.

'I hope I wasn't disappointing.'

'Don't ever think that,' I said. 'It was the first time. We were both nervous. And it was hardly terrible. "Tomorrow is another day," and all that.'

The next morning we found a nice rhythm together. A fast-maturing complicity. Afterwards I ran out for the Sunday *New York Times* and provisions. Back in the apartment I scrambled eggs, toasted bagels, prepared two Bloody Marys and a pot of French press coffee.

'Our first breakfast together,' she said, leaning over to kiss me.

I liked the fact that we sat at the table for two hours exchanging sections of the paper, talking, talking, talking. I liked the ease between us. The sense that I could see us five, ten years down the line at this table, the remains of a weekend brunch in front of us, talking, talking, talking, still deeply connected and passionate about each other. I knew this was the romantic in me envisaging a future. I knew I still had so much to learn about Ms Williams, as she did about me. But . . . this was nice. And not complicated. And from all that I had heard and observed during our four evenings out before she spent the night, I sensed someone who was aware of her shortcomings – she admitted to struggling with anxiety and much self-doubt when it came to believing she deserved happiness. Just as I admitted that I had walked into my marriage sensing that there were evident structural flaws already there. And that I had turned hesitant and analytical when the one person with whom I felt an immense connection, but who had never held out any hope of a future, offered me that future.

'But you were reacting to her saying "no, no, no" to you for years,' Lorrie said.

'I was reacting to fear. Fear of getting exactly what I so wanted.'

'But then later on you were together.'

'Yes – but back on the old terms. A window opened with her. I pushed her away. It opened again – and this time we were with each other in a part-time way . . .'

'But you were still together. Full-time possession is, in my experience, tricky. Who knows how long anything will last, let alone any of us? We are all so transitory. Which is why a true connection – when and if it comes along – is so precious. And so fragile.'

I concurred with that world view. After a month of seeing each other, I was starting to think: this is lovely. Yes, she was now spending two to three nights a week *chez moi*, especially as The New School was a ten-minute walk from my place. Yes, we still had much to discover about life at close quarters together. But we were also not rushing anything. We were still at that early juncture where our respective complexities had yet to tangle. Maybe we'd be smart enough to keep them at bay, to respect each other's neuroses and learn how to integrate them into something durable. Or maybe, as with past chapters in my life, they'd overwhelm us. But the portents were good. We both agreed – without over-talking it – that we were going to simply let things play out the way they were going to play out.

Ethan was having a bumpy time at college. He found many of his peers shallow and far too party-oriented. He wanted a girlfriend. 'But I'm the weird deaf kid and who wants to date a deaf kid?' And after Manhattan and his regular visits to Paris this corner of Long Island struck him as suburban and sterile.

'So transfer to NYU next term,' I said.

'I want Columbia.'

'Then raise your academic game.'

'Who's the new girlfriend, Dad?' he asked me, changing the subject.

'What makes you think there's a new girlfriend?'

'You seem happy.'

'By which you mean . . . I haven't seemed happy for a while?'

'Not since Isabelle.'

Isabelle.

I did write her at Christmas – two or three paragraphs of greetings, along with the large-print edition of my life. I never talked about the women I was seeing, or the quiet despair that I still felt about the way that she had ended our life together. I updated her on Ethan, on my work, on life in New York. Without ever putting my cards on the table, I did let the subtext be known: I am still waiting for you. Isabelle replied with a few lines about Charles, and how he was simply getting older and more infirm. And how Émilie was walking again, was finding her way back to stability, and was even (according to last year's Christmas letter) back living in Paris. *We have hopes for her* was Isabelle's final comment before wishing me well for the coming year . . . never once revealing in this short missive what she was thinking, how she viewed her life, or giving me any hint whatsoever about her ongoing thoughts on us.

Isabelle.

Around a month after meeting Lorrie an observation took hold of me one morning while out for my daily run: I was no longer mourning Isabelle. Because I had met someone with whom I was glimpsing the elusive possibilities of reasonable contentment.

Then, out of nowhere, Isabelle was back in my life. On a Friday morning, I found myself canceling everything for the next few days and grabbing the last afternoon flight from JFK to Paris, racing off the plane to the address she had sent me in her email. An email that read:

My dearest Samuel
It seems that my turn has come.
I have days left . . . perhaps a week.
Here is my address. It will be my last address.

You know where to find me . . . if you can bear to after the wall I put up between us. But as I said a few sentences ago: time is not on our side.

Isabelle.

*

The flight landed just after dawn. I had emailed Isabelle from the airport in New York saying that I was on my way; that I would arrive with tomorrow's sun. A reply came back ten minutes later:

Morning visiting hours at the hospital: 10h00–12h00. But I have just spoken with the night nurse – who gets off at 08h00. If you get here before then he will get you in . . . especially given that you are coming from New York and the clock is running down. But I still await you.

I was in a taxi from the airport just before 6 a.m. Half an hour later I was in front of the American Hospital in Neuilly. I had texted Isabelle from the cab. She texted back, telling me that the nurse – a fellow named Loic – would be waiting in the main entrance of the hospital at six thirty and would get me upstairs without too many questions from the people at the front desk.

Try to disguise your shock when you see me, she said.

Loic had the air of someone living with perpetual insomnia. Which I suppose came with the territory of hospital night shifts. He was relieved to discover I spoke French.

'We must hurry,' he whispered as I came in. 'The people in charge start work soon – and are very rigid about rules, regulations.'

He got me to show my passport to the security guard on the door. I was waved through. Loic brought me down several back corridors, then up six floors in an big, empty service elevator.

'Madame was so pleased to hear that you were coming. It means a great deal to her. More than a great deal. You have done a good thing getting here.'

Once out of the service elevator Loic hurried me down another back corridor never seen by anyone not employed by the hospital. Then we came back into the public hallways.

'She is in room 242,' Loic said, glancing at his watch. 'The staff change happens at eight. So I will come by several minutes beforehand. She has a private room – and I will ensure that you are left alone. But if there is an emergency there is a buzzer by the bed.'

We reached the door. Her name – *de Monsambert* – had been written on white card and posted outside. I thought: was this the sum total of our lives – a last name written with a Sharpie on a piece of white card, to be tossed in the trash when that life was no more? I felt a moment of panic. I didn't want to face what was beyond that door . . . even though I'd flown through the night to do just that.

Loic knocked on the door. No reply. He opened it. The room was small. With a large institutional hospital bed engulfed in medical paraphernalia: drips and manifold wires and three high-tech monitors, a urine bag and trays of medications and a metronomic soundtrack of *beep, beep, beep*: the heartbeat of my Isabelle.

She was there amidst all this end-of-life technology. She had asked me in advance not to be thrown by what she'd

333

become. I failed. She was dressed in a print hospital gown that seemed three sizes too large for her – because she had shrunk so much. She was emaciated, gray, hollow-cheeked, cadaverous. An elegant silk scarf was tied around her head – something designer, once bought in a far too expensive boutique, now the single reminder of that time in life when an overpriced thing of beautiful silk was tied around the neck as part of the refined image she presented to the world. Maybe it was a gift from a husband, a lover. Now it was covering her hairless head. She had been dozing. Now she opened her eyes. It took a moment for them to focus, to discern who was in front of her. Then:

'If you tell me how good I look you are leaving.'

I suppressed a laugh that was going to turn into tears.

'I won't say that.'

'Good,' she said, motioning to the metal chair by her bed. Then with a nod toward Loic – who was still standing in the door frame – she indicated that we wanted to be alone. I sat down on the cold chair.

'Take my hand,' Isabelle said, extending fingers now anatomical, all bones. 'That is, if you don't mind holding hands with a skeleton.'

'Shut up,' I said, leaning over to kiss her. She tried to just give me a cheek to kiss. I touched her lips with mine. Lips that had been just about everywhere on each other's bodies.

'You are a romantic to the end, Samuel. Even if it means kissing a corpse.'

'Shut up,' I repeated, managing a smile. She managed a small smile back.

'I appreciate your spirit of normality . . . even if to me there is nothing normal about any of this. Though to the staff here, on this floor, this is *comme d'habitude*. They move you here when the endgame is nigh.'

'How long have you known . . .?'

'That I am going to die? Since I first found out about death when my great-aunt Véronique died when I was six years old. As I am sixty-six now I have lived with the knowledge of my impending mortality for sixty years.'

'I am pleased to see that your wit is still intact.'

'I am having a moment of rare clarity, perhaps linked to your arrival. But . . . how long have I had this fatal cancer? Eighteen months ago they found a tumor in my left lung. Surgery, chemo, radio, remission. The usual cancer dance steps. And then the discovery of another tumor. Only this one was not containable. It was metastasizing, spreading everywhere with a ferocity and determination that was breathtaking. Two months ago I was told perhaps a year if I was fortunate and chose to attack it aggressively. But my oncologist also told me I was in for a year of agony if I followed that route. Better to accept palliative care and make the most of the time remaining. Then that last "twelve months" prognosis became three months. Then six weeks. Then . . . "you have seven days if you are fortunate". Which is when I contacted you. When you told me you would arrive this morning I informed Loic: no morphine until later. Morphine is wonderful. The best end-of-life high going. But there is no clarity with morphine, no cognition, no language.'

'But there's pain without it?'

'Of course. But I can deal with it for a little while – as it allows me this brief window of lucidity with you.'

'I'm so sorry.'

'But why? Lung cancer is the usual result when you smoke between thirty and forty cigarettes a day for fifty years. This was to be expected. Especially as everyone did tell me: it is a stupid habit.'

Silence. I felt her fingers try to clutch around mine – but she had little strength. I gripped hers gently, afraid that they were so brittle they might just snap.

'I've asked for no funeral,' she said. 'No burial. My ashes to be scattered wherever Charles and Émilie see fit . . . if anywhere at all. No plaque on a tree. No urn to be interred in a cemetery. Nothing to mark my time here. And absolutely no memorial service later on. I just want to disappear.'

'I see.'

'You don't approve.'

'I am not you.'

'Ah, but you were an essential part of me. That I will carry with me into the great unknown.'

I bit down on my lip. I held back a sob.

'If you start to cry I am going to order you to leave. Do you know what Puccini wrote in the margin of the score of *La bohème* at that moment when Mimi dies? "*Sentiment, no sentimentality.*" I told the same thing to Charles the other day. And Émilie.'

'How is Émilie?'

'Let's start with Charles – who is asleep in the next room.'

'Really?'

'You should see your face. Like the bad-boy lover expecting the angry husband to burst in and challenge him to a duel. Charles will hardly be doing that, as he is an elderly man confined to a wheelchair . . . soon to be joining me on the other side. Émilie is taking this all very badly. She married her fellow last year. Jean-Pierre. She made such a full recovery from her injuries and here is the greatest miracle of them all: she is pregnant. Her doctors have told her that if she is very careful, her once-crushed frame can carry the child. She is due in four months.'

'Wonderful news,' I said.

'I always wanted to be a grandmother. All the pleasure with none of the immediate grief. But that too is being denied me.'

A wave of pain sideswiped her. Her body went into a small convulsion, the agony clawing its way across her sunken face. I was on my feet, about to hit the panic button.

'No, no,' she whispered. 'I can withstand a moment or two more.'

I pulled my chair closer to her bed, both her hands now in mine.

'Where was I?' she asked.

'It doesn't matter.'

'It matters. Where was I?'

'Émilie.'

Another convulsion of pain broadsided her. Now I did reach for the pain button, one of my hands still holding hers. Loic was in the room moments later. As he arrived Isabelle was hit with a third convulsion. He motioned for me to clear away. He was at work immediately, discerning her heart meter, whispering something into her ear, Isabelle giving him the smallest of nods, then him finding a plunger, calibrating a dosage, depressing it fully.

'Morphine?' I asked.

He nodded. I watched as the drugs cascaded through her, rendering her silent, tranquil, benumbed.

'Should I go?' I whispered to him.

'Stay,' he said, pointing to the chair. I sat back down. Isabelle was now staring upwards at the ceiling, her eyes as glassy as a lake in winter, the pain now elsewhere. Out of nowhere an image filled that space between my ears. Isabelle next to me in bed, a beatific post-coital smile on her face, a cigarette between her lips, staring up at the ceiling, telling me: 'Who needs drugs at a moment like this – when, for a moment or two, all in life is perfect?' And then thinking later that day, walking in the rain back to my little room in that half-star hotel: I have just known a moment of pure love.

I reached out and took both her hands again. Her lips moved imperceptibly. A smile? Hard to discern. Her hands were warm in mine. I sat back in the chair, not letting go of her. I shut my eyes for a moment, a surge of exhaustion breaking over me. When I opened them again I had an instant of general cognitive confusion. As in: where am I and what am I doing here? The bedside clock read: 06h48. I had been asleep for mere minutes. And my hands were linked with Isabelle's. And she was still staring up at the ceiling, that celestial smile still spread across her face. Only now she was motionless. No longer breathing.

I jolted upright. I reached over and touched that pulse point on her neck. Nothing. I glanced at the heart meter, now sending out a low monotonal screech as the once calibrating pulse indicator on the screen had been transformed into one endless flat line. I grabbed the panic button. Loic was with us seconds later. He saw what was happening; what had just happened. He motioned for me to step away. He went to work. Quietly. With clinical deliberation. Checking her vital signs. Using a stethoscope for one last listen of a heart that had ceased functioning. Turning off the electrocardiogram. Removing the pillow that was propping her up. Lowering her down so that she was now lying flat on the bed. Staring up into eternity. Until he closed her eyes.

I stood there, not knowing what to do. Except to leave. And to say:

'Thank you for getting me to her before . . .'

'She wanted to see you. She was waiting for you. You got here. She saw you. And now she has left us. She held on for you. Know that.'

I nodded, my head lowered, one hand against a wall. An attempt to find stability at a moment when I felt as if I was in free fall.

'I have to tell her husband,' Loic said; his hint that my time here was finished.

'Of course, of course.'

I looked down at Isabelle for one final time. Loic pulled the bedsheet over her. She was no more. Her story had ended. Mine would continue for a while longer. But with Isabelle always a profound part of it. As she had been from that moment of happenstance three decades ago in a bookshop on the boulevard Saint-Germain. A glance this way. A glance returned. And the entire trajectory of two lives altered in the process. But that is the way it all works. The music of chance bound up in that most human of pursuits: the search for a passionate connection that might just endure.

Loic coughed – a signal that I really did have to leave. I nodded. I picked up my shoulder bag. I walked out into the over-bright hospital corridor. And found myself facing a large, ancient man in a wheelchair – his face like a bas-relief found in an archeological dig, the flesh around his neck loose, copious, his eyes reflecting exhaustion yet still a sharp regard for the world around him. He glared at me. I froze. His gaze was ferocious: decades of concealed rage finally focused on that shadowy presence in his life. His wife's great other love. I met his gaze. Then Charles did something remarkable. He forced himself up from his wheelchair. A vast, painful struggle – but one that he was determined to do by himself. Once he was on his feet, holding one side of the wheelchair for ballast, I saw that he was still a tall man, trying to unhunch his hunched shoulders. His right hand reached out. It grasped my shoulder. He looked directly at me. No words. No exchanged commiserations. No tears. Just silent, profound grief. Shared for a moment.

Then he lowered himself back into his chair. The door opened. Loic came out. Charles looked in and could see the body in the bed, the sheet shrouding the face that was once Isabelle. He shut his eyes. Loic wheeled him into the room. The door closed behind them all. As I walked away I saw an orderly with a clipboard coming by and removing Isabelle's name from the slot by the door.

*

I left the hospital. As soon as my feet landed on the sidewalk outside I made a decision. No nostalgic wanderings through

Paris. No remembrances of things past. No musing on scenarios that should have played out; the alternative version we all seek. *Sentiment, not sentimentality.* And life ahead.

There was a row of taxis outside. I hopped in the first one and asked to go to the airport.

Traffic was light. I was there thirty minutes later. I went to the ticket counter. I asked to be put on the next flight to New York. I was told there was a seat available on the 11 h 05 service. I slid a piece of plastic across the counter. The transaction was finalized in minutes. Lorrie. Yesterday I had called her on my cell from the airport, saying that I was about to board a flight to Paris. When I explained why I was making this sudden trip across the Atlantic she had said nothing except:

'You must get to her. And call me day or night if you need to talk.'

Now I was texting her:

I got to Paris just in time. With mere minutes left. It's done. Now on my way back to New York. Air France 790. Arriving 1.15 p.m. I will call when I land. Thinking very much of you.

The flight back. A blur. I pulled a mask over my eyes. I inserted plugs in my ears. I surrendered to sleep after forty hours without sleep. A flight attendant woke me twenty minutes before we touched down at JFK. I peered out the window. Light snow had fallen on the vast geographic sprawl that is New York. The world was pristine. Bleached clean of all its imperfections. For a moment or two anyway.

And then we were on the ground. I moved fast through all the frontier formalities. No questions at passport control. A cursory glance at my shoulder bag at customs. I cleared officialdom.

I headed out into the New York world beyond. Electric doors swinging open for me. The noise and congestion of arrivals. All those comings and goings. The endless two-step that is life.

'Sam!'

Was someone calling my name? But I was expecting no one to meet me here.

'Sam!'

I turned around. There, on the far left of the arrivals area, was Lorrie. My bemusement at seeing her here, awaiting me, must have thrown her – she looked at me with concern, unease. Her face asking: *Did I overplay my hand by showing up like this?*

My reply . . .

A smile. And:

'Well, hello there!'

Her relief was palpable, vast. She was moving toward me, wanting to take me in her arms. As, yes, I wanted to take her in mine. With the knowledge: I will truly never know you. Just as you will never truly know me. Because the biggest mystery in life is not the one with whom you seek love. The biggest mystery is yourself.

And yet there she was. The possible felicitous future. The hope we all crave. Can we do this? Can we somehow find a way of making each other happy? And, in turn, remind ourselves: we are not alone in the dark.

It's what we all want.

Isn't it?